翻译前沿研究系列丛书

莎剧《哈姆雷特》
辞格辨析与文体鉴赏

Rhetorical Devices and Style of *Hamlet*

谢桂霞◎著

中山大学出版社
·广州·

版权所有　翻印必究

图书在版编目（CIP）数据

莎剧《哈姆雷特》辞格辨析与文体鉴赏：英文、中文/谢桂霞著．—广州：中山大学出版社，2020.10
（翻译前沿研究系列丛书）
ISBN 978 - 7 - 306 - 07010 - 4

Ⅰ.①莎…　Ⅱ.①谢…　Ⅲ.①《哈姆雷特》—文学翻译—研究　Ⅳ.①I046 ②H315.9

中国版本图书馆 CIP 数据核字（2020）第 206731 号

SHAJU《HAMULEITE》CIGE BIANXI YU WENTI JIANSHANG

出 版 人：	王天琪
策划编辑：	熊锡源
责任编辑：	熊锡源
封面设计：	林绵华
责任校对：	叶　枫
责任技编：	何雅涛
出版发行：	中山大学出版社
电　　话：	编辑部 020 - 84110779，84110283，84111997，84110771
	发行部 020 - 84111998，84111981，84111160
地　　址：	广州市新港西路 135 号
邮　　编：	510275　传　真：020 - 84036565
网　　址：	http：//www.zsup.com.cn　E-mail：zdcbs@mail.sysu.edu.cn
印 刷 者：	广州市友盛彩印有限公司
规　　格：	880mm×1230mm　1/32　11.75 印张　290 千字
版次印次：	2020 年 10 月第 1 版　2020 年 10 月第 1 次印刷
定　　价：	38.00 元

如发现本书因印装质量影响阅读，请与出版社发行部联系调换

前　言

莎士比亚生活的伊丽莎白时代，是英国修辞学蓬勃发展的时期。受到当时意大利和法国等文艺复兴先锋国家的作品的影响，许多英国学者也想借此机会丰富英国的诗学艺术，以振兴本国文学，而他们所共同关注的，便是文学创作的艺术。当时英国学校的人文初级必修的三个学科（the Trivium），即语法、逻辑和修辞，便是教授这些艺术规则的主要学科。

生活在这一时期的莎士比亚，也接受了深入全面的修辞学教学。学者们通过研究莎士比亚的生活轨迹，或者通过研究他的作品后发现，莎士比亚幼年时期曾就读语法学校，对古典修辞学家的作品有深入理解，并将这些修辞手法运用到他的戏剧和诗歌创作中。可以说，莎剧中修辞手法的频繁出现是伊丽莎白时期社会对修辞学重视程度的一个缩影。然而，莎士比亚的作品能够超越同时期的其他作品，成为公认的世界经典文学，则离不开莎士比亚本人的写作语言天赋，特别是对修辞使用的天赋。辞格在莎士比亚手中，已经不仅是一种"语言的艺术"，而且是他渲染主题和刻画人物的工具。因此，不管是从作品创作的时代背景，还是从莎士比亚个人专长的角度来看，修辞都是阅读莎剧的一个重要切入点。

本书基于对西方修辞学的简单回顾，聚焦于辞格这一修辞学中与文体和语言应用相关性最为紧密的方面。本书的前半部分（第一章至第三章）主要讨论辞格的各种分类和辨析标准，中间部分（第四章）为对《哈姆雷特》剧中辞格的辨析和简单的局部文体效果分析，后面部分（第五章）则从整体的角度，分析辞格如何帮助创设戏剧语言的多重解读和多重语域文体效果，并分析辞格在该剧主题渲染和人物塑造上的功能。作者认为，仅有对具体辞格在具体语境中的分析，虽然能够看到细微处的创意，但不足以展示莎剧的独特之处，对戏剧的文学性理解帮助也不大。因此，本书书写的基本原则为辞格的局部辨析和整体分析相结合，以期在为读者展示莎剧中丰富的辞格之余，也为读者揭示莎士比亚如何通过创造性地使用这些辞格来创造戏剧效果，使自己的作品成为"属于所有时代"的文学瑰宝。

本书的主要读者群体为莎剧的研究者和阅读爱好者，以及修辞的研究者和爱好者；《哈姆雷特》一剧的辞格辨析部分也能充当莎剧初学者的导读性材料，或莎剧辞格研究者的基础语料。本书为从辞格角度解读莎剧的一种尝试，感谢中山大学出版社熊锡源老师对这一研究的支持。书中如有错误和疏忽之处，也恳请学术界同仁和读者们不吝指正。

谢桂霞

2020年9月于珠海

目　录

第一章　莎士比亚与莎剧语言 ………………………………… 1
　　第一节　莎剧的传入与研究 …………………………… 1
　　第二节　莎剧语言特点 ………………………………… 4
　　第三节　莎剧《哈姆雷特》 …………………………… 6
　　第四节　内容和框架 …………………………………… 11

第二章　修辞学与辞格分类研究 ……………………………… 13
　　第一节　西方修辞学简介 ……………………………… 13
　　第二节　辞格的分类研究 ……………………………… 17

第三章　辞格的辨析 …………………………………………… 22
　　第一节　形变辞格（Schemes） ……………………… 23
　　第二节　义变辞格（Tropes） ………………………… 40

第四章　《哈姆雷特》辞格辨析 ……………………………… 59
　　第一幕 …………………………………………………… 62
　　第二幕 …………………………………………………… 130

I

第三幕 ·················· 178
　　第四幕 ·················· 246
　　第五幕 ·················· 292

第五章　辞格文体鉴赏 ·················· 337
　第一节　《哈姆雷特》辞格使用概述 ·················· 338
　第二节　辞格与主题渲染 ·················· 344
　第三节　辞格与人物塑造 ·················· 353

第六章　结语 ·················· 362

参考文献 ·················· 366

第一章 莎士比亚与莎剧语言

威廉·莎士比亚（William Shakespeare，1564—1616）是西方最著名的作家之一。哈里逊（G. B. Harrison）甚至指出，一个可以称为"拥有完备家当"的英国家庭里，都必不可少地藏有《圣经》和一部《莎士比亚作品集》（1959：11）。这两部书分别代表着英语国家的宗教和文化。随着大英帝国在全球的贸易与殖民，莎士比亚也随着英语语言的传播，逐渐成为代表英国文学文化的作家。本章主要介绍莎士比亚和莎剧在中文世界的传播和莎剧语言的特点，以及本书选择以《哈姆雷特》一剧作为分析对象的原因。

第一节 莎剧的传入与研究

在中文世界，早期莎士比亚的介绍主体主要为传教士。他们主要通过著作或译作向中国读者介绍这位英国作家。1856年，慕威廉（William Muirhead）在他翻译的《大英国志》中，将"莎士比亚"翻译为"舌克斯毕"，描述其为英国儒林中

"所著诗文,美善俱尽,至今无以过之也"的知名之士之一;1882年,谢卫楼(Davelle Z. Sheffield)在其所著的《万国通鉴》中,则翻译为"沙斯皮耳",认为他"善作戏文,哀乐罔不尽致,自侯美尔(即荷马)之后,无人几及也";1896年,艾约瑟(Joseph Edkins)编译《西学启蒙十六种》的中文译作中,有"英国一最著声称之词人,名曰筛斯比尔,凡所作词曲,于其人之喜怒哀乐,无一不口吻逼肖"的评价;1903年,李提摩太(Timothy Richard)主编的《广学类编》,则写着"沙基斯庇尔……世称之为诗中之王,亦为戏文中之大名家";李思·伦白·约翰(John Lambert Rees)编译的《万国通史》,将其名翻译为"夏克思芘尔",称其为"最著名之诗人","瑰词异藻,声振金石,其集传诵至今,英人中鲜能出其右者"。此外,当时中国的一些使臣和知名学者,也都介绍过莎士比亚。例如,清朝的驻英公使郭嵩焘便曾在日志中提及"舍克斯毕尔",称其为"善谱剧者,与希腊人何满(即荷马)得齐名"。1903年在上海出版的《东西洋尚友录》和《历代海外尚友录》,则有"索士比尔"为"英国第一诗人"和"英吉利国优人"的记录。严复称赞莎士比亚"其传作大为各国所传译、宝贵也"(2002:78);梁启超将莎士比亚与米尔顿等并列,称其作品"勿论文藻,即其气魄,固已夺人矣"(1998:4);鲁迅将莎士比亚与牛顿并列,认为两者分别代表科学和文学,能够"致人性于全,不使之偏倚"(2011:10)。而"莎士比亚"这个译名第一次出现是在梁启超的《饮冰室诗话》中。此后,这一译名便被广为接受。

中文读者对莎士比亚戏剧内容的接触,则首先通过一本名为《澥外奇潭》(1903)的文言文译著。该书以文言文的形式翻译了英国散文家兰姆姐弟(Charles Lamb, Mary Lamb)改写的《莎士比亚故事集》(*Tales from Shakespeare*) 中七个喜剧和两个悲剧。次年,林纾和魏易又合译了该故事集,译名为《英国诗人吟边燕语》(1904)。莎士比亚戏剧的足本翻译,则直到1921年才出现。田汉翻译的《哈姆莱特》,首次发表在《少年中国》第2卷第12期,次年又由中华书局出版了单行本。该译本成为莎士比亚戏剧的第一个白话文足本译本。此后,莎剧汉译一直吸引许多学者的参与。截至2020年,已经有四部莎剧全集问世。这些全集的译者、第一版出版社和出版年份信息分别为:朱生豪(世界书局,1947),梁实秋(台北远东,1968),方平(河北教育出版社,2000)和辜正坤(外语教学与研究出版社,2015)。近年来,许渊冲和傅光明也均在从事全集的翻译工作。另外,基于朱生豪译本的补译本和修订本则至少有五个版本,分别为:虞尔昌(台北世界书局,1957),吴兴华等(人民文学出版社,1978),苏福忠等(长春时代文艺出版社,1996),裘克安等(南京译林出版社,1998),陈才宇(浙江工商大学出版社,2015),等等。

　　从莎剧在中国的传播情况来看,莎剧已经成为中文翻译文学的重要组成部分,甚至被列入义务教育的必读书目,成功实现了经典化。那么,作为来自其他文化系统的文学作品,莎剧在中国的流传与接受的原因有哪些?除了上文提及的大英帝国在全球的贸易和英语的流行,也有学者认为,莎剧的传播得益于它本身的"弹性和韧性"(郝田虎,2014:83)。该"弹性和韧性"的其中一个体现方式,便是莎剧的语言。本书将聚焦莎剧原文的语言分析,并以"辞格"作为主要切入点,讨论莎士比亚戏剧语言中辞格的使用以及其使用的文体效果,从语言层面探讨莎士比亚的"弹性和韧性"。

第二节 莎剧语言特点

莎学学者詹姆士·夏碧罗（James Shapiro）曾这样说过："脱离莎士比亚的时代来讨论他，或者不去借助莎士比亚的洞察力去了解当时的社会情况，都是行不通的"（2006：xv - xvi）。虽然他讨论的是莎士比亚生活的社会背景，但这一论断也同样适用于对莎剧的语言研究。本书主要以《哈姆雷特》这一莎剧为例，讨论莎士比亚的辞格使用特征，这就需要在了解莎士比亚的语言风格之前，了解一下英国伊丽莎白时代的语言行文规范。

莎士比亚生活的伊丽莎白时期对当代英语语言规范的形成具有重要的影响。受到当时意大利和法国等文艺复兴先锋国家的作品的影响，许多英国学者也想借此机会丰富英国的诗学艺术，以振兴本国文学。而他们所共同关注的，便是文学创作的艺术（Joseph，1962：5）。例如，汤姆森·纳什（Thomas Nashe）（1567—1601）认为，没有艺术的话语是最让人生厌的（1950：335）。在这批复兴时期学者看来，文学创作艺术必不可少，同时，他们也认为艺术创作不完全是一个依赖灵感、虚无缥缈的东西，而是有规范和理论可循。在这里，"艺术"已经是一个具有规定性质的名词，用伊丽莎白时期著名的作家和文学批评家乔治·普登汉姆（George Puttenham）（1529—1590）的话说，艺术是"由理智所规定的，从实践中得来的某些规则"（2007：95），艺术创作则是对这些规则的习得和使用。当时人文初级必修的三个学科（the Trivium），即语法、逻辑和修辞，便是教授这些艺术规则（主要是演讲和作文）的主要学科，这三者也是英国所有语法学校（即小学）

的必修课程。

汤姆森·鲍德温（Thomas Baldwin）通过研究莎士比亚的背景和莎剧中具体诗句中的语言，证明莎士比亚年幼的时候，便曾就读于这类语法学校。他不但接受了当时语法学校修辞教育的熏陶，而且还熟知昆体良（Marcus Fabius Quintilianus）等古典修辞学家的作品（1944：378）。罗伯特·埃文斯（Robert Evans）也证明，莎士比亚关于如何使用修辞方面的知识，并不是通过对特定的几种辞格的特别钻研便能习得的（1966：5）。米里亚姆·约瑟夫（Miriam Joseph）（1962）则更有针对性地分析所有莎剧，并发现伊丽莎白时期语法学校中教授的一百多种修辞手法，都可以在莎剧中找到相应的例子。作为伊丽莎白时期的文学作品，莎士比亚戏剧以及其他同时期作品的共同特征之一便是辞格的频繁使用。因此从辞格角度去分析莎剧语言，也显得有一定的必要性。

然而，莎剧最终可以超越伊丽莎白时代诞生的其他戏剧作品，成为本·琼森（Ben Johnson）在诗中所预言的"属于所有时代"（1954：286），其中既有时代的原因，也有他自身的原因。约瑟夫认为，伊丽莎白时期，未完善的英语语言系统、流行的作文规范以及（莎士比亚）本人的语言天赋造就了他语言的生命力和丰富性（1962：2）。伊丽莎白时期的英国，政治、经济和文化得到了空前的发展，成为英国历史上的"黄金时代"，英语语言也开始活跃地从其他语言中吸取不同的因素，语法结构因此也相对不稳定。但这些不稳定的因素，也是莎士比亚语言取得成就的契机。乔治·戈登（George Gordon）曾说，因为英语语法的不稳定，"莎士比亚才可以对英语语法为所欲为，从它们的不完善之中找到美和力量。并在这种繁杂的语言中，找到了主动的机会，时而很有风度地对待这语言，时而则近乎专制"（转引自 Evans，1964：xi），而正是他的语言天赋和对语言使用的"专制"精神，使得他在使用古典修辞创作戏剧时，不是一味地遵循传统的做法，受修辞的束缚，而是将修辞为己所用，使其成为他创作的工具。有时，莎士比亚甚至会跳出常规来使用某些辞格，以向观众传递他的意思（Evans，1966：6）。如果说，莎士比亚创作初期还有模仿古典修辞的迹象，到了后期，他使用修辞的手法便达到炉火纯青的程度。沃尔夫冈·克莱门（Wolfgang H. Clemen）对莎士比亚使用隐喻有如下的观察：

  在他手中，隐喻渐渐地发展为一个越来越有效的工具：在初始它只是用来实现几个简单的功能，到后来，便变为可以同时间实现多个目标的语言工具，并且在戏剧角色性格塑造和戏剧主题表达方面，起到决定性的作用。（1966：5）

辞格在莎剧中，已经不像古典修辞那样，仅仅是为了提高语言的艺术性，而是莎士比亚戏剧创作、人物塑造以及主题揭示的工具，透过辞格的分析，可以更加深刻地理解莎剧的内涵以及莎剧语言的精华；研究莎剧中的辞格也有助于更加深刻地解读莎剧的人物和主题。

第三节　莎剧《哈姆雷特》

本书选取莎士比亚的《哈姆雷特》作为分析文本。《哈姆雷特》为莎士比亚的四大悲剧之一，在三十九部莎剧中知名度最高。

《哈姆雷特》一剧的故事以丹麦国夜间出现刚去世的先王老哈姆雷特的鬼魂开始,通过鬼魂的控诉,王子哈姆雷特了解到现今的国王克劳狄斯(Claudius)可能是杀父娶母的凶手。在一系列印证鬼魂控诉真实性的事件中,哈姆雷特装疯卖傻的行为引起克劳狄斯的怀疑。他利用哈姆雷特的女友莪菲莉娅(Ophelia)试探他发疯的原因,遣派他的密友监视他的行为。在哈姆雷特借助"戏中戏"证实了克劳狄斯的罪行后,克劳狄斯让其母葛特露(Gertrude)与之说理。在谈话中,哈姆雷特误杀了偷听的普隆涅斯(Polonius),也即莪菲莉娅的父亲。克劳狄斯以此为借口,表面上以保护哈姆雷特为由将他送往英国,暗地里则试图借英王之手杀害哈姆雷特。但该阴谋被哈姆雷特发现,在路上趁机逃回丹麦,但回来后又落入克劳狄斯设定的圈套,引诱他和想为父亲普隆涅斯报仇的勒替斯(Laertes)比武。在比武过程中,葛特露误喝毒酒身亡,而哈姆雷特和勒替斯也双双被毒剑击中。在毒性发作之前,哈姆雷特终于杀死了克劳狄斯,并承诺将丹麦国交给挪威王子福丁布拉斯(Fortinbras)管理。

《哈姆雷特》深受读者喜爱,其中一个原因是其故事情节的繁复有序。这一故事除了哈姆雷特为父复仇这一条主线之外,还包含其他的复仇情节:因为其父普隆涅斯在偷听哈姆雷特和其母的辩论被误杀,勒替斯向哈姆雷特寻求复仇,用毒剑刺中哈姆雷特;挪威王子福丁布拉斯因老挪威王败于老哈姆雷特被罚割地赔偿,而准备起兵攻打丹麦国复仇,但后来不用任何武力而得到管理丹麦国的权利,实现了另一种复仇;在剧中演员的表演中,也隐藏一段复仇故事,即皮拉斯(Pyrrhus)谋杀特洛伊国王普莱安(Priam),为被普莱安之子杀害的父亲阿奇里斯（Achilles）报仇。此外，故事还有多种试探，如哈姆雷特对克劳狄斯的罪行试探，普隆涅斯利用女儿对哈姆雷特的爱情试探，哈姆雷特两位好友对哈姆雷特的内在意图试探，等等，就如同哈姆雷特所说的"捕鼠器"（mousetrap）一般，各种圈套、各种试探，使整个故事险象迭生、引人入胜。

至于《哈姆雷特》一剧的创作时间，则是备受争论的话题之一。一些学者根据相关的历史记录和事件对该剧的创作时期进行推断。弗朗西斯·米尔斯（Francis Meres）在1598年编的有关莎士比亚创作的图书《智慧的宝藏》（*Palladis Tamia*：*Wits Treasury*）里并没有提及《哈姆雷特》，因此欧内斯特·霍尼曼（Ernest Honigmann）推测，《哈姆雷特》可能写于1599年年末到1600年早期之间（1956：33）。还有学者借助《哈姆雷特》的第一个四开本中提到的童伶得势这个事件，结合1600—1601年剧院相争这一真实历史事件（因为当时的剧院是人们了解时事的一个途径），推测出该剧的创作时间应该是在1601年中期之后。然而，其中最具说服力的根据应该是来自张伯伦公爵保护下的剧团的"剧目登记本"（Stationers' Register）。登记本中提到1602年7月26日有一部戏剧名为《丹麦哈姆雷特王子复仇记》（Revenge of Hamlet, Prince of Denmark），被认为是对莎士比亚这部戏剧的书面记录（Thompson & Taylor, 2007：49）。

此外，也有学者参考其他莎剧或者同时期其他戏剧的信息，来推测该剧的创作时间。例如，《哈姆雷特》剧中涉及对凯撒死前罗马景象的描述（第一幕第一场）和普隆涅斯提及自己扮演过凯撒（第三幕第二场）两个情节，因此被认为是对当时的新剧《凯撒大帝》（*Julius Caesar*）的宣传，从而推断《哈姆雷特》一剧应该创作于《凯撒大帝》上演时间的

1599年左右；也有学者从《哈姆雷特》与当时莎士比亚的竞争对手约翰·马斯顿（John Marston）创作的《安东尼之复仇》（*Antonio's Revenge*）（约1601）之间的各种情节关联，推断出主题相似的《哈姆雷特》应出现在1599—1600年左右；查尔斯·卡斯卡特（Charles Cathcart）则选择分析马斯顿创作的《安东尼与梅里达》（*Antonio and Mellida*）（约1599—1600），以及他参与创作的《欲望的权利》（*Lust's Dominion*）（约1600）与《哈姆雷特》之间的语言关联，推断出该剧应创作于1599年（2011：359）。因此，综合各种讨论，《哈姆雷特》一剧的大约创作时间应该是1599—1600年之间。

本书选取《哈姆雷特》作为辞格分析对象，则有以下三个方面的原因：

首先，《哈姆雷特》一剧深受中西方学者的关注。《哈姆雷特》是最受关注的一部莎剧，这不仅表现在该作品在学者和学生心中所能唤起的那种敬畏感，更表现在那些不计其数的研究数量上（Horvei，1984：126）。根据哈拉尔·哈维（Harald Horvei）1960年的统计，"关于《哈姆雷特》的作品比任何其他的莎剧都要多"（ibid）。在20世纪60年代，波恩汉姆·卡特（Burnham Carter）也指出，平均每十二天，世上便有一篇新的《哈姆雷特》批评作品出现（1961：13）。这一数据在今天应该也是有增无减。这些研究和出版方面的数据，也从侧面反映出《哈姆雷特》一剧在莎剧中的地位。在中国，《哈姆雷特》不仅是莎剧中第一部全文被翻译成白话文的戏剧，而且翻译这部作品的译者数量在所有莎剧中也是人数最多的，按照目前出版的译者姓名统计，共有16个不同译者。在这些译者当中，有剧作家（田汉）、诗人（卞之琳）、评论家（林同济）和散文家（梁实秋）等。从时间上看，他们翻译

《哈姆雷特》的时间从1922年到最近的2019年,跨越了近一个世纪,从这一现象中也可以管窥该剧在中国读者和译者心中的重要性。

其次,《哈姆雷特》也是莎士比亚的一部重要作品。弗兰克·克尔莫德(Frank Kermode)认为,在1599—1600年期间,莎士比亚取得一个新的创作高度和难度,而《哈姆雷特》和《凤凰与斑鸠》(*Phoenix and Turtledove*)这两部作品就是这个转折点的代表作(2000:ix)。卞之琳也认为这部戏剧"牵涉到莎士比亚前后期作品的各个方面,它提供了莎士比亚思想发展的来龙去脉,它展出了莎士比亚艺术成就的各种特征",因此是莎士比亚的一部"中心作品",是莎士比亚从早期以喜剧和历史剧为主向后期以悲剧为主的创作转向的一个标志(1980:41-42)。把该剧作为研究文本,更能全面看到莎士比亚这位文学天才在创作上的特点。

最后,《哈姆雷特》大约写于1599—1600年间,属于莎士比亚创作成熟期的一部作品,其语言特征也值得研究。作品中语言形式多样化,既有无韵诗,也有散文、民谣和古戏体,这些不同语域的语言随着剧情的变化而交替使用,共同推动戏剧的发展,完成人物性格的塑造(Kermode,2000:97)。在修辞方面,约瑟夫在研究了莎剧的修辞后发现,莎士比亚早期语言中有很多模仿古典拉丁文作品的痕迹,到了他创作的成熟阶段,便显示出同时期作家无法相比的对戏剧语言准确度的把握,和对深刻思想的细腻表达等特点(1962:285-286)。从修辞格的角度来研究莎剧,分析作者如何使用不同的修辞格来塑造人物、推进情节,把《哈姆雷特》作为文本便是一个很好的选择。

第四节 内容和框架

关于莎士比亚的语言研究,特别是修辞研究,一直是学者们热衷的话题之一。早期的如上文提到和引用到的约瑟夫(1962)和爱弗·埃文斯(Ifor Evans)(1964)便是系统研究莎士比亚修辞语言的重要学者。也有学者专注某一部莎剧的语言研究,如罗伯特·埃文斯(1966)对《罗密欧与朱丽叶》一剧中修辞格的研究等。近年的一些研究中,莎士比亚的语言也是绕不开的话题,如弗兰克·克尔莫德(2000)对莎士比亚语言的研究,其他相关性较大的还有保罗·坎特(Paul Cantor)(2004)的《哈姆雷特》专题研究等。国内对莎剧语言的专著研究,主要集中在戏剧中的著名对白或者名言的翻译和分析,如马常纲(1992),或者一些特定的语言修辞手段在不同的莎剧或莎诗中的应用,如吾文泉(2002)、徐鹏(2001)等。

以上大部分研究的特点是使用莎士比亚的所有剧本作为语言或修辞手段的案例来源。本书则聚焦《哈姆雷特》一剧,辨析这部戏剧中修辞手段的使用情况。本书整体上更像是一项梳理性的工作,并基于这些第一手梳理得出的数据,分析该剧中修辞语言使用的特点和作用。由于聚焦的是辞格,其他非辞格的语言因素,或者其他更为宏观的因素,虽然对戏剧的效果和人物的塑造同样具有重要的作用,但仍不属于本书的分析范围。同时,由于辞格的种类多样,有些辞格关注点较为细微,如"词首脱落"(aphaeresis)关注的是词语构成方面形成的修辞,如莎剧行文中常见的用"tween"来代替"between",起到节省音节的作用;也有一些辞格关注的落脚点比较宏大,如

"交换对白"（stichomythia）常以一大段的对话为单位，以突出人物之间的亲密关系或者冲突。这两种关注点较为细微或较为宏大的辞格，也不在本书的辨析范围。本书主要关注的，仍然是最为常见和主要的修辞格，如隐喻、对仗和头韵等，并尝试通过具体的辨析，寻找莎士比亚对这些辞格的创造性使用方式。

　　本书分为六章。第一章主要介绍莎士比亚如何传入中国、莎剧语言的整体特点，以及聚焦在《哈姆雷特》一剧辞格辨析的原因；第二章介绍辞格的主要分类和辨析方法，其中包括对西方修辞学的概述，以及对不同辞格分类的梳理；第三章聚焦两大类辞格的辨析，即形变辞格和义变辞格的辨析，并以《哈姆雷特》剧中的内容作为案例；第四章按照幕为单位，从文本层面对《哈姆雷特》一剧中的辞格做局部和微观的辨析和文体分析；第五章则从整体和宏观的角度，对整部戏剧中的辞格使用情况作概述，并分析辞格使用对该剧的主题渲染和人物塑造的文体效果；第六章结语则对全书内容作回顾总结，以及提出书中存在的不足。

第二章 修辞学与辞格分类研究

辞格属于西方修辞学的一部分，也是和语言使用关系最密切、也相对较为局部的一部分。然而，对莎剧行文辞格的局部分析，并不仅仅是为了分析局部的辞格文体效果，而是为了更深刻地解读莎士比亚如何使用辞格来推进情节、塑造人物和创设氛围。换言之，"只有把局部方面的修辞与整体布局的修辞结合起来考虑，才能使局部方面的修辞有意义"（胡曙中，2008：1）。本章从整体角度简单介绍西方修辞学，以及辞格在整个西方修辞学中的位置，并聚焦于辞格的分类和辨析。本章是本书第三章文本层面的辞格分析以及第四章辞格文体鉴赏的基础。

第一节　西方修辞学简介

修辞学在西方具有悠久的传统，与语法和逻辑并列为西方传统文科教育的三学科（the Trivium），为语法学校的主要讲授内容。关于修辞，亚里士多德（Aristotle）的定义是："在任何情况下，使用可利用的方法来进行劝说的能力"（2007：37），将其定位为与演说息息相关的一门学问。因此，修辞可以被笼统地定义为一种"劝说"的语言能力。传统西方修辞学的内容主要围绕这些"可利用的方法"如何分门别类，具有规定性和实用性的特点。

在西方修辞学的发展历程中，其与口语和书面语的关系密切程度不断变化。古典时期的修辞学主要关注演说语体，主要以古希腊的柏拉图、亚里士多德和西塞罗的论述为代表。其中，亚里士多德的"理性诉求"（logos）、"情感诉求"（pathos）和"品格诉求"（ethos）影响力较大。"理性诉求"主要指"用词和辩论的证据，以及演讲的逻辑性"；"情感诉求"指"感情和情绪上赋予劝说性信息能量的诉求，使信息能够影响听众，使其付诸行动"；最后的"品格诉求"指在演讲过程中，"讲者的性格和个人信用所具有的劝说潜力"（Herrick, 2008：82-84）。亚里士多德对修辞艺术的系统化讨论在古典时期"最全面和最具真知灼见"（ibid.：87-88）。这三类诉求对现当代修辞学仍具有影响力。

古典修辞学影响较大的学者还有古罗马时期的昆体良和西塞罗（Marcus Tullius Cicero）。昆体良把修辞看作公民教育的一部分，这一主张使修辞在很长时间内成为西方教育的主要成分；西塞罗则提出较为具体的"演说五大准则"（canons of oratory），将演说分为五个阶段，即"取材"（invention）、"谋篇"（disposition）、"文体"（style）、"记忆"（memory）和"讲演"（delivery）（ibid.：97），从如何发掘有效的论题、安排论述步骤、使用语言表达论点、从认知上把握论题和语言，以及到最后如何通过声音和肢体动作来演说论点等方面，都有详细的论述。西塞罗的这五个阶段说将修辞学的实用性推到了新的高度。简言之，对古罗马学者来说，修辞可以简单理解为有效地、清晰地说和写的能力。

基督教统治下的中世纪时期，西方修辞学的发展基本沿着古罗马的方向，即将修辞作为教育的一个重要组成部分，主要代表学者包括奥古斯丁（St. Augustine）。奥古斯丁认为修辞有助于有效传播基督教的真理。一方面，随着宗教对生活各个方面影响的深入，布道的需求促进了修辞和宗教传播的结合；另一方面，对语言艺术性的追求也使修辞与写作和诗歌创作相结合。詹姆士·墨菲（James Murphy）甚至将"布道"（the art of preaching）、"写作"（the art of letter writing）和"写诗"（the art of poetry）看作修辞的三种艺术样式。"装饰"功能一时成为修辞的主要特征。

在文艺复兴时期，修辞已经深入到社会教育的方方面面，成为"写作和劝说的方法指南、个人修养提升的方法、民商事务的管理方法，以及研读古今各类文学文本的重要方法"（Herrick，2008：146）。这一时期，修辞在影响范围和价值上均取得前所未有的发展。其中对教育领域的影响尤为深入，甚至可以说，整个教育体系开始建立在修辞学基础之上；能否熟练使用修辞也被看作是衡量一个人受教育程度的标准之一，演说家则被看作是成功教育的典范。这一时期对修辞的辨析也达到前所未有的精确度，例如，布莱恩·维克斯（Brian Vickers）便指出，1559年出版的《修辞汇编》（*Thesaurus Rhetoricae*）便列举了多达5000种与修辞相关的术语。修辞学的发展也促使学者对修辞本质进行思考。这一时期出现了三个主要流派：传统派（the Traditionalists）、拉米斯派（the Ramists）和修辞手段派（the Figurists）。这三大流派的主要区别在于对修辞学性质的理解和研究的关注点不同。传统派以西塞罗的

"五大准则"为基础和研究内容；拉米斯派则将"取材"和"谋篇"归为逻辑学内容，把"表达"和"讲演"作为主要研究对象；修辞手段派则主要以比喻修辞手段为主要兴趣。文艺复兴时期，英国对修辞艺术也异常感兴趣，在1500年至1600年的一百年间，先后出现了伦纳德·考克斯（Leonard Cox）、里查德·谢礼（Richard Sherry）、汤姆森·威尔逊（Thomas Wilson）、理查德·雷诺德（Richard Reinolde）、罗杰·阿斯克姆（Roger Ascham）、嘉百利·哈维（Gabriel Harvey）和亨利·皮查姆（Henry Peacham）等学者的修辞专题著作。

启蒙时期的修辞学发展基本沿用了文艺复兴的基础，同时也增加了对修辞的"科学性"和人类"心理"的思考，主要代表学者有乔治·坎贝尔（George Campbell）等。詹姆士·赫里克（James Herrick）将这一时期的修辞学转变总结为"从单纯产出公共语篇到提高语篇使用效果的转变，从发现修辞知识到应对其他学科中发现的修辞知识的转变，以及从关注外部公共语篇问题到关注内在思想和想象力的转变"（2008：190）。换言之，在启蒙时期，修辞学的研究对象已经开始聚焦其"科学性"的问题，并与相邻的学科开始产生关联。

进入近现代，修辞学曾有一段时间经历了与演说分离的情况，变得更为聚焦在书面写作，甚至被简化为基本的写作技巧，但很快现当代学者发现了其中的局限性，并开始重新发掘修辞学的古典因素。20世纪80年代以艾弗·理查兹（I. A. Richards）和肯尼斯·伯克（Kenneth Burke）为代表的"新修辞学"的出现，进一步拓展了修辞学的研究范围。正如伯克所说的，"古典修辞的关键词是'劝说'（persuasion），其强调的是蓄意的设计；而新修辞的关键词是'同一/认同'（identification），包含感染（appeal）中的部分'无意识'的因素"(1951: 203)。可以说,近现代的修辞研究与心理学和语言学等学科的关系更为紧密,将修辞学从关注语言使用方法,扩展到修辞使用背后的心理特征和原因分析,以及其可能产生的文体效果,进一步拓宽了修辞学的研究范围。

纵观西方修辞学的发展,我们可以看到修辞在西方的重要地位。修辞学已经不仅仅是一门演说的艺术,而是渗入了西方文化、教育和生活等各个方面,是我们阅读和欣赏西方文学作品的一个重要切入点。在英国,修辞教育与其他西方国家相比,甚至有过之而无不及,在传统英国教育中扮演着重要的角色(Vickers, 1971: 83)。莎士比亚在学期间,也接受过系统的修辞学教育,熟知昆体良等古典修辞学家的作品(Baldwin, 1944: 378)。可以说,不管是有意识还是无意识,修辞学都是莎士比亚戏剧创作的基础。当我们从修辞的角度来欣赏莎剧时,传统意义上的修辞学,即修辞为语言劝说的艺术,可以帮助我们更好地欣赏莎士比亚的戏剧语言,了解莎士比亚对语言炉火纯青的应用能力;从新修辞的角度来看,则可以帮助我们窥看莎士比亚使用这些修辞手段背后显性或隐性的创作动机。本书的第四章可以理解为较为传统的辞格辨析;第五章则从文体的视角,探讨这些修辞可能产生的文体效果。

第二节 辞格的分类研究

辞格是本书讨论莎剧修辞的微观切入点。辞格是"文体"中最小的结构单位(structural units),在不同的文本类型中,我们都能找到使用辞格的例子(Plett, 2001: 324)。需要指出的是,不管是在典型的文学文本,如莎剧,还是在最为规定性的学术语言使用中，如学术论文，我们都可以找到辞格的身影，唯一的不同可能是其种类和密集程度的不一。因此，辞格并不是文学文本的专利，而是在不同语境下均可出现的语言现象。

　　根据西塞罗的"五大准则"，辞格属于修辞学"文体"准则下的内容，与语言的使用关系最为直接。针对辞格的定义，不同学者看法不一。昆体良将辞格（figure）定义为"通过艺术的手法给表达以新的内容"（1959：353），仍将辞格看作是一种"艺术"的行为。但笼统来说，辞格（figures of speech/rhetorical devices）指的是"词语使用的特殊和不寻常的方法：可以是对词语的异常的安排（arrangement），也可以是使词语拥有特别的、异常的意义（meaning）的方法"（Harris, 2018：2）。换言之，辞格就是对语言的常规组织形式和常规意义的偏离，以达到原来组织形式和意义所没有的文体效果。例如，当哈姆雷特说出 O that this too too solid flesh would melt, /thaw, and resolve itself into a dew! 时，他连续使用三个动词，melt, thaw 和 resolve，形成一种特殊安排，构成形变辞格排比；他同时也将自己的身躯，this solid flesh, 和冰块的溶解相比，赋予身体不同的意象和意义，构成义变辞格隐喻。

　　辞格也有多种分类的方法。例如，昆体良就将辞格分为"思想格"（figure of thought）和"语言格"（figure of speech）两大类。而更为常见的是基于辞格的定义，将辞格分为"形变辞格"（schemes/figures）和"义变辞格"（tropes）。前者指通过改变词语的安排获得修辞效果，后者则指通过改变意义获得修辞效果。不同时期的学者对辞格的分类方法和标准也各有不同。文艺复兴时期修辞学发展进入精细阶段，乔治·普登汉姆（George Puttenham）在他的《英诗的技巧》（*The Arte of English Poesie*）（1589）中，根据辞格对人产生的不同类型的感染力，将辞格分为听觉类（aurucular）、感觉类（sensable）和听觉感觉类（sententious），突出辞格在感官感染方面的作用；米里亚姆·约瑟夫（Miriam Joseph）（1962）认为，辞格和五大阶段中的"取材"阶段息息相关，则在"形变辞格"和"义变辞格"的基础上，从逻辑的角度进一步细分文艺复兴时期发现的辞格。她将"形变辞格"分为"语法层面辞格"（schemes of grammar）和"重复辞格"（figures of repetition），如"插说"由于打断原来的句子结构，属于"语法层面辞格"；"排比"是由三个以上的相同结构成分构成，属于"重复辞格"。约瑟夫又将"义变辞格"进一步分为"相似与不同类"（similarities and dissimilarities）、"类与属类"（genus and species）、"因与果类"（cause and effect）、"整体与部分类"（whole and part）、"主体与属性类"（subject and adjuncts）、"词源和词形变化类"（notation and conjugates）、"对比类"（comparison）和"相互矛盾类"（contraries and contradictory）等。例如，隐喻辞格是在对比两事物的相似点的逻辑思维基础上形成的辞格，属于"相似与不同类"；换义双关属于"词源和词形变化类"。

按照辞格内在逻辑分类，仍然是现当代辞格相关著作的主要分类方法。在《现代学生的古典修辞》（*Classical Rhetoric for the Modern Student*）（1999）一书中，爱德华·科贝特（Edward P. J. Corbett）和罗伯特·康纳斯（Robert J. Connors）对形变辞格的讨论较为简练，他们把形变辞格分为"词语形变辞格"（schemes of words）和"结构形变辞格"（schemes of construction）。然后又将"结构形变辞格"继续分为"平衡形变辞格"（schemes of balance）、"词序倒装形变辞格"（schemes of unusual or inverted word order）、"省略形变辞格"（schemes of omission）和"反复形变辞格"（schemes of repetition）等四类。

除了按照辞格构成的逻辑来分类之外，在20世纪六七十年代语言学迅猛发展的影响下，一些学者也使用语言学的框架来对辞格作分类，最具代表性的学者要属茨维坦·托多罗夫（Tzvetan Todorov）和杰弗里·利奇（Geoffrey Leech）。在他们同时期的作品中，托多罗夫（1967）和利奇（1966）都采用从"规则违背"（rule violating）和"规则增强"（rule-reinforcing）这个思路，结合语言学的各种语言层次，构成详细的辞格分类模型。例如，隐喻对托多罗夫来说，属于语义方面的"规则违背"，同位语属于句法方面的"规则增强"。利奇受到语言学家约翰·弗斯（John Firth）和韩礼德（Michael Halliday）的影响，则建议从语法、词汇、语音、拼写和语义等语言学层面来对辞格作分类（1966：147）。同样，海恩里希·普莱特（Heinrich Plett）（2010）也将辞格系统地按照语言学层次来分类，分为"语音辞格"（phonological figures）、"形态辞格"（morphological figures）、"句法辞格"（syntactic figures）、"语义辞格"（semantic figures）、"字形辞格"（graphemic figures）、"语篇辞格"（text figures）、"互文辞格"（intertextual figures）。例如，头韵属于"语音辞格"，引用则属于"互文辞格"等。

可以看到，与古典修辞按照逻辑或语言结构和语义的分类相比，语言学的分类方法更为系统和细致。然而，上述的这些分类虽然有助于对辞格的辨析和梳理，但从文体的角度来说，其作用可能不如按照逻辑的分类大。例如，约瑟夫将隐喻归类为根据"相似性"的辞格,而利奇将隐喻归为"语义辞格",相比之下,约瑟夫的分类标准更能使隐喻构成的背后逻辑一目了然。本书第三章有关辞格的讨论,也将从逻辑的角度来对辞格进行分类,并辅以《哈姆雷特》剧中的案例加以说明。

可以看到,与古典修辞按照逻辑或语言结构和语义的分类相比,语言学的分类方法更为系统和细致。然而,上述的这些分类虽然有助于对辞格的辨析和梳理,但从文体的角度来说,其帮助可能不如按照逻辑的分类大。例如,约瑟夫将隐喻归类为根据"相似性"的辞格,而利奇将隐喻归位"语义辞格",相比之下,约瑟夫等的分类标准更能使隐喻构成的背后逻辑一目了然。本书第三章有关辞格的讨论,也将从逻辑的角度来对辞格进行分类,并辅以《哈姆雷特》句中的案例加以说明。

第三章的案例,以及第四章的原文内容均基于安·汤普森(Ann Thompson)和尼尔·泰勒(Neil Taylor)编、2007年出版的阿登版莎士比亚(The Arden Shakespeare)系列之《哈姆雷特》(*Hamlet*)。该版本不详或不确定的内容,则同时参考史蒂芬·格林布拉特(Stephen Greenblatt)等编、2005年出版的《诺顿莎士比亚全集》(*The Norton Shakespeare*)。文本的文字拼写主要根据阿登版,标点符号方面则综合两个版本的理解,在阿登版基础上做了修改。

第三章　辞格的辨析

辞格的数量众多，如第二章提到的，出版于 1559 年的《修辞汇编》中，便包含 5000 多种辞格。辞格数量如此之多，一方面是因为学者们对语言中的各种表达方式，即使是最为普通的语言使用，都冠以一个具体的辞格名称；另一方面也是因为辞格辨析过程中，有的学者对同一种辞格又继续作细致入微的分析和区别。如出自《哈姆雷特》的例 1 和例 2：

例 1：

…To die: to sleep—
No more, and by a sleep to say we end
The heartache, and the thousand natural shocks
That flesh is heir to: 'tis a consummation
Devoutly to be wished. To die: to sleep—
To sleep, perchance to dream—ay, there's the rub,
For in that sleep of death what dreams may come
When we have shuffled off this mortal coil
Must give us pause…

例 2：
I will speak daggers to her but use none.

例 1 为哈姆雷特最著名的独白，是他对于人生死的一次思考。在辞格分析中，我们一般考虑的是行文语言的具体辞格，而在伊丽莎白时期，这种对自我做法和思想的怀疑和思考也被归为"理性诉求"类别下的"自我质疑"（aporia）辞格，而这类辞格现在较少被提及。例 2 中的 speak daggers 的搭配不符合惯常的规范，属于对语义的转移，即将恶毒的、让人伤心的语言，与被匕首刺痛的感觉相比拟，属于基于"相似性"的一类辞格。在伊丽莎白时期，这类辞格被称为"误用"（catachresis）辞格，是一种含蓄的隐喻辞格。从例 1 和例 2 可以看到，语言的各种使用方式，对修辞学家来说，都可以看作某种类别的辞格，而同一种辞格，也可以进一步细分为更为精确的辞格。然而，本书并不计划以这些细微的辞格类型作为辨析对象，而是聚焦在一些较为常用和普遍的辞格分析上。尽管如此，我们也会发现莎士比亚在行文过程对辞格的密集使用和灵活处理。下文将基于最基本的"形变辞格"和"义变辞格"的分类，同时结合约瑟夫与科贝特对两者的进一步分类，对两大类别的辞格进行定义和文体分析。

第一节　形变辞格（Schemes）

形变辞格指的是以"对词语的常规结构和安排的偏离"（Corbett & Connors，1999：379）取得一定修辞效果的辞格类型。科贝特将形变辞格分为"词语形变辞格"和"结构形变辞格"两大类。其中,"词语形变辞格"也被其他修辞学家称为"书写辞格"(orthographical schemes),指:①在词语的前、中和后部分增加或减少字母或音节,或②转变词语的读音(ibid.:428)。例如,在 climate 的词末尾添加一个音节,构成 climature,这是属于"词尾添音"(proparalepsis)辞格。然而,词语是语言较为活跃的单位,会随着时间的变化而发生转变,词语形变辞格也因此变得较难把握。特别是在莎士比亚创作的伊丽莎白时期,英语语言形式还处于不稳定的状态(Joseph,1962:1),莎士比亚本人也是造字能手,更使得对词语形变辞格的判断很难有一个较为稳定的标准,因此,本书将不对词语形变辞格作讨论。

"结构形变辞格"立足在句法上,指通过变换句子的常规结构,取得一定修辞效果的辞格。科贝特将"结构形变辞格"分为"平衡形变辞格""词序倒装形变辞格""省略形变辞格"和"反复形变辞格"四类,并对各类包含的辞格做了简单介绍。下文参考科贝特的著作,对这四个类别之下的常见辞格分别加以分析。

一、平衡形变辞格

平衡形变辞格主要是通过两个以上的结构相同、意义相似或相反的句子,排列成串而成的辞格。平衡的句子结构有利于借用相同的结构,减轻读者阅读的困难,以达到更清晰地传递信息的目的;同时,平衡的句子结构也能创造一种音韵效果,使行文在音韵上更加流畅。平衡形变辞格主要有两种,即排比和对仗。

1. 排比 (parallelism)

排比指的是使用两个以上的结构相似和内容相关的词语、

短语和小句构成的辞格。排比是和语法相关的辞格，借助平行的结构来反映一系列有规律的思维模式，能够增强语言的气势，从而加强表达的效果，如例3、例4和例5。

例3：

Hamlet：
O that this too too sallied flesh would <u>melt</u>,
<u>Thaw</u> and <u>resolve</u> itself into a dew,
Or that the Everlasting had not fixed
His canon 'gainst self-slaughter. O God, God,
How <u>weary</u>, <u>stale</u>, <u>flat</u> and <u>unprofitable</u>
Seem to me all the uses of this world!

例4：

Hamlet：
For who would bear <u>the whips and scorns of time</u>,
<u>Th' oppressor's wrong</u>, <u>the proud man's contumely</u>,
<u>The pangs of despised love</u>, <u>the law's delay</u>,
<u>The insolence of office</u> and the spurns
That patient merit of th' unworthy takes,
When he himself might his quietus make
With a bare bodkin.

例5：

Hamlet：
I have heard of your paintings well enough. God hath given you one face and you make yourselves another. <u>You jig and</u>

amble and you lisp; you nickname God's creatures and make your wantonness your ignorance.

例3、例4和例5分别为词语、短语和小句构成的排比辞格。例3中，第一处排比辞格由 melt、thaw 和 resolve 三个动词构成；第二处由 weary、stale、flat 和 unprofitable 四个形容词构成。例4中，其中的四处"the…of…"短语结构和三个's所有格结构构成排比辞格。例5中由三个 you 引领的小句构成。这一系列的排比能够帮助表意更加深入和全面，也能够使行文语势更加强而有力。

在各种排比句中，如果构成排比的成分不但结构相同，而且每部分使用的字数或者音节数量都相同的话，则构成"同一语法反复辞格"（isocolon），如上面例4即为一处同一语法反复辞格。可以说，同一语法反复辞格为更加整齐的排比结构。

2. 对仗（antithesis）

对仗是用相同或相似的结构将意义相反的成分排列在一起的辞格。在英文的对仗中，意思的相反为对仗辞格的主要特征，而结构是否对应，则不如中文严格，如例6和例7。

例6：
Hamlet：
But to my mind, though I am native here
And to the manner born, it is a custom
More honoured in the breach than the observance.

例7：

Hamlet：

So again, good night.

I must <u>be cruel only to be kind</u>.

在例6中，breach（摒弃）和observance（遵循）两个词的语义相反，例7中，cruel（残忍）和kind（友善）两词语义相反，构成了对仗辞格。对仗辞格的使用有助于"创造一种警句般的工整效果，也能体现说话人的智慧"（Corbett and Connors, 1999：383）。在例6和例7中，虽然"（酗酒的）习俗摒弃比遵守更让人敬仰"、"我必须残忍才能变得友善"等在表达上比较反常，但却能将事物的两个方面工整地表达出来，并通过相互对照，产生使用普通语言所无法实现的修辞效果。

二、词序倒装形变辞格

词序倒装形变辞格主要是通过颠倒或打乱句子结构的惯常位置，以获得不同修辞效果的形变辞格。这类辞格主要包括倒装、插说和同位语。同样，由于莎剧所处的时代英语语言还没有定型，有些句法结构与现代英语存在差别，因此，倒装在本书也不作讨论。下文主要讨论插说和同位语两个辞格。

1. 插说（parenthesis）

插说通过在正常的句子中插入一些内容，打断句子的正常语序，从而构成一定的修辞效果。插说的主要功能在于能够在行文中补充新的内容，因此，我们可以"听到作者的声音、评论、意见，并使句子具有原来所没有的情感成分"（Corbett and Connors, 1999：385）。如例8和例9：

例8：

Claudius：

Hamlet, this deed for thine especial safety—
Which we do tender, as we dearly grieve
For that which thou hast done—must send thee hence.

例9：

Horatio：

Our last King,
Whose image even but now appeared to us,
Was, as you know, by Fortinbras of Norway—
Thereto pricked on by a most emulate pride—
Dared to the combat, in which our valiant Hamlet
(For so this side of our known world esteemed him)
Did slay this Fortinbras, ...

例8和例9的下划线部分为插说辞格。例8中，克劳狄斯在表达将哈姆雷特送去英国的句子中，插入which we do tender as we dearly grieve for that which thou hast done（我们对你的所作所为感到非常痛心），在说出结果之前，插入自己的感受。在例9中，as you know（如你所知）为较为常见的插说用语，提醒下方信息为对方所了解的，另一处为for so this side of our known world esteemed him，则插入将老哈姆雷特尊为valiant Hamlet（神勇哈姆雷特）的说法由来，使自己的语言有了出处。这两个例子的插说辞格，都为原来的陈述句子增添了一些"个人"的因素。此外，插说辞格在句子中往往有较为明显的符号标志，如例8中是由破折号引出，例9的例子则分别通过逗号和括号隔开。

2. 同位语（apposition）

同位语指将两个并列的、内容相同或相似的成分放在一起，其中位于后面的成分往往对前面的作补充和说明。这一辞格最常用于人物或事物的介绍。如例 10 和例 11：

例 10：

Hamlet：

That is <u>Laertes</u>, <u>a very noble youth</u>.

例 11：

Hamlet：

I have of late—but wherefore I know not—lost all my mirth, forgone all custom of exercises and, indeed, it goes so heavily with my disposition that <u>this goodly frame</u> <u>the earth</u> seems to me a sterile promontory, …

例 10 和例 11 中的下划线部分均为同位语。例 10 中，Laertes 和 a very noble youth 构成同位语，后者是对前者的信息补充，即对这个青年的评价；例 11 中，this goodly frame 和 the earth 构成同位语，前者为借代的手法，然后通过后面的 the earth 这一同位语点名所指对象。

三、省略形变辞格

省略形变辞格是通过故意省略词语构成的辞格，听众或读者往往可以通过上下文的语境补充所省略的部分。省略辞格是

■ 莎剧《哈姆雷特》辞格辨析与文体鉴赏

"一种充满艺术性和引人注意的方法,使行文更加简洁"(Corbett & Connors, 1999: 387),其包含的主要辞格是省略(ellipsis),如例12和例13。

例 12:

Hamlet:

Armed, say you?

Marcellus:

[with Bernado] Armed, my lord.

Hamlet:

From top to toe?

Marcellus:

[with Bernado] My lord, from head to foot.

例 13:

Hamlet:

What is a man
If his chief good and market of his time
Be but to sleep and feed? A beast—no more.

例12为哈姆雷特和两个守夜卫士的对话,其中 Armed 的完整句子应该为"Was he armed?","From top to toe"和"from head to foot"应为"He was armed from top to toe."和"He was armed from head to foot."。省略在这里的使用使得对话更加紧凑,增强了紧张、急促的效果。例13中哈姆雷特的自问自答中,a beast 的完整句子应该是"He is a beast.",这处的省略有助于突出保留的部分,即 a beast。从这两个例子可

30

以看到，省略辞格常用于对话中，有助于语言的简炼紧凑，也有助于将次要的、可以通过语境获得的内容省去，以凸显所要强调的内容。

此外，如果句子所省略的部分为连接词，则该类省略也名为"连词省略"（asyndeton）。如例 14：

例 14：
Ophelia：
The courtier's, scholar's, soldier's, eye, tongue, sword,
Th' expectancy and rose of the fair state,
The glass of fashion and the mould of form,
Th' observ'd of all observers——quite, quite down.

按照英语的语法，当列举到最后一个词的时候，需要添加连接词 and，即例 14 中的 courtier's, scholar's, soldier's 和 eye, tongue, sword 需要分别在 soldier's 和 sword 之前添加 and，因此此处属于连词省略辞格。连接词的省略能够使行文更加规整，从而取得不同的效果，如最为著名的有亚伯拉罕·林肯的 government of the people, by the people, for the people, 以及恺撒大帝的"I came, I saw, I conquered"。在例 14 中，除了使用连词省略取得简练的效果之外，莎士比亚使用该辞格还可能是受到了每行十个音节的五步格的约束。

四、重复形变辞格

科贝特和康纳斯认为，"重复是情绪高涨时的语言特征之一"（1969：392）。在讨论重复形变辞格时，他将声音重复类和词语重复类的辞格放在一起讨论。声音类主要讨论的是头韵

（alliteration）和元音韵（assonance），词语重复类主要包含首语重复（anaphora）、尾语重复（epistrophe）、首尾重复（epanalepsis）、链形重复（anadiplosis）、回环重复（antimetabole）和同根异形重复（polyptoton）等。下文讨论声音重复类时，则主要聚焦于头韵和尾韵。尾韵（rhyming）和元音韵有相似之处，但也有不同之处。相似之处是当一个构成韵的词语词尾没有辅音时，两者基本没有差别，如 he 和 be 构成的韵。而尾韵则除了这类没有辅音尾音的词语之外，也包含有辅音尾音的词语，如 peace 和 tease，因此，本书主要讨论尾韵。在词语重复中，除了科贝特提及的六种特殊的重复辞格之外，还存在其他的较为普通的重复辞格，分别是直接重复（epizeuxis）和间隔重复（diacope）。下文将逐一举例说明。

1. 声音重复形变辞格

（1）头韵（alliteration）

头韵指一个词组、诗行甚至句子中，相邻或相近的两个或两个以上词语，其开头字母或音节相同。头韵有节奏和音律上的修辞效果。如例 15 和例 16。

例 15：
Father's Ghost：
I am thy father's spirit,
Doomed for a certain term to walk the night,
And for the day confined to <u>fast</u> in <u>fires</u>
Till the <u>foul</u> crimes done in my days of nature
Are burnt and purged away.

例 16：

First Player：

　　　　　　　　　　　　　Anon he finds him,
Striking too short at Greeks. His antique sword,
Rebellious to his arm, lies where it falls,
Repugnant to command.

例 15 构成头韵的词语首字母相同，即 fast、fires 和 foul 三个词语首字母都是 f；例 16 中，构成头韵的词语不仅首字母相同，首音节也相同，即 rebellious 和 repugnant。头韵比较明显，能够使读者感受到构成头韵的几个词语之间有较为密切的关系，阅读起来不但有一种韵律之美，而且有时候也能产生一种语义上的呼应。如例 16 中，rebellious 和 repugnant 不仅首音节发音相同，在语义上也都属于贬义词，构成语义上的呼应。

（2）尾韵（rhyming）

与头韵相反，尾韵指一个词组、诗行甚至句子中，相邻或相近的两个或两个以上词语，其结尾的音节相同，如例 17 和例 18。

例 17：

Hamlet：

O cursed spite
That ever I was born to set it right!

例 18：

Player King：

Full thirty times hath Phoebus' cart gone round

> Neptune's salt wash and Tellus' orbed <u>ground</u>
> And thirty dozen moons with borrowed <u>sheen</u>
> About the world have times twelve thirties <u>been</u>
> Since love our hearts, and Hymen did our <u>hands</u>
> Unite commutual in most sacred <u>bands</u>.

例 17 中的 spite 和 right 构成尾韵。在莎剧中，相连两行构成尾韵一般用来预示该场或该幕的结束。此外，和头韵相似，押韵的两个词语之间，有时也构成语义关联。如例 17 中，两个词语的语义关联可以理解为"set the spite right"，这有助于加深对戏剧语言的深层理解。莎剧中主要使用的是抑扬五步格自由诗，而在剧中，也有部分地方使用了对句押韵，使用尾韵除了预示该场或该幕的结束之外，也有区分不同文体的作用。如在剧中的歌谣和剧中剧部分，均使用了尾韵辞格。例 18 中，round 和 ground，sheen 和 been，hands 和 bands 分别构成三处尾韵辞格。

2. 词语重复形变辞格

词语重复形变辞格的判断一般与该重复词语在句中的不同位置相关，根据其位置的特殊程度，可以分为四组：第一组为间接重复和直接重复，这两种辞格的判断标准主要是其是否存在重复，以及重复的词语是否相邻或者间隔；第二组为首语重复、尾语重复和首尾重复，主要以重复部分发生在句首或句尾作为参照；第三组较为特殊，是链形重复和回环重复，主要体现为重复之间是否构成链接和呼应；第四组为同根异形重复，主要是词语的内部词根的重复，是所有重复辞格中最为精细的一种辞格。下文将一一举例说明。

(1) 间隔重复（diacope）和直接重复（epizeuxis）

间隔重复指一个句子或几个句子中，重复的词语或短语中间被其他句子成分隔开；而直接重复则指这些重复的词语和短语没有被其他句子成分隔开。在分析过程中，直接重复和间接重复经常交织在一处出现，如例 19、例 20 和例 21。

例 19：

Laertes:

If with too credent ear you list his songs

Or lose your heart, or your chaste treasure open

To his unmastered importunity.

Fear it, Ophelia, fear it, my dear sister,

And keep you in the rear of your affection

Out of the shot and danger of desire

例 20：

Hamlet:

O all you host of heaven, O earth—What else? —

And shall I couple hell? Hold, hold, my heart, …

例 21：

Polonius:

What do you read, my lord?

Hamlet:

Words, words, words.

例 19 中，勒替斯说出 fear it 时，使用了间隔重复辞格，两处 fear it 之间插入了他妹妹的名字 Ophelia。例 20 和例 21 则为直接重复，重复词语之间没有被其他词语间隔开。在例 20 中，哈姆雷特重复了 hold 两次；在例 21 中，他重复了 words 三次。间隔重复和直接重复辞格的使用，一般为强调被重复的词语。该辞格的使用和说话者的感情相关性较大，一般为有感而发。

（2）首语重复（anaphora）、尾语重复（epistrophe）和首尾重复（epanalepsis）

与间隔重复和直接重复相比，首语重复和尾语重复运用的刻意性比较大。通过首语重复的使用，说话人为系列句子建立了韵律，同时也取得了强烈的感情效果；尾语重复同样建立了韵律，起到对重复部分的强调作用（Corbett & Connors, 1999：391）；而首尾重复辞格与前两者相比，可能传递的情绪更为强烈，但对首尾重复的使用，科贝特强调要"时机合适"（when the time is appropriate），"当你发现自己刻意地使用首尾重复时，不要用它"（Corbett & Connors, 1999：392）。如例 22、例 23 和例 24。

例 22：

Hamlet：

Doubt thou the stars are fire,
Doubt that the sun doth move,
Doubt truth to be a liar,
But never doubt I love.

例 23：

Claudius：

Farewell, and let your haste commend your duty.

Cornelius：[with Voltemand]
In that and all things will we show our duty.

例 24：
Polonius：
My liege, and madam, to expostulate
What majesty should be, what duty is,
Why day is day, night is night, and time is time,
Were nothing but to waste night, day, and time; ...

例22、例23和例24分别是首语重复、尾语重复和首尾重复辞格。在例22中，哈姆雷特在句首重复了doubt，借助这一词语的重复，使三句话成为一个并列关系的句群；例23中，朝臣科尼利厄斯（Cornelius）重复克劳狄斯句子的最后一个词duty，构成尾语重复辞格，也对duty一词起到强调的效果；例24中，普隆涅斯的day is day, night is night和time is time构成首尾重复辞格。然而，值得指出的是，普隆涅斯对该辞格的使用有些刻意，因此凸显出来的并不是他充沛的感情，而是语言的啰唆。科贝特在书中举了一个父亲失去儿子的例子，当时父亲发出"He was flesh of my flesh, bone of my bone, blood of my blood"，为肺腑之言，所传达的感情也更为充沛真实，因此说明该辞格的使用贵在自然。

(3) 链形重复（anadiplosis）和回环重复（antimetabole）

链形重复指第一句的末尾词语在第二句的开头出现，形成链形的效果，类似于汉语的"顶真"格；回环重复则指在下一个句中，以颠倒过来的结构重复上一句的词语，类似于汉语的"回文"。如例25和例26：

例 25：

Player Queen：
Where love is great, the littlest doubts are fear,
Where little fears grow great, great love grows there.

例 26：

Hamlet：

For this same lord
I do repent, but heaven hath pleased it so
To punish me with this, and this with me,
That I must be their scourge and minister.

例 27：

Hamlet：

What devil was't
That thus hath cozened you at hoodman-blind?
Eyes without feeling, feeling without sight,
Ears without hands or eyes, smelling sans all,
Or but a sickly part of one true sense
Could not so mope.

例 25 中，第一小句以 great 结尾，第二小句以 great 开头，构成了链形重复；例 26 中，me with this 和 this with me 构成回环重复；例 27 与例 26 有些不同，eyes without feeling 和 feeling without sight 在回环重复的过程中，eyes 变为同义词 sight，属于一种较为灵活的回环重复辞格。这两种重复辞格都使行文更加简练，且创造了一种警句的效果。

(4) 同根异形重复 (polyptoton)

同根异形重复指所重复的词语词根相同,如同一词根的不同屈折变化等。同根异形重复可以创造一种类似文字游戏的效果。如例 28 和例 29:

例 28:

Polonius:

See you now—
Your bait of falsehood takes this carp of truth,
And thus do we of wisdom and of reach,
With windlasses and with assays of bias,
By indirections find directions out: ...

例 29:

Polonius:

And now remains
That we find out the cause of this effect—
Or rather say, the cause of this defect,
For this effect defective comes by cause.

例 28 中,indirections 和 directions 属于同词根词语,两者在此处构成同根异形重复辞格;例 29 中,effect, defect 和 defective 三个词语都包含词根"fect",构成了同根异形重复辞格。这些同根异形重复辞格的使用,能创设一种睿智的效果;但过度的使用,则有卖弄的嫌疑。如例 28 和例 29 中,普隆涅斯对这一辞格就有过度使用的嫌疑。辞格的使用是为了更清晰、更简练、更生动地表达观点,但普隆涅斯的这两处则不但

39

没有使表达更加清晰，反而影响了听者的理解。

第二节　义变辞格（Tropes）

义变辞格指"对词语的常规和主要语义的偏离"（Corbett & Connors，1999：379），从而获得原来语义没有的修辞效果的辞格。参考约瑟夫的分类，以及对常见义变辞格构成逻辑的分析，本书将义变辞格分为相似类、替代类、双关类、层递类和对比类等类型。下文讨论每类辞格下的具体辞格类型。

一、相似类义变辞格

相似类义变辞格在这里指建立在"相似性"这一逻辑基础上的辞格，包括隐喻、明喻和拟人，这三种辞格都是建立在事物之间的相似性之上。其中，隐喻和明喻的主要区别在于事物之间的对比是明确地通过喻词 like 或 as 等表达出来，还是通过行文暗示而得到的。

1. 隐喻（metaphor）

隐喻指在原来不同的两种事物中发现相似性而建立起来的对比辞格。隐喻在修辞学中有很多的讨论。亚里士多德甚至将能够熟练使用隐喻、在不同的事物之间发现相似点看作是"天才"的特征。隐喻最基本的形式是用 A 事物指认 B 事物，如例 30 和例 31：

例 30：

Hamlet：

Fie on't! Ah, fie, 'tis an unweeded garden
That grows to seed, things rank and gross in nature
Possess it merely.

例 31：

Hamlet：

…but that I love thee best, O most best, believe it. Adieu. Thine evermore, most dear lady, whilst this machine is to him.

例 30 中，哈姆雷特用 'tis is an unweeded garden（杂草丛生的花园）来描述丹麦王国，构成一处隐喻辞格；例 31 中，哈姆雷特则把自己的身体比喻为一台机器。两个例子都是基于"A 是 B"的结构构成。虽然说这是隐喻的经典结构，但隐喻并不总是这么明显，有时候则是通过句子中的其他成分表达出来，如例 32、例 33 和例 34：

例 32：

Polonius：

       And then I prescripts gave her,
That she should lock herself from his resort,
Admit no messengers, receive no tokens；
Which done, she took the fruits of my advice, …

例 33：

Polonius：

I would fain prove so. But what might you think
When I had seen this hot love on the wing—
As I perceived it (I must tell you that)
Before my daughter told me—, what might you, …

例 34：

Bernado：

Looks it not like the King? Mark it, Horatio.

Horatio：

Most like. It harrows me with fear and wonder.

在例 32 中，普隆涅斯的隐喻是通过一个修饰语表达出来，即 the fruits of my advice（我的建议的果实），将建议被采纳比喻为建议结出了果实；例 33 中，隐喻是通过一个介宾短语传递出来，即 this hot love on the wing（插上翅膀的热恋），将迅速升温的爱情比喻为仿佛长了翅膀一般；例 34 中，隐喻则通过谓语动词传递出来，"It harrows me with fear and wonder."（恐惧和惊讶耙过我的心），将受到鬼魂惊吓的心理比喻为被农具钉耙耙过一般。这 3 例都是较为隐晦的隐喻辞格，其对比的两种事物并没有直接表达出来，而是需要根据用词来推测。有些比较特殊的隐喻，还被专门冠以另一个名称。例如，当"喻体第一次出现后，或作为第二本体，继之以一个或多个喻体相喻；或进一步设喻揭示喻体的多方面特征"（李亚丹、李定坤，2005：143），这类隐喻被称为进喻（extended metaphor），或扩展隐喻，如例 35 和 36：

例 35：

Bernado： Sit down awhile,
And let us once again <u>assail your ears</u>
<u>That are so fortified against our story</u>
What we two nights have seen.

例 36：

Laertes： Think it no more.
<u>For nature crescent</u> does not grow alone
In thews and bulk, but as <u>this temple waxes</u>
<u>The inward service of the mind and soul</u>
<u>Grows wide withal.</u>

例 35 中，博纳多（Bernado）用动词 assail（攻打）来比喻向同伴讲述遇到鬼魂的事情，采用的是军事的意象；在接下来的说话中，他进一步拓展这个隐喻，继续将不相信这个故事的情况比喻为耳朵被 fortified（严防死守），进一步延伸原来的军事比喻，属于隐喻中的进喻辞格。例 36 中，勒替斯首先用 nature crescent（新月）的变圆来比喻哈姆雷特的成长；进而又使用 temple（庙宇），并将该隐喻延伸，用庙宇的扩大和 service（供品）的需求增加来比喻随着其成长，个人欲望也会变多。

隐喻的使用能够使行文更加生动，好的隐喻也能够揭示事物的本质。隐喻的种类多样，有的被修辞学家冠以精确的名称，但在本书中，均作为隐喻来辨析和讨论。

2. 明喻（simile）

明喻即是比较显化的比喻，通常可以借助喻词 like 或 as

来确认。明喻和隐喻一样,都是借助对两种不同事物的对比来发现事物之间相似点的辞格,为行文增添生动性。如例37和例38:

例37:

Hamlet:

My fate cries out
And makes each petty artery in this body
As hardy as the Nemean lion's nerve.

例38:

First Player:

Roasted in wrath and fire,
And thus o'ersized with coagulate gore,
With eyes like carbuncles, the hellish Pyrrhus
Old grandsire Priam seeks.

例37中,哈姆雷特由于听了鬼魂的控诉之后,心情激动,身体充满了复仇的能量,因此将其比喻为身体的经络如同复仇女神的狮子那般强壮,整个比喻通过对比的结构"as hardy as"构成;例38中,演员在讲述希腊皮拉斯王子为父亲复仇的过程,将他充满杀气的眼睛比喻为如红宝石般红艳,也为一处明喻,通过like的喻词实现。

3. 拟人(personification)

拟人辞格指将物品或动物比拟为人,赋予其人的思想和行为特征。通过将其他物品和动物比拟为人,使行文变得更加生动有趣，同时也能使描述增添情感成分，如例39。

例39：

Hamlet：
Thus conscience does make cowards—
And thus the native hue of resolution
Is sicklied o'er with the pale cast of thought,
And enterprises of great pith and moment
With this regard their currents turn awry…

例39中，哈姆雷特将resolution（行动力）比拟为人，将行动力的不足，比拟为生病的人，脸色苍白，奄奄一息。

在汉语中，除了拟人，还区分了拟物辞格，即将人比喻为动物或者没有生命的物体，在本书中，将把拟物归为隐喻辞格来辨析。相似类义变辞格的整体特征是在不同事物中寻找共同点，它们也是义变辞格中数量较为庞大、较为常见的一类辞格。

二、替代类义变辞格

替代类义变辞格指辞格的构成背后逻辑为将A事物替代B事物，这类辞格主要包括借代、提喻和换说。

1. 借代（metonymy）

借代指用事物的主要特征或者最为相关的物品指代该事物的辞格，如用容器指代所盛物品，用处所指代居于处所的人或事，用工具或器官指代该工具和器官的功能等，最为经典的借代辞格有用"笔杆子"指代"作家"，用"酒瓶"指代"喝

酒"等。莎剧中也有许多借代辞格,如例40和例41:

例40:
Claudius:
I have sent to seek him and to find the body.
How dangerous is it that this man goes loose!
Yet must not we put the strong law on him:
He's loved of the distracted multitude,
Who like not in their judgment, but their eyes, ...

例41:
Rosencrantz:
These are now the fashion, and so berattle the common stages (so they call them) that many wearing rapiers are afraid of goose-quills and dare scarce come thither.

例40中,克劳狄斯用eyes(眼睛)来指代能用眼睛这一人体器官看到的外貌,即群众感性地喜欢哈姆雷特的外貌,并不用他们的理性来判断他行为是否正确。这处辞格是用与事物关联性较大的其他事物来指代原来事物。例41中有两处借代辞格:第一处使用wearing rapiers(佩戴长剑)指代当时的时髦年轻人,第二处用goose-quills(鹅毛笔)指代用鹅毛笔写作的作家。借代可以突出描写对象的主要特征,以增加行文的生动性和变化性。

2. 提喻(synecdoche)

提喻指用事物的类别和种类、整体和部分、抽象和具体、材料和材料造成的物品等之间的相互替代，如用"武器"这一整体总称指代"手枪"这一种具体的武器，如用"屋顶"这一房屋的部分构成指代整栋房屋，用"葡萄"指代用葡萄制成的"葡萄酒"等。提喻的使用需要基于语境来判断，才能确定所指代的具体对象。如例 42 和例 43：

例 42：

Rosencrantz:

Faith, there has been much to-do on both sides, and <u>the nation</u> holds it no sin to tarre them to controversy.

例 43：

Hamlet:

He would drown the stage with tears
And cleave the general ear with horrid speech,
Make mad the guilty and appal the free,
Confound the ignorant and amaze indeed
The very faculties of <u>eyes and ears</u>.

例 42 中，使用整体的 the nation（全国）来指代全国的人民，属于用整体指代个体；例 43 中，用 eyes and ears 指代舞台下的观众，属于用部分指代整体。

值得指出的是，提喻和借代两个辞格较难区分，简单来说，借代辞格是建立在关联性基础上的替代，相互替代的事物不存在相互从属的关系，或者属于同一类别的事物；而提喻是建立在相关性上的辞格，相互替代的事物之间具有直接的关系。如例 40 和例 43 中，都涉及使用人体器官来替代其他事

47

物,由于例40中的eyes所替代的是发挥该器官的功能而得到的结果,即用眼睛看到的外貌,是通过两者之间的关联产生的替代,因此属于借代辞格;而例43中,则是用eyes and ears来指代拥有这些器官的台下观众,属于用部分替代整体,是建立在相关性上的替代,是提喻辞格。鉴于这两个辞格有类似这里提到的重叠和难以辨析的地方,有些修辞学家甚至建议不对两者加以区分。而在必须区分这两者的时候,则需要根据上下文,仔细分析替代物和被替代事物之间是有相关性还是有关联性来判断。

3. 换说(perphrasis)

换说也是一种基于替代逻辑构成的辞格,指"用某专有名词的主要描述词或短语来替代该专有名词,或者用该专有名词来指代该专有名词包含的相关性质特征"(Corbett & Connors,1999:401),如用"雷锋"指代乐于助人的人等。莎剧中也有换说的案例,如例44和例45:

例44:

Horatio:

As stars with trains of fire and dews of blood,
Disasters in the sun; and the moist star
Upon whose influence Neptune's empire stands
Was sick almost to doomsday with eclipse.

例45:

Hamlet:

I would have such a fellow whipped for o'erdoing Termagant—It out-herods Herod. Pray you avoid it.

例44中，霍拉旭（Horatio）用Neptune's empire（海神的国度）来指代大海。在莎剧中，有较多的使用希腊神话中的人物来指代所描述的对象，如用幸运女神指代命运等；例45中，哈姆雷特用Termagant（特码根，脾气暴躁的神灵）来指代演员表演彪悍暴躁的角色，用Herod（希律王）来指代演员表演残忍凶狠的角色。两个例子中，例44借用的是专有名词的描述语，例45则是借用专有名词的相关特征。换说能够给原来平淡的，甚至是滥俗的表达增添一些新颖性，甚至幽默性。

三、双关类义变辞格

双关类义变辞格指词语使用的时候，有多于两种意义，构成多重解读的效果。双关类义变辞格根据词语制造多义性的方法，可以分为换义双关、谐音双关和一笔双叙双关。

1. 换义双关（antanaclasis）

换义双关指同一个词语在不同的使用语境中具有不同的意义。换义双关和其他双关的最大区别是该词语重复使用的次数多于一次。如例46和例47：

例46：

Gertrude：

If it be,

Why seems it so particular with thee?

Hamlet：

'Seems', madam—nay it is, I know not 'seems'.

'Tis not alone my inky cloak, good mother,
…
Together with all forms, moods, shapes of grief,
That can denote me truly. These indeed 'seem',
For they are actions that a man might play, …

例 47:

Gertrude:

Hamlet, thou hast thy father much offended.

Hamlet:

Mother, you have my father much offended.

例 46 中,葛特露使用的 seems,用的是其表示"似乎"的意思,但哈姆雷特在下文重复使用该词时,使用的是其表示"外在样子""努力扮出的样子"的意思,表示所有的悲伤行为都是表面的,而不能代表他心底真实的悲伤;例 47 中,offended 构成了换义双关。葛特露使用 offended 用的是"伤害感情"的意思,哈姆雷特重复使用该词时,选取的是"冒犯"的意思。

2. 谐音双关(paronomasia)

谐音双关指借用不同词语之间在读音上的相似性,创设一种多重解读的修辞效果,如例 48 和例 49:

例 48:

Claudius:

But now, my cousin Hamlet, and my son—

Hamlet:〔aside〕

A little more than kin, and less than kind.

Claudius:

How is it that the clouds still hang on you?

Hamlet:

Not so much, my lord, I am too much in the sun.

例 49：

Polonius:

I did enact Julius Caesar; I was kill'd i'th' Capitol; Brutus killed me.

Hamlet:

It was a brute part of him to kill so capital a calf there

例 48 中，有两处谐音双关，第一处由 kin（亲属）和 kind（良善）构成，两者在发音上有相似性，第二处由 son（儿子）和 sun（太阳）构成。从语义上来说，则与英语俗语"The nearer in kin, and the less in kindness."表达内容相似，即指克劳狄斯与葛特露这桩叔嫂的婚姻，使克劳狄斯与哈姆雷特在原来叔侄关系基础上，又多了继父和养子的关系，因此比亲戚更亲一层，但他对哈姆雷特的怀疑和伤害，则不足以体现其为良善之举。

例 49 也有两处谐音双关：第一处是哈姆雷特用 brute（残忍）和 Brutus（罗马政治家布鲁特斯）构成，第二处是 capital（庞大的）和 Capitol（议会）谐音构成。哈姆雷特在此处借助两处谐音双关，起到对普隆涅斯的调侃效果。

3. 一笔双叙双关（syllepsis）

一笔双叙双关指一个词语在行文中有多于两种的解读。莎剧中有较多的一笔双叙辞格的使用例子，如例 50 和例 51：

例 50：

Guildenstern：

Is in his retirement, marvellous <u>distempered</u>.

Hamlet：

With drink, sir?

Guildenstern：

No, my lord, with <u>choler</u>.

Hamlet：

Your wisdom should show itself more richer to signify this to the doctor, for for me to put him to his purgation would perhaps plunge him into far more <u>choler</u>.

例 51：

First Clown：

Faith, e'en with losing his wits.

Hamlet：

Upon what <u>ground</u>?

First Clown：

Why, here in Denmark.

例 50 的 distempered 是一处一笔双叙双关。distempered 一方面可以理解为"生气，发脾气"；另一方面可以理解为喝酒过多而生病，而当哈姆雷特在回答时，取的是"生病"的意思。例51中的ground也有两种解读，一方面可以理解为"地点"，另一方面可以理解为"原因"，而当答案是here in Denmark的时候，则选取的是其"地点"的意思。此外，例49中的calf，也是一处一笔双叙，因为该词可以同时理解为"牛犊"和"愚蠢的人"。

  一笔双叙双关和换义双关有相同的地方，也有不同的地方。相同之处在于两者都是建立在词语本身的多义性上，不同之处在于换义双关为同一词语的多次使用，每次使用采用其中一种意义，而一笔双叙指该词语在一次使用过程中，就产生多种解读的可能。然而，这两个辞格有时候也有难以辨析的地方，如在例50中，choler一方面可以理解为"生气，暴怒"，另一方面也可以理解为因为酗酒胆病发作。哈姆雷特的朋友在第一次使用时，选取的是其"生气"的意思，而这个词再次出现在哈姆雷特的对话中时，则有两种解读，即哈姆雷特认为，他去见克劳狄斯会让他更生气，这时候，choler和distempered都是选取"生气"这个意思；哈姆雷特的另一种解读则选取两个词语"酗酒生病""酒后胆病发作"的意思，理解为哈姆雷特的到来，不但不能帮他治愈酗酒后的病，而且可能让他胆病暴发。这时，第二处choler可以理解为一笔双叙，但如果和前面第一次出现的choler相联系时，又可以理解为换义双关，造成辞格辨析的模糊性。在本书中，将主要根据多义词出现的次数来区别一笔双叙和换义双关，即多义词在行文中出现两次以上构成双关的，为换义双关，按照这个标准，则该处为换义双关。

四、层递类义变辞格

层递类义变辞格在本书指基于程度大小的逻辑基础上的辞格,是通过将原来的事物的重要性或其他方面的程度加大或缩小,从而获得一定的强调效果。层递类义变辞格主要代表为夸张和弱陈。

1. 夸张(hyperbole)

夸张指用夸大的词语以达到强调的目的。如例 52 和例 53:

例 52:

Horatio:
Do not, my lord!

Hamlet:
 Why, what should be the fear?
I do not set my life at a pin's fee;
And for my soul, what can it do to that,
Being a thing immortal as itself?

例 53:

Guildenstern:
Good my lord, vouchsafe me a word with you.

Hamlet:
Sir, a whole history.

在例 52 中,哈姆雷特将自己的生命看作比别针还便宜,属于夸张的手法,表示他对自己生死的漠视;例 53 中,当朋友说想和哈姆雷特说话时,哈姆雷特回答道 a whole history (一整部历史),表示可以跟他朋友聊一部历史那么多的内容,为夸张手法。

2. 弱陈（litotes）

与夸张相反的辞格为弱陈,表示使用轻描淡写的方法（一般为否定的形式）,来给听众留下不同的印象,从而起到强调的作用。如例 54 和例 55:

例 54:

Claudius:

Co-leagued with this dream of his advantage—
He hath <u>not failed</u> to pester us with message
Importing the surrender of those lands
Lost by his father, with all bands of law,
To our most valiant brother.

例 55:

Cornelius: [with Voltemand]
In that and all things will we show our duty.
Claudius:
We <u>doubt it nothing</u>. Heartily farewell.

例 54 的 not fail'd to（没有忘记）为弱陈辞格,通过故意弱化的方式,强调福丁布拉斯并没有忘记复仇;而例 55 中的 doubt it nothing 也同样用两个否定的辞格,表示克劳狄斯对两个使臣的信任。弱陈借助否定的方式，起到强调的效果。

五、对比类义变辞格

对比类义变辞格指通过词语或句子意思正反面的对比，达到强调的修辞效果。本书中，本类辞格包括反问句和逆喻。

1. 反问句（rhetorical questions）

反问句指说话人明知故问，通过发问的方式来达到对原来观点的肯定，如例56和例57：

例56：

Hamlet：

That if you be honest and fair, your honesty should admit no discourse to your beauty.

Ophelia：

Could Beauty, my lord, have better commerce than with Honesty?

例57：

Hamlet：　　　　　Nay, do not think I flatter,
For what advancement may I hope from thee
That no revenue hast but thy good spirits
To feed and clothe thee? Why should the poor be flattered?

例56中，"Could beauty have better commerce than with honesty?"为反问句，表示莪菲莉娅认为beauty（美貌）和honesty（忠诚）的结合是最好的品质；例 57 中有两处反问句，第一句表示哈姆雷特认为好友霍拉旭除了一身正气之外，没有钱财等其他因素让他为了达到其他目的而来夸奖他。第二句用反问的方式，表达了哈姆雷特对霍拉旭人格魅力的肯定，认为他并不是因为拥有财富才受到夸奖。"反问句常常比直接的陈述更有效，更具备说服力"（Corbett & Connors, 1999：405），这两个例中的反问句辞格，都通过问句的形式强调说话人的观点，使原本的观点显得更有说服力。

2. 逆喻（oxymoron）

逆喻指的是将语义相反的词语放在一处使用，从而达到一种警句的效果。逆喻辞格建立在对比的基础上，同时也和形似类辞格有一定的关系，即说话人能够在语义相对的词语中，发现共同点。如例 58：

例 58：
Hamlet：
Would I had met my dearest foe in heaven
Or ever I had seen that day, Horatio!

在例 58 中，哈姆雷特将自己要面对母亲葛特露改嫁他的叔父克劳狄斯的心境之糟糕，让他即使见到敌人也感到亲近。

逆喻一般用来表达一种细腻的感情，行文会比普通的语言更加具有感染力。如例 7 中，哈姆雷特的"I must be cruel, only to be kind."，如果用逆喻的形式，可以将这种感情表达为 cruel kindness。

■ 莎剧《哈姆雷特》辞格辨析与文体鉴赏

　　本章分别就"形变辞格"和"义变辞格"中较为常见的辞格做定义和文体分析,第四章则将从辞格使用的角度,分析上述各种辞格在莎剧《哈姆雷特》中的具体使用及局部文体效果。

第四章 《哈姆雷特》辞格辨析

本章主要根据第三章整理的两大类"形变辞格"和"义变辞格",在莎剧《哈姆雷特》中找到相应的案例,并做简单的辨析,属于对文本局部辞格的文体分析。

在辞格辨析过程中,本书主要根据以下的三个标准:

第一,其他学者是否曾讨论过该辞格。这方面主要参考了不同版本的《哈姆雷特》剧本或译作,或一些关于莎士比亚的研究著作(如,Hibbard, 1987; Jenkins, 1982; Joseph, 1962; Kermode, 2000; Spencer, 1980; Thompson & Taylor, 2007; Wilson, 1952/2009; 黄国彬, 2013),对于这些版本或译作中提到的辞格,大部分将包括到辞格辨析中。然而,这些学者讨论的辞格,有些需要依赖剧本之外的语境来解释,如有学者认为剧中提到的 globe 可以作为双关理解,因为其在剧中的情景下指"地球",也可以理解为莎士比亚在指代当时英国表演莎剧的"环球剧院",因此可以理解为双关辞格。但在本书中,将不把这些依赖剧本之外情景的辞格包含在内。又比如,剧中普隆涅斯在和"发疯的"哈姆雷特对话时,发现疯人说出来的话也有些哲理,便说了一句"How pregnant sometimes his replies are!",有学者认为 pregnant 在此处表示"有意义,有道理"的同时,也表示"怀孕"的意思(黄国彬,2013:304)。而在本书中,对辞格构成的考虑,主要是剧中说话人是否对该辞格有"故意"的行为,而不是简单依赖词语本身是否存在多义性这一个标准上。

第二,该辞格是否符合辞格的构成方法。在剧中,在其他学者讨论过的辞格之外,也有许多辞格是他们没有讨论过的。例如,在不同版本中,学者们最经常提及的是双关和隐喻辞格,而对其他的辞格,如排比或借代等,除了个别学术论著的分析过程提及外,几乎没有系统的讨论。本文对这部分辞格的辨析,主要依赖辞格的构成标准来判断,同时根据该辞格的解读是否符合上下文的理解来确定。

第三,该辞格是否为常见辞格。有学者发现,莎士比亚的戏剧语言几乎涵盖了所有文艺复兴时期的修辞手段。然而,如上文第三章所述,很多辞格在现当代读者眼中,可能已经不再具有特殊性,因此,本书则主要聚焦在第三章讨论的辞格,并在《哈姆雷特》剧中找到它们相应的例子并作简单的文体解读。

本章对辞格的辨析更类似一种梳理性的工作。在辨析的过程也统一了标注的格式。具体格式如下面例 1 和例 2:

例 1:

隐喻(Thomson & Taylor, 2007: 147)。Nay, answer me. Stand and **unfold** yourself. 此处为剧中关于衣物的比喻,即把展示个人身份的过程,比喻为展开衣物的过程。

例2：

排比，借代（1）（2）（3）和夸张。**Caps, hands, and tongues** applaud it to the clouds. 此处有三种辞格。第一种由 caps，hands 和 tongues 三个名词构成的排比；第二种是由这三个名词分别指代兴奋的场景，即帽子高飞表示庆祝，鼓掌和大声疾呼等，构成三处借代辞格；第三种是由 to the clouds 表示呼叫声之大，直冲云霄，属于夸张的辞格。

例1和例例2分别是两次辨析的案例。每处辞格辨析都包含辞格的类型，辞格名称，辞格的出处（如有），辞格的所在内容（加粗），辞格的分析等。对于没有具体出处的、为辨析者的判断的，则没有夹注标明出处。当一个句段中的某一种辞格出现多次时，如例2中的借代辞格，则在其后面标注序号，以方便辨析过程的指代，也方便研究者或读者统计。

对莎剧来说，行数也是编辑过程需要考虑的重要因素，方便在书中相互引用。然而，该剧同时包含诗体和散文体两种行文方式。诗体的行数比较固定，也容易标注，而散文体部分则受到排版的影响。在本书则根据自身的排版情况来划定行数，而没有参考其他经典的版本，这也是不同版本的莎剧所采用的行数标注方法。其他格式方面还包括本章以该剧的幕为单位分析，同时，辨析过程中人名使用英文，以与戏剧正文相对应，而其他分析章节则使用汉译名。

第一幕

Act I, Scene 1

Elsinore. A platform before the Castle.

Enter two Sentinels—［first］, Francisco,［who paces up and down at his post; then］Bernado,［who approaches him］.

Bernado: Who's there?
Francisco: Nay, answer me. Stand and unfold yourself. ①
Bernado: Long live the King.
Francisco: Bernado?
Bernado: He.
Francisco: You come most carefully upon your hour.
Bernado: 'Tis now struck twelve. Get thee to bed, Francisco.
Francisco: For this relief much thanks. 'Tis bitter cold
And I am sick at heart.
Bernado: Have you had quiet guard?
Francisco: Not a mouse stirring.
Bernado: Well, good night.

【辞格辨析】

①隐喻（Thomson & Taylor, 2007: 147）。Nay, answer me. Stand and **unfold** yourself. 此处为剧中关于衣物的比喻，即把展示个人身份的过程，比喻为展开衣物的过程。

If you do meet Horatio andMarcellus,

The rivals of my watch, bid them make haste. ①

[Enter Horatio and Marcellus.]

Francisco: I think I hear them. Stand ho, Who is there?

Horatio: Friends to this ground.

Marcellus: And liegemen to the Dane.

Francisco: Give you good night.

Marcellus: O, farewell, honest soldiers.

Who hath relieved you?

Francisco: Bernado hath my place.

Give you good night. [Exit.]

Marcellus: Holla, Bernado!

Bernado: Say—

What, is Horatio there?

Horatio: A piece of him.

Bernado: Welcome Horatio, welcome good Marcellus.

Marcellus: What, has this thing appeared again tonight?

Bernado: I have seen nothing.

Marcellus: Horatio says 'tis but our fantasy

【辞格辨析】

①同位语。If you do meet **Horatio and Marcellus**, /**the rivals of my watch**, bid them make haste. 同位语为违反或打乱正常语序的形变辞格。同位语的使用给说话人提供补充信息，并借以表达个人态度。在这两个并列的名词短语中，后一处为对前一处的信息扩充。

莎剧《哈姆雷特》辞格辨析与文体鉴赏

And will not let belief take hold of him ①
Touching this dreaded sight twice seen of us.
Therefore I have entreated him along
With us to watch the minutes of this night
That, if again this apparition come,
He may approve our eyes and speak to it.
Horatio: Tush, tush, 'twill not appear.
Bernado: Sit down awhile,
And let us once again assail your ears
That are so fortified against our story
What we two nights have seen. ②
Horatio: Well, sit we down,
And let us hear Bernado speak of this.
Bernado: Last night of all,
When yond same star that's westward from the pole
Had made his course t' illume that part of heaven
Where now it burns, Marcellus and myself,
The bell then beating one— [Enter Ghost.]

【辞格辨析】

①拟人。…And will not let **belief take hold** of him…在此处拟人形变辞格中，belief 这一抽象概念被赋予了生命，能够做出 take hold（抓住）的动作。

②隐喻（Thompson & Taylor, 2007: 150）。…And let us once again **assail** your ears, /that are so **fortified** against our story, /…此处的 assail 和 fortified 为两处动词隐喻，共同构成了军事隐喻。

Marcellus：Peace, break thee off! Look where it comes again.
Bernado：In the same figure, like the King that's dead.
Marcellus：Thou art a scholar—speak to it, Horatio.
Bernado：Looks 'a not like the King? ① Mark it, Horatio.
Horatio：Most like. It harrows me with fear and wonder. ②
Bernado：It would be spoke to.
Marcellus：　　　　　　　Speak to it, Horatio.
Horatio：What art thou that usurp'st this time of night
Together with that fair and warlike form
In which the majesty of buried Denmark
Did sometimes march? ③ By heaven, I charge thee speak.
Marcellus：It is offended.
Bernado：　　　　　　See, it stalks away.

【辞格辨析】

①反问句。Looks 'a not like the King? 反问句并不要求听众回答，但能够使听众对所讨论话题更加关注（Corbett & Connors, 1999：269），同时，相比直接陈述，如"It is like the King."，反问句也是一种让听众赞同说话人的有效劝说手段（ibid.：405）。

②隐喻。It **harrows** me with fear and wonder. 农业隐喻（Thompson & Taylor, 2007：152）。Harrow 在此处为动词隐喻，指心情像土地被犁田的工具耙过一般。

③提喻。... In which the majesty of **buried Denmark**/did sometimes march? 此处以集体替代个体，即以丹麦国来替代丹麦先王老哈姆雷特。

■ 莎剧《哈姆雷特》辞格辨析与文体鉴赏

Horatio: Stay, speak, speak, I charge thee speak. ① ［Exit Ghost.］
Marcellus: 'Tis gone and will not answer.
Bernado: How now, Horatio, You tremble and look pale.
Is not this something more than fantasy? ②
What think you on't?
Horatio: Before my God, I might not this believe
Without the sensible and true avouch
Of mine own eyes.
Marcellus:　　　Is it not like the King? ③
Horatio: As thou art to thyself.
Such was the very armour he had on
When he the ambitious Norway combated.
So frowned he once when, in an angry parle,
He smote the sledded Polacks on the ice.
'Tis strange.

【辞格辨析】

①直接重复和间接重复。Stay, **speak, speak**, I charge thee **speak**! 此处为直接重复和间接重复的结合。直接反复的使用渲染了紧迫的气氛。

②反问句。Is not this something more than fantasy? 反问句往往为明知故问。该辞格给说话者质疑反对者的机会 (Crowley & Hawhee, 2004: 299)。

③反问句。Is it not like the King? 反问句除了反驳作用，还能将注意力引导谈话的主题（Crowley & Hawhee, 2004: 299）。这里，Marcellus 借助反问句，把话题从鬼魂出现转移到鬼魂和先王的关系。

Marcellus: Thus twice before, and jump at this dead hour,
With martial stalk hath he gone by our watch.
Horatio: In what particular thought to work, I know not,
But in the gross and scope of my opinion
This bodes some strange eruption to our state.
Marcellus: Good now, sit down, and tell me he that knows,
Why this same strict and most observant watch
So nightly toils the subject of the land, ①
And why such daily cast of brazen cannon
And foreign mart for implements of war,
Why such impress of shipwrights, whose sore task
Does not divide the Sunday from the week.
What might be toward, that this sweaty haste
Doth make the night joint-labourer with the day? ②
Who is't that can inform me? ③

【辞格辨析】

①拟人。…So nightly **toils** the subject of the land. Toil 为生命主体才能发出的动作，此处将森严的看守这一行为赋予生命，使其变成能够折磨士兵的主体。

②拟人。…Doth make the night **joint-labourer** with the day。Joint-labor 需要一个生命主体作主语，而此处赋予 the night 人的感情，指不分日夜的艰辛工作。

③首语重复。Why … /and why …, /Why … /What … /Who…该辞格强调重复的词语 why，从而突出 Marcellus 的疑惑的重心为这些一系列事件的原因。

莎剧《哈姆雷特》辞格辨析与文体鉴赏

Horatio：　　　　　　　　That can I.
At least, the whisper goes so. Our last king,
Whose image even but now appeared to us,
Was, as you know, by Fortinbras of Norway—
Thereto prick'd on by a most emulate pride—
Dared to the combat, in which our valiant Hamlet
(For so this side of our known world esteemed him) ①
Did slay this Fortinbras, who by a sealed compact
Well ratified by law and heraldry
Did forfeit with his life all those his lands
Which he stood seized of to the conqueror;
Against the which a moiety competent
Was gaged by our King, which had returned
To the inheritance of Fortinbras
Had he been vanquished, as, by the same co-mart
And carriage of the article designed,
His fell to Hamlet. Now, sir, young Fortinbras,

【辞格辨析】

①插说。…in which our valiant Hamlet/ (**for so this side of our known world esteemed him**) /did slay this Fortinbras. 插说为对正常语序的强制性中断，其插入的内容也与所中断部分没有太多的关联，主要功能在于让说话人发出声音和作出评价，从而使行文更具感情色彩。此处的插说加入了 Horatio 对已故丹麦老国王评价的补充说明，可以侧面看出 Horatio 对使用评价性语言的严谨态度。

Of unimproved mettle hot and full, ①
Hath in the skirts of Norway, here and there,
Sharked up a list of lawless resolutes ②
For food and diet to some enterprise
That hath a stomach in't, which is no other,
As it doth well appear unto our state, ③

【辞格辨析】

①谐音双关（Thompson & Taylor, 2007: 157；黄国彬, 2013: 161）。…Of unimproved **mettle** hot and full. 此处可以理解为和 metal 的谐音双关。Mettle 在该剧中意思为"精神、性情和气质"（Crystal & Crystal, 2002: 281），然而其后面的形容词 hot 和 full 又使其与 metal 发生关联。此处可以理解为 Fortinbras 的战争气焰高涨，也可以理解为他性情暴躁，如一块热铁一般火烫。

②隐喻（Thompson & Taylor, 2007: 157）。Now, sir, young Fortinbras …hath …**sharked up** a list of lawless resolutes, …to some enterprise/that hath a **stomach** in't. Shark up 与下文的 food and diet, stomach 等在语义上相回应，为饮食动作相关隐喻。突出 Fortinbras 为了准备战争，良莠不齐地收集人手充当军力，这一做法与鲨鱼捕食相类似。

③插说。…which is no other, /**as it doth well appear unto our state**, /but to recover of us by strong hand…此处插说为说话人提供发表看法的作用，使行文中的推理更显严谨。

莎剧《哈姆雷特》辞格辨析与文体鉴赏

But to recover of us, by strong hand
And terms compulsatory those foresaid lands
So by his father lost. ① and this, I take it,
Is the main motive of our preparations,
The source of this our watch and the chief head
Of this post-haste and romage in the land. ②
Bernado: I think it be no other but e'en so.
Well may it sort that this portentous figure
Comes armed through our watch, so like the King
That was and is the question of these wars.
Horatio: A mote it is to trouble the mind's eye. ③
In the most high and palmy state of Rome
A little ere the mightiest Julius fell
The graves stood tenantless, and the sheeted dead

【辞格辨析】

①提喻。But to recover of us, by strong **hand**, /and terms compulsatory those foresaid lands/…此处用 strong hand 指代强硬手段,也被看作是对 Fortinbras 这个人名的内涵意思的明晰化 (Thompson & Taylor, 2007: 158)。

②排比。…and this, I take it, /is **the main motive of** …/ **the source of** …, and **the chief head**/of …此处用相同的语法结构"the … of …"形成排比辞格,其中 motive, source 和 chief head 在语境中均为近义表达。排比在这里增强表达效果。

③隐喻。A **mote** it is to trouble the mind's eye。此处隐喻和上文联系密切,即将上文中提到的有关 old Hamlet 与 old Fortinbras 之间的争斗,比喻为一颗灰尘,意指说话人没有抓住事情的重点,被表面现象所迷惑。

Did squeak and gibber in the Roman streets;
As stars with trains of fire and dews of blood,
Disasters in the sun; and the moist star
Upon whose influence Neptune's empire stands ①
Was sick almost to doomsday with eclipse. ②
And even the like precurse of fierce events,
As harbingers preceding still the fates
And prologue to the omen coming on,
Have heaven and earth together demonstrated
Unto our climature and countrymen. ③　　[Enter Ghost again.]
But soft, behold, lo, where it comes again;
I'll cross it, though it blast me.—Stay illusion. [Spreads his arms.]
If thou hast any sound or use of voice,
Speak to me.

【辞格辨析】

①换说（1）　（2）。...and **the moist star**/upon whose influence **Neptune's empire** stands. 换说即使用一些描述语来替代专有名词，此处用 moister star 来替代月亮，用 Neptune's empire 来指代大海。

②拟人。...and the **moist star**/.../was **sick almost to doomsday with eclipse**. 将月亮拟人化，看作一个因为生病而脸色苍白、面容消瘦的人。

③隐喻。...**as harbingers preceding still the fates**/and **prologue to the omen coming on**,/have **heaven and earth together demonstrated/unto our climature and countrymen**...在此处，Horatio 将天地展示的各种不同寻常的情景，比喻为预言家对命运和灾难的预告。

莎剧《哈姆雷特》辞格辨析与文体鉴赏

If there be any good thing to be done
That may to thee do ease and grace to me,
Speak to me.
If thou art privy to thy country's fate
Which happily foreknowing may avoid,
O, speak.
Or if thou hast uphoarded in thy life
Extorted treasure in the womb of earth— ①
For which, they say, you spirits oft walk in death— ②
　　　　　　　　　　　　　　[The cock crows.]
Speak of it, stay and speak. Stop it, Marcellus! ③
Marcellus: Shall I strike at it with my partisan?
Horatio: Do, if it will not stand.
Bernado:　　　　　　　'Tis here.
Horatio:　　　　　　　　　　'Tis here. [Exit Ghost.]

【辞格辨析】

①拟人和换说。Or if thou hast uphoarded in thy life/extorted treasure in the **womb of earth**. 此处可以理解为换说和拟人的结合。从换说角度，即用 womb of earth 来指代土地。拟人则是将大地比喻为人，而将地里比喻为人的子宫。

②插说。…extorted treasure in the womb of earth/**for which, they say, you spirits oft walk in death**—/Speak of it,…此处插说为补充信息。

③排比和首尾语重复。If …, /Speak to me. /If …, /Speak to me. /If …, /O, speak. /Or if…, /Speak of it. 此处排比也糅合了首尾语重复。使用排比提升了 Horatio 说话的气势，同时辞格的使用也符合他作为同伴心目中的"学者"形象。

Marcellus: 'Tis gone.
We do it wrong, being so majestical
To offer it the show of violence,
For it is as the air, invulnerable, ①
And our vain blows malicious mockery.
Bernado: It was about to speak, when the cock crew.
Horatio: And then it started, like a guilty thing
Upon a fearful summons. ② I have heard
The cock, that is the trumpet to the morn ③
Doth with his lofty and shrill-sounding throat
Awake the god of day; and at his warning,
Whether in sea or fire, in earth or air,
Th' extravagant and erring spirit hies
To his confine—and of the truth herein
This present object made probation.

【辞格辨析】

①明喻。…for it is **as the air**, invulnerable, /and our vain blows malicious mockery. 此处将鬼魂比喻为空气, 缥缈不定, 不可捕获。

②明喻。And then it started, **like a guilty thing**/upon a fearful summons. 将鬼魂听到公鸡鸣叫声后的状态比喻为罪犯听到传唤一般。

③隐喻。…the cock, that is the **trumpet to the morn**, /doth with his lofty and shrill-sounding throat/awake the god of day. 此处将公鸡早晨的鸣叫声, 比喻为叫醒白天之神的号角。

莎剧《哈姆雷特》辞格辨析与文体鉴赏

Marcellus: It faded on the crowing of the cock.
Some say that ever, 'gainst that season comes
Wherein our Saviour's birth is celebrated,
The bird of dawning singeth all night long, ①
And then, they say, no spirit dare stir abroad,
The nights are wholesome, then no planets strike,
No fairy takes, nor witch hath power to charm,
So hallowed and so gracious is the time. ②
Horatio: So have I heard and do in part believe it.
But look, the morn in russet mantle clad
Walks o'er the dew of yon high eastward hill. ③
Break we our watch up; and by my advice
Let us impart what we have seen tonight

【辞格辨析】

①换说。…**the bird of dawning** singeth all night long, …此处用 the bird of dawning 来指代公鸡。从文体效果来看,起到避免行文单一的作用。

②排比。… and then, they say, **no spirit dare stir abroad**, /the nights are wholesome, then **no planets strike**, /**no fairy takes, nor witch hath power to charm**, /…排比辞格使用起到强调"no …"这一内容的作用,突出当时耶稣诞生时的圣洁美好。

③拟人。But, look, **the morn, in russet mantle clad**, /**walks o'er** the dew of yon high eastward hill. 此处将清晨比作裹着红色斗篷走来的人物,增加了语言的形象化。

Unto young Hamlet, for, upon my life
This spirit dumb to us will speak to him.
Do you consent we shall acquaint him with it
Marcellus: As needful in our loves, fitting our duty?
Let's do't, I pray, and I this morning know
Where we shall find him most conveniently.　　　　〔Exeunt.〕

Act I, Scene 2
Elsinore. A room of state in the Castle.
Flourish. 〔Enter Claudius, King of Denmark, Gertrude the Queen, Hamlet, Polonius, Laertes and his sister Ophelia, Voltemand, Cornelius, Lords Attendant.〕

Claudius: Though yet of Hamlet our dear brother's death ①
The memory be green, and that it us befitted
To bear our hearts in grief, and our whole kingdom
To be contracted in one brow of woe, ②

【辞格辨析】

①同位语。Though yet of Hamlet **our dear brother's** death …此处为同位语，即 our dear brother（亲爱的兄长）放在 Hamlet 之后，说明 Claudius 和老王之间的兄弟关系。

②拟人和提喻（Thompson & Taylor, 2007: 165）。…and **our whole kingdom/to be contracted in one brow of woe**. 此处有两种辞格，第一处将 our whole kingdom（整个国家）比拟为拥有感情的人，能够因为悲伤而眉头紧锁，是拟人辞格；第二处为提喻，借用 brow（眉毛）这一局部来指代悲伤的面容。

莎剧《哈姆雷特》辞格辨析与文体鉴赏

Yet so far hath discretion fought with nature ①
That we with wisest sorrow think on him
Together with remembrance of ourselves.
Therefore our sometime sister, now our Queen,
Th' imperial jointress to this warlike state, ②
Have we, as 'twere with a defeated joy,
With an auspicious and a dropping eye,
With mirth in funeral and with dirge in marriage, ③
In equal scale weighing delight and dole, ④

【辞格辨析】

①拟人。Yet so far hath **discretion fought with nature**…此处将抽象的 discretion（谨慎）赋予生命，使其和 nature（本性）能够相互抗争。

②同位语。…**th' imperial jointress to this warlike state**. 此处为上文 our queen 的同位语，为对前文信息的补充。

③逆喻（1）（2）（3）和对仗。…have we, as 'twere with **a defeated joy**, /…/with **mirth in funeral**, and with **dirge in marriage**…Defeated 和 joy 之间语义相反，构成逆喻辞格。下文的逆喻还包括 mirth in funeral 和 dirge in marriage。同时，此处的 **with an auspicious, and a dropping eye,** /**with mirth in funeral, and with dirge in marriage** 等语义相对的成分也构成对仗辞格，与逆喻一起传达出说话人的矛盾心情。

④隐喻和插说。In **equal scale weighing** delight and dole,…此处将 delight（欢乐）和 dole（悲伤）比喻为可以用秤来衡量重量的事物。这一行也是一处插入语，补充说明说话人的思考过程，以及做出决定的不易。

Taken to wife. ① Nor have we herein barred
Your better wisdoms, which have freely gone
With this affair along. For all, our thanks.
Now follows that you know: young Fortinbras,
Holding a weak supposal of our worth
Or thinking by our late dear brother's death
Our state to be disjoint and out of frame— ②
Co-leagued with this dream of his advantage—
He hath not fail'd to pester us with message ③
Importing the surrender of those lands
Lost by his father with all bands of law
To our most valiant brother. So much for him.
Now for ourselves, and for this time of meeting,
Thus much the business is: we have here writ

【辞格辨析】

①排比。…have we, as 't were **with** a defeated joy, /**with** …, /**with** …and **with** …, /… /taken to wife. 此处主要通过使用相同的语法结构，即由 with 引出的一系列表达构成排比。排比增强了论述的气势。

②隐喻（Thompson & Taylor, 2007: 166）。…our state to **be disjoint** and **out of frame**。此处通过 disjoint 和 out of frame 两个词，将国家比喻为家具，可以因为脱臼和变形而坏掉。

③弱陈。…he hath **not failed** to pester us with message/ importing the surrender of those lands/lost by his father…这里的弱陈通过否定对立面来增强听众对所讨论对象的印象。

莎剧《哈姆雷特》辞格辨析与文体鉴赏

To Norway, uncle of young Fortinbras— ①
Who impotent and bedrid scarcely hears
Of this his nephew's purpose to suppress
His further gait herein, in that the levies,
The lists and full proportions are all made
Out of his subject; ② and we here dispatch
You, good Cornelius, and you, Voltemand,
For bearers of this greeting to old Norway,
Giving to you no further personal power
To business with the King, more than the scope
Of these dilated articles allow.

　　　　　　　　　　　　　　[Gives a paper.]

Farewell, and let your haste commend your duty.
Cornelius:〔with Voltemand〕
In that and all things will we show our duty. ③

【辞格辨析】

①同位语。…to Norway, **uncle of young Fortinbras/**…此处 uncle of young Fortinbras 为 Norway 的同位语，补充说明 Fortinbras 和挪威王的关系。

②排比。… in that **the levies, /the lists,** and **full proportions** are all made/out of his subjects;…此处的三处结构相同的词组并列构成排比关系，达到增强语势的效果。

③尾语重复。Farewell, and let your haste commend your **duty**. /in that and all things will we show our **duty**. 此处尾语重复不但有押韵效果，也能突出说话人强调的内容，即 duty。

78

第四章 《哈姆雷特》辞格辨析

Claudius: We doubt it nothing. Heartily farewell. ①

　　　　　　　　[Exeunt Voltemand and Cornelius.]

And now, Laertes, what's the news with you?
You told us of some suit—What is't, Laertes?
You cannot speak of reason to the Dane ②
And lose your voice. ③ What wouldst thou beg, Laertes,
That shall not be my offer, not thy asking? ④
The head is not more native to the heart,
The hand more instrumental to the mouth,
Than is the throne of Denmark to thy father. ⑤

【辞格辨析】

①弱陈和插说。We doubt it nothing. 此处 Claudius 借助 doubt 和 nothing 两个表示否定的词语，表示对使臣的信任，对他的工作能力不存在任何怀疑。

②提喻。You cannot speak of reason to **the Dane**…用整体指代个体的提喻，即用整个丹麦国来指代 Claudius。

③借代。…and lose your **voice**. 用与发表意见和请求关联最为相近的 voice（声音）来指代 Laertes 的请求。

④反问句和弱陈。**What wouldst thou beg**, Laertes, /**that shall not be my offer, not thy asking**? 通过使用反问句，强调丹麦王对 Laertes 的请求无所不应；此处的第二处辞格为弱陈，即借助两个 not 的使用，起到借助否定来强调的目的。

⑤隐喻。**The head is not more native to the heart, /the hand more instrumental to the mouth, /than is the throne of Denmark to thy father**. 此处把 Claudius 与 Polonius 的关系，比喻为头与心、手与口的关系，从而突出两人的亲密。

莎剧《哈姆雷特》辞格辨析与文体鉴赏

What wouldst thou have, Laertes?

Laertes： My dread lord,
Your leave and favour to return to France,
From whence though willingly I came to Denmark
To show my duty in your coronation,
Yet now I must confess, that duty done,
My thoughts and wishes bend again toward France
And bow them to your gracious leave and pardon.

Claudius：Have you your father's leave? What says Polonius?

Polonius：He hath, my lord, wrung from me my slow leave
By laboursome petition, ① and at last
Upon his will I sealed my hard consent. ②
I do beseech you give him leave to go.

Claudius：Take thy fair hour, Laertes, time be thine
And thy best graces spend it at thy will.
But now, my cousin Hamlet, and my son—

【辞格辨析】

①隐喻。He hath [...] **wrung** from me my slow leave…此处为动词隐喻,通过使用 wring(拧干)一词,将 Polonius 答应 Laertes 返回学校的请求,比喻为拧干布料或衣物,表示 Laertes 获得他父亲这一许可的不易。

②隐喻和一笔双叙双关。… /upon his **will** I **sealed** my hard consent。Polonius 将同意儿子的请求比喻为在文件或书信盖上印章。此处的 will 为一笔双叙双关。Will 可以解读可为 Laertes 的"意愿",也可以理解为法律角度的"意愿",和后面 seal my consent 等法律用语相呼应。

Hamlet:[aside] A little more than kin, and less than kind. ①

Claudius: How is it that the clouds still hang on you? ②

Hamlet: Not so much, my lord, I am too much in the 'son'. ③

Gertrude: Good Hamlet, cast thy nighted colour off

And let thine eye look like a friend on Denmark. ④

Do not for ever with thy vailed lids

Seek for thy noble father in the dust. ⑤

【辞格辨析】

①谐音双关，一笔双叙双关（黄国彬，2013：178）和对仗。A little more than **kin**, and less than **kind**。此处可以理解为谐音双关，即利用 kin 和 kind 在发音上的相似，构成谐音双关；第二处双关为 kind 的多义性构成，该词同时表示"厚道，亲切"，也可以表示"自然的，天性的"；此处把结构相同语义相反的内容结合在一起，构成对仗辞格。

②隐喻。How is it that the **clouds** still hang on you. 此处将 Hamlet 脸上的忧愁，比喻为被云朵笼罩的阴影。

③谐音双关（Thompson & Taylor, 2007：170）。...and my **son**...I am too much in the '**son**'。这一句中 son 和 sun 是谐音双关。既表达 Hamlet 被 Claudius 称为 son 的一种反抗，也与前文的 clouds still hang on you 相呼应，对这句话的一种反驳。

④提喻。And let thine eye look like a friend on **Denmark**. 这里用整体指代局部，用丹麦国指代 Claudius。

⑤隐喻（Thompson & Taylor, 2007：171）。Do not for ever with thy **vailed lids**/seek for thy noble father in the dust. 此处将 Hamlet 的下垂眼睑比喻为放下来的帷幔或窗纱。

莎剧《哈姆雷特》辞格辨析与文体鉴赏

Thou knowst 'tis common all that lives must die,
Passing through nature to eternity.
Hamlet:Ay, madam, it is common. ①
Gertrude:　　　　　　　　If it be,
Why seems it so particular with thee?
Hamlet:'Seems', madam, Nay, it is. I know not 'seems'. ②
'Tis not alone my inky cloak, cold mother,
Nor customary suits of solemn black,
Nor windy suspiration of forced breath,
No, nor the fruitful river in the eye, ③
Nor the dejected havior of the visage, ④

【辞格辨析】

①换义双关。Thou knowst 'tis **common**. ... / ... /Ay, madam, it is **common**. 此处的两个common意义不同。第一处为Gertrude说出，指生老病死为"平常"的自然现象，而Hamlet重复该字，则可以理解为"粗俗"等意思，属于换义双关。

②换义双关。If it be, /why **seems** it so particular with thee? /'**Seems**', madam, Nay, it is. I know not '**seems**'。Gertrude使用的seems意思为"似乎"，但Hamlet则意指"努力扮出的样子"，与下文各种空有其样的悲伤形式相呼应。

③隐喻。No, nor **the fruitful river** in the eye. 此处将流下脸庞的眼泪比喻为一条滚滚的河流。

④首语重复和排比。**Nor** ... /**Nor** ... /No, **nor** ... /**Nor** ... 此处可以看作首语重复和排比的结合。通过在每句句首重复nor字，起到对该重复词语的强调作用。同时通过nor引起的结构相似的排比句，进一步增强Hamlet的辩论气势。

Together with all forms, moods, shapes of grief, ①

That can denote me truly. These indeed 'seem',

For they are actions that a man might play,

But I have that within which passeth show,

These but the trappings and the suits of woe. ②

Claudius: 'Tis sweet and commendable in your nature, Hamlet,

To give these mourning duties to your father,

But you must know your father lost a father,

That father lost his, and the survivor bound

In filial obligation for some term

To do obsequious sorrow; but to persever

In obstinate condolement is a course

Of impious stubbornness, 'tis unmanly grief,

It shows a will most incorrect to heaven,

A heart unfortified, ③ a mind impatient,

【辞格辨析】

①排比。…together with all **forms**, **moods**, **shows** of grief/…此处为三个相同语义词语构成的排比。

②隐喻。These but **the trappings and the suits of woe**. 此处 Hamlet 将各种悲伤的外在表现，如穿黑色衣服、无法喘气、流泪等，比喻为悲伤的装饰和外衣，指这些外在的表现无法表达他内心真实的痛苦。

③隐喻。It shows a will most incorrect to heaven, /a heart **unfortified**…此处为军事意象隐喻。将悲伤不止的心情比喻为一座失守的城堡。

莎剧《哈姆雷特》辞格辨析与文体鉴赏

An understanding simple and unschooled; ①
For what we know must be, and is as common
As any the most vulgar thing to sense—
Why should we in our peevish opposition
Take it to heart? Fie! 'tis a fault to heaven,
A fault against the dead, a fault to nature,
To reason most absurd, ② whose common theme
Is death of fathers, and who still hath cried
From the first corse till he that died today
'This must be so.' We pray you throw to earth
This unprevailing woe, ③ and think of us
As of a father, for let the world take note
You are the most immediate to our throne,

【辞格辨析】

①排比和头韵。It shows **a will most incorrect to heaven, /a heart unfortified, a mind impatient, /an understanding simple and unschool'd;** …通过系列结构相同的名词短语构成排比,增强语气。此外 incorrect, unfortified, impatient, unschooled 等词语的前缀也构成语音上的头韵。

②排比。Fie! 'tis **a fault to heaven, /a fault against the dead, a fault to nature,** /to reason most absurd, …相同结构短语的重复构成排比,增强语气。

③隐喻(Thompson & Taylor, 2007: 173)。We pray you **throw to earth**/this unprevailing woe; …此处用摔跤意象,将悲伤比喻为具体的、可以摔到地上的事物。

And with no less nobility of love

Than that which dearest father bears his son

Do I impart toward you. For your intent

In going back to school in Wittenberg

It is most retrograde to our desire, ①

And we beseech you bend you to remain

Here in the cheer and comfort of our eye,

Our chiefest courtier, cousin, and our son. ②

Gertrude: Let not thy mother lose her prayers, Hamlet. ③

I pray thee stay with us, go not to Wittenberg.

Hamlet: I shall in all my best obey you, madam.

Claudius: Why, 'tis a loving and a fair reply.

Be as ourself in Denmark. Madam, come—

【辞格辨析】

①隐喻。…it is most **retrograde** to our desire…指天体的逆向运转，在此处将 Hamlet 计划回学校的意愿与 Claudius 和 Gertrude 希望他留下来的意愿，比喻为逆向运行的天体。

②夸张（1）（2），排比和头韵。…and with no less nobility of love/than that which **dearest** father bears his son/…/our **chiefest courtier**, **cousin**, and **our son**. 此处的两处最高级，即 dearest 和 chiefest，有强调的作用，为夸张辞格；第二处由 courtier、cousin 和 our son 构成的排比；第三处为 courtier 和 cousin 构成的头韵辞格。

③弱陈。Let **not** thy mother **lose** her prayers, Hamlet. 此处 Gertrude 使用两个表示否定含义的辞格，not 和 lose，构成弱陈辞格，起到强调的作用。

■ 莎剧《哈姆雷特》辞格辨析与文体鉴赏

This gentle and unforced accord of Hamlet
Sits smiling to my heart, ① in grace whereof
No jocund health that Denmark drinks today
But the great cannon to the clouds shall tell
And the King's rouse the heaven shall bruit again,
Respeaking earthly thunder. ② Come away.

[Exeunt all but Hamlet.]

Hamlet: O that this too too solid flesh would melt,
Thaw, and resolve itself into a dew, ③
Or that the Everlasting had not fixed
His canon 'gainst self-slaughter. O God, God,
How weary, stale, flat, and unprofitable
Seem to me all the uses of this world! ④

【辞格辨析】

①拟人。This gentle and unforced accord of Hamlet/**sits smiling** to my heart, …把 Hamelt 答应留在丹麦拟人化，使行文更为生动。

②拟人。…but **the great cannon to the clouds shall tell**/ …/**respeaking earthly thunder**. 把礼炮拟人化，将礼炮对天空的声音比拟为向天空说话，并得到来自地面的回应。

③隐喻和排比。O that this too too solid flesh would **melt**,/**thaw**, and **resolve** itself into a dew, …此处将身体比喻为可融化的物品。此处的三个动词也构成排比，增强说话语气。

④排比。How **weary**, **stale**, **flat**, and **unprofitable**/seem to me all the uses of this world! 三个词性相同的词语构成排比，增强语气。

Fie on't! ah, fie, 'tis an unweeded garden
That grows to seed, things rank and gross in nature
Possess it merely. ① That it should come to this:
But two months dead—nay, not so much, not two—
So excellent a king, that was to this
Hyperion to a satyr, so loving to my mother
That he might not beteem the winds of heaven
Visit her face too roughly. ② Heaven and earth,
Must I remember? Why, she would hang on him
As if increase of appetite had grown③
By what it fed on. And yet within a month

【辞格辨析】

①隐喻（Thompson & Taylor, 2007: 176）。'Tis an **unweeded garden**/that **grows to seed**; things **rank and gross** in nature…这里的隐喻将丹麦比喻为一个没有修剪的、杂草丛生的花园。

②拟人。…that he might not beteem **the winds of heaven/ visit her face** too roughly。此处将风拟人化，把风拂面比拟为到脸上走动。

③明喻（Thompson & Taylor, 2007: 177）。Why, she would hang on him, /**as if increase of appetite had grown/by what it fed on**。此处把 Gertrude 对已故老王的欲望比喻为吃到美食后胃口大开。

莎剧《哈姆雷特》辞格辨析与文体鉴赏

(Let me not think on't! Frailty, thy name is woman) —①
A little month, or e're those shoes were old
With which she followed my poor father's body,
Like Niobe, all tears. Why she—
O God! A beast that wants discourse of reason
Would have mourned longer—married with my uncle, ②
My father's brother (but no more like my father
Than I to Hercules). Within a month,
Ere yet the salt of most unrighteous tears
Had left the flushing in her galled eyes,
She married. ③ O most wicked speed! To post
With such dexterity to incestuous sheets,

【辞格辨析】

①插说和拟人（Thompson & Taylor, 2007: 177）。(Let me not think on't! **Frailty, thy name is woman**) …此处有两个辞格。一为插说，通过插说 Hamlet 发表自己的观点；二为拟人，即将抽象的 frailty（懦弱）比拟为女人。

②插说和拟人。**O God! A beast, that wants discourse of reason,** /would have mourn'd longer…此处为插说，Hamlet 发表自己的观点。此处也是拟人，将 beast 赋予人的特征，能追求理性。

③重复。…and yet, **within a month**… /A little month, / … /Than I to Hercules. **within a month**, …此处在不同的地方重复 within a month，凸显时间短暂。有学者认为此处为夸张手法，因为根据剧情发展，老王去世和 Gertrude 再婚时隔不止一个月（Thompson & Taylor, 2007: 177）。

It is not, nor it cannot come to good;
But break my heart, for I must hold my tongue. ①

[Enter Horatio, Marcellus, and Bernado.]

Horatio: Hail to your lordship.

Hamlet: I am glad to see you well.
Horatio, or I do forget myself.

Horatio: The same, my lord, and your poor servant ever.

Hamlet: Sir, my good friend, I'll change that name with you.
And what make you from Wittenberg, Horatio?
Marcellus!

Marcellus: My good lord.

Hamlet: I am very glad to see you. [To Bernado] Good even, sir.—
But what in faith make you from Wittenberg?

Horatio: A truant disposition, good my lord.

Hamlet: I would not hear your enemy say so,
Nor shall you do my ear that violence
To make it truster of your own report ②
Against yourself. I know you are no truant; ③
But what is your affair in Elsinore?

【辞格辨析】

①借代。But break, my heart, for I must hold my **tongue**. 用 tongue 指代说话，发表观点的行为。

②拟人。...to make it **truster** of your own report...将耳朵比拟为人，可以成为成为"信托人"。

③弱陈。I know you are **no truant**; —but what is your affair in Elsinore? 通过否定来强调 Horatio 不是喜欢逃学之人。

89

莎剧《哈姆雷特》辞格辨析与文体鉴赏

We'll teach you to drink deep ere you depart.

Horatio: My lord, I came to see your father's funeral.

Hamlet: I prithee do not mock me, fellow student.
I think it was to see my mother's wedding.

Horatio: Indeed, my lord, it followed hard upon.

Hamlet: Thrift, thrift, Horatio, The funeral baked meats
Did coldly furnish forth the marriage tables. ①
Would I had met my dearest foe in heaven ②
Or ever I had seen that day, Horatio.
My father, methinks I see my father.

Horatio: Where, my lord?

Hamlet: In my mind's eye, Horatio.

Horatio: I saw him once—'a was a goodly king.

Hamlet: 'A was a man, take him for all in all.
I shall not look upon his like again.

Horatio: My lord, I think I saw him yesternight.

Hamlet: Saw, who?

Horatio: My lord, the King your father.

Hamlet: The King my father?

Horatio: Season your admiration for a while

【辞格辨析】

①对仗。The funeral **baked** meats/did **coldly** furnish forth the marriage tables. 通过反义词构成对仗,增强冲突感。

②逆喻。Would I had met my **dearest foe** in heaven……此处使用 dearest 和 foe 这对语义相反的词语,构成逆喻,凸显 Hamlet 对参加母亲再婚婚礼的排斥。

90

With an attent ear, till I may deliver

Upon the witness of these gentlemen ①

This marvel to you.

Hamlet: For God's love let me hear!

Horatio: Two nights together had these gentlemen,

Marcellus and Bernado, on their watch, ②

In the dead vast and middle of the night

Been thus encountered: a figure like your father

Armed at point exactly, cap-a-pie,

Appears before them and with solemn march

Goes slow and stately by them; ③ Thrice he walked

By their oppress'd and fear-surprised eyes

Within his truncheon's length whilst they distilled

Almost to jelly with the act of fear, ④

Stand dumb and speak not to him. This to me

【辞格辨析】

①插说。…with an attent ear, till I may deliver, /**upon the witness of these gentlemen**, /this marvel to you。此处插说为Horatio一处誓言，表达了他接下来所说内容的真实性。

②同位语。Two nights together had these gentlemen/**Marcellus and Bernardo**, on their watch…此处同位语是these gentlemen 的信息补充。

③头韵。…goes **slow** and **stately** by them。Slow 和 stately 构成头韵。

④隐喻。whilst they **distill'd**/almost **to jelly** with the act of fear。此处把人因受惊吓而僵硬不动，比喻为凝固了的胶状物。

In dreadful secrecy impart they did,

And I with them the third night kept the watch

Where, as they had delivered, both in time,

Form of the thing, each word made true and good,

The apparition comes. I knew your father,

These hands are not more like.

Hamlet: But where was this?

Marcellus: My lord, upon the platform where we watch.

Hamlet: Did you not speak to it?

Horatio: My lord, I did,

But answer made it none. Yet once methought

It lifted up it head and did address

Itself to motion, like as it would speak.

But even then the morning cock crew loud

And at the sound it shrunk in haste away

And vanish'd from our sight.

Hamlet: 'Tis very strange.

Horatio: As I do live, my honour'd lord, 'tis true,

And we did think it writ down in our duty

To let you know of it.

Hamlet: Indeed, sirs, but this troubles me.

Hold you the watch tonight?

Marcellus: [with Bernado]   We do, my lord.

Hamlet: Armed, say you?

Marcellus: [with Bernado]   Armed, my lord.

Hamlet: From top to toe?

Marcellus: [with Bernado] My lord, from head to foot.

第四章 《哈姆雷特》辞格辨析

Hamlet：Then saw you not his face.

Horatio：O, yes, my lord, he wore his beaver up.

Hamlet：What looked he—browningly?

Horatio：A countenance more in sorrow than in anger.

Hamlet：Pale or red?

Horatio：Nay, very pale.

Hamlet：　　　　　And fixed his eyes upon you?

Horatio：Most constantly. ①

Hamlet：　　　　　　　　　I would I had been there.

Horatio：It would have much amazed you.

Hamlet：　　　　　　　　Very like Stay'd it long?

Horatio：While one with moderate haste might tell a hundred.

Marcellus：[with Bernado] Longer, longer.

Horatio：Not when I saw't.

Hamlet：　　　　　His beard was grizzled, no?

Horatio：It was as I have seen it in his life,

【辞格辨析】

①省略（1）-（7）。Armed, say you? /Armed, my lord. /From top to toe? /My lord, from head to foot. /…What look'd he—Frowningly? /A countenance more in sorrow than in anger. /Pale or red? /Nay, very pale. /And fixed his eyes upon you? /Most constantly. 此处的对话有7处省略。省略内容可以根据情景来补充。这些省略不仅可以使得表达简练，符合口语的特点，也能够突出 Hamlet 听到鬼魂出现时惊讶的心理，以及迫切想了解具体情况的心情。

A sable silvered.

Hamlet: I will watch tonight.
Perchance 'twill walk again.

Horatio: I warrant it will.

Hamlet: If it assume my noble father's person
I'll speak to it, though hell itself should gape
And bid me hold my peace. ① I pray you all,
If you have hitherto conceal'd this sight
Let it be tenable in your silence still
And whatsoever else shall hap tonight
Give it an understanding but no tongue, ②
I will requite your loves. So, fare you well.
Upon the platform 'twixt eleven and twelve,
I'll visit you.

All: Our duty to your honour.

Hamlet: Your loves, as mine to you, farewell.

[Exeunt, all but Hamlet.]

My father's spirit—in arms! All is not well;
I doubt some foul play. Would the night were come.

【辞格辨析】

①拟人。I'll speak to it, though **hell itself should gape/and bid me hold my peace**. 此处将 hell 拟人化，比拟为一个可以开口说话，要求 Hamlet 闭嘴的人。

②借代。Give it an understanding but no **tongue**, …用说话器官指代语言。

Till then sit still, my sou—Foul deeds will rise

Though all the earth o'erwhelm them to men's eyes. ①

[Exit.]

Act I, Scene 3

Elsinore. A room in the house of Polonius.

[Enter Laertes and Ophelia.]

Laertes：My necessaries are embarked. Farewell.

And sister, as the winds give benefit ②

And convoy is assistant, do not sleep

But let me hear from you.

Ophelia：　　　　　　　Do you doubt that?

Laertes：For Hamlet and the trifling of his favour,

Hold it a fashion and a toy in blood,

A violet in the youth of primy nature,

【辞格辨析】

①拟人和尾韵。Till then **sit still, my soul.** Foul deeds will **rise**, /though all the earth o'erwhelm them, to men's **eyes**. 此处将 my soul 赋予生命，比拟为蠢蠢欲动的生物，而在事出蹊跷的关头，Hamlet 则需要他的 soul 冷静下来；此外，rise 和 eyes 也构成尾韵，表示该场结束。

②拟人。And sister, **as the winds give benefit**/and convoy is assistant, do not sleep, /…此处将 wind 赋予生命，能够作出 assistant（给予帮助）的行为。

莎剧《哈姆雷特》辞格辨析与文体鉴赏

Forward, not permanent, —sweet, not lasting, ①
The perfume and suppliance of a minute,
No more.

Ophelia：　　　No more but so. ②

Laertes：　　　　　　　　Think it no more.
For nature crescent does not grow alone
In thews and bulk, but as this temple waxes
The inward service of the mind and soul
Grows wide withal. ③ Perhaps he loves you now,

【辞格辨析】

①隐喻和对仗。For Hamlet, and the trifling of his favour, / hold it [...] /**a violet in the youth of primy nature**, /**forward, not permanent, sweet, not lasting** ... 此处为植物隐喻，将 Hamlet 对待 Ophelia 的感情，比喻为阳春的紫罗兰，虽然艳丽但不持久。此处另一种辞格为对仗，forward not permanent, sweet not lasting 两个短语结构相同，语义相反，构成对仗，进一步凸显紫罗兰的特点，并以此来比拟 Hamlet 的感情。

②省略。No more but so. 省略掉根据情景能够推测的内容，增强对话的现场感。

③隐喻（1）（2）（黄国彬，2013：204）。For **nature crescent** does not grow alone/in thews and bulk; but as this **temple waxes**, /the inward **service** of the mind and soul/grows wide withal. 此处有两处比喻。第一，将 Hamlet 的成长与月亮渐满相比较，体现在词汇 crescent 与 wax 的呼应上；第二，将 Hamlet 心智的成熟，需求的增长比喻扩大的庙宇需要更多的供奉，体现在 temple 和 services 的呼应上。

And now no soil nor cautel doth besmirch

The virtue of his will; ① but you must fear,

His greatness weighed, ② his will is not his own.

For he himself is subject to his birth.

He may not, as unvalued persons do,

Carve for himself, for on his choice depends

The safety and health of this whole state, ③

And therefore must his choice be circumscribed

Unto the voice and yielding of that body

Whereof he is the head. ④ Then if he says he loves you

【辞格辨析】

①隐喻。...and now **no soil** nor cautel doth **besmirch**/the virtue of his will;...此处将不好的行为，比喻为玷污 Hamlet 美德的泥土。

②隐喻。...but you must fear,/his greatness **weighed**,...将 Hamlet 的高贵身份，具体化为可以用来称重的具体物品。

③隐喻（Wilson, 2009: 154）和拟人。He may not, as unvalued persons do, /**carve for himself**, for on his choice depends/**the safety and health of this whole state**. 此处的比喻较为隐晦，即将人的存在，比喻为被雕刻出来的塑像。另一处为拟人，将国家看作有生命的个体，也有安全和健康的问题需要考虑。

④借代和拟人。...unto the **voice** and yielding of **that body**/whereof he is the **head**. 用 voice 指代通过声音表达的"意见"。此外，that body 和 head 将国家比拟为身体，而将未来的国王 Hamlet 比作该身体的头部。

It fits your wisdom so far to believe it
As he in his particular act and place
May give his saying deed, which is no further
Than the main voice of Denmark goes withal. ①
Then weigh what loss your honour may sustain
If with too credent ear you list his songs ②
Or lose your heart, or your chaste treasure open
To his unmastered importunity. ③
Fear it, Ophelia, fear it, my dear sister ④
And keep you in the rear of your affection
Out of the shot and danger of desire. ⑤

【辞格辨析】

①借代。…than the main **voice** of Denmark goes withal. 同上,也是使用 voice 指代"意见"。

②借代。…if with too credent **ear** you list his songs…用 ear 指代轻易相信别人的话语,此处劝告 Ophelia 不要轻易相信 Hamlet 的甜言蜜语。

③隐喻。… or lose your heart, Or **your chaste treasure open**/to his unmastered importunity. 把处女的童真比喻为未被发现的宝藏。

④间隔重复。**Fear it**, Ophelia, **fear it**, my dear sister…重复词语 fear it 之间加入 Ophelia。

⑤隐喻(Thompson & Taylor, 2007: 192)…and keep you **in the rear** of your affection/out of **the shot** and danger of desire. 此处使用了军事的意象,如 rear 和 shot 等,将 Hamlet 对 Ophelia 的追求比喻为军队的进攻。

第四章 《哈姆雷特》辞格辨析

The chariest maid is prodigal enough
If she unmask her beauty to the moon.
Virtue itself scapes not calumnious strokes. ①
The canker galls the infants of the spring
Too oft before their buttons be disclosed, ②
And in the morn and liquid dew of youth
Contagious blastments are most imminent. ③
Be wary then: best safety lies in fear, ④
Youth to itself rebels, though none else near.
Ophelia: I shall the effect of this good lesson keep
As watchman to my heart. ⑤ But, good my brother,

【辞格辨析】

①拟人。**Virtue itself scapes** not calumnious strokes. 将 virtue 拟人化，能够做出 scape（逃离）的动作。

②拟人。The canker galls the **infants** of the spring/Too oft before their buttons be disclosed, …将春天的新发的花蕊比拟为春天的宝宝，凸显其娇嫩的同时，也强调 canker 对待放花蕊的侵害。

③隐喻。… and **in the morn** and liquid dew of youth/contagious blastments are most imminent. 将青春比喻为早晨。

④逆喻。…**best safety lies in fear**, …Safety 和 fear 这对语义上有些相冲突的词语，一起构成逆喻，蕴含一些哲理的味道。

⑤拟人。I shall the effect of this good lesson keep, /as **watchman** to my heart. Ophelia 将 Laertes 劝告的话语比拟为一个心门的守护人，使表述更为生动。

莎剧《哈姆雷特》辞格辨析与文体鉴赏

Do not as some ungracious pastors do
Show me the steep and thorny way to heaven ①
Whiles, like a puff'd and reckless libertine,
Himself the primrose path of dalliance treads ②
And recks not his own rede.
Laertes:　　　　　　O, fear me not.
　　　　　　　　　　　〔Enter Polonius〕
I stay too long. But here my father comes.
A double blessing is a double grace:
Occasion smiles upon a second leave. ③
Polonius: Yet here, Laertes? Aboard, aboard for shame!
The wind sits in the shoulder of your sail ④
And you are stayed for. There, my blessing with thee,
And these few precepts in thy memory

【辞格辨析】

①隐喻。…show me **the steep and thorny way** to heaven…将恋爱过程遇到的各种不测比喻为陡峭且布满荆棘的路。

②隐喻。…himself **the primrose path** of dalliance treads。将寻欢作乐的生活态度比喻为踏上铺满报春花的路。

③拟人（Thompson & Taylor, 2007: 194）。**Occasion smiles** upon a second leave. 将再次道别赋予生命，能够做出微笑的动作。

④拟人。**The wind sits in the shoulder of your sail.** 此处有两处拟人，一是将 wind 赋予生命，能够 sit（坐）在某处；二是将船帆赋予生命，并且拥有 shoulder。

Look thou character：① Give thy thoughts no tongue ②
Nor any unproportioned thought his act.
Be thou familiar, but by no means vulgar；
Those friends thou hast, and their adoption tried,
Grapple them unto thy soul with hoops of steel, ③
But do not dull thy palm with entertainment
Of each new-hatched, unfledged comrade. ④ Beware
Of entrance to a quarrel but, being in,
Bear't that th' opposed may beware of thee.
Give every man thine ear but few thy voice; ⑤

【辞格辨析】

①拟人。…and these few precepts in thy memory/**look thou character**：…将训诫拟人化（同上 watchman 的例子），能够监视一个人的行为。

②借代。Give thy thoughts no **tongue**…将用说话的器官 tongue 指代发表意见。

③隐喻（Thompson & Taylor, 2007：195）。…**grapple them unto thy soul with hoops of steel**, …将和经过考验的朋友保持友谊比喻为用钢圈把木桶箍紧。

④借代和隐喻。… but do not **dull thy palm with** entertainment/of each **new-hatched**, **unfledged** comrade. 用握手的动作指代结识新朋友。将刚认识、未经考验的朋友比喻为刚孵出来的小鸟。

⑤借代（1）（2）。Give every man thine **ear** /but few thy **voice**. 用倾听的器官 ear 和说话的行为 voice 指代倾听和表达观点行为。

101

莎剧《哈姆雷特》辞格辨析与文体鉴赏

Take each man's censure but reserve thy judgment.
Costly thy habit as thy purse can buy
But not expressed in fancy—rich, not gaudy;
For the apparel oft proclaims the man
And they in France of the best rank and station
Are most select and generous, chief in that.
Neither a borrower nor a lender, boy,
For loan oft loses both itself and friend
And borrowing dulleth th'edge of husbandry. ①
This above all, to thine own self be true
And it must follow as the night the day ②
Thou canst not then be false to any man. ③
Farewell, my blessing season this in thee.
Laertes: Most humbly do I take my leave, my lord.

【辞格辨析】

①隐喻。…and borrowing **dulls the edge** of husbandry. 此处把勤俭比喻为一把刀,而借贷则会使这把刀变钝。

②明喻和省略。…and it must follow, **as** the night the day…此处有两个辞格。第一,Claudius 要求他儿子 Laertes 遵循他的训诫如同黑夜紧跟白天一样,借用 as 构成明喻;第二,as the night the day 省略了动词 follow。此处省略辞格可以看作为了让语言表意清晰,也可能因为受到每行固定音节的约束。

③弱陈。…and it must follow, as the night the day, /thou canst **not** then be **false** to any man. Not 和 false 双重否定,构成弱陈,起到强调的作用。

Polonius: The time invites you. ① Go, your servants tend.

Laertes: Farewell, Ophelia, and remember well

What I have said to you.

Ophelia: 'Tis in my memory locked, ②

And you yourself shall keep the key of it.

Laertes: Farewell. 　　　　　　　　　　　[Exit.]

Polonius: What is't, Ophelia, he hath said to you?

Ophelia: So please you, something touching the Lord Hamlet.

Polonius: Marry, well bethought:

'Tis told me he hath very oft of late

Given private time to you, and you yourself

Have of your audience been most free and bounteous.

If it be so—as so 'tis put on me,

And that in way of caution—I must tell you ③

You do not understand yourself so clearly

As it behooves my daughter and your honour.

What is between you? Give me up the truth.

【辞格辨析】

①拟人。The time invites you. 将 time 拟人化，能够发出 invite 的动作。

②隐喻。'Tis in my memory **locked**, /and you yourself keep **the key** of it. Ophelia 将记住 Laertes 的劝告比喻为将它锁在记忆中。

③插说。If it be so— **as so 'tis put on me, /and that in way of caution**—I must tell you...此处插说补充了 Polonius 的心声，接下来他将阻止 Ophelia 和 Hamlet 的交往。

莎剧《哈姆雷特》辞格辨析与文体鉴赏

Ophelia: He hath, my lord, of late made many tenders
Of his affection to me.
Polonius: Affection? Pooh, you speak like a green girl
Unsifted in such perilous circumstance. ①
Do you believe his 'tenders', as you call them?
Ophelia: I do not know, my lord, what I should think.
Polonius: Marry, I will teach you; think yourself a baby
That you have ta'en these tenders for true pay
Which are not sterling. Tender yourself more dearly
Or—not to crack the wind of the poor phrase,
Running it thus—② you'll tender me a fool. ③

【辞格辨析】

①隐喻。…**unsifted** in such perilous circumstance. 此处把 Ophelia 涉世未深比喻为未经 sift（筛选）的事物。

②隐喻和插说。Not to **crack the wind** of the poor phrase. 此处把一个词语（即 tender）比喻为一匹马，然后把重复使用该词语比喻为驱赶该马，使得它气喘吁吁。这里也是一处插说，Polonius 插入自己的一些想法。

③换义双关（黄国彬，2013：216）和一笔双叙双关（Raffel，2003：33；Thompson & Taylor，2007：198）。…of late made many **tenders**/…/That you have ta'en these **tenders** for true pay, /…**Tender** yourself more dearly; /…/you'll **tender** me **a fool**. 此处的 tender 分别表示"爱慕""清偿""照顾"和"使……成为"等。在这里，Polonius 借该词的多义性，玩了一把文字游戏；另一处双关为 a fool，同时表示"大傻瓜"和"小婴儿"的意思。

Ophelia: My lord, he hath importuned me with love
In honourable fashion.
Polonius: Ay, 'fashion' you may call it. Go to, go to. ①
Ophelia: And hath given countenance to his speech, my lord,
With almost all the holy vows of heaven.
Polonius: Ay, springes to catch woodcocks! ② I do know
When the blood burns, how prodigal the soul
Lends the tongue vows. ③ These blazes, daughter,
Giving more light than heat, extinct in both
Even in their promise as it is a-making,
You must not take for fire. ④ From this time

【辞格辨析】

①换义双关（Thompson & Taylor, 2007: 199; 黄国彬, 2013: 217）。…in honourable **fashion**/Ay, **fashion** you may call it; …Ophelia 使用 fashion 时, 取的是该词"方式"的语义, 而 Polonius 则选取其"流行"的意思, 把该词变为贬义。

②隐喻。**Ay, springes to catch woodcocks!** 此处 Polonius 将甜言蜜语比喻为抓捕丘鹬鸟而设置的圈套。

③拟人。When the blood burns how prodigal **the soul/lends the tongue vows.** 将 soul 拟人化, 使其变成能够发出 lend（帮助）动作的个体。

④隐喻。**These blazes**, daughter, /giving **more light than heat, extinct** in both/…/you must not take for **fire**. 此处隐喻将 Hamlet 热烈但不恒久的爱情比喻为烈焰, 主要迸发出光芒, 而不是热量, 且会很快熄灭。

莎剧《哈姆雷特》辞格辨析与文体鉴赏

Be something scanter of your maiden presence;
Set your entreatments at a higher rate
Than a command to parley. ① For Lord Hamlet,
Believe so much in him, that he is young
And with a larger tether may he walk ②
Than may be given you. In few, Ophelia,
Do not believe his vows, for they are brokers ③
Not of that dye which their investments show
But mere implorators of unholy suits
Breathing like sanctified and pious bonds

【辞格辨析】

①隐喻（Jenkins, 1982: 206; Hibbard, 1987: 179）。…set your **entreatments** at a higher rate/than a command to parley. 此处为使用军事意象的隐喻，把 Ophelia 答应和 Hamlet 见面比喻为军事中的谈判请求。

②隐喻。…and with **a larger tether** may he **walk**…此处将 Hamlet 作为王子所拥有的生活自由度和宽广度比喻为用更长的拴绳拴住的动物，拥有更大的活动空间。

③拟人（Thompson & Taylor, 2007: 200）。…do not believe his vows; for they are **brokers**…此处把 Hamlet 的爱情誓言比拟为 broker，即"掮客"或"代理商"。

The better to beguile. ④ This is for all:
I would not, in plain terms, from this time forth
Have you so slander any moment leisure
As to give words or talk with the Lord Hamlet.
Look to't, I charge you. Come your ways.
Ophelia: I shall obey, my lord.

[Exeunt.]

【辞格辨析】

①一笔双叙双关（1）-（6）。For they are **brokers**, /not of that **dye** which their **investments** show, /but mere **implorators** of unholy **suits**, /breathing like sanctified and pious **bonds**, /the better to beguile. 此处由 brokers 等一系列词语构成的双关。这几行至少有两种理解：第一，broker 作为生意的中间人理解，investments，implorators，suits 和 bonds 均可以从商业的语境来分别理解为"投资""仲裁者""诉求"和"债券"，整句话可以理解为"誓言就如同生意中间人一般，兜售各种看似可靠的债券来从中牟利"。第二，broker 作销售旧衣服的商人理解，dye，investments 和 suits 等词则全都可以从"衣物"相关语义来理解，理解为"颜色""衣服"和"套装"，整句话又可以理解为"誓言就像兜售旧衣物的商人一样，所卖的衣物并不是外在颜色所展示的"。因此，brokers，dye，investments，implorators，suits 和 bonds 可以理解为六处一笔双叙双关。

■ 莎剧《哈姆雷特》辞格辨析与文体鉴赏

Act I, Scene 4

Elsinore. The platform before the Castle.

Enter Hamlet, Horatio, and Marcellus.

Hamlet: The air bites shrewdly; ① it is very cold.

Horatio: It is a nipping and an eager air.

Hamlet: What hour now?

Horatio: I think it lacks of twelve.

Marcellus: No, it is struck.

Horatio: Indeed, I heard it not.

It then draws near the season

Wherein the spirit held his wont to walk.

[A flourish of trumpets, and two pieces go off.]

What does this mean, my lord?

Hamlet: The King doth wake to-night and takes his rouse,

Keeps wassail, and the swaggering upspring reels,

And as he drains his draughts of Rhenish down ②

The kettledrum and trumpet thus bray out

The triumph of his pledge. ③

【辞格辨析】

①拟人。The air **bites** shrewdly; it is very cold. 将寒冷的空气描述为能够发出 bite（咬人）动作的个体。

②隐喻。… and, as he **drains** his draughts of Rhenish down…此处将 Claudius 喝酒的动作比喻为水管排水。

③隐喻。…the kettledrum and trumpet thus **bray out**…Bray out 为动物叫声，特别是驴的叫声。此处将庆祝国王干杯的鼓乐声比喻为动物吵闹乱叫声。

Horatio: Is it a custom?

Hamlet: Ay, marry, is't,
But to my mind, though I am native here
And to the manner born, it is a custom
More honoured in the breach than the observance. ①
This heavy-headed revel east and west ②
Makes us traduced and taxed of other nations:
They clepe us drunkards and with swinish phrase
Soil our addition, and indeed it takes
From our achievements, though performed at height,
The pith and marrow of our attribute. ③
So oft it chances in particular men
That, for some vicious mole of nature in them, ④
As in their birth wherein they are not guilty
(Since nature cannot choose his origin), —

【辞格辨析】

①对仗。…it is a custom/more honor'd in the **breach** than the **observance**. Breach（摒弃）和 observance（遵循）构成对仗关系。

②借代。This **heavy-headed** revel east and west…用 heavy-headed，即喝酒后醉醺醺的模样，指代酗酒行为。

③隐喻。…the **pith** and **marrow** of our attribute. Hamlet 将丹麦人的优良品质比喻为脊髓精华。

④隐喻。…that, for some **vicious mole** of nature in them,／…Hamlet 此处将丹麦人的缺陷（即酗酒）比喻为随生而来的胎痣。

■ 莎剧《哈姆雷特》辞格辨析与文体鉴赏

By the o'ergrowth of some complexion
Oft breaking down the pales and forts of reason, ①
Or by some habit that too much o'erleavens ②
The form of plausive manners—that these men,
Carrying, I say, the stamp of one defect
(Being nature's livery, or Fortune's star), ③
His virtues else, be they as pure as grace,
As infinite as man may undergo, ④
Shall in the general censure take corruption
From that particular fault. The dram of eale
Doth all the noble substance often doubt
To his own scandal.　　　　　　　　[Enter Ghost.]
Horatio:　　　　Look, my lord, it comes.

【辞格辨析】

①隐喻。…oft breaking down the **pales** and **forts** of reason。此处将抽象的理智物化，使其如同一个地方一样拥有藩篱和堡垒，因此理智的僭越就如同翻越藩篱或推翻堡垒一般。

②隐喻（Thompson & Taylor, 2007: 204）。…or by some habit that too much **o'erleavens**/the form of plausive manners。Hamlet 在此处将过度放纵的行为，即酗酒，比喻为过度发酵。

③隐喻和插说。…being nature's **livery** or fortune's star。此处将一个民族的优点比喻为自然的外套。此处也是插说，Hamlet 在评说过程，插入让步的语言。

④插说。…their virtues else, **be they as pure as grace /as infinite as man may undergo**,…此处插说为对前面 virtue 的补充和强调。

Hamlet: Angels and ministers of grace defend us!
Be thou a spirit of health or goblin damned,
Bring with thee airs from heaven or blasts from hell,
Be thy intents wicked or charitable, ①
Thou com'st in such a questionable shape
That I will speak to thee. I'll call thee Hamlet,
King, father, royal Dane. O answer me?
Let me not burst in ignorance ② but tell
Why thy canonized bones hearsed in death, ③
Have burst their cerements, why the sepulchre
Wherein we saw thee quietly inurned,
Hath oped his ponderous and marble jaws
To cast thee up again. ④ What may this mean

【辞格辨析】

①首语重复。**Be thou** a spirit of health… /**Be thy** intents wicked or charitable, …此处重复使用 be thou/thy 的结构,构成首语重复,起到对重复内容的强调作用。

②隐喻。Let me not **burst** in ignorance. 将抽象的 ignorance 物化,将其比喻为可以膨胀充斥一个空间的事物。

③提喻。Why thy **canonized bones**, hearsed in death, …用 cannonized bone(裹尸布里的骨头)指代已故先王身躯。

④拟人。…why **the sepulchre**, /wherein we saw thee quietly inurned, /hath **oped his ponderous and marble jaws**, /to cast thee up again. 此处将 sepulchre(坟墓)赋予生命,使其能够发出 open(张开)和 cast(投射出)的动作。

111

莎剧《哈姆雷特》辞格辨析与文体鉴赏

That thou, dead corpse, again in complete steel,
Revisits thus the glimpses of the moon, ①
Making night hideous, and we fools of nature ②
So horridly to shake our disposition
With thoughts beyond the reaches of our souls?
Say, why is this? Wherefore? What should we do? ③

[Ghost beckons Hamlet.]

Horatio: It beckons you to go away with it
As if it some impartment did desire
To you alone.
Marcellus: Look with what courteous action
It waves you to a more removed ground.

【辞格辨析】

①同位语和拟人。…that thou, **dead corpse**, again in complete steel/revisits thus **the glimpses of the moon**, …Dead corpse 为 thou 的同位语,为对 thou 的补充和说明。The glimpses of the moon 为拟人,将月光暗淡的夜晚,比拟为月亮在偷看,因此漏出来的光亮不多。

②同位语。…making night hideous, and we **fools of nature**/so horridly …同位语,对 we 作补充说明。

③首语重复和排比。…but tell/**why** thy canoniz'd bones, …/**have** burst their cerements; **why** the sepulchre/… /**hath** op'd …. **What** may this mean/… /Say, **why** is this? 此处可以理解为借用 why 开篇的首语重复,同时,也可以理解为借助重复的 why… v. …结构构成的排比。这两重辞格的结合使用增强了语势。

But do not go with it.

Horatio: No, by no means.

Hamlet: It will not speak; Then will I follow it.

Horatio: Do not, my lord.

Hamlet: Why, what should be the fear?
I do not set my life at a pin's fee, ①
And for my soul, what can it do to that,
Being a thing immortal as itself?
It waves me forth again. I'll follow it.

Horatio: What if it tempt you toward the flood, my lord,
Or to the dreadful summit of the cliff
That beetles o'er his base into the sea, ②
And there assume some other horrible form
Which might deprive your sovereignty of reason ③
And draw you into madness? Think of it.
The very place puts toys of desperation

【辞格辨析】

①夸张。I do not set my life **at a pin's fee**. Hamlet 将自身生命价值比为比喻别针还便宜,是夸张的手法。

②拟人(Thompson & Taylor, 2007: 208)。…or to the dreadful summit of **the cliff/that beetles o'er his base** into the sea. 此处将 cliff 赋予生命,将其描绘为能够发出 beetle (悬挂)这一动作的主体。

③隐喻。…which might deprive your **sovereignty of reason** …此处将一个人的理性比喻为一个拥有主权的国度,而丧失理智就如同失去主权。

莎剧《哈姆雷特》辞格辨析与文体鉴赏

Without more motive into every brain ①
That looks so many fathoms to the sea
And hears it roar beneath. ②
Hamlet: It waves me still. Go on. I'll follow thee.
Marcellus: You shall not go, my lord.
Hamlet: Hold off your hands!
Horatio: Be ruled. You shall not go.
Hamlet: My fate cries out
And makes each petty artery in this body
As hardy as the Nemean lion's nerve. ③

　　　　　　　　　　　　［Ghost beckons.］

Still am I called. Unhand me, gentlemen—
By heaven, I'll make a ghost of him that lets me! -
I say, away! —Go on! I'll follow thee.

【辞格辨析】

①借代。The very place puts toys of desperation, /without more motive, into every **brain**…这里将人脑来指代理性。

②拟人。…that looks so many fathoms to **the sea**/and hears it **roar** beneath. 此处将大海比拟为生命体,能够发出 roar（咆哮）的动作。

③拟人和明喻。**My fate cries out** /and makes each petty artery in this body/**as** hardy **as** the Nemean lion's nerve. 此处 Hamlet 赋予自己的命运这一抽象概念以生命,使其能够做出 cry out（哭喊）动作。另一处为明喻,即将自己追随鬼魂离开的决心比喻为狮子奋起的神经。

[Exeunt Ghost and Hamlet.]
Horatio: He waxes desperate with imagination.
Marcellus: Let's follow. 'Tis not fit thus to obey him.
Horatio: Have after. To what issue will this come?
Marcellus: Something is rotten in the state of Denmark. ①
Horatio: Heaven will direct it.
Marcellus: Nay, let's follow him.   [Exeunt.]

Act I, Scene 5
Elsinore. The Castle. Another part of the fortifications.
Enter Ghost and Hamlet.

Hamlet: Whither wilt thou lead me? Speak! I'll go no further.
Father's Ghost: Mark me.
Hamlet: I will.
Father's Ghost: My hour is almost come,
When I to sulphurous and tormenting flames
Must render up myself.
Hamlet: Alas, poor ghost.
Father's Ghost: Pity me not, but lend thy serious hearing

【辞格辨析】

　　①隐喻。Something is **rotten** in the state of Denmark. 此处把发生在丹麦国的坏事比喻为会腐烂的事物。

To what I shall unfold. ①

Hamlet: Speak, I am bound to hear.

Father's Ghost: So art thou to revenge when thou shalt hear.

Hamlet: What?

Father's Ghost: I am thy father's spirit,

Doomed for a certain term to walk the night

And for the day confined to fast in fires

Till the foul crimes done in my days of nature ②

Are burnt and purg'd away. But that I am forbid

To tell the secrets of my prison house

I could a tale unfold whose lightest word

Would harrow up thy soul, freeze thy young blood, ③

【辞格辨析】

①隐喻（1）（2）。Pity me not, but **lend thy serious hearing**/to what I shall **unfold**. 此处有两处隐喻。第一处为将 hearing（倾听）这一动作物化，比喻为可以 lend（借用）的物品，另一处是 unfold 这一衣物相关的隐喻。

②头韵。…confined to **f**ast in **f**ires/till the **f**oul crimes done in my days of nature…此处 fast, fires 和 foul 构成头韵，增强这两行诗句的音韵感。

③夸张和隐喻（Thompson & Taylor, 2007：212）。…I could a tale unfold whose **lightest** word/would **harrow up** thy soul,…此处有两处辞格。第一处用最高级的 lightest word 和列举的系列反应相对照，凸显地狱情况惊人，为夸张手法；第二处借用 harrow up 这一农业意象，表示地狱中的事件会让人灵魂被"耙"空。

Make thy two eyes like stars start from their spheres, ①
Thy knotted and combined locks to part
And each particular hair to stand on end
Like quills upon the fretful porcupine. ②
But this eternal blazon must not be
To ears of flesh and blood. ③ List, list, O list! ④
If thou didst ever thy dear father love—
Hamlet: O God!
Father's Ghost: Revenge his foul and most unnatural murther!
Hamlet: Murther?
Father's Ghost: Murther most foul—as in the best it is—
But this most foul, strange, and unnatural. ⑤

【辞格辨析】

①明喻。…make **thy two eyes, like stars, start from their spheres**, …此处借用天文行星跃出轨道的意象来比喻人们听到骇人听闻的事件后眼部的表情动作。

②明喻。…and each particular hair to stand on end, /l**ike quills upon the fretful porcupine**. 此处将因为听到惊讶事件害怕而使头发竖立的形象，比喻为竖起尖刺的豪猪。

③借代和提喻。But this eternal blazon must not be/to **ears of flesh and blood**. 此处 ear 指代"听"这一动作，为借代；flesh and blood 指代活着的人，为部分代替整体的提喻。

④间隔重复。**List**, Hamlet, **list**, o **list**! 此处重复三次 listen，增强感叹语气。

⑤排比。…but this most **foul**, **strange**, and **unnatural**. 此处由三个词构成排比，对谋杀事件的凶恶起到烘托作用。

莎剧《哈姆雷特》辞格辨析与文体鉴赏

Hamlet: Haste me to know't that I with wings as swift
As meditation or the thoughts of love ①
May sweep to my revenge.

Father's Ghost: I find thee apt;
And duller shouldst thou be than the fat weed
That rots itself in ease on Lethe wharf ②
Wouldst thou not stir in this. Now, Hamlet, hear:
'Tis given out that, sleeping in my orchard,
A serpent stung me. So the whole ear of Denmark
Is by a forged process of my death
Rankly abused. ③ But know, thou noble youth,
The serpent that did sting thy father's life
Now wears his crown. ④

【辞格辨析】

①明喻。Haste me to know't, that I, with wings **as swift/as meditation or the thoughts of love/**…此处 Hamlet 将自己报仇速度与思绪和联想的速度相比拟，突出行动的果断和快捷。

②隐喻。**And duller shouldst thou be than the fat weed/**that rots itself in ease on Lethe wharf/…此处将听到谋杀后无动于衷的情形比喻为阴间遗忘河旁的野草。

③借代和提喻。So **the whole ear of Denmark/**is by a forged process of my death/rankly abused. 此处有两种辞格，第一为借代，用 ear 指代"听"这一动作，第二为提喻，用整体的 Denmark 指代所有丹麦人民。

④隐喻。**The serpent** that did sting thy father's life…此处鬼魂将 Claudius 比喻为 the serpent。

第四章 《哈姆雷特》辞格辨析

Hamlet： O my prophetic soul! ①
My uncle!
Father's Ghost：Ay, that incestuous, that adulterate beast,
With witchcraft of his wit, with traitorous gifts— ②
O wicked wit and gifts, ③ that have the power
So to seduce ④ —won to his shameful lust
The will of my most seeming-virtuous Queen.
O Hamlet, what a fallingoff was there,
From me whose love was of that dignity
That it went hand in hand even with the vow ⑤
I made to her in marriage, and to decline

【辞格辨析】

①拟人。O my **prophetic soul**! 此处将 soul 赋予生命，拥有预知的能力。

②逆喻。... with **witchcraft of his wit**, with **traitorous gifts**—...使用 witchcraft 和 wit，以及 traitorous 和 gift 这两对语义相反的词语，构成逆喻。

③逆喻和头韵。O **wicked wit** and gifts, ...此处有两处辞格，wicked 和 wit 构成的头韵；两者语义上相反，也构成逆喻。

④插说。...with traitorous gifts—/O **wicked wit and gifts, that have the power/so to seduce**—won to his shameful lust...此处的插说一方面有补充信息的作用，另一方面也是鬼魂个人观点的抒发和强调。

⑤拟人。...that it **went hand in hand** even with the vow/...将先王对 Gertrude 的爱情和尊重赋予生命，能够作出 hand in hand 的动作，比喻爱和尊重并举。

Upon a wretch whose natural gifts were poor
To those of mine.
But Virtue, as it never will be moved,
Though lewdness court it in a shape of heaven,
So lust, though to a radiant angel linked,
Will sate itself in a celestial bed
And prey on garbage. ①
But soft, methinks I scent the morning air.
Brief let me be. Sleeping within my orchard—
My custom always of the afternoon—②
Upon my secure hour thy uncle stole
With juice of cursed hebona in a vial
And in the porches of my ears did pour
The leperous distilment ③ whose effect
Holds such an enmity with blood of man
That swift as quicksilver it courses through

【辞格辨析】

①拟人（Thompson & Taylor, 2007: 215）。But **Virtue, as it never will be mov'd/… /so lust**, though to a radiant angel link'd, /… /and **prey** on garbage. 此处将 virtue（美德）和 lust（欲望）赋予生命，能够被感动，也能够觅食。

②插说。Brief let me be. Sleeping within my orchard, /**my custom always of the afternoon**/upon my secure hour…此处插说补充信息，告诉听者在果园午休为鬼魂生前的习惯。

③隐喻。… and in **the porches** of my ears did pour/The leperous distilment。此处将耳朵的耳道比喻为走廊。

The natural gates and alleys of the body ①
And with a sudden vigour it doth possess
And curd like eager droppings into milk ②
The thin and wholesome blood. So did it mine
And a most instant tetter barked about
Most lazar-like, with vile and loathsome crust
All my smooth body. ③
Thus was I sleeping by a brother's hand
Of life, of crown, of queen, at once dispatched;
Cut off even in the blossoms of my sin,

【辞格辨析】

①拟人，明喻和隐喻。…whose effect/**holds such an enmity with** blood of man/that **swift as quicksilver** it courses through/…/the **natural gates** and **alleys** of the body, …这一句的辞格比较密集。首先是将毒水的毒性赋予生命，描述其与人的血液有深仇大恨，即能严重破坏人体血液；其次是明喻，将毒水在身体中的流动速度比喻为如水银般变幻莫测；最后是隐喻，将血管比喻为门户和走廊，回应上面隐喻意象。

②明喻。…and curd **like** eager droppings into milk. 将毒水和血液结合后，在皮肤上凝结的情形比喻为酸性物质滴入牛奶形成凝固状物体的过程。

③隐喻（Thompson & Taylor, 2007: 217）。…and a most instant tetter **bark'd about**, /most lazar-like, …将身体长出的硬皮比喻为树皮。

莎剧《哈姆雷特》辞格辨析与文体鉴赏

Unhouseled, disappointed, unaneled, ①
No reckoning made but sent to my account
With all my imperfections on my head.
O, horrible, O horrible! Most horrible! ②
Father's Ghost: If thou hast nature in thee bear it not,
Let not the royal bed of Denmark be
A couch for luxury and damned incest.
But, howsoever thou pursuest this act
Taint not thy mind nor let thy soul contrive
Against thy mother aught. ③ Leave her to heaven,

【辞格辨析】

①排比和隐喻。Thus was I, sleeping, by a brother's hand/**of life, of crown, of queen**, at once dispatched; /cut off even **in the blossoms of my sin**, /Unhouseled, disappointed, unaneled, /no reckoning made, but sent to my account/with all my imperfections on my head. 此处有三处辞格,首先是 of life, of crown 和 of queen 三个平行结构构成的排比;其次是将死前没有祷告(基督教的仪式)而使得生前罪恶没有消减的情况,比喻为罪恶如花般开放;最后是由 unhouseled, disappointed 和 unaneled 三个以否定前缀开头的词语构成的排比。这些辞格增强了行文的语气,突出先王在描述过程的气愤之情。

②间隔重复。O, **horrible**, O, **horrible**! Most **horrible**! 间隔重复突出了 Hamlet 听到先王控诉之后的惊讶之情。

③拟人。…taint not thy mind, **nor let thy soul contrive/against thy mother aught**. 将灵魂比拟为有生命和智力的生命体,能够 contrive(谋划)阴谋。

And to those thorns that in her bosom lodge
To prick and sting her. ① Fare thee well at once.
The glow-worm shows the matin to be near
And 'gins to pale his uneffectual fire.
Adieu, adieu, adieu, remember me.   [Exit.]
Hamlet: O all you host of heaven, O earth! What else?
And shall I couple hell? Hold, hold, my heart, ②
And you, my sinews, grow not instant old
But bear me stiffly up. ③ Remember thee?
Ay, thou poor ghost, while memory holds a seat
In this distracted globe. ④ Remember thee?

【辞格辨析】

①隐喻。…and to **those thorns that in her bosom** lodge/to **prick and sting** her. 将 Gertrude 心中可能存在的愧疚比喻为生长在心中的刺，能够刺痛人。

②直接重复。**Hold, hold,** my heart！直接重复，突出 Hamlet 此时亢奋的心情。

③拟人。And you, **my sinews, grow not instant old**/but bear me stiffly up. 把人的肌腱赋予生命，能够变老。

④拟人和隐喻。While **memory holds a seat**/in **this distracted globe**。此处有两处辞格，第一是拟人，将 memory（记忆）赋予生命，能够在头脑中占有一席；第二是隐喻，即 Hamlet 将自己的头脑比喻为 globe。也有学者将此处的 globe 与莎士比亚的环球剧场相联系，如果按此理解，则又有借代的含义。也有学者将此处的 globe 作为双关看待，如 Thompson & Taylor（2007）等。

莎剧《哈姆雷特》辞格辨析与文体鉴赏

Yea, from the table of my memory ①
I'll wipe away all trivial fond records,
All saws of books, all forms, all pressures past ②
That youth and observation copied there
And thy commandment all alone shall live
Within the book and volume of my brain
Unmixed with baser matter. ③ Yes, by heaven,
O most pernicious woman,
O villain, villain, smiling, damned villain, ④
My tables! Meet it is I set it down

【辞格辨析】

①隐喻(Thompson & Taylor, 2007: 219)(Wilson, 2009: 162)。Yea, from **the table of my memory**/I'll wipe away all trivial fond records. 此处将记忆比作用于书写的 table（伊丽莎白时期用于书写的器具）。

②排比。I'll wipe away all trivial fond records, /**all saws of books, all forms, all pressures past** …此处借助 all saws, all forms 和 all pressures past 等结构相同的短语，构成排比。

③隐喻和拟人。…and thy **commandment all alone shall live**/within **the book and volume of my brain**, /unmixed with baser matter. 这句话有两种辞格。第一种是拟人，即将老王告诉 Hamlet 的 commandment 赋予生命，能够生存在脑海中，意为 Hamlet 将记住这些告诫；第二种是隐喻，即将头脑的记忆比喻为书本。

④直接重复和间接重复。O **villain**, **villain**, smiling, damned **villain**! 此处的两个 villain 构成直接和间接重复。

That one may smile and smile and be a villain—①
At least I am sure it may be so in Denmark.   [Writes.]
So, uncle, there you are. Now to my word.
It is 'Adieu, adieu, remember me.'
I have sworn't.

Horatio: [within] My lord, my lord! [Enter Horatio and Marcellus.]
Marcellus: Lord Hamlet!
Horatio: Heaven secure him!
Hamlet: So be it!
Marcellus: Illo, ho, ho, my lord!
Hamlet: Hillo, ho, ho, boy! Come, bird, come!
Marcellus: How is't, my noble lord?
Horatio: What news, my lord?
Marcellus: O, wonderful.
Horatio: Good my lord, tell it.
Hamlet: No, you will reveal it.
Horatio: Not I, my lord, by heaven.
Marcellus: Nor I, my lord.
Hamlet: How say you then—Would heart of man once think it? — But you'll be secret?
Marcellus: [with Horatio]   Ay, by heaven, my lord.
Hamlet: There's never a villain dwelling in all Denmark

【辞格辨析】

①间隔重复。O villain, villain, **smiling**, … /… /that one may **smile**, and **smile**, and be a villain. 此处 smile 为间隔重复，和 villain 构成对 smiling villain（笑面恶棍）强调的作用。

But he's an arrant knave.

Horatio: There needs no ghost, my lord, come from the grave
To tell us this.

Hamlet: Why, right! You are in the right!
And so, without more circumstance at all
I hold it fit that we shake hands and part—
You as your business and desires shall point you
(For every man hath business and desire
Such as it is) ① and for my own poor part
I'll go pray.

Horatio: These are but wild and whirling words, my lord.

Hamlet: I am sorry they offend you—heartily,
Yes, faith, heartily.

Horatio: There's no offence, my lord.

Hamlet: Yes, by Saint Patrick, but there is, Horatio,
And much offence too. Touching this vision here
It is an honest ghost—that let me tell you.
For your desire to know what is between us
O'ermaster as you may. And now, good friends,
As you are friends, scholars, and soldiers ②

【辞格辨析】

①插说。…**for every man hath business and desire**，/**such as it is** and for my own poor part，/I will go pray. 此处插说补充了原因信息，使 Hamlet 突然要告别其他人有了理由。

②排比。As you are **friends, scholars,** and **soldiers,** /give me one poor request. 此处用一系列名词构成排比。

第四章 《哈姆雷特》辞格辨析

Give me one poor request.

Horatio: What is't, my lord? We will.

Hamlet: Never make known what you have seen tonight.

Marcellus: [with Horatio] My lord, we will not.

Hamlet: Nay, but swear't.

Horatio: In faith, my lord, not I.

Marcellus: Nor I, my lord, in faith.

Hamlet: Upon my sword.

Marcellus: We have sworn, my lord, already.

Hamlet: Indeed, upon my sword, indeed. ①

Ghost cries under the stage.

Father's Ghost: Swear.

Hamlet: Aha boy, sayst thou so? Art thou there, truepenny? ②
Come on, you hear this fellow in the cellarage?
Consent to swear.

Horatio: Propose the oath, my lord.

Hamlet: Never to speak of this that you have seen.

【辞格辨析】

①省略。**Upon my sword.** /We have sworn, my lord, already. /Indeed, **upon my sword**, indeed. 此处完整的句子应该是"Swear upon my sword.",省略还原对话的真实性。

②换说。Art thou there, **truepenny**? Truepenny 为 Nicholas Udall 的戏剧 Ralph Roister Doister（c. 1553）中一个诚实可信的角色（Thompson & Taylor, 2007: 224），此处使用换说的手法,表示 Hamlet 对老王的鬼魂在此时发声,帮助他让同伴发誓的行为的赞同。

127

莎剧《哈姆雷特》辞格辨析与文体鉴赏

Swear by my sword.

Father's Ghost:〔beneath〕Swear.

Hamlet: *Hic et ubique*? Then we'll shift our ground.

　　Come hither, gentlemen, and lay your hands

　　Against upon my sword. Swear by my sword.

　　Never to speak of this that you have heard.

Father's Ghost:〔beneath〕Swear by his sword.

Hamlet: Well said, old mole! Canst work i' th' earth so fast?
A worthy pioner! ① Once more remove, good friends.

Horatio: O day and night, but this is wondrous strange.

Hamlet: And therefore as a stranger give it welcome. ②
There are more things in heaven and earth, Horatio,
Than are dreamt of in your philosophy.
But come!
Here as before: never—so help you mercy,
How strange or odd some'er I bear myself

【辞格辨析】

①省略和隐喻（Thompson & Taylor, 2007: 225）。**A worthy pioneer.** 此处是"You/Thou are a worthy pioneer."的省略辞格，同时也是将老王的鬼魂比喻为善挖地道的动物或挖地道的士兵，突出其漂浮不定，行动快速。

②一笔双叙双关（黄国彬，2013: 261；Spencer, 1980: 242）。And therefore as **a stranger give it welcome**. 这句话为英语谚语"Give the stranger welcome."的灵活表达方式，在这里可以作两种理解，第一种表示欢迎陌生人，第二种表示不要问问题。

(As I perchance hereafter shall think meet
To put an antic disposition on) —
That you at such times seeing me, never shall
With arms encumbered thus, ① or this head-shake,
Or by pronouncing of some doubtful phrase
As 'Well, well, we know,' or 'We could an if we would',
Or 'If we list to speak', or 'There be, an if they might',
Or such ambiguous giving out ② to note
That you know aught of me. This do swear,
So grace and mercy at your most need help you,
Swear.

Father's Ghost: [beneath] Swear.　　　　　[They swear.]
Hamlet: Rest, rest, perturbed spirit! So, gentlemen,
With all my love I do commend me to you,
And what so poor a man as Hamlet is
May do t' express his love and friending to you
God willing, shall not lack. Let us go in together
And still your fingers on your lips, ③ I pray.

【辞格辨析】

①插说。How strange or odd some'er I bear myself, / (**as I perchance hereafter shall think meet/to put an antic disposition on**) /that you at such times seeing me never shall/with arms encumbered thus...插说，补充原因信息。

②首语重复。As... /or... /or..., or..., /or ...此处在每句的开头重复 or 这一词，构成首语重复，帮助列举出各种情形。

③借代。...and still your **fingers on your lips**. 将保守秘密的行为用 fingers on your lips 这一动作来指代。

The time is out of joint. ① O cursed spite
That ever I was born to set it right! ②
Nay, come, let's go together.　　　　　　　　　[Exeunt.]

第二幕

Act II, Scene 1

Elsinore. A room in the house of Polonius.
Enter Polonius and Reynaldo.

Polonius: Give him this money and these notes, Reynaldo.
Reynaldo: I will, my lord.
Polonius: You shall do marvellous wisely, good Reynaldo,
Before You visit him, to make inquire
Of his behaviour.
Reynaldo:　　　　My lord, I did intend it.
Polonius: Marry, well said, very well said. Look you, sir,
Enquire me first what Danskers are in Paris,

【辞格辨析】

①隐喻（Thompson & Taylor, 2007：227）。The time is **out of joint**. 这里是一个医学的隐喻，将时代的混乱比喻为脱臼的骨骼；也可以看作是木工隐喻，将时代比喻为脱榫或变形的家具。

②尾韵。O cursed **spite**/that ever I was born to set it **right**! 此处 spite 和 right 构成尾韵。在莎剧中，尾韵有表示结尾的作用，常用于一幕或一场的结尾处。

And how, and who, what means, and where they keep,
What company, at what expense; ① and finding
By this encompassment and drift of question
That they do know my son, come you more nearer
Than your particular demands will touch it;
Take you as 'twere some distant knowledge of him,
As thus, 'I know his father and his friends
And in part him'—do you mark this, Reynaldo?

Reynaldo: Ay, very well, my lord.

Polonius: 'And in part him, but', you may say, 'not well.
But if 't be he I mean he's very wild
Addicted so and so', and there put on him
What forgeries you please. Marry, none so rank
As may dishonour him—take heed of that—②
But, sir, such wanton, wild and usual slips
As are companions noted and most known
To youth and liberty.

Reynaldo: As gaming, my lord?

【辞格辨析】

①排比。And how, and **who, what means**, and **where they keep**, / **what company, at what expense**;…此处通过系列疑问词引出结构相似的成分,构成排比。

②插说。Marry, none so rank/as may dishonour him—**take heed of that**—…此处插说为Polonius对家奴Reynaldo的提醒,让他在打探Laertes国外生活情况的时候,不要捏造过分的以至于玷污Laertes名声的内容。

■ 莎剧《哈姆雷特》辞格辨析与文体鉴赏

Polonius: Ay, or drinking, fencing, swearing, quarrelling, Drabbing. You may go so far.
Reynaldo: My lord, that would dishonour him.
Polonius: Faith, no, as you may season it in the charge. ①
You must not put another scandal on him
That he is open to incontinency—
That's not my meaning—② But breathe his faults so quaintly
That they may seem the taints of liberty,
The flash and outbreak of a fiery mind,
A savageness in unreclaimed blood
Of general assault. ③
Reynaldo: But, my good lord—

【辞格辨析】

①隐喻（Wilson, 2009: 285）。…as you may **season** it in the charge. 此处为饮食意象相关的隐喻，用给菜肴调味的行为比喻 Reynaldo 对自己的语言加以修饰和把控，不至于说话内容过于没有节制，影响 Laertes 的名声。

②插说。…that he is open to incontinency. /**that's not my meaning**. But breathe his faults so quaintly/…Polonius 插入 "That's not my meaning"，在陈述过程表达了自己的观点。

③隐喻（1）（2）和排比。…that they may seem **the taints of liberty**, /**the flash and outbreak of a fiery mind**, /**a savageness in unreclaimed blood**, /**Of general assault**. 此处是将缺点比喻为自由个性所带来的 taint（污点）；第二处是将炽热性情比喻为火光电石，会发光甚至爆炸；另外由同一结构的名词短语"the …of …"构成排比，增强语势。

Polonius: Wherefore should you do this?
Reynaldo: Ay, my lord,
I would know that.
Polonius: Marry, sir, here's my drift,
And I believe it is a fetch of wit.
You laying these slight sullies on my son ①
As 'twere a thing a little soiled with working, ②
Mark you, your party in converse, him you would sound,
Having ever seen in the prenominate crimes
The youth you breathe of guilty, be assured
He closes with you in this consequence:
'Good sir,' or so, or 'friend,' or 'gentleman,'
According to the phrase or the addition
Of man and country—
Reynaldo: Very good, my lord.
Polonius: And then, sir, does 'a this—'a does—What was I about to say? By the mass, I was about to say something! Where did I leave?
Reynaldo: At 'closes in the consequence', at 'friend or so', and 'gentleman'.

【辞格辨析】

①隐喻。You laying these slight **sullies** on my son … 将 Reynaldo 为了打探 Laertes 在国外生活情况而随意捏造的一些个性小缺陷比喻为瑕疵,污点等。

②明喻。You laying these slight sullies on my son/**as** 'twere a thing a little soil'd i' th' working, …Polonius 将一个人身上的小缺点,比喻为一件物品在被触碰后留下污渍。

Polonius: At 'closes in the consequence'—Ay, marry.
He closes thus: 'I know the gentleman.
I saw him yesterday, or th'other day,
Or then, or then, with such or such; ① and, as you say
There was 'a gaming, there o'ertook in's rouse,
There falling out at tennis', ② or perchance
'I saw him enter such a house of sale',
Videlicet a brothel, or so forth.
See you now—
Your bait of falsehood takes this carp of truth, ③
And thus do we of wisdom and of reach,
With windlasses and with assays of bias, ④

【辞格辨析】

①直接重复和间隔重复。…**Or then, or then,** …由 or then 构成直接重复；with **such** or **such**, 由 such 构成间隔重复, 在这里也表示列举。

②首语重复。…**there** was 'a gaming; **there** o'ertook in's rouse; /**there** falling out at tennis', …There 引出各种假设情景。

③隐喻。**Your bait of falsehood takes this carp of truth**。将真理或事实比喻为一条大鱼, 而将这些编造的谎言比喻为用来诱惑大鱼上钩的诱饵。

④隐喻 (1)(2)(Thomson & Taylor, 2007: 232; Wilson, 2009: 262)。…**with windlasses** and **with assays of bias**, …此处有两处隐喻。第一处将侧面旁敲套出对话人信息的行为, 比喻为 windlasses (卷扬机) 的操作过程, 即通过迂回的方法达到目的。另一处则将迂回套话行为比喻为草地保龄球的击球技巧, 即通过曲线性的路径击中目标。

By indirections find directions out. ①

So by my former lecture and advice

Shall you my son. ② You have me, have you not?

Reynaldo: My lord, I have.

Polonius:　　　　　　God buy ye, fare ye well.

Reynaldo: Good my lord.

[Going.]

Polonius: Observe his inclination in yourself.

Reynaldo: I shall, my lord.

Polonius:　　　　　　And let him ply his music.

Reynaldo: Well, my lord.

Polonius: Farewell.

[Exit Reynaldo, enter Ophelia]

How now, Ophelia? What's the matter?

Ophelia: O my lord, my lord, I have been so affrighted.

Polonius: With what, i' th' name of God?

Ophelia: My lord, as I was sewing in my closet

Lord Hamlet, with his doublet all unbraced,

No hat upon his head, his stockings fouled,

【辞格辨析】

①同根异形重复。...by **indirections** find **directions** out. 此处 indirection 和 direction 为同根词，只有前缀的不同，属于同根反复。

②省略。So by my former lecture and advice/**shall you my son**. 此处辞格的后面部分省略了动词谓语。根据上下文，这里的谓语可以理解为 find my son's directions out。

135

莎剧《哈姆雷特》辞格辨析与文体鉴赏

Ungartered and down-gyved to his ankle, ①
Pale as his shirt, ② his knees knocking each other,
And with a look so piteous in purport
As if he had been loosed out of hell ③
To speak of horrors, he comes before me.

Polonius: Mad for thy love?

Ophelia: My lord, I do not know,
But truly I do fear it.

Polonius: What said he?

Ophelia: He took me by the wrist and held me hard,
Then goes he to the length of all his arm
And, with his other hand thus o'er his brow
He falls to such perusal of my face
As he would draw it. ④ Long stayed he so.
At last, a little shaking of mine arm
And thrice his head thus waving up and down,

【辞格辨析】

①隐喻。Ungartered, and **down-gyved** to his ankle, …此处将垂落到脚踝到吊袜带比喻为脚镣。

②明喻。…Pale **as** his shirt, …将Hamlet苍白的脸色与他穿的白色上衣颜色相比拟。

③明喻。…**as if** he had been loosed out of hell…将Hamlet的神情比喻为从地狱跑出来的鬼魂。

④明喻。…he falls to such perusal of my face/**as** he would draw it. 将Hamlet凝视Ophelia的专注神情比喻为画家准备绘画前的专注观察。

He raised a sigh so piteous and profound
As it did seem to shatter all his bulk ①
And end his being. That done, he lets me go
And withhis head over his shoulder turned
He seem'd to find his way without his eyes
For out o' doors he went without their help
And to the last bended their light on me. ②
Polonius: Come, go with me. I will go seek the King.
This is the very ecstasy of love,
Whose violent property fordoes itself
And leads the will to desperate undertakings ③
As oft as any passion under heaven

【辞格辨析】

①头韵和隐喻。He raised a sigh so **piteous** and **profound**/as it did seem to **shatter all his bulk** …此处 piteous 和 profound 构成头韵。另外，此处还将 Hamlet 的身躯比喻为一个容器，他发出的感叹声能够震碎这个身躯。

②拟人和借代。He seemed to find his way without his eyes, /for out o' doors he went without **their help**/and to the last bended **their light** on me. 此处将 Hamlet 的眼睛拟人化，将它们从 Hamlet 的身体抽离出来，变成能帮助 Hamlet 走路的主体。此外用 their light 指代目光，用将光线朝向 Ophelia 表示将目光落在她的身上。

③拟人。…and leads **the will** to desperate undertakings…此处将 will 拟人化，描述为能够做出一些摧毁性实践的主体。

莎剧《哈姆雷特》辞格辨析与文体鉴赏

That does afflict our natures. I am sorry—
What, have you given him any hard words of late?
Ophelia: No, my good lord, but, as you did command
I did repel his letters and denied
His access to me.
Polonius: That hath made him mad.
I am sorry that with better heed and judgment
I had not quoted him. I fear'd he did but trifle
And meant to wrack thee—but beshrew my jealousy—①
By heaven, it is as proper to our age
To cast beyond ourselves in our opinions
As it is common for the younger sort
To lack discretion. ② Come, go we to the King.
This must be known which, being kept close, might move
More grief to hide than hate to utter love.
Come.   [Exeunt.]

【辞格辨析】

①拟人。But beshrew my **jealousy**—...Polonius 将妒忌赋予生命,会提防他人。

②隐喻(Greenblatt et. al., 2005: 1103; Hibbard, 1987: 202)。...it is **as proper to our age/to cast beyond ourselves** in our opinions/as it is common for the younger sort/to lack discretion. 此处为狩猎隐喻,cast about 指的是寻找消失的气味,Polnoius 此处将自己错怪 Hamlet 对 Ophelia 的感情不真诚,比喻为如同狩猎时猎犬没有跟踪快消失的气味那样判断不准确。

138

Act II, Scene 2

Elsinore. A room in the Castle.

Flourish. [Enter King and Queen, Rosencrantz and Guildenstern].

Claudius: Welcome, dear Rosencrantz and Guildenstern.
Moreover that we much did long to see you
The need we have to use you did provoke
Our hasty sending. Something have you heard
Of Hamlet's transformation. So I call it,
Sith nor th'exterior nor the inward man
Resembles that it was. ① What it should be
More than his father's death, that thus hath put him
So much from th' understanding of himself
I cannot dream of. I entreat you both
That, being of so young days brought up with him
And sith so neighboured to his youth and haviour, ②
That you vouchsafe your rest here in our court
Some little time, so by your companies
To draw him on to pleasures and to gather

【辞格辨析】

①插说。…of Hamlet's transformation. **So I call it**, /sith nor th' exterior nor the inward man/resembles that it was. Claudius 插入信息, 补充 transformation 为他自己的措辞。

② 隐喻。… and since so **neighbored** to his youth and haviour, …此处将 Rosencrantz 和 Guildenstern 与 Hamlet 的亲密关系, 具体化为如邻居般紧密。

139

So much as from occasion you may glean, ①
Whether aught to us unknown afflicts him thus
That, opened, lies within our remedy.
Gertrude: Good gentlemen, he hath much talked of you
And sure I am two men there are not living
To whom he more adheres. If it will please you
To show us so much gentry and good will
As to expend your time with us awhile
For the supply and profit of our hope,
Your visitation shall receive such thanks
As fits a king's remembrance.
Rosencrantz: Both your Majesties
Might by the sovereign power you have of us
Put your dread pleasures more into command
Than to entreaty.
Guildenstern: But we both obey,
And here give up ourselves, in the full bent ②

【辞格辨析】

①隐喻（Thomson & Taylor, 2007: 238）。…and to gather/so much as from occasion you may **glean**, …此处将收集信息比喻为在刚收割完的稻田中收集稻穗的行为。

②隐喻（Thomson & Taylor, 2007: 239; Greenblatt et. al., 2005: 1103）。…and here give up ourselves, **in the full bent**…此处为包含射箭意象的隐喻，将 Rosencrantz 和 Guildenstern 准备好为 Claudius 服务比喻为拉满的弓，随时可以射出箭。

To lay our service freely at your feet
To be commanded.
Claudius: Thanks, Rosencrantz and gentle Guildenstern.
Gertrude: Thanks, Guildenstern and gentle Rosencrantz.
And I beseech you instantly to visit
My too much changed son. Go, some of you,
And bring these gentlemen where Hamlet is.
Guildenstern: Heavens make our presence and our practices
Pleasant and helpful to him. ①
Gertrude:　　　　　　Ay, amen!
　　　[Exeunt Rosencrantz and Guildenstern, enter Polonius.]
Polonius: Th' ambassadors from Norway, my good lord,
Are joyfully returned.
Claudius: Thou still hast been the father of good news.
Polonius: Have I, my lord? Assure you, my good liege
I hold my duty as I hold my soul,
Both to my God and to my gracious King;
And I do think, or else this brain of mine
Hunts not the trail of policy so sure

【辞格辨析】

①头韵。Heavens make our **presence** and our **practices/pleasant** and helpful to him. 此处为头韵，由 presence, practices 和 pleasant 三个词语构成。头韵除了有音韵上的重复之外，也有通过声音的相似，强调关键词的作用。这里三个头韵的词语，可以构成 pleasant presence and practice 的解读，传递出 Rosencrantz 和 Guildenstern 的良好初衷。

莎剧《哈姆雷特》辞格辨析与文体鉴赏

As it hath us'd to do, that I have found
The very cause of Hamlet's lunacy. ①
Claudius: O, speak of that! That do I long to hear.
Polonius: Give first admittance to th' ambassadors.
My news shall be the fruit to that great feast. ②
Claudius: Thyself do grace to them and bring them in. ③
He tells me, my dear Gertrude, he hath found [Exit Polonius.]
The head and source of all your son's distemper.
Gertrude: I doubt it is no other but the main—
His father's death and our hasty marriage. ④

【辞格辨析】

①隐喻和插说。…and I do think, or else **this brain of mine/hunts not the trail of policy so sure /as it hath us'd to do**,…此处 Polonius 将自己的判断能力比喻为猎狗寻味狩猎,为一处隐喻辞格;其次,此处内容通过破折号引出,插入行文之中,为插说辞格,起到补充的作用。

②隐喻。My news shall be the **fruit to that great feast**. 此处 Polonius 将自己知道 Hamlet 发疯的消息比喻为宴后果品。

③一笔双叙双关(Hibbard, 1987: 205; Jenkins, 1982: 239)Thyself do **grace** to them, and bring them in. Grace 根据上下文语境有两种理解方式,第一种表示"给客人荣耀",即 Claudius 让 Polonius 把使臣带进来,是给他们荣耀;第二种表示餐前的祈祷,回应上文 Polonius 的饮食隐喻意象。

④同位语。I doubt it is no other but the main/**his father's death and our hasty marriage**. 此处同位语为对 the main 的信息补充。

Claudius: Well, we shall sift him.
[Enter Polonius, Voltemand, and Cornelius.]
Welcome, my good friends.
Say, Voltemand, what from our brother Norway?
Voltemand: Most fair return of greetings and desires. ①
Upon our first he sent out to suppress
His nephew's levies, which to him appeared
To be a preparation 'gainst the Polack,
But better looked into, he truly found
It was against your Highness; whereat grieved,
That so his sickness age and impotence
Was falsely borne in hand, ② sends out arrests
On Fortinbras; which he, in brief, obeys,
Receives rebuke from Norway and in fine,
Makes vow before his uncle never more
To give th' assay of arms against your Majesty.
Whereon old Norway, overcome with joy,
Gives him three thousand crowns in annual fee

【辞格辨析】

①省略。Most fair return of greetings and desires. 此处为对"Most fair return of greetings and desires from Norway"的省略形式。省略让行文简洁，此处也可能是诗行音节数量的限制。

②排比。…whereat grieved, /that so his **sickness**, **age** and **impotence**/was falsely borne in hand. 此处由三个名词构成排比结构，强调挪威王在病弱期间被 Fortinbras 蒙蔽的痛心。

莎剧《哈姆雷特》辞格辨析与文体鉴赏

And his commission to employ those soldiers
So levied as before against the Polack,
With an entreaty herein further shown　　　　[Gives a paper.]
That it might please you to give quiet pass
Through your dominions for this enterprise
On such regards of safety and allowance
As therein are set down.

Claudius:　　　　　　It likes us well;
And at our more considered time we'll read,
Answer and think upon this business. ①
Meantime we thank you for your well-took labour.
Go to your rest, at night we'll feast together. ②
Most welcome home.　[Exeunt Ambassadors.]
Polonius:　　　This business is well ended.
My liege and madam, to expostulate
What majesty should be, what duty is,

【辞格辨析】

①排比。…and at our more considered time we'll **read**, / **answer**, and **think** upon this business. 此处三个动词 read, answer 和 think 构成了排比句式。

②尾韵（Thomson & Taylor, 2007: 243）。Meantime we thank you for your well-took **labour**. /Go to your rest; at night we'll feast **together**. 此处 labour 和 together 构成尾韵。在莎剧的辞格使用中，尾韵常用于一场或一幕的结尾，这里 Claudius 用了尾韵，暗指要结束和两位使臣的谈话。

144

Why day is day, night is night, and time is time,
Were nothing but to waste night, day and time. ①
Therefore, since brevity is the soul of wit ②
And tediousness the limbs and outward flourishes, ③
I will be brief. Your noble son is mad.
Mad call I it; for, to define true madness,
What is't but to be nothing else but mad? ④

【辞格辨析】

①排比（1）（2）和间接重复（1）（2）（3）。My liege, and madam, to expostulate/**what** majesty should be, **what** duty is, / **why day is day**, **night is night**, and **time is time**. /Were nothing but to waste night, day, and time. 此处有两处排比辞格和三处重复辞格。第一处是由 what 和 why 等疑问词引领的小句，第二处为"…is…"的三个结构相同的小句构成。此外，day, night 和 time 三个词语又构成了间接重复辞格。这部分语言简单，但辞格密集，凸显了 Polonius 好用修辞的特点。

②拟人。…since **brevity is the soul of wit**…此处赋予 wit 生命，将 brevity 看作它的 soul（灵魂），即最重要部分。该辞格在上下文语境中，也有讽刺的修辞效果，因为 Polonius 虽然说出简练是智慧的灵魂，但他说话却非常繁琐拖沓。

③隐喻。… and **tediousness the limbs and outward flourishes**, …此处为植物意象的隐喻，将沉闷冗长的修辞比喻为旁逸斜出的枝叶。

④同根异形重复。Your noble son is **mad**. /**Mad** call I it; for, to define true **madness**, /…be nothing else but **mad**? 此处使用 mad（疯狂的）的不同形式，构成同根异形重复。

145

莎剧《哈姆雷特》辞格辨析与文体鉴赏

But let that go.
Gertrude: More matter, with less art.
Polonius: Madam, I swear I use no art at all.
That he is mad, 'tis true; 'tis true 'tis pity,
And pity 'tis 'tis true. ① A foolish figure!
But farewell it, for I will use no art. ②
Mad let us grant him then, and now remains
That we find out the cause of this effect—
Or rather say, the cause of this defect,
For this effect defective comes by cause. ③

【辞格辨析】

①回环重复和间隔重复。That he is mad, 'tis true; **'tis true 'tis pity; / And pity 'tis 'tis true.** 此处为回环重复和间隔重复，通过 true 和 pity 构成。在上下文语境中与 Polonius 提出的简练原则形成对比，进一步加强讽刺的效果。

②拟人。But **farewell it.** 此处将修辞的使用比拟为有生命的主体，并能和说话人 farewell（告别），在这里表示 Polonius 不再使用修辞。

③同根异形重复和插说。That we find out the cause of this **effect—/or rather say, the cause of this defect,** /for this **effect defective** comes by cause. 此处的辞格利用同根的词语 effect，defect，defective 等构成。根据上下文语境，Polonius 刚决定不再使用修辞，转而又开始使用，为行文增添了一些诙谐的效果；同时，这句话中，or rather say, the cause of this defect 也构成插说辞格，补充其他可能信息。

Thus it remains, and the remainder thus. ① Perpend,
I have a daughter (have while she is mine), ②
Who in her duty and obedience, mark,
Hath given me this. Now gather and surmise. [Reads the letter.]
To the celestial and my soul's idol, the most beautified Ophelia, —
That's an ill phrase, a vile phrase, 'beautified' is a vile phrase. But you shall hear—③ *thus in her excellent white bosom, these,* etc.
Gertrude: Came this from Hamlet to her?
Polonius: Good madam, stay awhile. I will be faithful. [Reads.]
Doubt thou the stars are fire,
Doubt that the sun doth move,
Doubt truth to be a liar, ④

【辞格辨析】

①同根异形重复。Thus it **remains**, and the **remainder** thus. 此处的 remain 和 remainder 为同根异形重复。与上面的同根异形重复效果相同，都有创设诙谐效果的作用。

②插说。I have a daughter (**have while she is mine**). 此处插说为补充信息。然而，这处信息补充显得比较冗余。

③尾语重复和插说。The most beautified Ophelia, —/ **That's an ill phrase, a vile phrase; 'beautified' is a vile phrase.** But you shall hear—…此处 phrase 重复三次，构成尾语重复。此处还是插说，补充 Polonius 自己的观点。

④首语重复和拟人。**Doubt** … /**Doubt** … /**Doubt truth to be a liar**…此处重复以 doubt 开头构成首语重复辞格。Truth to be a liar 则赋予 truth（真理）赋以人的特征，能够撒谎。

莎剧《哈姆雷特》辞格辨析与文体鉴赏

But never doubt I love.
O dear Ophelia, I am ill at these numbers. I have not art to reckon my groans, ① *but that I love thee best, O most best, believe it. Adieu. Thine evermore, most dear lady, whilst this machine is to him. Hamlet.* ②

This in obedience hath my daughter shown me;
And more above hath his solicitings
As they fell out by time, by means and place,
All given to mine ear. ③

Claudius：　　　　But how hath she
Received his love?
Polonius：　　　What do you think of me?
Claudius：As of a man faithful and honourable. ④

【辞格辨析】

①借代和隐喻。O dear Ophelia, I am ill at these **numbers**, I have not art to **reckon my groans**, …此处用 numbers 指代有韵律的诗歌。Reckon my groans 为隐喻，与 numbers 相关联。在 reckon my groans 这里，Hamlet 将抽象的、无形的 groans（呻吟）具体化，变成能被按照韵律来计算的事物。

②隐喻。Whilst this **machine** is to him. 在此处将自己的身躯比喻为一台机器。

③排比。… as they fell out **by time, by means, and place**, /all given to mine ear. 此处借助 by time, by means 和省略了 by 的 place, 构成排比句式。

④省略。As of a man faithful and honourable. 此句为对 Polonius 的回复，完整句子是 "I think of you as a man faithful and honorable."省略使行文紧凑，从而更逼真地还原对话情景。

Polonius: I would fain prove so. But what might you think,
When I had seen this hot love on the wing ①
(As I perceiv'd it, I must tell you that,
Before my daughter told me), what might you, ②
Or my dear Majesty your Queen here, think,
If I had played the desk or table book,
Or given my heart a winking, mute and dumb,
Or looked upon this love with idle sight?
What might you think? ③ No, I went round to work
And my young mistress thus I did bespeak:
'Lord Hamlet is a prince, out of thy star. ④

【辞格辨析】

①隐喻。…when I had seen this hot love **on the wing**…此处将热恋比喻为长出翅膀的主体,形容 Hamlet 和 Ophelia 之间的恋情发展迅速。

②插说。…when I had seen this hot love on the wing/ (**as I perceiveed it, I must tell you that, / before my daughter told me**), what might you …此处 Polonius 用插说来说明自己具有先见之明。

③重复和排比。But **what might you think, /… /what might you, /or …, /… /or … /or …What might you think**?此处 what might you think 构成重复辞格;另外,由 or 引出不同情景,列出 Polonius 假设的情景,构成排比辞格。

④隐喻。Lord Hamlet is a prince, **out of thy star**. 此处用天文隐喻,将 Hamlet 和 Ophelia 社会地位的不同比喻为天体在不同的轨道上。

莎剧《哈姆雷特》辞格辨析与文体鉴赏

This must not be.' And then I prescripts gave her
That she should lock herself from his resort,
Admit no messengers, receive no tokens. ①
Which done, she took the fruits of my advice, ②
And he, repelled, a short tale to make,
Fell into a sadness, then into a fast, ③
Thence to a watch, thence into a weakness,
Thence to a lightness, and by this declension
Into the madness wherein now he raves,
And all we mourn for. ④

【辞格辨析】

①排比。…and then I prescripts gave her, /that she should **lock** herself from his resort, /**admit** no messengers, **receive** no tokens. 此处三个动词构成排比辞格,列出 Polonius 要求 Ophelia 做到的一系列行为。

②隐喻。…she took the **fruits** of my advice。此处 Polonius 将 Ophelia 接受并执行他的建议比喻为建议结出果实。

③插说。…and he, repelled, **a short tale to make**, /fell into a sadness, then into a fast, …此处插入 Polonius 的补充信息。Polonius 在陈述 Hamlet 和 Ophelia 的恋爱过程时,用语冗长繁琐,此处的插说 a short tale to make 有反讽的效果。

④排比。fell **into** a sadness, **then into** a fast, /**thence to** a watch, **thence into** a weakness, /**thence to** a lightness, … /**Into** the madness wherein now he raves, /and all we mourn for. 此处使用 "into …" 的结构,构成排比辞格,起到层层推进的作用,说明 Hamlet 从失恋悲伤发展成癫狂的过程。

Claudius: Do you think 'tis this?
Gertrude: It may be, very like.
Polonius: Hath there been such a time—I would fain know that—
That I have positively said 'tis so
When it prov'd otherwise? ①
Claudius: Not that I know.
Polonius: Take this from this if this be otherwise.
[Points to his head and shoulder]
If circumstances lead me I will find
Where truth is hid, though it were hid indeed
Within the centre. ②
Claudius: How may we try it further?
Polonius: You know sometimes he walks for hours together
Here in the lobby.
Gertrude: So he does indeed.
Polonius: At such a time I'll loose my daughter to him. ③

【辞格辨析】

①插说。Hath there been such a time—**I would fain know that**—/that I have positively said 'tis so/... 此处插说补充了 Polonius 的观点，说明他对自己的推测充满自信。

②拟人（1）（2）。If **circumstances lead** me, I will find/where **truth is hid**, though it were hid indeed/... 此处将 circumstances 和 truth 分别比拟为具有生命的主体，circumstances 能够 lead（带领）Polonius，truth 能够躲藏起来。

③隐喻。At such a time I'll **loose** my daughter to him. 此处将 Ophelia 比喻为动物，能够被 loose（释放）出来。

■ 莎剧《哈姆雷特》辞格辨析与文体鉴赏

Be you and I behind an arras then,
Mark the encounter: If he love her not
And be not from his reason fall'n thereon ①
Let me be no assistant for a state
But keep a farm and carters. ③
Claudius: We will try it.
〔Enter Hamlet, reading on a book.〕
Gertrude: But look where sadly the poor wretch comes reading.
Polonius: Away, I do beseech you, both away
I'll board him presently. O, give me leave.
〔Exeunt King and Queen, with Attendants.〕
How does my good Lord Hamlet?
Hamlet: Well, God-a-mercy.
Polonius: Do you know me, my lord?
Hamlet: Excellent well. You are a fishmonger. ②
Polonius: Not I, my lord.
Hamlet: Then I would you were so honest a man.

【辞格辨析】

①隐喻（Thomson & Taylor, 2007：249）。If he love her not, /and he not **from his reason fall'n** thereon, /…此处将疯癫这一抽象概念具体化，形容其能够从高处 fall（跌落）。

②一笔双叙双关。You are a **fishmonger**. Fishmonger 有两种解读，第一种可以理解为卖鱼的贩子，第二种可以理解为拉皮条者。Hamlet 在这里借该词的多义性讽刺 Polonius 用女儿来引诱他。

152

Polonius: Honest, my lord? ①

Hamlet: Ay, sir. To be honest as this world goes is to be one man picked out of ten thousand. ②

Polonius: That's very true, my lord.

Hamlet: For if the sun breed maggots in a dead dog, being a god kissing carrion ③—Have you a daughter?

Polonius: I have, my lord.

Hamlet: Let her not walk i' th' sun: conception is a blessing but not as your daughter may conceive. Friend, look to't. ④

【辞格辨析】

①省略。**Honest**, my lord. 此处是"I am an honest man"的省略形式。

②明喻。To be honest, **as this world goes**, is to be one man pick'd out of ten thousand. 此处将诚实的人比喻为如地球一般有规则地运转。

③同位语。For if the sun breed maggots in a dead dog, **being a god kissing carrion**. 此处 being a god kissing carrion 为 a dead dog 的同位语,起到修饰和补充信息的作用。

④谐音双关(Thomson & Taylor, 2007: 251),一笔双叙双关(Hubbard, 1989: 213)和同根异形重复。Let her not walk i' th' **sun. conception** is a blessing, but not as your daughter may **conceive**. 此处的 sun(太阳)和 son(儿子)构成谐音双关,表示不能让 Ophelia 在太阳下走路,也表示不能和 Hamlet 接触;第二处为 conception 和 conceive 构成的一笔双叙,这两个词可以同时理解为"构思的能力"和"怀孕";最后,conception 和 conceive 也是同根重复辞格。

Polonius: [aside] How say you by that? Still harping on my daughter. Yet he knew me not at first, 'a said I was a fishmonger! 'A is far gone, far gone! And truly in my youth I suffered much extremity for love—very near this. I'll speak to him again.—What do you read, my lord?

Hamlet: Words, words, words. ①

Polonius: What is the matter, my lord?

Hamlet: Between who?

Polonius: I mean, the matter that you read, my lord. ②

Hamlet: Slanders, sir. For the satirical rogue says here that old men have grey beards, that their faces are wrinkled, their eyes purging thick amber and plum-tree gum, ③ and that they have a plentiful lack of wit together with most weak hams. All which, sir, though I most powerfully and potently believe, yet I hold it not honesty to have it thus set down. For you yourself, sir, should be old as I am if, like a crab, you could go backward. ④

【辞格辨析】

①直接重复。**Words, words, words.** 此处为直接重复，强调被重复的词语 word。

②换义双关。What is the **matter**, my lord? /Between who? /I mean, the **matter** that you read, my lord. 此处 Polonius 使用 matter，取的是该词的"主题"这一意义，但 Hamlet 将其理解为"发生事端"。

③隐喻。Their eyes purging **thick amber** and **plum-tree gum**, ...此处将老年人眼睛分泌物比喻为老树流出的树脂。

④明喻。...**like a crab, you could go backward.** Hamlet 将人的年龄倒退比喻为螃蟹的倒退式的行走方式。

Polonius:〔aside〕Though this be madness yet there is a method in't. —Will you walk out of the air, my lord?

Hamlet: Into my grave. ①

Polonius: Indeed, that is out of the air.〔Aside〕How pregnant sometimes his replies are—a happiness that often madness hits on, which reason and sanity could not so prosperously be delivered of. I will leave him and suddenly contrive the means of meeting between him and my daughter. —My honourable lord, I will most humbly take my leave of you.

Hamlet: You cannot, sir, take from me anything that I will more willingly part withal—except my life, except my life, except my life. ② 〔Enter Rosencrantz and Guildenstern.〕

Polonius: Fare you well, my lord.

Hamlet: These tedious old fools.

Polonius: You go to seek the Lord Hamlet? There he is.

Rosencrantz:〔to Polonius〕God save you, sir. 〔Exit Polonius.〕

Guildenstern: My honour'd lord.

【辞格辨析】

①省略和一笔双叙双关。Will You walk **out of the air**, my lord? /Into my grave！此处为对话过程的省略。Into my grave 完整可以理解为"I walk into my grave."。另外，out of the air 也有双关的意思，Polonius 在此处表示不要在风大的地方呆太久，而 Hamlet 将其理解为不要在有空气的地方呆，因此回复说要到坟墓中去。

②直接重复。You cannot, sir, take from me anything that I will more willingly part withal—**except my life, except my life, except my life**. 直接重复，强调了 except my life 这几个词。

莎剧《哈姆雷特》辞格辨析与文体鉴赏

Rosencrantz: My most dear lord.

Hamlet: My excellent good friends. How dost thou, Guildenstern? Ah, Rosencrantz! Good lads, how do ye both.

Rosencrantz: As the indifferent children of the earth.

Guildenstern: Happy in that we are not over-happy. On Fortune's cap we are not the very button.

Hamlet: Nor the soles of her shoe? ①

Rosencrantz: Neither, my lord.

Hamlet: Then you live about her waist, or in the middle of her favours.

Guildenstern: Faith, her privates we. ②

Hamlet: In the secret parts of Fortune? O! Most true—she is a strumpet. What news?

Rosencrantz: None, my lord, but that the world's grown honest.

Hamlet: Then is doomsday near—but your news is not true. Let me question more in particular. What have you, my good friends, deserved at the hands of Fortune that she sends you to prison hither?

【辞格辨析】

①隐喻（1）和（2）。On Fortune's cap **we are not the very button**. /Nor **the soles of her shoe**? 此处将生活中受到幸运女神眷顾的情况比喻为幸运女神帽子顶上的小纽扣，将生活不如意的情况比喻为幸运女神鞋子的底部。

②一笔双叙双关（Jenkins, 1982: 249）。Faith, her **privates** we. 此处双关有两层意思，第一层指幸运女神的私处（因为Rosencrantz和Guildenstern描述自己的生活不好也不坏，即不再帽顶也不在鞋底，则应该在身体的中间部位），另一层指私密亲信，这里则和两人此时的身份相呼应。

Guildenstern: Prison, my lord?

Hamlet: Denmark's a prison. ①

Rosencrantz: Then is the world one.

Hamlet: A goodly one, in which there are many confines, wards, and dungeons—Denmark being one o' th' worst.

Rosencrantz: We think not so, my lord.

Hamlet: Why, then 'tis none to you; for there is nothing either good or bad, but thinking makes it so. To me it is a prison.

Rosencrantz: Why, then your ambition makes it one: 'tis too narrow for your mind.

Hamlet: O God, I could be bounded in a nutshell and count myself a king of infinite space—were it not that I have bad dreams.

Guildenstern: Which dreams, indeed, are ambition; for the very substance of the ambitious is merely the shadow of a dream.

Hamlet: A dream itself is but a shadow. ②

Rosencrantz: Truly, and I hold ambition of so airy and light a quality that it is but a shadow's shadow.

【辞格辨析】

①隐喻。What have you, my good friends, deserved at the hands of Fortune that she sends you to prison hither?/.../ Denmark's a **prison**. 此处 Hamlet 将丹麦国比喻为一座监狱。

②隐喻（1）（2）。Which dreams indeed are ambition; for the very substance of **the ambitious is merely the shadow of a dream. /A dream itself is but a shadow**. 此处将 ambition（抱负）比喻为梦，而 Hamlet 将梦比喻为影子。

莎剧《哈姆雷特》辞格辨析与文体鉴赏

Hamlet: Then are our beggars bodies, and our monarchs and outstretched heroes the beggars' shadows. Shall we to th' Court? For, by my fay, I cannot reason.

Rosencrantz: [with Guildenstern] We'll wait upon you. ①

Hamlet: No such matter. I will not sort you with the rest of my servants, for, to speak to you like an honest man, I am most dreadfully attended. ② But in the beaten way of friendship, what make you at Elsinore?

Rosencrantz: To visit you, my lord, no other occasion.

Hamlet: Beggar that I am, I am even poor in thanks, but I thank you, and sure, dear friends, my thanks are too dear a halfpenny. ③

【辞格辨析】

①一笔双叙双关（Wilson, 2009: 174） We'll wait upon you. Wait upon 有两种理解，第一种可以理解为"跟随"，第二种也可以理解为"监视"，甚至"埋伏等候"等。

②插说和一笔双叙双关（Thomson & Taylor, 2007: 467）。 …**for, to speak to you like an honest man**, I am most **dreadfully attended**. Hamlet 此处插说表达观点；此外，dreadfully attended 可以理解为 Hamlet 近期经常做梦，也可以理解为他意识到被监视，第二种理解与 wait upon 回应。

③隐喻和一笔双叙双关（黄国彬, 2013: 311）。 **Beggar that I am, …my thanks are too dear a halfpenny**. Hamlet 将自己比喻为乞丐，人微言轻，连感谢也不值钱。第二处为 too dear a halfpenny 构成双关，可理解为 Hamlet 自认为乞丐，因此感谢不值钱；第二种理解为他意识到两名好友为国王派来监视自己，因此 a halfpenny 对两名奸细来说还有些多。

Were you not sent for? Is it your own inclining? Is it a free visitation? Come, deal justly with me. ① Come, come, nay, speak.

Guildenstern: What should we say, my lord?

Hamlet: Anything—but to th' purpose. You were sent for, and there is a kind of confession in your looks, which your modesties have not craft enough to colour. ② I know the good King and Queen have sent for you.

Rosencrantz: To what end, my lord? ③

Hamlet: That you must teach me. But let me conjure you by the rights of our fellowship, by the consonancy of our youth, by the obligation of our ever-preserved love, and by what more dear a better proposer could charge you withal, be even and direct with me, whether you were sent for or no. ④

【辞格辨析】

①隐喻。Come, **deal** justly with me. Hamlet 要求两个朋友向他说实话, 就如同公平买卖一般。

②拟人。...which **your modesties have not craft enough to colour**. 将 modesties（谦逊）比拟为能够掩饰自己表情的主体。此处 Hamlet 表示, 两个好友的谦逊本性流露出他们到来的真正目的。

③省略。I know the good King and Queen have sent for you. /**To what end**, my lord. 此处的 to what end 为省略句, 完整的句子可表达为 "What end do the good King and Queen have sent us for you to？"。

④排比。...**by** ..., **by** ..., **by** ..., and **by** ...此处由介词 by 引导出的四个短语, 构成排比辞格, 形成递进的效果。

Rosencrantz: [aside to Guildenstern] What say you?

Hamlet: [aside] Nay then, I have an eye of you. —If you love me, hold not off.

Guildenstern: My lord, we were sent for.

Hamlet: I will tell you why. So shall my anticipation prevent your discovery, and your secrecy to the King and Queen moult no feather. ① I have of late, but wherefore I know not, lost all my mirth, ② forgone all custom of exercises and, indeed, it goes so heavily with my disposition that this goodly frame the earth seems to me a sterile promontory, ③ this most excellent canopy the air, look you, this brave o'erhanging firmament, this majestical roof fretted with golden fire, ④

【辞格辨析】

①隐喻。…and your secrecy to the King and Queen **moult no feather**. 此处将 secrecy（秘密）比喻为禽类动物，会掉羽毛。Hamlet 表示，他会将这个秘密（即已经知晓两人为国王派遣而来）保守好，使 Rosencrantz 和 Guildenstern 在国王面前不会被质疑。

②插说。I have of late, **but wherefore I know not**, lost all my mirth…Hamlet 插入了自己的想法。

③同位语和隐喻。…that **this goodly frame, the earth, seems to me a sterile promontory**…此处有两处辞格，第一处即 the earth 为 this goodly frame 的同位语，起到对 frame 的说明作用；第二处为隐喻，将 the earth 比喻为海中的岬角。

④隐喻。…**this most excellent canopy**, the air, look you, this brave o'erhanging firmament, …此处将天空（或表演时的剧院）比喻为一张天蓬华盖。

第四章 《哈姆雷特》辞格辨析

why, it appeareth nothing to me than a foul and pestilent congregation of vapours. ① What a piece of work is a man—how noble in reason! How infinite in faculties! in form and moving how express and admirable! In action how like an angel! In apprehension how like a god! The beauty of the world, the paragon of animals! ② And yet to me what is this quintessence of dust? ③ Man delights not me—no, nor woman neither, though by your smiling you seem to say so.

Rosencrantz: My lord, there was no such stuff in my thoughts.

Hamlet: Why did you laugh then, when I said 'Man delights not me'?

Rosencrantz: To think, my lord, if you delight not in man, what lenten entertainment the players shall receive from you. We coted them on the way ④ and hither are they coming to offer you service.

Hamlet: He that plays the King shall be welcome—his Majesty shall have tribute of me—the Adventurous Knight shall use his foil

【辞格辨析】

①隐喻。Why, **it appeareth no other thing to me than a foul and pestilent congregation of vapours.** Hamlet 将整个天空比喻为一团水汽。

②排比。**How…! How…! …how…! …how…! …how…!** 此处借助 how 引出一系列的句子构成排比，描述人类这件作品的伟大。

③隐喻。And yet to me what is this **quintessence of dust**? Hamlet 将人类比喻为一团尘土。

④隐喻。We **coted** them on the way…此处 Rosencrantz 把在路上遇到演员并将他们邀请到宫廷来的行为比喻为用栅栏将牲畜围起来。

161

and target; the Lover shall not sigh gratis; the Humorous Man shall end his part in peace; the Clown shall make those laugh whose lungs are tickle o' th' sere; and the Lady shall say her mind freely, or the blank verse shall halt for't. ① What players are they?

Rosencrantz: Even those you were wont to take such delight in, the tragedians of the city.

Hamlet: How chances it they travel? Their residence, both in reputation and profit, was better both ways.

Rosencrantz: I think their inhibition comes by the means of the late innovation.

Hamlet: Do they hold the same estimation they did when I was in the city? Are they so followed?

Rosencrantz: No, indeed are they not.

Hamlet: How comes it? Do they grow rusty? ②

Rosencrantz: Nay, their endeavour keeps in the wonted pace. But there is, sir, an eyrie of children, little eyases, ③

【辞格辨析】

①排比。He that plays the king **shall** ...—his Majesty **shall** ...; the Adventurous Knight **shall** ...; the Lover **shall** ...; the Humorous Man **shall** ...; the Clown **shall** ...; and the Lady **shall** ..., or the blank verse **shall** ...此处通过相同的句式,即...shall ...,构成了排比。

②隐喻。Do they grow **rusty**? 此处将演员演技生疏比喻为金属生锈。

③同位语和隐喻。There is, sir, **an eyrie of children, little eyases**, ...Little eyases 为 an eyrie of children 的同位语。同时,这两处也是一处隐喻,将小演员比喻为一群雏鹰。

that cry out on the top of question and are most tyrannically clapped for't. These are now the fashion, and so berattle the common stages (so they call them) that many wearing rapiers are afraid of goosequills and dare scarce come thither. ①

Hamlet: What, are they children? Who maintains 'em? How are they escoted? Will they pursue the quality no longer than they can sing? Will they not say afterwards if they should grow themselves to common players—as it is most like, if their means are no better—their writers do them wrong to make them exclaim against their own succession? ②

Rosencrantz: Faith, there has been much to do on both sides, and the nation holds it no sin to tarre them to controversy. ③ There was, for a while, no money bid for argument unless the poet and the player went to cuffs in the question.

Hamlet: Is't possible?

【辞格辨析】

①插说和借代（1）（2）。…and so berattle the common stages (**so they call them**) that many wearing **rapiers** are afraid of **goosequills** …So they call them 为插说辞格，补充了观点出处。此外，rapiers 和 goosequills 分别指代佩挂长剑的时髦年轻人，goosequills 指代使用羽毛笔写作的作家或写手。

②插说。…to common players (**as it is most like, if their means are no better**)，their writers …此处插入 Hamlet 的个人观点，表达了对这群儿童演员哗众取宠的做法的担忧。

③提喻和隐喻。**The nation** holds it no sin to **tarre** them to controversy. 此处用整体的 nation 指代这个国家的人民。此外，这句话也将纵容各方相争比喻为为争闹添加燃料。

莎剧《哈姆雷特》辞格辨析与文体鉴赏

Guildenstern: O, there has been much throwing about of brains. ①
Hamlet: Do the boys carry it away?
Rosencrantz: Ay, that they do, my lord—Hercules and his load too.
Hamlet: It is not very strange, for my uncle is King of Denmark, and those that would make mouths at him while my father lived give twenty, forty, fifty, a hundred ducats apiece for his picture in little. 'Sblood, there is something in this more than natural if philosophy could find it out. 　[Flourish for the Players.]
Guildenstern: There are the players!
Hamlet: Gentlemen, you are welcome to Elsinore. Your hands, come! Th'appurtenance of welcome is fashion and ceremony. Let me comply with you in this garb lest my extent to the players (which I tell you must show fairly outwards) should more appear like entertainment than yours. You are welcome. But my uncle-father and aunt-mother are deceived.
Guildenstern: In what, my dear lord?
Hamlet: I am but mad north-north-west. When the wind is southerly I know a hawk from a handsaw.　[Enter Polonius.]
Polonius: Well be with you, gentlemen!
Hamlet: Hark you, Guildenstern—and you too—at each ear a hearer. That great baby you see there is not yet out of his swaddling clouts. ②

【辞格辨析】

①借代。O, there has been much throwing about of **brains**. 此处用 brain 这一用来思考的人体器官指代人的思考的行为。

②隐喻。**That great baby** you see there is not yet out of **his swaddling clouts.** ... an old man is twice **a child.** 此处将 Polonius 比喻为一个还在襁褓中的婴儿。

Rosencrantz: Happily he's the second time come to them, for they say an old man is twice a child.

Hamlet: I will prophesy he comes to tell me of the players. Mark it. —You say right, sir; a Monday morning, 'twas so indeed.

Polonius: My lord, I have news to tell you.

Hamlet: My lord, I have news to tell you. When Roscius was an actor in Rome—

Polonius: The actors are come hither, my lord.

Hamlet: Buzz, buzz.

Polonius: Upon my honour—

Hamlet: Then came each actor on his ass—

Polonius: The best actors in the world, either for tragedy, comedy, history, pastoral, pastoral-comical, historical-pastoral, tragical-historical, tragical-comical-historical-pastoral, scene individable, or poem unlimited. Seneca cannot be too heavy, nor Plautus too light. For the law of writ and the liberty, these are the only men.

Hamlet: *O Jephthah, judge of Israel, what a treasure hadst thou?* ①

Polonius: What treasure had he, my lord?

Hamlet: Why,

'One fair daughter, and no more,

The which he loved passing well.'

Polonius: [aside] Still on my daughter.

【辞格辨析】

①同位语。O Jephthah, **judge of Israel**, what a treasure hadst thou! 此处的 judge of Isreal 是 Jephthah 的同位语,是对他身份的补充说明。

Hamlet: Am I not i' th' right, old Jephthah?
Polonius: If you call me Jephthah, my lord, I have a daughter that I love passing well.
Hamlet: Nay, that follows not.
Polonius: What follows then, my lord?
Hamlet: Why,
'As by lot, God wot,' ①
and then, you know,
'It came to pass, as most like it was.'
The first row of the pious chanson will show you more, for look where my abridgment comes.　　[Enter four or five Players.] You are welcome, masters, welcome, all. I am glad to see thee well. Welcome, good friends. O, my old friend, why, thy face is valanced since I saw thee last. ② Com'st' thou to beard me in Denmark? What, my young lady and mistress? By'r Lady, your ladyship is nearer to heaven than when I saw you last by the altitude of a chopine. Pray God your voice, like a piece of uncurrent gold, be not crack'd within the ring. ③ —Masters, you are all welcome.

【辞格辨析】

①尾韵。As by **lot**, God **wot**. 此处的 lot 和 wot 构成尾韵。

②隐喻。Why, thy face is **valanced** since I saw thee last. 此处 Hamlet 将脸上长出胡须比喻为挂了帷幔。

③明喻和一笔双叙双关（Raffel, 2003: 82）。Your voice, **like** a piece of uncurrent gold, be not crack'd within the **ring**. 此处将演员青春期变声，无法饰演女性角色的情况，比喻为一枚因破损而失去价值的钱币；Ring 也构成一笔双叙，指金币上国王头像周边的一圈花饰，也指男演员的声音。

We'll e'en to't like French falconers—fly at anything we see. ①
We'll have a speech straight. Come, give us a taste of your quality.
Come, a passionate speech.

First Player: What speech, my good lord?

Hamlet: I heard thee speak me a speech once, but it was never acted, or if it was, not above once, for the play I remember pleased not the million, 'twas caviary to the general. ② But it was (as I received it, and others, whose judgments in such matters cried in the top of mine) an excellent play, well digested in the scenes, ③ set down with as much modesty as cunning. I remember one said there were no sallets in the lines to make the matter savoury, ④ nor no matter in the phrase that might indict the author of affectation,

【辞格辨析】

① 明喻。We'll e'en to't **like French falconers**—fly at anything we see. 此处 Hamlet 将接下来随性的表演比喻为捕猎者训练猎鹰随处追赶猎物。

② 隐喻。'Twas **caviary** to the general. 此处将不受大众欢迎的戏剧或选段，比喻为不受大众欢迎的鱼子酱。

③ 插说和隐喻。（**As I received it, and others, whose judgments in such matters cried in the top of mine**）an excellent play, **well digested** in the scenes, …此处插说补充信息，说明一些比 Hamlet 更有戏剧修养的人也喜欢该剧。Digest 则是将好戏剧比喻为各部分充分消化的食物。

④ 隐喻。One said there were no **sallets** in the lines to make the matter **savoury**, …此句将对语言的过渡修饰比喻为给菜肴添加佐料。在文中指这段不受大众欢迎的戏剧选段没有过多的文饰。

but called it an honest method, as wholesome as sweet, and by very much more handsome than fine. One speech in't I chiefly loved. 'Twas Aeneas' tale to Dido, and thereabout of it especially where he speaks of Priam's slaughter. If it ① live in your memory, begin at this line—let me see, let me see.

'*The rugged Pyrrhus like th' Hyrcanian beast—*' ②
'Tis not so. It begins with Pyrrhus.
The rugged Pyrrhus, he whose sable arms,
Black as his purpose, ③ *did the night resemble*
When he lay couched in the ominous horse,
Hath now this dread and black complexion smeared
With heraldry more dismal. ④ *Head to foot*
Now is be total gules, horridly tricked
With blood of fathers, mothers, daughters, sons,

【辞格辨析】

①拟人。If it **live** in your memory,…此处将戏剧的台词赋予生命,能够居住在人的记忆中,表示演员记住台词。

②明喻。The rugged Pyrrhus, **like th' Hyrcanian beast**—…此处将 Pyrrhus 比喻为 Hyrcanian beast(赫卡尼亚地区的老虎)一般凶猛。

③明喻。…he whose sable arms, /black **as** his purpose,…将武器的黑色与 Pyrrhus 阴暗的计谋相比。

④隐喻。… hath now this dread and black complexion **smear'd/with heraldry more dismal**. 此处将干了黏在皮肤上的鲜血比喻为身上的印章。

*Baked and impasted with the parching streets*①
That lend a tyrannous and a damned light
To their lord's murther. Roasted in wrath and fire,
And thus o'ersized with coagulate gore
With eyes like carbuncles, ② *the hellish Pyrrhu*s
Old grandsire Priam seeks. '
So, proceed you.
Polonius: Fore God, my lord, well spoken, with good accent and good discretion.
First Player: '*Anon he finds him,*
Striking too short at Greeks. His antique sword,
Rebellious to hisarm, lies where it falls,
Repugnant to command. ③ *Unequal matched,*

【辞格辨析】

①排比。... with blood of **fathers, mothers, daughters, sons,** ...此处由 fathers, mothers, daughters 和 sons 等四个词语构成的排比。这些具体身份更显出 Pyrrhus 杀人如麻。

②隐喻和明喻。**Roasted in wrath and fire**, /.../with **eyes like carbuncles**, the hellish Pyrrhus/old grandsire Priam seeks. Roasted in wrath and fire 将一个人生气的样子比喻为在火上炙烤,为隐喻辞格;此外,此处把因为发怒而变红的眼睛比喻为红色的石榴石,为明喻。

③拟人和头韵。His antique sword, /**rebellious to his arm,** ..., /**repugnant to command.** 此处第一处是拟人辞格,将剑比拟为能够反叛主人的意愿和指示的主体;第二处是头韵,由 rebellious 和 repugnant 构成,有强调的作用。

Pyrrhus at Priam drives, in rage strikes wide,
But with the whiff and wind of his fell sword ①
Th' unnerved father falls. Then senseless Ilium,
Seeming to feel this blow, with flaming top
Stoops to his base and with a hideous crash
Takes prisoner Pyrrhus' ear. ② *For lo, his sword,*
Which was declining on the milky head
Of reverend Priam seemed i' th' air to stick. ③
So, as a painted tyrant, Pyrrhus stood ④
Like a neutral to his will and matter,

【辞格辨析】

①头韵。But with the **whiff** and **wind** of his fell sword/…此处的 whiff 和 wind 构成头韵。

②拟人，借代和拟人。**Then senseless Ilium,/seeming to feel this blow,** with flaming top/…/takes **prisoner** Pyrrhus' ear. 此处将 Illium 城（伊利昂或特洛伊）赋予生命，在 Priam 倒下的时候，也发出响声；第二处为提喻辞格，用 ear 指听觉，即城堡因为燃烧坍塌的响声震响 Pyrrhus 的耳朵；第三处为拟人辞格，即将 Pyrrhus 的听觉比拟为人，将听到巨响比拟为被逮捕。

③隐喻和明喻。Which was declining on **the milky head**/of reverend Priam, **seemed i' th' air to stick.** 此处的 milky head 为隐喻辞格，即将花白的头发比喻为银河的颜色；另一处为明喻，将剑停驻在半空比喻为剑被粘在空中。

④明喻。So, **as** a painted tyrant, Pyrrhus stood, …此处将 Pyrrhus 比喻为一尊画像。

第四章 《哈姆雷特》辞格辨析

Did nothing.
But as we often see against some storm
A silence in the heavens, the rack stand still,
The bold winds speechless, and the orb below
As hush as death—anon the dreadful thunder
Doth rend the region, ① *so, after Pyrrhus' pause*
Aroused vengeance sets him new awork
And never did the Cyclops' hammers fall
On Mars's armour, forged for proof eterne,
With less remorse than Pyrrhus' bleeding sword
Now falls on Priam.
Out, out, thou strumpet Fortune! ② *All you gods*
In general synod take away her power,
Break all the spokes and fellies from her wheel
And bowl the round nave down the hill of heaven
As low as to the fiends!

【辞格辨析】

①明喻（Wilson, 200）拟人（1）（2）和排比。But, as we often see, against some storm, a silence in the heavens, **the rack stand still, the bold winds speechless,** and **the orb below as hush as death**—anon the dreadful thunder/doth rend the region, …此处将 rack（舒卷中的云朵）和 wind 拟人化，赋予能够站立和说话的动作；此外，句中的三处主谓结构也构成了排比辞格。

②直接重复。**Out, out,** thou strumpet Fortune! 直接重复 out, 表达了愤慨之情。

■ 莎剧《哈姆雷特》辞格辨析与文体鉴赏

Polonius: This is too long.
Hamlet: It shall to the barber's with your beard. —Prithee say on. He's for a jig or a tale of bawdry, or he sleeps. Say on, come to Hecuba.
First Player: '*But who, O who, had seen the mobled queen—*'
Hamlet: '*The mobled queen*'?
Polonius: That's good! '*Mobled queen*' is good.
First Player: '*Run barefoot up and down, threat'ning the flames*
With bisson rheum, a clout upon that head
Where late the diadem stood, and for a robe,
About her lank and all o'erteemed loins,
A blanket in the alarm of fear caught up.
Who this had seen, with tongue in venom steeped
'Gainst Fortune's state would treason have pronounced.
But if the gods themselves did see her then,
When she saw Pyrrhus make malicious sport
In Mincing with his sword her husband's limbs,
The instant burst of clamour that she made
(Unless things mortal move them not at all)
Would have made milch the burning eyes of heaven
And passion in the gods.' ①

【辞格辨析】

①插说和借代。(**Unless things mortal move them not at all**) would have made milch **the burning eyes of heaven**/and passion in the gods. 此处插入一些评论式的语言，说明屠杀场面非常惨烈，连天体都为之动容；第二处为借代，用 burning eyes of heaven 指代太阳。

Polonius: Look, where he has not turn'd his colour and has tears in's eyes. Prithee no more!

Hamlet: 'Tis well. I'll have thee speak out the rest of this soon. ——Good my lord, will you see the players well bestowed? Do you hear? Let them be well used; for they are the abstract and brief chronicles of the time. ① After your death you were better have a bad epitaph than their ill report while you live.

Polonius: My lord, I will use them according to their desert.

Hamlet: God's bodykins, man, much better! Use every man after his desert and who should scape whipping? Use them after your own honour and dignity. The less they deserve, the more merit is in your bounty. ② Take them in.

Polonius: Come, sirs.

Hamlet: Follow him, friends. We'll hear a play tomorrow.

[Exeunt Polonius and Players except the First.]
Dost thou hear me, old friend? Can you play *The Murther of Gonzago*?

First Player: Ay, my lord.

Hamlet: We'll ha't tomorrow night. You could for a need study a speech of some dozen or sixteen lines which I would set down and insert in't, could you not?

【辞格辨析】

①隐喻。...for they are **the abstract** and **brief chronicles of the time**. 将演员比喻为时代的缩影和历史。

②对仗。**The less** they deserve, **the more** merit is in your bounty. 此处通过 the less 和 the more 对比，构成对仗辞格。

Hamlet: Very well. Follow that lord—and look you mock him not.
First Player: Ay, my lord.　　　　　[Exit First Player.]
Hamlet: My good friends, I'll leave you till night. You are welcome to Elsinore.
Rosencrantz: Good my lord.
Hamlet: Ay, so, God buy to you.
　[Exeunt Rosencrantz and Guildenstern]
　　　　　　　　　　　　　　Now I am alone.
O what a rogue and peasant slave am I!
Is it not monstrous that this player here,
But in a fiction, in a dream of passion,
Could force his soul so to his own conceit
That from her working all his visage wanned,
—Tears in his eyes, distraction in's aspect,
A broken voice, and his whole function suiting
With forms to his conceit— ① and all for nothing—
For Hecuba?
What's Hecuba to him, or he to her,
That he should weep for her? What would he do
Had he the motive and the cue for passion

【辞格辨析】

①排比。…that, from her working, all **his visage wann'd, —tears in his eyes, distraction in's aspect, a broken voice,** and **his whole function suiting with forms to his conceit—**…此处五个名词短语构成排比,描述演员在表演过程中的神情。

That I have? He would drown the stage with tears
And cleave the general ear with horrid speech,
Make mad the guilty and appal the free,
Confound the ignorant and amaze indeed ①
The very faculties of eyes and ears. Yet I,
A dull and muddy-mettled rascal, ② peak
Like John-a-dreams, unpregnant of my cause,
And can say nothing. No, not for a king,
Upon whose property and most dear life
A damned defeat was made. Am I a coward?
Who calls me villain, breaks my pate across,
Plucks off my beard and blows it in my face,
Tweaks me by th' nose, gives me the lie i' th' throat

【辞格辨析】

①排比，借代（1）（2）。He would **drown the stage** with tears/and **cleave the general ear** with horrid speech, /**make** mad the guilty and **appal** the free, /.../**confound** the ignorant, and **amaze** indeed/...此处有三处辞格：第一为由 drown, cleave, make, appal, confound 和 amaze 等构成的排比；第二处为借代，用整体的 the stage 指代演员的表演；第三处也为借代，用 the general ear 指代舞台下观众的听觉。

②同位语。Yet I, /**a dull and muddy-mettled rascal**, peak/like John-a-dreams, ...此处的 a dull and muddy-mettled rascal 为 I 的同位语，对 I 作修饰说明作用。

175

莎剧《哈姆雷特》辞格辨析与文体鉴赏

As deep as to the lungs? ① Who does me this,
Ha? 'Swounds, I should take it! For it cannot be
But I am pigeon-livered and lack gall ②
To make oppression bitter, or ere this
I should have fatted all the region kites
With this slave's offal—bloody, bawdy villain,
Remorseless, treacherous, lecherous, kindless villain! ③
Why, what an ass am I: this is most brave,
That I, the son of a dear father murdered, ④
Prompted to my revenge by heaven and hell,
Must like a whore unpack my heart with words
And fall a-cursing like a very drab,

【辞格辨析】

①排比。Am I a coward? /Who calls me villain? Breaks my pate across? /Plucks off my beard and blows it in my face? /Tweaks me by th' nose? Gives me the lie i' th' throat/as deep as to the lungs? 此处系列疑问句构成排比辞格，增强语气。

②隐喻。But I am **pigeon-liver'd and lack gall**…Hamlet 在这里将自己比喻为温和且缺少勇气的鸽子。

③尾语重复，排比和尾韵。With this slave's offal—bloody, bawdy **villain**, **remorseless**, **treacherous**, **lecherous**, **kindless villain!** 这两行末尾重复了 villain；第二，四个修饰 villain 的形容词构成排比；第三，四个修饰语中，remorseless 和 kindless，treacherous 和 lecherous 分别有尾韵效果。

④同位语。That I, **the son of a dear father murdered**, …此处 the son of a dear father murdered 修饰为 I 的同位语。

第四章 《哈姆雷特》辞格辨析

A scullion! Fie upon't! Foh! About, my brain!
Hum, I have heard
That guilty creatures sitting at a play,
Have by the very cunning of the scene
Been struck so to the soul that presently
They have proclaimed their malefactions.
For murder, though it have no tongue, will speak
With most miraculous organ. ① I'll have these Players
Play something like the murder of my father
Before mine uncle. I'll observe his looks,
I'll tent him to the quick. ② If he but blench
I know my course. The spirit that I have seen
May be a devil, and the devil hath power
T'assume a pleasing shape. Yea, and perhaps
Out of my weakness and my melancholy,
As he is very potent with such spirits, ③

【辞格辨析】

①拟人。For **murther**, though it have no tongue, **will speak**/with most miraculous organ. 此处将罪行赋予生命，虽然没有发声器官，但能够说出罪行。

②隐喻（Thompson & Taylor, 2007：278）。I'll **tent him to the quick**. Hamlet 在此处将试探 Claudius 内心最为不安的部分比喻为查看病人的伤口。

③插说。Out of my weakness and my melancholy, /**as he is very potent with such spirits**, /…此处插说补充 Hamlet 认为鬼魂能够利用他，主要因为它能操纵人的灵魂。

Abuses me to damn me. I'll have grounds
More relative than this. The play's the thing
Wherein I'll catch the conscience of the King. ①

[Exit.]

第三幕

Act III, Scene 1
Enter King, Queen, Polonius, Ophelia, Rosencrantz, Guildenstern, and Lords.

Claudius: And can you by no drift of circumstance
Get from him why he puts on this confusion,
Grating so harshly all his days of quiet
With turbulent and dangerous lunacy? ②
Rosencrantz: He does confess he feels himself distracted
But from what cause he will by no means speak.
Guildenstern: Nor do we find him forward to be sounded

【辞格辨析】

①尾韵。The play's the **thing**/wherein I'll catch the conscience of the **King**. 此处为尾韵，预示本幕的结束。

②隐喻。… **grating** so harshly all his days of quiet/with turbulent and dangerous lunacy? 此处 Claudius 将给平静的生活带来麻烦比喻为碾磨器粉碎食物的过程。

But with a crafty madness keeps aloof
When we would bring him on to some confession
Of his true state.

Gertrude:　　　　　Did he receive you well?

Rosencrantz: Most like a gentleman. ①

Guildenstern: But with much forcing of his disposition.

Rosencrantz: Niggard of question, but of our demands
Most free in his reply.

Gertrude: Did you assay him to any pastime?

Rosencrantz: Madam, it so fell out that certain players
We o'erraught on the way. Of these we told him
And there did seem in him a kind of joy
To hear of it. They are here about the court,
And, as I think, they have already order
This night to play before him.

Polonius:　　　　　　　'Tis most true,
And he beseeched me to entreat your Majesties
To hear and see the matter.

Claudius: With all my heart, and it doth much content me
To hear him so inclined.

【辞格辨析】

①省略。**Did he receive you well?** /**Most like a gentleman.** /But with much forcing of his dispostition. /…此处 Gertrude 和 Rosencrantz 两人的对话可以看作一句话，为省略了开头主谓部分的句子。完整句子为"He received us most like a gentleman …"。

■ 莎剧《哈姆雷特》辞格辨析与文体鉴赏

Good gentlemen, give him a further edge
And drive his purpose on to these delights.
Rosencrantz: We shall, my lord.
[Exeunt Rosencrantz and Guildenstern.]
Claudius: Sweet Gertrude, leave us too.
For we have closely sent for Hamlet hither,
That he, as 'twere by accident, may here ①
Affront Ophelia.
Her father and myself—lawful espials ②
Will so bestow ourselves that, seeing unseen,
We may of their encounter frankly judge
And gather by him, as he is behaved,
If't be th' affliction of his love or no
That thus he suffers for.
Gertrude: I shall obey you.
And for your part, Ophelia, I do wish
That your good beauties be the happy cause

【辞格辨析】

①插说。That he, **as 'twere by accident**, may here. 此处插说表示信息补充。

②同位语和隐喻。Her father and myself—**lawful espials**…此处有两处辞格：第一处是 lawful espials 作为 her father and myself 的同位语，起到补充说明的作用；第二处是 lawful espials 作为隐喻，即把 Polonius 和 Claudius 躲藏起来偷听的行为，比喻为侦探。

Of Hamlet's wildness. So shall I hope your virtues
Will bring him to his wonted way again
To both your honours.

Ophelia： Madam, I wish it may. [Exit Queen]
Polonius： Ophelia, walk you here. ——Gracious, so please you,
We will bestow ourselves. —— [To Ophelia] Read on this book,
That show of such an exercise may colour
Your loneliness. ——We are oft to blame in this,
'Tis too much proved, that with devotion's visage
And pious action we do sugar o'er
The Devil himself. ①
Claudius：[aside] O, 'tis too true！
How smart a lash that speech doth give my conscience！ ②
The harlot's cheek, beautied with plast'ring art ③
Is not more ugly to the thing that helps it

【辞格辨析】

①隐喻。...that with devotion's visage/and pious action we do **sugar o'er**/the devil himself. 此处比喻将给坏事安上好的借口比喻为为食物添加糖。

②隐喻（Thomson & Taylor, 2007：283）。How smart **a lash** that ...此处 Claudius 将听到对自己良知有触动的语言, 比喻为鞭子抽到身体。

③隐喻。**The harlot's cheek, beautied with plast'ring art**, /...此处为隐喻, 将掩饰性语言比喻为被 painted（涂画）的文字。

181

■ 莎剧《哈姆雷特》辞格辨析与文体鉴赏

Than is my deed to my most painted word. ①
O heavy burthen!
Polonius: I hear him coming. Let's withdraw, my lord.
[Exeunt King and Polonius. Enter Hamlet.]
Hamlet: To be, or not to be—that is the question; ②
Whether 'tis nobler in the mind to suffer
The slings and arrows of outrageous fortune
Or to take arms against a sea of troubles
And by opposing end them. ③ To die—to sleep—
No more, and by a sleep to say we end
The heartache, and the thousand natural shocks

【辞格辨析】

①弱陈。The harlot's cheek, beautied with plast'ring art, /is **not more ugly** to the thing ...此处为弱陈，即 Claudius 使用 not 和 ugly 两个否定词语，进一步强调其行为的丑陋。

②对仗。To be or not to be—that is the question; ...此处利用 to be 和 not to be 构成对仗辞格。

③对仗，提喻和隐喻（1）（2）（Wilson, 2009: 191; 黄国彬, 2013: 365）。**Whether** 'tis nobler in the mind to suffer/**the slings and arrows** of outrageous fortune/**or** to take arms against **a sea of troubles**, /and by opposing, end them. 这句话中有四处辞格。第一处，借用 whether...or...的句式，提出两个选择，构成对仗辞格；第二处，用 slings 和 arrows 指代弹弓和弓箭，构成部分指代整体的提喻辞格；第三处，这一句中也把生活中受到的各种打击比喻为被弹弓或弓箭射击；第四处，把遇到的许多麻烦与烦恼和大海相比，形容数量之多。

That flesh is heir to. ① 'Tis a consummation

Devoutly to be wish'd. To die—to sleep— ②

To sleep—perchance to dream: ay, there's the rub, ③

For in that sleep of death what dreams may come

When we have shuffled off this mortal coil ④

Must give us pause. There's the respect

That makes calamity of so long life. ⑤

For who would bear the whips and scorns of time, ⑥

【辞格辨析】

①拟人。…that flesh **is heir to.** 此处将肉体比拟为接班人，而痛苦和打击则是肉体继承而来的。

②普通重复。**To die—to sleep**—No more；…/…/**To die—to sleep**. 这段话中，重复了两次 to die, to sleep, 构成普通重复辞格。

③隐喻（Hibbard，1987：240）。To sleep, perchance to dream: Ay, there's the **rub,** …此处将人们对死后世界的无知影响人们自杀的决心，比喻为木球游戏过程影响木球旋转路径的障碍物。

④隐喻（Jenkins，1982：278）。…when we have shuffled off this mortal **coil**…此处将摆脱生活烦恼比喻为纠缠的事物。

⑤拟人。Must give us pause. There's the respect/that makes **calamity of so long life.** 将灾难比拟为拥有生命的主体，而人们对自杀的迟疑，即是延长灾难的生命。

⑥拟人。For who would bear the **whips and scorns of time,** …将时代赋予生命，能够鞭打和辱骂人们。

Th' oppressor's wrong, the proud man's contumely,
The pangs of despised love, the law's delay,
The insolence of office and the spurns
That patient merit of th' unworthy takes,
When he himself might his quietus make
With a bare bodkin? ① Who would these fardels bear
To grunt and sweat under a weary life
But that the dread of something after death—
The undiscovered country, from whose bourn
No traveller returns②—puzzles the will,

【辞格辨析】

①排比和隐喻（Thomson & Taylor, 2007: 286）。For who would bear **the whips and scorns of time/th' oppressor's wrong, the pround man's contumely,** /**the pangs of dispised love, the law's delay,** /**the insolence of office** and **the spurns/that patient merit of th' unworthy takes**, /when he himself might his **quietus** make/with a bare bodkin? 此处有两种辞格。第一处为七个名词短语构成的排比辞格，列举了人活在世上所要经历的各种磨难；第二处为隐喻，即将结束生命比喻为 quietus（清算）账目。

②隐喻（1）（2）（Jenkins, 1982: 491）。…/**The undiscovered country,** from whose bourn/**no traveller** returns. 此处将人死去后的世界比喻为 undiscovered country（未被发现的国度），将去世的人比喻为旅客。

And makes us rather bear those ills we have
Than fly to others that we know not of.
Thus conscience does make cowards of us all,
And thus the native hue of resolution
Is sicklied o'er with the pale cast of thought, ①
And enterprises of great pith and moment
With this regard their currents turn awry ②
And lose the name of action. —Soft you now,
The fair Ophelia! —Nymph, in thy orisons
Be all my sins remembered.

Ophelia: Good my lord,
How does your honour for this many a day?
Hamlet: I humbly thank you, well, well, well. ③
Ophelia: My lord, I have remembrances of yours
That I have longed long to re-deliver.

【辞格辨析】

①拟人（Thompson 1987：107；Thomson & Taylor, 2007：287）。…and thus the native hue of resolution/**is sicklied o'er with the pale cast of thought**, …此处将人（寻死）的决心比拟为因为生病而脸色惨白的人。

②隐喻。…with this regard **their currents turn awry**…此处将思绪比喻为水流，将人们因为对死后世界的未知导致的不敢下定决心自杀的行为比喻为水流改变流动方向。

③直接重复。I humbly thank you, **well, well, well.** 此处为直接重复。Jenkins 将此处的重复解读为 Hamlet 的不耐烦（见 Thomson & Taylor, 2007：288）。

莎剧《哈姆雷特》辞格辨析与文体鉴赏

I pray you, now receive them.

Hamlet: No, not I! I never gave you aught.

Ophelia: My honoured lord, you know right well you did,

And with them words of so sweet breath composed

As made the things more rich. Their perfume lost, ①

Take these again, for to the noble mind

Rich gifts wax poor when givers prove unkind. ②

There, my lord.

Hamlet: Ha, ha! Are you honest?

Ophelia: My lord?

Hamlet: Are you fair? ③

Ophelia: What means your lordship?

Hamlet: That if you be honest and fair,

【辞格辨析】

①隐喻。… and with them **words of so sweet breath** compos'd/…their **perfume** lost. 此处将情话比喻为香甜的事物，会因为 Hamlet 的爱情的消失而失去香气。

②尾韵和对仗。…for to the noble **mind** /rich gifts wax poor when givers prove **unkind**. 这句话中，第一处辞格是 mind 和 unkind 构成的尾韵，在这里预示着谈话的结束或爱情的终止；第二处辞格为对仗，即 rich gifts 和 poor, unkind 等词构成的对仗。

③一笔双叙双关（1）（2）。Ha, ha! Are you **honest**?/My lord?/Are you **fair**? 此处的 honest 和 fair 构成两个一笔双叙双关辞格。Honest 同时表示忠诚和贞洁两个意思，fair 同时表示漂亮和善良的意思。

your honesty should admit no discourse to your beauty. ①

Ophelia: Could Beauty, my lord, have better commerce than with Honesty? ②

Hamlet: Ay, truly; for the power of Beauty will sooner transform Honesty from what it is to a bawd than the force of Honesty can translate Beauty into his likeness. This was sometime a paradox, but now the time gives it proof. I did love you once.

Ophelia: Indeed, my lord, you made me believe so.

Hamlet: You should not have believ'd me. For virtue cannot so inoculate our old stock but we shall relish of it. ③ I loved you not.

Ophelia: I was the more deceived.

【辞格辨析】

①同根异形重复和拟人。That if you be **honest** and fair, your **honesty** should **admit no discourse** to your beauty. 此处的 honest 和 honesty 为同根异形重复辞格；另外，这一句也将 honesty 和 beauty 拟人化，能够相互接触。

②拟人，反问句和一笔双叙双关。Could Beauty, my lord, **have better commerce** than with Honesty? 此处有三处辞格。第一处和上文相同，将 beauty 和 honesty 拟人化，能够相互建立关系；另一处是反问句，为 Ophelia 对 Hamlet 的反驳；第三处为一笔双叙的双关，主要借助 commerce 这一词语同时有交易和建立性关系的意义，表达了两种共存的意思，成为双关。

③隐喻（Thomson & Taylor, 2007：290）。... for virtue cannot so **inoculate our old stock** but we shall relish of it. 此处将美德和罪恶的结合与新枝嫁接老树桩相比。

莎剧《哈姆雷特》辞格辨析与文体鉴赏

Hamlet: Get thee to a nunnery! ① Why wouldst thou be a breeder of sinners? I am myself indifferent honest but yet I could accuse me of such things that it were better my mother had not borne me. I am very proud, revengeful, ambitious, with more offences at my beck than I have thoughts to put them in, imagination to give them shape, or time to act them in. ② What should such fellows as I do, crawling between earth and heaven? We are arrant knaves all—believe none of us. Go thy ways to a nunnery. Where's your father?
Ophelia: At home, my lord.
Hamlet: Let the doors be shut upon him that he may play the fool nowhere but in's own house. Farewell.
Ophelia: O, help him, you sweet heavens!
Hamlet: If thou dost marry, I'll give thee this plague for thy dowry: be thou as chaste as ice, as pure as snow, ③ thou shalt not escape calumny. Get thee to a nunnery. Go, farewell. Or if thou wilt needs marry,

【辞格辨析】

①一笔双叙双关。Get thee to a **nunnery.** 此处为一笔双叙的双关。Nunnery 在这里一方面表示女子修道院，另一方面也可以理解为妓院。

②排比（1）（2）。I am very **proud**, **revengeful**; **ambitious**, with more **offences** at my beck than I have **thoughts to put them in, imagination to give them shape,** or **time to act them in.** 这句话有两处排比，第一处为 proud, revengeful 和 ambitious 三个构成，第二处为三个 "…to…" 的结构构成。

③明喻（1）（2）。Be thou **as chaste as ice, as pure as snow.** 此处将贞洁比喻为冰，将纯洁化作雪。

marry a fool; for wise men know well enough what monsters you make of them. To a nunnery, go, and quickly too. Farewell.

Ophelia: O heavenly powers restore him!

Hamlet: I have heard of your paintings well enough. God hath given you one face and you make yourselves another. You jig, you amble and you lisp; you nickname God's creatures and make your wantonness your ignorance. ① Go to, I'll no more on't! it hath made me mad. I say, we will have no more marriages. Those that are married already—all but one—shall live. The rest shall keep as they are. To a nunnery, go.　　　　　　　　　　　　　　　　[Exit.]

Ophelia: O, what a noble mind is here o'erthrown! ②
The courtier's, scholar's, soldier's eye, tongue, sword, ③
Th' expectancy and rose of the fair state,
The glass of fashion and the mould of form,

【辞格辨析】

①排比。You **jig**, you **amble**, and you **lisp**; and you **nickname** God's creatures and **make** your wantonness your ignorance. 此处用系列动词，即 jig、amble、lisp、nickname 和 make 等构成排比辞格。

②隐喻。What a noble mind is here **o'erthrown**! Ophelia 将一个人的思想具体化，比喻为可以推翻的事物，如建筑等。

③排比和借代。The **courtier's**, **soldier's**, **scholar's eye**, **tongue**, **sword**, … 此处由 courtier、soldier、scholar 和 eye、tongue 和 sword 构成的排比。此外，此处的 eye、tongue 和 sword 也分别指代 Hamlet 的外貌、口才和武艺。

莎剧《哈姆雷特》辞格辨析与文体鉴赏

Th' observ'd of all observers—quite, quite down. ①
And I, of ladies most deject and wretched,
That suck'd the honey of his music vows, ②
Now see that noble and most sovereign reason
Like sweet bells jangled out of tune and harsh— ③
That unmatched form and feature of blown youth
Blasted with ecstasy. ④ O, woe is me
T' have seen what I have seen, see what I see. ⑤

【辞格辨析】

①排比，隐喻（1）（2）（3），同词异义重复和直接重复。…/**th' expectancy and rose of the fair state,/the glass of fashion** and **the mould of form,/th' observ'd of all observers—quite, quite** down! 由四个"…of…"名词结构构成的排比。同时，将 Hamlet 比喻为国家的玫瑰、时尚的镜子、行为的典范等，分别构成隐喻；此外，observ'd 和 observer 构成同根异形重复；最后，两个 quite 构成直接重复辞格。

②隐喻。…that **suck'd the honey of his music vows**. 此处 Ophelia 将听了 Hamlet 的爱情盟誓比喻为蜂蜜和音乐。

③拟人和明喻。…now see that **noble and most sovereign reason**, /**like sweet bells jangled, out of tune and harsh**. 此句有两处辞格，第一处将 reason（理性）比拟为身体的统治者；第二处为明喻，将 Hamlet 失去理性比喻为铃铛音调失调。

④隐喻。That unmatched form and feature of **blown** youth/blasted with ecstasy. 此处将年轻人比喻为植物开花。

⑤同根异形重复。…T' **have seen** what I **have seen**, …此处使用了 see 的不同形式，构成同根异形重复。

[Enter King and Polonius.]
Claudius: Love? His affections do not that way tend.
Nor what he spake, though it lacked form a little,
Was not like madness. There's something in his soul
O'er which his melancholy sits on brood ②
And I do doubt the hatch and the disclose
Will be some danger—which for to prevent,
I have in quick determination
Thus set it down: he shall with speed to England
For the demand of our neglected tribute.
Haply the seas and countries different
With variable objects shall expel
This something-settled matter in his heart
Whereon his brains still beating puts him thus
From fashion of himself. What think you on't?
Polonius: It shall do well. But yet do I believe
The origin and commencement of his grief
Sprung from neglected love. How now, Ophelia?
You need not tell us what Lord Hamlet said—
We heard it all. My lord, do as you please,
But if you hold it fit after the play

【辞格辨析】

①隐喻（Thomson & Taylor, 2007: 293-294）。... o'er which his melancholy **sits on brood**;/... 此处 Claudius 怀疑 Hamlet 心中有秘密没有透露出来，具有不确定的危险性，所以将这种情况比喻为还没有孵出来的动物。

莎剧《哈姆雷特》辞格辨析与文体鉴赏

Let his queen mother all alone entreat him
To show his grief. Let her be round with him
And I'll be placed, so please you, in the ear
Of all their conference. ① If she find him not,
To England send him; or confine him where
Your wisdom best shall think.

Claudius: It shall be so.
Madness in great ones must not unwatched go. ②　　［Exeunt.］

Act III, Scene 2
Elsinore. hall in the Castle. Enter Hamlet and three of the Players.

Hamlet: Speak the speech, I pray you, as I pronounced it to you, trippingly on the tongue. ③ But if you mouth it, as many of our players do, I had as lief the town crier spoke my lines.

【辞格辨析】

①插说和借代。…and I'll be placed, **so please you**, in **the ear**/of all their conference. 此处第一处辞格为插说，补充 Polonius 的态度；第二处辞格为借代，用 ear 指代偷听行为。

②尾韵和弱陈。It shall be **so**. /Madness in great ones must **not unwatched go**. 此处的 so 和 go 构成了尾韵，表示本节结束；另外一处辞格是由 not 和 unwatched 两个表示否定的词语构成，Claudius 强调对发疯的 Hamlet 更需要严加看管。

③插说。Speak the speech, **I pray you, as I pronounced it to you**, trippingly on the tongue. 此处插说补充说明了 Hamlet 的态度。

第四章 《哈姆雷特》辞格辨析

Nor do not saw the air too much with your hand, thus, but use all gently; for in the very torrent, tempest, and (as I may say) whirlwind of your passion, you must acquire and beget a temperance that may give it smoothness. ① O, it offends me to the soul to hear a robustious periwig-pated fellow tear a passion to tatters, to very rags, to split the ears of the groundlings, ② who (for the most part) are capable of nothing but inexplicable dumb shows and noise. I would have such a fellow whipped for o'erdoing Termagant. It out-herods Herod. Pray you avoid it. ③

【辞格辨析】

①排比，插说，隐喻和头韵。…the very **torrent**, **tempest**, and (**as I may say**) **whirlwind** of your **passion**, … beget a **temperance** that …此句中有四处使用了辞格，第一处为 torrent、tempest 和 whirlwind 三个词构成排比；第二处，as I may say 为表达 Hamlet 观点的插入语；第三处为将 passion（激情）比喻为湍流的隐喻；第四处，由 torrent、tempest 和 temperance 三个词构成头韵。

②隐喻和借代。…to hear a robustious periwig-pated fellow **tear a passion to tatters**, **to very rags**, to split **the ears** of the groundlings, …此处将 passion（激情）具体化，比喻为可以撕成碎片的东西；第二次辞格是借代，用 ears 指代观众的听觉，表示台上粗糙吵闹的表演，把观众的耳朵听觉振聋。

③换说（1）（2）。…whipped for **o'erdoing Termagant**. It **out-herods Herod**. Pray you avoid it. 这里有一处换说，即用 Termagant（特码根，脾气暴躁的神灵）来指代表演彪悍暴躁的角色；另一处用 Herod（希律王）来指代残忍凶狠的角色。

193

■ 莎剧《哈姆雷特》辞格辨析与文体鉴赏

First Player: I warrant your honour.

Hamlet: Be not too tame neither, but let your own discretion be your tutor. ① Suit the action to the word, the word to the action, ② with this special observance, that you o'erstep not the modesty of nature. For anything so overdone is from the purpose of playing, whose end, both at the first and now, was and is to hold as 'twere, the mirror up to Nature ③ to show Virtue her own feature, Scorn her own image, and the very age and body of the time his form and pressure. ④ Now this overdone, or come tardy off, though it make the unskilful laugh,

【辞格辨析】

①拟人。…but let your own discretion **be your tutor**. 此处赋予 discretion（谨慎）人的特征，能够充当演员的 tutor（导师）。Hamlet 意为让演员不要夸张地表演。

②回环重复。Suit the <u>action</u> to the <u>word</u>, the <u>word</u> to the <u>action</u>, …此处为回环重复，第一小句以 action 开始，word 结尾，第二小句以 word 开始，action 结尾，构成回环重复。

③明喻。…and is, to hold, **as** 'twere, the mirror up to nature …此处将戏剧表演的"真"比喻为给自然照镜子。

④排比和拟人（1）（2）（3）。… to show **Virtue** her own feature, **scorn** her own image and the very **age** and **body of the time** his form and pressure. 此处由 Virtue，scorn 和 time 等三处名词短语构成排比；另外也将这几类抽象事物比拟为拥有生命的主体。

第四章 《哈姆雷特》辞格辨析

cannot but make the judicious grieve, ① the censure of the which one must in your allowance o'erweigh a whole theatre of others. O, there be players that I have seen play, and heard others praise, and that highly (not to speak it profanely), that neither having the accent of Christians nor the gait of Christian, pagan nor man ② have so strutted and bellowed that I have thought some of Nature's journey men had made men, and not made them well, they imitated humanity so abominably.

First Player: I hope we have reformed that indifferently with us, sir.

Hamlet: O, reform it altogether! And let those that play your clowns speak no more than is set down for them. For there be of them that will themselves laugh, to set on some quantity of barren spectators to laugh too, though in the mean time some necessary question of the play be then to be considered. That's villanous and shows a most pitiful ambition in the fool that uses it. Go make you ready.

[Exeunt Players.]
[Enter Polonius, Rosencrantz, and Guildenstern]

【辞格辨析】

①借代（1）（2）。...though it make **the unskilful** laugh; cannot but make **the judicious** grieve, ...用 unskillful 和 the judicious 分别指代不懂戏剧和对表演理解充分的两类观众。

②插说。...and that highly (**not to speak it profanely**), that, neither having the accent of Christians, nor the gait of Christian, pagan, nor man, ...此处 Hamlet 的插入语表示他意识到将这群表演夸张的演员定义为非 Christian, pagan 和 man 的不妥。

How now, my lord? Will the King hear this piece of work?

Polonius: And the Queen too, and that presently.

Hamlet: Bid the players make haste.

〔Exit Polonius.〕

Will you two help to hasten them?

Rosencrantz: 〔with Guildenstern〕 We will, my lord.

〔Exeunt they two. Enter Horatio.〕

Hamlet: What, ho, Horatio!

Horatio: Here, sweet lord, at your service.

Hamlet: Horatio, thou art e'en as just a man

As e'er my conversation cop'd withal.

Horatio: O, my dear lord!

Hamlet: Nay, do not think I flatter,

For what advancement may I hope from thee

That no revenue hast but thy good spirits

To feed and clothe thee? Why should the poor be flattered? ①

No, let the candied tongue lick absurd pomp

And crook the pregnant hinges of the knee

【辞格辨析】

①反问句（1）（2）和拟人。…that no revenue hast but thy **good spirits**/to feed and clothe thee? Why should the poor be flattered? 第一个问句为反问句，表示对内容的强调，突出 Horatio 的 good spirits 是他所赖以生存的一切；第二个问句也为反问句，Hamlet 进一步说明夸奖 Horatio 并不是为了奉承他；第三处为拟人，把 good spirits 赋予人的特征，能够给 Horatio 提供粮食和衣物。

Where thrift may follow fawning. ① Dost thou hear?
Since my dear soul was mistress of her choice
And could of men distinguish, her election
Hath sealed thee for herself. ② For thou hast been
As one in suff'ring all that suffers nothing— ③
A man that Fortune's buffets and rewards
Hast ta'en with equal thanks; and blest are those
Whose blood and judgment are so well commingled
That they are not a pipe for Fortune's finger
To sound what stop she please. ④ Give me that man

【辞格辨析】

①隐喻（1）（2）。Let the **candied** tongue lick the absurd pomp,／and crook the pregnant **hinges of the knee**／where thrift may follow fawning. 此处将说出奉承语言的话比喻为吃了甜肉的舌头，试图通过奉承继续索取食物（Wilson, 2009: 197）；第二处将双膝的合并（跪下）比喻为铰链的启合。

②拟人。Since **my dear soul was mistress of her choice**／and could of men distinguish, **her election**／hath seal'd thee **for herself**. 此处 Hamlet 将自己的灵魂比拟为人，能够辨识和挑选自己的朋友。

③同根异形重复。…as one, **in suffering all, that suffers nothing**. 此处的 suffering 和 suffers 为同根词语的异形重复。

④隐喻。…that they are not **a pipe** for Fortune's finger/to sound what stop she please. 此处将听从命运摆布的人比喻为命运女神手中的笛子，而 Hamlet 认为，Horatio 不是任由命运摆布的人。

莎剧《哈姆雷特》辞格辨析与文体鉴赏

That is not passion's slave and I will wear him
In my heart's core, ay, in my heart of heart,
As I do thee. ① Something too much of this:
There is a play tonight before the King.
One scene of it comes near the circumstance
Which I have told thee of my father's death.
I prithee when thou seest that act afoot,
Even with the very comment of thy soul
Observe my uncle. If his occulted guilt
Do not itself unkennel in one speech ②
It is a damned ghost that we have seen
And my imaginations are as foul
As Vulcan's stithy. ③ Give him heedful note,

【辞格辨析】

　　①隐喻和普通重复。Give me that man/that is not **passion's slave**, and I will wear him/in my **heart's** core, ay, in my **heart** of **heart**, /as I do thee. 此处 Hamlet 将听从激情摆布的人比喻为 passion's slave（激情的奴隶）；另一处辞格为三个 heart 构成的重复辞格。

　　②隐喻和弱陈。If his occulted guilt/do **not** itself **unkennel** in one speech. 此处 Hamlet 将 Claudius 流露罪恶内心比喻为动物从洞穴中被逼迫出来；另一处辞格是由 not 和 unkennel 构成，表示 Hamlet 认为戏中戏肯定会让 Claudius 暴露自己的罪行。

　　③明喻。And my imaginations are **as foul** /as Vulcan's stithy. 此处 Hamlet 将自己内心的黑暗比喻为铁匠 Vulcan 黑漆漆的打铁店。

第四章 《哈姆雷特》辞格辨析

For I mine eyes will rivet to his face ①
And after we will both our judgments join
In censure of his seeming.
Horatio: Well, my lord.
If he steal aught the whilst this play is playing
And scape detecting I will pay the theft.

Sound a flourish. [Enter Trumpetsand Kettledrums. Danish march. Enter King, Queen, Polonius, Ophelia, Rosencrantz, Guildenstern, and other Lords attendant, with the Guard carrying torches.]

Hamlet: They are coming to the play. I must be idle. Get you a place.
Claudius: How fares our cousin Hamlet?
Hamlet: Excellent, i'faith! Of the chameleon's dish. I eat the air, promise-crammed. You cannot feed capons so. ②

【辞格辨析】

①隐喻。…for I mine eyes will **rivet** to his face. Hamlet 将自己目光注视 Claudius 的行为比喻为如被铆钉固定住一般。

②一笔双叙双关和谐音双关（Thomson & Taylor, 2007: 303; Wilson, 2009: 198）。How **fares** our cousin Hamlet? /... of the chameleon's dish. I eat the **air**, promise-crammed. 这里有两处双关：第一处为由 fare 构成的一笔双叙双关。Claudius 说出 fares 时表示问候，Hamlet 回答时取该词表示食物的意思；第二处为由 air 和 heir 构成谐音双关，表面上表示 Hamlet 吃了靠吃 air（空气）为生的变色龙，深层则讥讽 Claudius 抢夺了他这个 heir（王位继承人）的位子。

199

莎剧《哈姆雷特》辞格辨析与文体鉴赏

Claudius: I have nothing with this answer, Hamlet. These words are not mine.

Hamlet: No, nor mine now. [to Polonius] My lord, you played once i' th' university, you say?

Polonius: That did I, my lord, and was accounted a good actor.

Hamlet: What did you enact?

Polonius: I did enact Julius Caesar. I was killed i' th' Capitol; Brutus killed me.

Hamlet: It was a brute part of him to kill so capital a calf there. ① Be the players ready?

Rosencrantz: Ay, my lord. They stay upon your patience.

Gertrude: Come hither, my dear Hamlet, sit by me.

Hamlet: No, good mother. Here's metal more attractive. ②

Polonius: [to the King] O, ho! Do you mark that?

Hamlet: Lady, shall I lie in your lap?

[Sits down at Ophelia's feet.]

【辞格辨析】

①谐音双关（1）（2）和一笔双叙双关。I did enact Julius Caesar; I was killed i' th' **Capitol**; **Brutus** killed me. It was a **brute** part of him to kill so **capital** a **calf** there. 此处有三处双关：其中两处是 Hamlet 用 brute（残忍）和 Brutus（罗马政治家布鲁特斯），capital（庞大的）和 Capitol（议会）的谐音构成两处谐音双关辞格，起到对 Polonius 调侃的效果；另外一处是借助 calf 同时表示小牛和愚蠢的人的多义性，构成一处一笔双叙双关。

②隐喻。Here's **metal** more attractive. 此处 Hamlet 将 Ophelia 对他的吸引力比喻为磁铁的引力。

Ophelia: No, my lord.

Hamlet: I mean, my head upon your lap?

Ophelia: Ay, my lord.

Hamlet: Do you think I meant country matters?

Ophelia: I think nothing, my lord.

Hamlet: That's a fair thought to lie between maids' legs. ①

Ophelia: What is, my lord?

Hamlet: Nothing.

Ophelia: You are merry, my lord. ②

【辞格辨析】

①一笔双叙双关（1）（2）（3）（4）（Thomson & Taylor, 2007：304-305；Raffel, 2003：111）。Lady, shall I **lie in your lap**? /... /Do you think I meant **country matters**? /I think **nothing**, my lord. /That's a **fair** thought to **lie** between maids' legs. 此处对话为 Hamle 对 Ophelia 的戏裘，对话充满猥亵语，其中的 lie, country matter, nothing 和 fair 等词分别表示"躺在膝上""粗野事情""没事"和"合适的"等，另一方面也各有其他意思，甚至性暗示，构成不同种类的双关。Lie in your lap 也可以理解为男欢女爱，为一笔双叙双关；country 在伊丽莎白时期也曾被 Ben Johnson 用来指代女性隐私部位，为谐音双关；而 nothing 中的 thing 则常被用来作为男性性器官的委婉语，属于一笔双叙双关；fair 也可以表示"愉悦的，欢快的"，属于一笔双叙双关。

②一笔双叙双关（Raffel, 2003：112）。You are **merry**, my lord. 此处的 merry 有两种理解，一方面是"开心"，另一方面是"微醉"。

Hamlet: Who, I?

Ophelia: Ay, my lord.

Hamlet: O God, your only jig-maker! What should a man do but be merry? For look you how cheerfully my mother looks, and my father died within's two hours.

Ophelia: Nay 'tis twice two months, my lord.

Hamlet: So long? Nay then, let the devil wear black, for I'll have a suit of sables. O heavens! Die two months ago, and not forgotten yet? Then there's hope a great man's memory may outlive his life half a year. ① But, by'r Lady, he must build churches then, or else shall he suffer not thinking on, with the hobby-horse, whose epitaph is 'For O, for O, the hobby-horse is forgot!'

[Hautboys play. The dumb show enters.]

Enter a King and a Queen very lovingly; the Queen embracing him and he her. She kneels, and makes show of protestation unto him. He takes her up, and declines his head upon her neck. He lays him down upon a bank of flowers. She, seeing him asleep, leaves him. Anon comes in a fellow, takes off his crown, kisses it, pours poison in the sleeper's ears, and leaves him. The Queen returns, finds the King dead, and makes passionate action. The Poisoner with some three or four Mutes, comes in again, seem to condole with her. The dead body is carried away.

【辞格辨析】

①拟人。Then there's hope a great man's memory may **outlive his life** half a year. 此处 Hamlet 将记忆拟人化，比拟为具有生命的主体。

The Poisoner wooes the Queen with gifts; she seems harsh and unwilling awhile, but in the end accepts his love.

[Exeunt.]

Ophelia: What means this, my lord?

Hamlet: Marry, this is munching mallico! It means mischief.

Ophelia: Belike this show imports the argument of the play.

[Enter Prologue.]

Hamlet: We shall know by this fellow. The players cannot keep counsel; they'll tell all.

Ophelia: Will he tell us what this show meant?

Hamlet: Ay, or any show that you'll show him. Be not you ashamed to show, he'll not shame to tell you what it means. ①

Ophelia: You are naught, you are naught! I'll mark the play.

Prologue: *For us, and for our tragedy,*

Here stooping to your clemency,

We beg your hearing patiently. [Exit.]

Hamlet: Is this a prologue, or the posy of a ring?

Ophelia: 'Tis brief, my lord.

【辞格辨析】

①换义双关。Will he tell us what this **show** meant? /Ay, or any **show** that you'll **show** him. Be not you ashamed to **show**, he'll not shame to tell you what it means. 此处 Ophelia 询问 Hamlet 表演的内容,而 Hamlet 则用 show 一词的多义性来创造双关。Show 除了表示"表演"之外,还可以指"展示",而 Hamlet 此处暗指一些亲密的(甚至是性方面)的展示(Thomson & Taylor, 2007: 309)。

■ 莎剧《哈姆雷特》辞格辨析与文体鉴赏

Hamlet: As woman's love. ①
[Enter two Players as King and Queen.]
Player King: *Full thirty times hath Phoebus' cart gone round*
Neptune's salt wash and Tellus' orbed ground,
And thirty dozen moons with borrowed sheen
About the world have times twelve thirties been
Since love our hearts, and Hymen did our hands
Unite comutual in most sacred bands. ②
Player Queen: *So many journeys may the sun and moon*

【辞格辨析】

①省略和明喻。'Tis brief, my lord. /**As** woman's love. 此处对话有两处辞格,第一处为 Hamlet 回答过程省略部分内容,完整句子可以是"'Tis brief as woman's love."。第二处辞格为明喻,即把开场介绍的简短比喻为女人的爱情。

②换说（1）（2）（3）（4）和尾韵（1）—（3）。Full thirty times hath **Phoebus' cart** gone round/**Neptune's salt wash** and **Tellus' orbed ground**, /and thirty dozen moons with borrowed **sheen**/about the world have times twelve thirties **been**, /since love our hearts, and **Hymen did our hands**, /**unite comutual in most sacred bands**. 此处 Phoebus' cart, Neptune's salt wash, Tellus' orbed ground, 和 Hymen did our hands unite comutual in most sacred bands 四处分别指代太阳、大海、大地和结婚等事物或事件,属于换义辞格。这部分还有三处尾韵,分别由 round 和 ground, sheen 和 been, 以及 hands 和 bands 构成。这些尾韵和每一幕最后的对句不同,这里,以及下面部分的尾韵,均为戏中戏的语言,与戏剧其他部分的语言有所区分。

204

第四章 《哈姆雷特》辞格辨析

Make us again count o'er ere love be done. ①
But woe is me! you are so sick of late,
So far from cheer and from your former state,
That I distrust you. Yet, though I distrust,
Discomfort you, my lord, it nothing must.
For women's fear and love holds quantity,
Either none in neither aught, or in extremity.
Now what my love is, proof hath made you know
And as my love is sized, my fear is so.
Where love is great, the littlest doubts are fear;
Where little fears grow great, great love grows there. ②
Player King：*Faith, I must leave thee, love, and shortly too,*
My operant powers their functions leave to do.
And thou shalt live in this fair world behind,
Honour'd, belov'd, and haply one as kind! ③

【辞格辨析】

①隐喻。So many **journeys** may the sun and moon/make us again count o'er ere love be done！此处 Player Queen 将时间比喻为旅途。

②链形重复和尾韵（1）—（6）。Where little fears grow **great, great** love grows there. 此处第一小句以 great 结尾，第二小句以 great 开头，构成链形重复。这部分还有六处尾韵，分别由 moon 和 done，late 和 state，distrust 和 must，quantity 和 extremity，know 和 so，以及 fear 和 there 构成。

③尾韵（1）（2）。这部分有两处尾韵，分别由 too 和 do，behind 和 kind 构成。

莎剧《哈姆雷特》辞格辨析与文体鉴赏

For husband shalt thou—

Player Queen: *O, confound the rest!*
Such love must needs be treason in my breast.
When second husband let me be accurst:
None wed the second but who killed the first. ①
Hamlet: [aside] *Wormwood, wormwood!*
Player Queen: *The instances that second marriage move*
Are base respects of thrift, but none of love.
A second time I kill my husband dead
When second husband kisses me in bed. ②
Player King: *I do believe you think what now you speak.*
But what we do determine oft we break.
Purpose is but the slave to memory,

【辞格辨析】

①尾韵（1）（2）。这部分有两处尾韵，分别由 rest 和 breast，accurst 和 first 构成。

②普通重复和尾韵（1）（2）。When **second** husband ... / None wed the **second** but who kill'd the first. /... /The instances that **second** marriage move/... /A **second** time ... /when **second** husband kisses me in bed. 此处使用了五个 second，构成普通重复辞格。这部分还有两处尾韵，分别由 move 和 love，dead 和 bed 构成。其中 move 和 love 可以在阅读的过程变音，也可以看作是一处视韵（eye rhyme），下面其他尾韵也有类似情况。

Of violent birth, but poor validity, ①
Which now, like fruit unripe, sticks on the tree
But fall unshaken when they mellow be. ②
Most necessary 'tis that we forget
To pay ourselves what to ourselves is debt.
What to ourselves in passion we propose,
The passion ending, doth the purpose lose.
The violence of either grief or joy
Their own enactures with themselves destroy.
Where joy most revels, grief doth most lament;
Grief joys, joy grieves, on slender accident.
This world is not for aye, nor 'tis not strange
That even our loves should with our fortunes change;
For 'tis a question left us yet to prove,
Whether love lead fortune, or else fortune love. ③

【辞格辨析】

①拟人。**Purpose is but the slave to memory,** /…此处 Player King 把决心比作记忆的奴隶。

②明喻。…which now, **like fruit unripe**, sticks on the tree! But fall unshaken when they mellow be. 此处 Player King 将决心比作树上的果实，还没有成熟的时候紧粘着树枝，而一旦成熟了，即使不用摇晃都会自行脱落。

③拟人。…whether **love lead fortune**, or else fortune love. 此处 Player King 将 love（爱情）和 fortune（命运）等都拟人化，能够相互引领。

莎剧《哈姆雷特》辞格辨析与文体鉴赏

The great man down, you mark his favourite flies, ①
The poor advanced makes friends of enemies,
And hitherto doth love on fortune tend,
For who not needs shall never lack a friend,
And who in want a hollow friend doth try,
Directly seasons him his enemy.
But, orderly to end where I begun,
Our wills and fates do so contrary run
That our devices still are overthrown.
Our thoughts are ours, their ends none of our own:
So think thou wilt no second husband wed
But die thy thoughts when thy first lord is dead. ②
Player Queen: *Nor earth to me give food, nor heaven light,*
Sport and repose lock from me day and night,

【辞格辨析】

①隐喻。The great man down, you mark **his favourite flies**. 此处 Player King 将一个伟人的宠臣们比喻为飞蚊,在伟人倒下后都各处飞散。

②拟人和尾韵(1)—(15)。But **die thy thoughts** when thy first lord is dead. 此处 Player King 将思想赋予生命,会有死亡的时刻。这部分还有 15 处尾韵,分别由 speak 和 break, memory 和 validity, tree 和 be, forget 和 debt, purpose 和 lose, joy 和 destroy, lament 和 accident, strange 和 change, prove 和 love, flies 和 enemies, tend 和 friend, try 和 enemy, begun 和 run, overthrown 和 own, wed 和 dead 构成。

An anchor's cheer in prison be my scope,
To desperation turn my trust and hope,
Each opposite that blanks the face of joy ①
Meet what I would have well, and it destroy,
Both here and hence pursue me lasting strife
If, once a widow, ever I be wife. ②

Hamlet: If she should break it now!

Player King: 'Tis deeply sworn. Sweet, leave me here awhile.
My spirits grow dull, and fain I would beguile ③
The tedious day with sleep.

Player Queen:　　　　Sleep rock thy brain,
And never come mischance between us twain. ④　　[Exit.]

Hamlet: Madam, how like you this play?

Gertrude: The lady doth protest too much, methinks.

Hamlet: O, but she'll keep her word.

【辞格辨析】

①拟人。Each opposite that blanks the face of joy. 此处 Player King 将 joy（欢乐）赋予生命，遇到不如意脸色发白。

②尾韵（1）—（4）。这部分有四处尾韵，分别由 light 和 night, scope 和 hope, joy 和 destroy, strife 和 wife 构成。

③尾韵。'Tis deeply sworn. Sweet, leave me here **awhile**. / My spirits grow dull, and fain I would **beguile**. 此处的 awhile 和 beguile 构成尾韵。

④尾韵。Sleep rock thy **brain**, /And never come mischance between us **twain.** 此处的 brain 和 twain 构成尾韵。

Claudius: Have you heard the argument? Is there no offence in't? ①

Hamlet: No, no! They do but jest, poison in jest; ② no offence i' th' world.

Claudius: What do you call the play?

Hamlet: '*The Mousetrap*.' Marry, how? Tropically. ③ This play is the image of a murther done in Vienna. Gonzago is the duke's name; his wife, Baptista. You shall see anon. 'Tis a knavish piece of work, but what o' that? Your Majesty, and we that have free souls, it touches us not. Let the galled jade winch; our withers are unwrung.

[Enter Lucianus.] This is one Lucianus, nephew to the King.

Ophelia: You are as good as a chorus, my lord.

Hamlet: I could interpret between you and your love if I could see the puppets dallying.

【辞格辨析】

①一笔双叙双关。Is there no **offence** in't? 此处的 offence 可以理解为一处一笔双叙双关，即 offence 可以同时理解为"不合适的行为"，也可以理解为"罪行"。

②普通重复。They do but **jest**, poison in **jest**. Hamlet 在这里重复了两处 jest，构成普通重复辞格，起到强调作用。

③隐喻（Raffel，2003：118）和谐音双关（黄国彬，2013：414）。'*The Mouse-trap*.' Marry, how? Tropically. Hamlet 将这部戏名为"捕鼠器"，有隐喻内涵，即将用戏中戏来引诱 Claudius 泄漏罪行比喻为摆放捕鼠器捉老鼠；第二处辞格为谐音双关，即 tropically 可以理解为"trope"一字的形容词，指比喻的说法，也可以谐音"trappical"，指"陷阱"。

第四章 《哈姆雷特》辞格辨析

Ophelia：You are keen, my lord, you are keen.
Hamlet：It would cost you a groaning to take off my edge. ①
Ophelia：Still better and worse.
Hamlet：So you must take your husbands. ② —Begin, murtherer; leave thy damnable faces, and begin! Come, 'the croaking raven doth bellow for revenge'.
Lucianus：*Thoughts black, hands apt, drugs fit, and time agreeing,*
Confederate season, else no creature seeing,
Thou mixture rank, of midnight weeds collected,
With Hecate's ban thrice blasted, thrice infected, ③

【辞格辨析】

①间隔重复和一笔双叙双关（1）（2）。You are **keen**, my lord, you are **keen**. /It would cost you a groaning to take off my **edge**. 此处辞格，第一处为 you are keen 的间隔重复；第二处为 keen 和 edge 构成的两处双关。Ophelia 说 keen 的时候取的是"话语犀利"的意思，下文哈姆雷特取"犀利"的意思，与 edge 作"刀锋"意思解时构成双关，将"话语犀利"变成"刀锋犀利"，用于暗指男性生殖器官。

②谐音双关。So you **must take** your husbands. 此处的 must take 是谐音双关，第一种可以理解为对结婚誓言 take somebody as husband/wife 这句话的戏袭，对 Ophelia 的 still better and worse 的回应；第二种是 must take 和 mistake 谐音，指作出错误的选择，认错了丈夫。

③间隔重复。With Hecate's ban **thrice** blasted, **thrice** infected. 此处间隔重复两次 thrice，突出毒药药性的厉害。

211

莎剧《哈姆雷特》辞格辨析与文体鉴赏

Thy natural magic and dire property
On wholesome life usurp immediately. ①
[Pours the poison in his ears.]
Hamlet: He poisons him i' th' garden for 's estate. His name's Gonzago. The story is extant, and written in very choice Italian. You shall see anon how the murtherer gets the love of Gonzago's wife.
Ophelia: The King rises.
Hamlet: What, frighted with false fire? ②
Gertrude: How fares my lord?
Polonius: Give o'er the play.
Claudius: Give me some light! Away!
All: Lights, lights, lights! ③

      [Exeunt all but Hamlet and Horatio.]
Hamlet: Why, let the strucken deer go weep,
The hart ungalled play,
For some must watch, while some must sleep.
Thus runs the world away.

【辞格辨析】

①隐喻。…on wholesome life **usurp** immediately. 此处将用毒药夺走生命比喻为篡夺政权。

②省略。The King rises. /What, frightened with false fire? 此处的 frightened with false fire 完整的句子应该是"Is the King frightened with false fire?"。

③直接重复。**Lights, lights, lights!** 此处直接重复了三个 light 构成直接重复。

第四章 《哈姆雷特》辞格辨析

Would not this, sir, and a forest of feathers—if the rest of my fortunes turn Turk with me ① —with two provincial roses on my razed shoes, get me a fellowship in a cry of players, sir?

Horatio: Half a share.

Hamlet: A whole one, I!
For thou dost know, O Damon dear,
This realm dismantled was
Of Jove himself, and now reigns here
A very, very—pajock.

Horatio: You might have rhymed.

Hamlet: O good Horatio, I'll take the ghost's word for a thousand pound! Didst perceive?

Horatio: Very well, my lord.

Hamlet: Upon the talk of the poisoning?

Horatio: I did very well note him.

Hamlet: Aha! Come, some music! Come, the recorders!
For if the King like not the comedy,
Why then, belike he likes it not, perdie.
Come, some music!

[Enter Rosencrantz and Guildenstern.]

Guildenstern: Good my lord, vouchsafe me a word with you.

【辞格辨析】

①拟人和换说。If the rest of my fortunes turn **Turk** with me. 此处的 Turk（土耳其人，突厥人）指背叛基督教而改信伊斯兰教的人。此处 Hamlet 将 fortune（命运）拟人化，同时通过换说的辞格，表达了"如果命运叛变了我"的意思。

213

莎剧《哈姆雷特》辞格辨析与文体鉴赏

Hamlet: Sir, a whole history. ①
Guildenstern: The King, sir—
Hamlet: Ay, sir, what of him?
Guildenstern: —is in his retirement, marvellous distempered.
Hamlet: With drink, sir?
Guildenstern: No, my lord; rather with choler. ②
Hamlet: Your wisdom should show itself more richer to signify this to the doctor.

【辞格辨析】

①夸张。Sir, **a whole history**. Hamlet 听到 Guidenstern 要和他说话是,用夸张的手法,说他们可以和他谈整部历史。

②省略 (1)(2)(3) 和换义双关 (1)(2)。…is in his retirement marvellous **distempered**. /**With drink**, sir? /No, my lord; **rather with choler**. 此处有两处省略,即 with drink 和 rather with choler 两句都省略主谓部分,完整句子应该是 "The King is marvellous distempered with drink?" 和 "The King is marvellous distempered rather with choler." 此处的 distempered 和 choler 是两处双关。Distempered 可以理解为"发脾气",也可以理解为喝酒过多而生病,为一笔双叙双关;choler 可以理解为"生气,暴怒",也可以理解为因酗酒胆病发作。Guildenstern 在使用的时候,选取的是"生气,暴怒"的意思,Hamlet 在重复时,选取的是"酗酒胆病爆发"的意思,属于换义双关。在接下来的对话中,Hamlet 故意继续选取 distempered 和 choler 作"生气"和"发病"方面解读。

for me to put him to his purgation would perhaps plunge him into far more choler. ①

Guildenstern: Good my lord, put your discourse into some frame and start not so wildly from my affair. ②

Hamlet: I am tame, sir; pronounce.

Guildenstern: The Queen, your mother, in most great affliction of spirit hath sent me to you.

Hamlet: You are welcome.

Guildenstern: Nay, good my lord, this courtesy is not of the right breed. If it shall please you to make me a wholesome answer, I will do your mother's commandment. If not, your pardon and my return shall be the end of my business.

Hamlet: Sir, I cannot.

Guildenstern: What, my lord?

【辞格辨析】

①一笔双叙双关。...for me to put him to his **purgation** would perhaps plunge him into far more choler. 此处 purgation 是一笔双叙双关。Hamlet 故意将 Claudius 发脾气理解为酒后病发，使用 purgation 第一层意思理解为"通便"，以使身体舒服，第二层意思是"洗罪"，让他变得清白。Hamlet 表面上对 Guildenstern 说他过去见国王无法帮助他恢复健康，另一层意思表示无法帮他洗去罪行。

②隐喻。Good my lord, put your discourse **into some frame** ...Guildenstern 在这里将语言比喻为可以塑形的事物，让 Hamlet 不要说疯话，而是将语言说得更加"成形"一些，即更加明白一些。

莎剧《哈姆雷特》辞格辨析与文体鉴赏

Hamlet: Make you a wholesome answer; my wit's diseased. ① But, sir, such answer as I can make, you shall command. Or rather, as you say, my mother. Therefore no more, but to the matter! My mother, you say—

Rosencrantz: Then thus she says. Your behaviour hath struck her into amazement and admiration. ②

Hamlet: O wonderful son that can so 'stonish a mother! But is there no sequel at the heels of this mother's admiration? Impart.

Rosencrantz: She desires to speak with you in her closet ere you go to bed.

Hamlet: We shall obey, were she ten times our mother. Have you any further trade with us? ③

Rosencrantz: My lord, you once did love me.

Hamlet: And do still, by these pickers and stealers.

Rosencrantz: Good my lord, what is your cause of distemper? You do surely bar the door upon your own liberty, ④ if you deny your griefs to your friend.

【辞格辨析】

①拟人。Make you a wholesome answer; my **wit's diseased**. Hamlet 将自己的心智拟人化，将自己心智烦乱比喻为人生病。

②头韵。Then thus she says: your behaviour hath struck her into **amazement** and **admiration**. 此处的 amazement 和 admiration 构成一处头韵。

③隐喻。Have you any further **trade** with us? 此处 Hamlet 将 Guildenstern 和他的对话比喻为商品交易。

④隐喻。You do surely **bar the door** upon your own liberty. 此处将拒绝敞开心扉比喻为关闭了自由之门。

第四章 《哈姆雷特》辞格辨析

Hamlet: Sir, I lack advancement.

Rosencrantz: How can that be, when you have the voice of the King himself for your succession in Denmark? ①

Hamlet: Ay, sir, but 'while the grass grows'—the proverb is something musty.　　　　[Enter the Players with recorders.] O, the recorders! Let me see one. To withdraw with you—why do you go about to recover the wind of me, as if you would drive me into a toil? ②

Guildenstern: O my lord, if my duty be too bold, my love is too unmannerly.

Hamlet: I do not well understand that. Will you play upon this pipe?

Guildenstern: My lord, I cannot.

Hamlet: I pray you.

Guildenstern: Believe me, I cannot.

Hamlet: I do beseech you.

Guildenstern: I know, no touch of it, my lord.

【辞格辨析】

①借代。How can that be, when you have the **voice** of the king...此处用 voice（声音）来指代国王的许可。

②隐喻（Crystal, 2002: 498）。Why do you go about to **recover the wind of me**, as if you would drive me into a toil? 此处为包含打猎意象的隐喻，Hamlet 将 Guildenstern 和 Rosencrantz 旁敲侧击地打探他内心想法的行为，比喻为打猎过程，猎人通过站在风口让猎物闻到气息，引诱猎物为了躲避猎人而往猎人设定陷阱的反方向逃走。

莎剧《哈姆雷特》辞格辨析与文体鉴赏

Hamlet: It is as easy as lying. ① Govern these ventages with your fingers and thumbs, give it breath with your mouth, and it will discourse most eloquent music. Look you, these are the stops.

Guildenstern: But these cannot I command to any utterance of harmony. I have not the skill.

Hamlet: Why, look you now, how unworthy a thing you make of me! You would play upon me! You would seem to know my stops, you would pluck out the heart of my mystery, you would sound me from my lowest note to the top of my compass, and there is much music, excellent voice, in this little organ. Yet cannot you make it speak. ②

【辞格辨析】

①明喻。It is **as** easy **as** lying. 此处 Hamlet 将表演风琴比喻如说谎般容易,有讽刺的修辞效果。

②首语重复,隐喻(1)(2),一笔双叙双关(1)(2)(3)。**You would play** upon me;**you would seem** to know my stops;**you would pluck** out the heart of my mystery;**you would sound** me from my lowest note to the top of my compass…此处有较多的辞格。首先是由 you would 构成的首语重复(也可看作排比)辞格;其次是 the heart of my mystery 隐喻中,把秘密比喻为心脏,在 from my lowest note to the top of my compass 隐喻中,Hamlet 将两人对自己全方位的监视和询问比喻为从低音演奏至高音;最后是分别由 play,pluck 和 sound 三个词构成的三处一笔双叙双关。其中,play 可以理解为演奏乐器和玩弄人;pluck 可以理解为拨弄琴弦和掠夺财产;sound 可以理解为弹奏乐器,也可以理解为通过间接手段从某人身上找到想要的信息。

第四章 《哈姆雷特》辞格辨析

'Sblood, do you think I am easier to be played on than a pipe? Call me what instrument you will, though you can fret me, you cannot play upon me. ①

[Enter Polonius]

God bless you, sir!

Polonius: My lord, the Queen would speak with you, and presently.
Hamlet: Do you see yonder cloud that's almost in shape of a camel?
Polonius: By th' mass, and 'tis like a camel indeed.
Hamlet: Methinks it is like a weasel.
Polonius: It is backed like a weasel.
Hamlet: Or like a whale.
Polonius: Very like a whale.
Hamlet: Then will I come to my mother by-and-by. ——They fool me to the top of my bent. ② ——I will come by-and-by.
Polonius: I will say so.   [Exit.]
Hamlet: 'By-and-by' is easily said. ——Leave me, friends.

[Exeunt all but Hamlet]

'Tis now the very witching time of night,
When churchyards yawn, and hell itself breathes out

【辞格辨析】

①一笔双叙双关。Call me what instrument you will, though you can **fret** me, you cannot play upon me. 此处 Hamlet 借用 fret 的多义性,构成双关。表层上表示按住风琴的定音品,深层意思表示使人发怒和厌烦。

②隐喻。They fool me to the top of my **bent**. 此处 Hamlet 将自己的忍耐性比喻为一张弓,而他对众人的怒气,就如同一张被拉满的弓一般。

219

Contagion to this world. ① Now could I drink hot blood
And do such bitter business as the day
Would quake to look on. ② Soft! Now to my mother.
O heart, lose not thy nature; ③ let not ever
The soul of Nero enter this firm bosom.
Let me be cruel, not unnatural: ④
I will speak daggers to her, but use none. ⑤
My tongue and soul in this be hypocrites. ⑥

【辞格辨析】

①拟人（1）（2）。When churchyards **yawn**/and hell itself **breathes out**/contagion to this world. 此处将墓地和地狱分别赋予生命，能够作出 yawn（打呵欠）和 breath out（呼气）的动作。

②拟人。… as the day/would **quake to look on**. 此处 Hamlet 将 the day（白昼）比拟为人，会受到惊吓。

③拟人。O heart, lose not thy nature. 此处 Hamlet 将他的心赋予生命，拥有良善的本性。

④换说和弱陈。Let not ever/**the soul of Nero** enter this firm bosom./Let me be cruel, **not unnatural**: …此处 Hamlet 用 the soul of Nero 来指代暴力行为；另外，用 not 和 unnatural 表示强调，说明即使用残忍手段，也不要失去人性。

⑤隐喻。I will **speak daggers** to her, but use none. 此处 Hamlet 将使人伤心的语言比喻刀子，能刺痛人心。

⑥拟人。My **tongue** and **soul** in this be **hypocrites**. 此处 Hamlet 将 tongue（语言）和 soul（灵魂）比为伪君子，表示他会故意言不由衷。

How in my words somever she be shent

To give them seals never my soul consent. ①

[Exit.]

Act III, Scene 3

A room in the Castle. Enter King, Rosencrantz, and Guildenstern.

Claudius: I like him not, nor stands it safe with us

To let his madness range. Therefore prepare you.

I your commission will forthwith dispatch

And he to England shall along with you. ②

The terms of our estate may not endure

Hazard so near us as doth hourly grow

Out of his lunacies.

Guildenstern: We will ourselves provide.

Most holy and religious fear it is

To keep those many many bodies safe

That live and feed upon your Majesty.

【辞格辨析】

①尾韵。How in my words somever she be **shent**, /To give them seals never, my soul, **consent**. 此处的 shent 和 consent 构成尾韵，意味着这部分的结束。

②省略（Corbett & Connors, 1999: 386）。... and **he to England** shall along with you. 此处的 he to England 省略了动词，完整表述应该为"He shall go to England along with you."。

221

■ 莎剧《哈姆雷特》辞格辨析与文体鉴赏

Rosencrantz: The single and peculiar life is bound
With all the strength and armour of the mind
To keep itself from noyance; but much more
That spirit upon whose weal depends and rests
The lives of many. The cesse of majesty
Dies not alone, but like a gulf doth draw ①
What's near it with it. It is a massy wheel ②
Fixed on the summit of the highest mount,
To whose huge spokes ten thousand lesser things
Are mortised and adjoined; which when it falls,
Each small annexment, petty consequence,
Attends the boisterous ruin. Never alone
Did the king sigh but with a general groan.
Claudius: Arm you, I pray you, to this speedy voyage
For we will fetters put upon this fear,
Which now goes too free-footed. ③

【辞格辨析】

①明喻。… but **like** a gulf …此处 Rosencrantz 将国王的去世比喻为漩涡，能够吞没周围的事物。

②隐喻。**It is a massy wheel**, …此处 Rosencrantz 将国王比喻为位于高山顶端的轮子，国王遇险就如同轮子滚下山坡，给轮子的各种部件带来重大的伤害。

③拟人和头韵。…for we will **fetters** put upon this **fear**, / which now goes too **free-footed**. 此处将 fear（恐惧）比喻为放任自由的主体，表示危险不受控制。另外，fetters, fear, free-footed 等词也构成头韵。

第四章 《哈姆雷特》辞格辨析

Rosencrantz：[with Guildenstern] We will haste us.
[Exeunt Gentlemen. Enter Polonius.]
Polonius：My lord, he's going to his mother's closet.
Behind the arras I'll convey myself
To hear the process. I'll warrant she'll tax him home
And, as you said, and wisely was it said,
'Tis meet that some more audience than a mother
(Since nature makes them partial) should o'erhear
The speech of vantage. Fare you well, my liege.
I'll call upon you ere you go to bed
And tell you what I know.
Claudius： Thanks, dear my lord.
[Exit Polonius.]
O, my offence is rank, it smells to heaven；①
It hath the primal eldest curse upon't,
A brother's murther. ② Pray can I not：
Though inclination be as sharp as will.
My stronger guilt defeats my strong intent ③

【辞格辨析】

①隐喻。O, my offence is **rank**, it smells to heaven；…这里 Claudius 将自己的 offence（罪行）比喻为四处漫长的植物。

②同位语。It hath the primal eldest curse upon't, **a brother's murder**！这里的 a brother's murder 和 the primal eldest curse 构成同位语，起到补充说明的作用。

③拟人。My stronger guilt **defeats** my strong intent, …这里 Claudius 将 guilt（罪恶）和 intent（意图）赋予生命，其中罪恶打败了他祈祷的意图。

223

莎剧《哈姆雷特》辞格辨析与文体鉴赏

And, like a man to double business bound
I stand in pause where I shall first begin
And both neglect. What if this cursed hand
Were thicker than itself with brother's blood?
Is there not rain enough in the sweet heavens
To wash it white as snow? ① Whereto serves mercy
But to confront the visage of offence?
And what's in prayer but this twofold force,
To be forestalled ere we come to fall
Or pardoned being down? Then I'll look up:
My fault is past. But, O, what form of prayer
Can serve my turn? 'Forgive me my foul murther'?
That cannot be, since I am still possessed
Of those effects for which I did the murther—
My crown, mine own ambition, and my Queen. ②
May one be pardon'd and retain th' offence?
In the corrupted currents of this world

【辞格辨析】

①明喻。Is there not rain enough in the sweet heavens/to wash it **white as snow**? 这里 Claudius 将洗去罪行后的清白比喻为如雪般洁白。

②同位语。Of those effects ... /**my crown, mine own ambition, and my Queen.** 这里的 my crown, mine own ambition, and my Queen 是前文 of those effects 的同位语，起到补充说明的作用。

Offence's gilded hand may shove by justice,
And oft 'tis seen the wicked prize itself
Buys out the law; ① but 'tis not so above:
There is no shuffling, there the action lies
In his true nature, and we ourselves compelled,
Even to the teeth and forehead of our faults,
To give in evidence. ② What then? What rests?
Try what repentance can. What can it not?
Yet what can it when one cannot repent?

【辞格辨析】

①隐喻（1）（2），拟人（1）（2）和谐音双关。In **the corrupted currents of this world**/offence's **gilded hand** may shove by justice,/and oft 'tis seen the wicked prize itself/**buys out the law**;……这一句有多处辞格。首先是两处隐喻，句中 the corrupted currents of this world 将一种腐败的作风比喻为洪流，buys out the law 则将法律比喻股票，能够被买卖；其次是两处拟人辞格，即将罪行和战利品比拟为具有生命的主体，拥有 hand（手），能够 shove（推动）公正，也能够 buy out（买断）法律的股份；最后还有一处双关辞格，即 gilded 和 guilty 构成谐音双关，一方面表示涂上金粉，另一方面表示罪恶的。

②隐喻（Thomson & Taylor, 2007：330）。We ourselves compelled,/even to **the teeth and forehead of our faults**,/to give in evidence. 此处将直面罪恶比喻为直接面对罪恶的牙齿和额头。

■ 莎剧《哈姆雷特》辞格辨析与文体鉴赏

O wretched state! O bosom black as death, ①
O limed soul, that, struggling to be free
Art more engaged! ② Help, angels! Make assay.
Bow, stubborn knees, and heart with strings of steel
Be soft as sinews of the new-born babe! ③
All may be well.   [Enter Hamlet.]
Hamlet: Now might I do it pat, now he is praying.
And now I'll do't. ④ And so he goes to heaven,
And so am I revenged. That would be scanned.

【辞格辨析】

①明喻。O bosom black **as** death, …此处将内心的黑暗和死亡相比。

②隐喻。O, **limed soul**, that, struggling to be free/art more engaged. 此处 Claudius 将自己的无法静心祷告的灵魂，比喻为被粘住的动物，越想挣脱，被粘得越紧。

③隐喻（Wilson, 2009：262）拟人和明喻。Help, angels! Make **assay**. /Bow, **stubborn knees**; and heart with strings of steel, /be **soft as sinews of the new-born babe!** 此处有三处辞格。第一处为 assay，为来自投球游戏（如保龄球）的动作意象，指球通过弧线射中目标；第二处是将 knees（双膝）拟人化，将不愿跪下祈祷比拟为性格固执的人；第三为明喻，将内心温顺的状态比喻为婴儿的筋骨一般柔软。

④普通重复。**Now** might I do it pat, **now** he is praying; /And **now** I'll do't. 此处重复的三个 now 构成普通重复辞格，强调"当下"的意思。

A villain kills my father, and for that
I, his sole son, do this same villain send
To heaven. ①
Why, this is hire and salary, not revenge.
He took my father grossly, full of bread
With all his crimes broad blown, as flush as May, ②
And how his audit stands who knows, save heaven? ③
But in our circumstance and course of thought
'Tis heavy with him; and am I then revenged
To take him in the purging of his soul
When he is fit and seasoned for his passage?
No.
Up, sword, and know thou a more horrid hent ④
When he is drunk, asleep or in his rage,

【辞格辨析】

①同位语。I, **his sole son**, do this same villain send/to heaven. 此处 his sole son 为 I 的同位语，有补充说明的作用。

②明喻。…with all his crimes broad blown, **as flush as** May. 此处 Hamlet 将一个人死前没有祷告，罪恶深重地去世比喻为五月繁茂的花朵。

③隐喻。… and how his **audit** stands, who knows save heaven? 此处 Hamlet 将还没有清算的罪恶（即没有在死前通过祈祷得到饶恕的罪行），比为账本上的账目。

④拟人。Up, sword, and **know** thou a more horrid hent…此处 Hamlet 将他的剑赋予生命，能够对情况作出判断。

Or in th' incestuous pleasure of his bed, ①
At gaming, swearing, or about some act
That has no relish of salvation in't—
Then trip him, that his heels may kick at heaven
And that his soul may be as damn'd and black
As hell, whereto it goes. My mother stays;
This physic but prolongs thy sickly days. ②　　　[Exit.]
Claudius:[rises] My words fly up, my thoughts remain below.
Words without thoughts never to heaven go. ③　　　[Exit.]

Act III, Scene 4
The Queen's closet. Enter Queen and Polonius.

【辞格辨析】

①排比和对仗。…when he is drunk asleep, **or in** his rage, / **Or in** th' incestuous pleasure of his bed, …此句由三处结构相似的短语，构成排比辞格。

②隐喻。…this **physic** but prolongs thy sickly days. Hamlet 在这里将 Claudius 的祈祷比喻为治疗生病躯体的药物。

③隐喻，对仗和尾韵。My words **fly up**, my thoughts remain **below**. /words without thoughts never to heaven **go**. 这句话有三种辞格：第一种是隐喻，Claudius 将自己无法静下来祈祷的状态比喻为语言飘起来但思想却沉下来；第二处为对仗，句子的平行结构，up 与 below 等语义相对的词语构成对比；第三处，below 和 go 构成尾韵，表示这部分的结束。

Polonius: He will come straight. Look you lay home to him. Tell him his pranks have been too broad to bear with, and that your Grace hath screened and stood between much heat and him. ① I'll silence me even here. Pray you be round.

Hamlet: [within] Mother, mother, mother! ②

Gertrude: I'll warrant you, fear me not. Withdraw, I hear him coming.

[Polonius hides behind the arras. Enter Hamlet.]

Hamlet: Now, mother, what's the matter?

Gertrude: Hamlet, thou hast thy father much offended.

Hamlet: Mother, you have my father much offended. ③

Gertrude: Come, come, you answer with an idle tongue.

【辞格辨析】

①隐喻（Thomson & Taylor, 2007: 334）和头韵。…that your grace hath **screened** and **stood** between much heat and him. 此处，Polonius 将 Gertrude 介于 Hamlet 和 Claudius 中间的状况，比喻为如同一个屏风将两者隔开；第二处辞格为由 screened 和 stood 构成的头韵辞格。

②直接重复。**Mother, mother, mother!** 此处三个 mother 构成直接重复辞格。

③换义双关。Hamlet, thou hast thy father much **offended**. / Mother, you have my father much **offended**. 此处为 offended 构成的换义双关。Gertrude 使用 offended 用的是"伤害感情"的意思，Hamlet 重复使用该词，但取"冒犯"的意思。

莎剧《哈姆雷特》辞格辨析与文体鉴赏

Hamlet: Go, go, you question with a wicked tongue. ①
Gertrude: Why, how now, Hamlet?
Hamlet: What's the matter now?
Gertrude: Have you forgot me?
Hamlet: No, by the rood, not so!
You are the Queen, your husband's brother's wife,
And (would it were not so!) you are my mother. ②
Gertrude: Nay, then I'll set those to you that can speak.
Hamlet: Come, come, and sit you down. You shall not budge.
You go not till I set you up a glass
Where you may see the inmost part of you.
Gertrude: What wilt thou do? Thou wilt not murther me?
Help, help, ho!
Polonius: [behind]   What, ho! help, help, help!

【辞格辨析】

①直接重复（1）（2）和对仗。**Come, come**, you answer with an idle tongue. /**Go, go**, you question with a wicked tongue. 此处 come 和 go 构成两处直接重复辞格；此外，这两句话通过使用相同的句法，也构成了对仗辞格。

②同位语和插说。You are the queen, **your husband's brother's wife**. /And (**would it were not so!**) you are my mother. 此句有两处辞格，第一处 your husband's brother's wife 作为 the queen 的同位语；第二处 would it were not so 作为插入语，表示补充说明。

Hamlet: How now? A rat! Dead for a ducat, dead!

[Makes a pass through the arras and kills Polonius.]

Polonius: [behind] O, I am slain!

Gertrude: O me, what hast thou done?

Hamlet: Nay, I know not. Is it the King?

Gertrude: O, what a rash and bloody deed is this!

Hamlet: A bloody deed—almost as bad, good mother,
As kill a king, and marry with his brother.

Gertrude: As kill a king? ①

Hamlet: Ay, lady, it was my word.

[Lifts up the arras and sees Polonius]

Thou wretched, rash, intruding fool, farewell! ②

I took thee for thy better. Take thy fortune.

Thou find'st to be too busy is some danger.

Leave wringing of your hands. Peace! Sit you down

And let me wring your heart. ③ For so I shall

【辞格辨析】

①省略。A bloody deed—almost as bad, goodmother, /as kill a king, and marry with his brother. /**As kill a king**？此处 Gertrude 说出的 as kill a king 为 a bloody deed as bad as kill a king 的省略，此处上下文突出了对话过程中，这一处信息对 Gertrude 的触动。

②排比。Thou **wretched**, **rash**, **intruding** fool, farewell! 此处三个形容词构成排比辞格。

③隐喻。And let me **wring** your heart. 此处 Hamlet 将质问 Gertrude 的过程比喻为拧干衣物的动作。

If it be made of penetrable stuff,
If damned custom have not brazed it so ①
That it is proof and bulwark against sense.
Gertrude: What have I done that thou dar'st wag thy tongue
In noise so rude against me? ②
Hamlet:　　　　　　　Such an act
That blurs the grace and blush of modesty;
Calls virtue hypocrite, ③ takes off the rose
From the fair forehead of an innocent love
And sets a blister there, ④ makes marriage vows

【辞格辨析】

①首语重复和拟人（Thompson，1987：106）。**If** it be made of penetrable stuff, /**if** damned **custom** have not brazed it so …此处有两种辞格：第一种为两个 if 构成的首语重复；第二处为将 custom（习惯）拟人化，赋予它能够给心灵镶上铜，以让心灵失去知觉。

②借代（1）（2）。What have I done that thou dar'st **wag thy tongue**/in **noise** so rude against me? 此处有两处借代辞格：第一处为使用 wag thy tongue（摇动舌头）这一动作指代说话；第二处为使用 noise 指代他说出来的话。

③拟人（1）（2）。… that blurs the grace and blush of **modesty**; /calls **virtue** hypocrite, …此处将 modesty（谦逊）和 virtue（美德）拟人化，分别会因为 Gertrude 的所作所为脸红或者变成伪君子。

④隐喻。And **sets a blister there**, …此处将 Gertrude 的不贞行为比喻为长在额头的水疱。

As false as dicers' oaths. ① O, such a deed
As from the body of contraction plucks
The very soul, and sweet religion makes
A rhapsody of words! Heaven's face doth glow
O'er, this solidity and compound mass
With tristful visage, as against the doom,
Is thought-sick at the act. ②
Gertrude: Ah me, what act,
That roars so loud and thunders in the index? ③
Hamlet: Look here upon th's picture, and on this,

【辞格辨析】

①排比和明喻。Such an act/that **blurs** ... /**calls** ...; **takes off** ... /... /and **sets a blister** there; **makes** marriage vows/**as false as dicers' oaths**. 此处由 blur、call、take off、set 和 make 构成动宾结构的排比辞格；此外，as false as dicers' oaths 中将不被遵守的婚誓比喻为赌徒的誓言。

②拟人和换说。**Heaven's face** doth glow; /Yea, **this solidity and compound mass**, /... /**is thought-sick** at the act. 此处第一处将 heaven（上天）比拟为人，因 Gertrude 的行为而变得脸色苍白；第二处是换说辞格，即用 this solidity and compound mass 指代 the heaven。

③隐喻（1）（2）。What act, /that **roars so loud and thunders in the index**? 这句话有两处隐喻，第一处是将责备比喻为会发出如雷响声的事物；第二处是将 Hamlet 还没有切入主题之前的这些语言，比喻为书的 index（前言）。

233

莎剧《哈姆雷特》辞格辨析与文体鉴赏

The counterfeit presentment of two brothers:
See what a grace was seated on this brow,
Hyperion's curls, the front of Jove himself, ①
An eye like Mars to threaten and command,
A station like the herald Mercury
New lighted on a heaven-kissing hill, ②
A combination and a form indeed
Where every god did seem to set his seal
To give the world assurance of a man.
This was your husband. Look you now what follows:
Here is your husband, like a mildewed ear
Blasting his wholesome brother. ③ Have you eyes?

【辞格辨析】

①拟人和换说（1）（2）。See what a grace was **seated** on this brow;/**Hyperion's curls**;the **front of Jove** himself;/an eye like Mars, to threaten and command,……此处将 grace（魅力）赋予生命，能够做出 seated（坐下）的动作；第二、第三处分别为换说，即用 Hyperion's curls（太阳神之父许珀里翁）和 front of Jove（朱庇特神）分别指代老王的头发和额头，从侧面衬托他的长相帅气伟岸。

②拟人。A station like the herald Mercury/new lighted on **a heaven-kissing** hill. 此处将 hill（山）赋予生命，将其高耸入云比喻为吻到上天。

③明喻。Here is your husband, **like a mildewed ear**/blasting his wholesome brother. 此处 Hamlet 将 Claudius 的模样比喻为得了霉病的玉米穗。

Could you on this fair mountain leave to feed
And batten on this moor? Ha! Have you eyes? ①
You cannot call it love for at your age
The heyday in the blood is tame, it's humble ②
And waits upon the judgment, and what judgment
Would step from this to this? ③ Sense sure you have,
Else could you not have motion; but sure that sense
Is apoplexed; ④ for madness would not err
Nor sense to ecstacy was ne'er so thralled
But it reserved some quantity of choice
To serve in such a difference. What devil was't

【辞格辨析】

①间隔重复和隐喻。**Have you eyes**?/Could you on **this fair mountain** leave to feed,/and batten on **this moor**? Ha! **Have you eyes**? 此处的 have you eyes 构成间隔重复；此外 Hamlet 将 Gertrude 离开帅气伟岸的先王，嫁给 Claudius 的行为，比喻为离开俊美的高山到荒野中觅食，属于隐喻辞格。

②换说。For at your age/the heyday in the blood is tame, it's humble…此处用 heyday in the blood（血液的兴盛期）指代性欲，为换说辞格。

③间隔重复。and waits upon the **judgement**; and what **judgement**/would step from this to this? 此外，两处 judgement 则构成间隔重复辞格。

④隐喻。but sure that sense/is **apoplexed**…此处将不理智的行为比喻为中风得病。

That thus hath cozened you at hoodman-blind?
Eyes without feeling, feeling without sight,
Ears without hands or eyes, smelling sans all,
Or but a sickly part of one true sense
Could not so mope. ①
O shame! where is thy blush?
Rebellious hell,
If thou canst mutine in a matron's bones
To flaming youth let virtue be as wax
And melt in her own fire; ② Proclaim no shame
When the compulsive ardour gives the charge,
Since frost itself as actively doth burn
And reason panders will. ③

【辞格辨析】

①排比和链形重复。Eyes **without feeling, feeling without** sight, /ears **without** hands or eyes, smelling sans all …此处三处"…without…"的名词短语构成排比结构；另外，eyes without feeling, feeling without sight 又构成链形重复。

②拟人，隐喻和明喻。**Rebellious hell,** /if thou canst **mutine** in a matron's bones/to **flaming youth** let virtue **be as wax**/ and melt in her own fire. 此处赋予 hell（地狱）以作出叛变的能力，为拟人；将 youth（青春）比喻为着了火一般充满激情，为隐喻；将火热青春的自我消磨比喻为蜡在火中熔化，为明喻。

③换说和拟人。Since **frost** itself as actively doth burn, /and **reason panders will**. 此处的 frost 指代上了年纪的人；另外，Hamlet 也将 reason（理性）拟人化，使其能做出拉皮条的事情。

第四章 《哈姆雷特》辞格辨析

Gertrude: O Hamlet, speak no more!
Thou turn'st mine eyes into my very soul
And there I see such black and grained spots
As will not leave their tinct. ①
Hamlet: Nay, but to live
In the rank sweat of an enseamed bed
Stewed in corruption, honeying and making love
Over the nasty sty! ②
Gertrude: O, speak to me no more!
These words like daggers enter in mine ears. ③
No more, sweet Hamlet!
Hamlet: A murtherer and a villain!
A slave that is not twentieth part the kith
Of your precedent lord, a vice of kings,
A cutpurse of the empire and the rule,

【辞格辨析】

①隐喻。…and there I see such **black and grained spots**/as will not leave their **tinct**. 此处 Gertrude 将自己意识到的缺点比喻为在灵魂中留下痕迹的黑点。有学者认为，句中的 grained 和 tinct 是来自染坊工业的术语，而下文的 enseamed 和 nasty sty 也为这些术语的延伸（Wilson, 2009: xxxviii）。

②隐喻。…stewed in corruption, honeying and making love/over **the nasty sty**! 此处 Hamlet 将乱伦之床比喻为肮脏的猪圈。

③明喻。These words **like** daggers enter in mine ears. Gertrude 将刺痛她内心的话语比喻为短刀。

That from a shelf the precious diadem stole

And put it in his pocket! ①

Gertrude:　　　　No more!

　　　　　　　　[Enter the Ghost in his nightgown.]

Hamlet:　　　　A king of shreds and patches! ——

Save me and hover o'er me with your wings,

You heavenly guards! What would your gracious figure?

Gertrude: Alas, he's mad!

Hamlet: Do you not come your tardy son to chide,

That, lapsed in time and passion, lets go by

Th' important acting of your dread command?

O, say!

Father's Ghost:　　　Do not forget. This visitation

Is but to whet thy almost blunted purpose. ②

But look, amazement on thy mother sits! ③

O, step between her and her fighting soul

【辞格辨析】

①排比和隐喻。**A murtherer** and **a villain**! /**A slave** that …/…**a vice of kings**;/**a cutpurse of the empire and the rule** …此处五个用来指代 Claudius 的名词构成排比；此外，a cutpurse of the empire 则是隐喻辞格，将篡位者比喻为小偷。

②隐喻。…is but to **whet** thy almost **blunted purpose**. 此处鬼魂将决心比喻为刀，而他这次的到来，就是为了使因 Hamlet 的延误而变钝的刀再次锋利起来。

③拟人。But look, amazement on thy mother **sits**! 将 Gertrude 的一脸惊愕比拟为惊愕坐在她脸上。

Conceit in weakest bodies strongest works. ①

Speak to her, Hamlet.

Hamlet: How is it with you, lady?

Gertrude: Alas, how is't with you,

That you do bend your eye on vacancy

And with th' encorporal air do hold discourse?

Forth at your eyes your spirits wildly peep, ②

And, as the sleeping soldiers in th' alarm

Your bedded hairs, like life in excrements

Start up and stand an end. ③ O gentle son,

Upon the heat and flame of thy distemper

Sprinkle cool patience! Whereon do you look?

Hamlet: On him, on him! ④ Look you how pale he glares!

【辞格辨析】

①拟人。O, step between her and her **fighting soul**/Conceit in weakest bodies strongest works. 此处将灵魂拟人化,将惊愕的心理比拟为灵魂用残弱的身躯做辛苦的工作。

②隐喻(Thomson & Taylor, 2007:346)。Forth at your eyes **your spirits wildly peep**. 此处 Gertrude 将 Hamlet 睁大眼睛比喻为他的灵魂在偷窥。

③明喻(1)(2)。And, **as the sleeping soldiers in th' alarm**, /your bedded hairs, **like life in excrements**, /start up and stand an end. 此处有两处明喻:第一处为将竖立起来的头发比喻为听到警报后站立起来的士兵;第二处为将竖立起来的头发比喻为生长在粪土中的茂盛直挺的花草。

④直接重复。**On him, on him!** 此处为直接重复。

His form and cause conjoined preaching to stones

Would make them capable. —Do not look upon me,

Lest with this piteous action you convert

My stern effects. Then what I have to do

Will want true colour—tears perchance for blood.

Gertrude: To whom do you speak this?

Hamlet: Do you see nothing there?

Gertrude: Nothing at all, yet all that is I see.

Hamlet: Nor did you nothing hear?

Gertrude: No, nothing but ourselves.

Hamlet: Why, look you there! Look how it steals away!

My father, in his habit as he lived!

Look where he goes even now out at the portal! [Exit Ghost.]

Gertrude: This is the very coinage of your brain.

This bodiless creation ecstasy

Is very cunning in. ①

Hamlet: Ecstasy?

My pulse as yours doth temperately keep time

And makes as healthful music. ② It is not madness

【辞格辨析】

①拟人。**This bodiless creation ecstasy**/is very cunning in. 此处 Gertrude 将癫狂比拟为一个狡猾的人,能够使人做出反常的行为。

②隐喻。My pulse as yours doth temperately keep time/and **makes as healthful music.** 此处将脉搏的规律跳动比喻为奏出音乐。

That I have uttered. Bring me to the test
And I the matter will reword, which madness
Would gambol from. Mother, for love of grace
Lay not that flattering unction to your soul
That not your trespass but my madness speaks.
It will but skin and film the ulcerous place
Whiles rank corruption mining all within
Infects unseen. ① Confess yourself to heaven,
Repent what's past; avoid what is to come,
And do not spread the compost on the weeds
To make them ranker. ② Forgive me this my virtue,
For in the fatness of these pursy times

【辞格辨析】

①隐喻。Lay not that flattering **unction** to your soul/... /It will but **skin and film the ulcerous place**,/whiles **rank** corruption, mining all within,/**infects** unseen. 此处 Hamlet 将 Gertrude 的乱伦罪行比喻为给溃烂的伤口，将她以他发疯为自己的乱伦罪行开脱比喻为伤口涂上膏油，虽然能在皮肤表层产生结痂，但底部仍然溃烂不堪。

②排比和隐喻。**Confess** yourself to heaven;/**repent** what's past;**avoid** what is to come;/and do **not spread the compost over the weeds**/to make them **ranker**. 此处有两处辞格：第一处为由 confess, repent, avoid, spread 的动词短语构成排比；第二处为将任由罪行泛滥比喻为往野草上泼洒肥料，任其疯狂生长。

莎剧《哈姆雷特》辞格辨析与文体鉴赏

Virtue itself of Vice must pardon beg— ①
Yea, curb and woo for leave to do him good.
Gertrude: O Hamlet, thou hast cleft my heart in twain. ②
Hamlet: O, throw away the worser part of it
And live the purer with the other half.
Good night—but go not to my uncle's bed;
Assume a virtue, if you have it not. ③
That monster Custom, who all sense doth eat
Of habits evil, is angel yet in this,
That to the use of actions fair and good
He likewise gives a frock or livery
That aptly is put on. ④ Refrain tonight

【辞格辨析】

①借代和拟人。…for in the **fatness** of these **pursy times**/virtue itself of vice must **pardon beg**—/…此处用 fatness of purse（膨胀的钱包）来指代唯利是图的时代，为借代辞格；此外，也将 virtue（美德）和 vice（罪恶）拟人化，指出在这样的时代中，美德仍要向罪恶妥协。

②隐喻。O Hamlet, thou hast **cleft my heart in twain**. 此处 Gertrude 将让她伤心比喻为她的心被切成两半。

③隐喻（Thomson & Taylor, 2007: 349）。… **assume** a virtue, if you have it not. 此处用了穿衣的意象，Hamlet 要求 Gertrude 即使没有美德，也应假装穿上一件美德的外衣。

④拟人。That **monster Custom**, who all sense doth eat…此处将 Custom（习惯）比拟能够 eat（吞噬）和嘉奖一些好的做法的主体，即要 Gertrude 习惯远离 Claudius 的生活。

第四章 《哈姆雷特》辞格辨析

And that shall lend a kind of easiness
To the next abstinence, the next more easy.
For use almost can change the stamp of nature
And either [master] the devil, or throw him out
With wondrous potency. Once more, good night,
And when you are desirous to be blest,
I'll blessing beg of you. —For this same lord
I do repent, but heaven hath pleas'd it so
To punish me with this, and this with me, ①
That I must be their scourge and minister.
I will bestow him, and will answer well
The death I gave him. So again, good night.
I must be cruel only to be kind; ②
Thus bad begins and worse remains behind.
One word more, good lady.

Gertrude: What shall I do?
Hamlet: Not this, by no means, that I bid you do:
Let the bloat King tempt you again to bed,
Pinch wanton on your cheek, call you his mouse,
And let him for a pair of reechy kisses,

【辞格辨析】

①回环重复。…but heaven hath pleas'd it so/to **punish me with this, and this with me**. 此处为回环重复。

②对仗。I must be **cruel** only to be **kind**. 此处的 cruel（残忍）和 kind（善良）构成对比，该句使用对仗辞格。

莎剧《哈姆雷特》辞格辨析与文体鉴赏

Or paddling in your neck with his damn'd fingers,
Make you to ravel all this matter out
That I essentially am not in madness
But mad in craft. ① 'Twere good you let him know,
For who that's but a queen, fair, sober, wise,
Would from a paddock, from a bat, a gib
Such dear concernings hide? ② Who would do so?
No, in despite of sense and secrecy,
Unpeg the basket on the house's top,
Let the birds fly, and like the famous ape
To try conclusions, in the basket creep
And break your own neck down.
Gertrude: Be thou assured, if words be made of breath
And breath of life, I have no life to breathe
What thou hast said to me. ③

【辞格辨析】

①排比。**Let** the bloat King **tempt** …, /**pinch** …; **call** …; /and **let** … /… /**make** … 此处为两个 let 和四个动词，tempt, pinch, call 和 make 构成的排比辞格。

②隐喻。…would from **a paddock, form a bat, a gib**/such dear concernings hide? Hamlet 在这句话中将 Claudius 比喻为 paddock（蟾蜍），bat（蝙蝠）和 gib（夜猫）。

③同根异形重复。If words be made of **breath**/And **breath** of life, I have no life to **breathe**/what thou hast said to me. 此处的 breathe 和 breath 构成了同根异形重复。

第四章 《哈姆雷特》辞格辨析

Hamlet: I must to England—you know that.
Gertrude: Alack,
I had forgot! 'Tis so concluded on.
Hamlet: There's letters sealed and my two schoolfellows,
Whom I will trust as I will adders fanged, ①
They bear the mandate, they must sweep my way
And marshal me to knavery. ② Let it work.
For 'tis the sport to have the enginer
Hoist with his own petard, and 't shall go hard
But I will delve one yard below their mines
And blow them at the moon. O, 'tis most sweet
When in one line two crafts directly meet. ③
This man shall set me packing;
I'll lug the guts into the neighbour room. —
Mother, good night indeed. This counsellor

【辞格辨析】

①明喻。Whom I will trust **as** I will adders fanged, …此处 Hamlet 将自己不信任两个旧日好友与不信任毒蛇相比。

②隐喻（Thomson & Taylor, 2007: 353）。…they must sweep my way/and **marshal** me to knavery. 此处 Hamlet 将两个好友准备陪同他到英国比喻为军事上的集结，准备战斗。

③一笔双叙双关（Jenkins, 1982: 332; Spencer, 1980: 302-303）。O, 'tis most sweet/when in one line two **crafts** directly meet. 此处 crafts 指"狡诈的密谋"; crafts 又同时可以指"船"，构成一笔双叙双关。

Is now most still, most secret and most grave, ①
Who was in life a foolish peating knave.
Come, sir, to draw toward an end with you.
Good night, mother.

[Exit the Queen, then exit Hamlet, tugging in Polonius.]

第四幕

Act IV, Scene 1

Elsinore. A room in the Castle.
Enter King and Queen, with Rosencrantz and Guildenstern.

Claudius: There's matter in these sighs, these profound heaves.
You must translate; 'tis fit we understand them.
Where is your son?
Gertrude: Bestow this place on us a little while.

[Exeunt Rosencrantz and Guildenstern]

Ah, mine own lord, what have I seen tonight!
Claudius: What, Gertrude? How does Hamlet?
Gertrude: Mad as the sea and wind when both contend

【辞格辨析】

①排比。This counsellor/is now **most still**, **most secret**, and **most grave**…此处三个形容词构成排比辞格。

Which is the mightier. ① In his lawless fit
Behind the arras hearing something stir,
Whips out his rapier, cries 'A rat, a rat!' ②
And in this brainish apprehension kills
The unseen good old man.

Claudius:　　　　　　　O heavy deed!
It had been so with us, had we been there.
His liberty is full of threats to all,
To you yourself, to us, to every one. ③
Alas, how shall this bloody deed be answered?
It will be laid to us, whose providence
Should have kept short, restrained, and out of haunt
This mad young man. ④ But so much was our love,

【辞格辨析】

①省略和拟人。Mad as **the sea and wind** when both **contend**/which is the mightier. 此处省略句子开头的主谓语，完整应该是"Hamlet is as mad as …"。此外此句也将 sea（大海）和 wind（风）比拟为有生命的主体，两者在斗争。

②省略（Thomson & Taylor, 2007: 356）。… behind the arras hearing something stir, /**whips out his rapier**, cries 'A rat, a rat!' 此处省略了主语 Hamlet。

③排比。His liberty is full of threats **to all**/ **to you yourself**, **to us**, **to everyone**. 此处由四处 to…构成排比辞格。

④排比。It will be laid to us, whose providence/should have kept **short**, **restrained**, **and out of haunt**/this mad young man. 此处由三处形容词和形容词短语，构成排比辞格。

莎剧《哈姆雷特》辞格辨析与文体鉴赏

We would not understand what was most fit,
But like the owner of a foul disease,
To keep it from divulging, let it feed
Even on the pith of life. ① Where is he gone?
Gertrude: To draw apart the body he hath killed; ②
O'er whom—his very madness like some ore
Among a mineral of metals base
Shows itself pure. —He weeps for what is done. ③
Claudius: O Gertrude, come away.
The sun no sooner shall the mountains touch
But we will ship him hence, ④ and this vile deed

【辞格辨析】

①明喻（Thomson & Taylor, 2007: 356）。...but, **like the owner of a foul disease**, /to keep it from divulging, let it feed/ even on the pith of life. 此处 Claudius 将掩盖杀人的行为比喻为患有隐疾的人为了掩饰病情，让病情在底下疯长。

②省略。To draw apart the body he hath kill'd. 此处省略了主语，应为"Hamlet has gone to draw apart the body he hath killed";...

③明喻。...o'er whom his very madness, **like some ore/ among a mineral of metals base**, /shows itself pure. 此处 Gertrude 将 Hamlet 为自己杀死 Polonius 而哭泣比喻为矿区中的宝贵的矿石一般，展现出他纯洁的一面。

④拟人。**The sun** no sooner shall the mountains **touch**...Claudius 此处将 sun（太阳）升上山头比拟为有生命的太阳触碰了山头。

第四章 《哈姆雷特》辞格辨析

We must with all our majesty and skill
Both countenance and excuse. Ho, Guildenstern!
　　　　　　　　　　［Enter Rosencrantz and Guildenstern］
Friends both, go join you with some further aid.
Hamlet in madness hath Polonius slain
And from his mother's closet hath he dragged him.
Go seek him out, speak fair and bring the body
Into the chapel. I pray you haste in this.
　　　　　　　　　［Exeunt Rosencrantz and Guildenstern］
Come, Gertrude, we'll call up our wisest friends
And let them know both what we mean to do
And what's untimely done. ［So haply slander—］
Whose whisper o'er the world's diameter,
As level as the cannon to his blank,
Transports his poisoned shot—may miss our name
And hit the woundless air. ① O, come away,
My soul is full of discord and dismay. ②　　　　［Exeunt.］

【辞格辨析】

① 换说和明喻。Whose **whisper o'er the world's diameter**, /**as level as the cannon to his blank**, /... 此处 Claudius 用 whisper o'er the world's diameter 指代社会舆论，为换说；他也将引导社会舆论引导到不伤害他和 Gertrude 的名声比喻为炮弹没有命中目标。

② 头韵和尾韵。O, come **away**! /My soul is full of **discord** and **dismay**. 此处的 discord 和 dismay 构成头韵；away 和 dismay 构成尾韵，预示本场结束。

Act IV, Scene 2

Elsinore. A passage in the Castle. Enter Hamlet.

Hamlet: Safely stowed.
Gentlemen: [within] Hamlet! Lord Hamlet!
Hamlet: But soft! What noise? Who calls on Hamlet? O, here they come.

[Enter Rosencrantz and Guildenstern.]

Rosencrantz: What have you done, my lord, with the dead body?
Hamlet: Compounded it with dust, whereto 'tis kin. ①
Rosencrantz: Tell us where 'tis, that we may take it thence and bear it to the chapel.
Hamlet: Do not believe it.
Rosencrantz: Believe what?
Hamlet: That I can keep your counsel and not mine own. Besides, to be demanded of a sponge! What replication should be made by the son of a king? ②

【辞格辨析】

①省略。What have you done, my lord, with the dead body? /Compounded it with dust, whereto 'tis kin. 此处 Hamlet 的回答省略了主语，完整应为"I compounded it with dust"。

②隐喻（Thomson & Taylor, 2007: 360）。Besides, to be demanded of **a sponge** what replication should be made by the son of a king? Hamlet 将 Rosencrantz 比喻为海绵，将他听取 Claudius 的命令并从中得到好处比喻为海绵吸水，而将没有利用价值，被国王抛弃的行为，比喻为往海绵身上挤出水分。

Rosencrantz: Take you me for a sponge, my lord?

Hamlet: Ay, sir—that soaks up the King's countenance, his rewards, his authorities. ① But such officers do the King best service in the end. He keeps them like an ape in the corner of his jaw, first mouthed, to be last swallowed. ② When he needs what you have gleaned, it is but squeezing you and, ③ sponge, you shall be dry again.

Rosencrantz: I understand you not, my lord.

Hamlet: I am glad of it. A knavish speech sleeps in a foolish ear. ④

Rosencrantz: My lord, you must tell us where the body is and go with us to the King.

【辞格辨析】

①排比。Ay, sir; that **soaks up** the King's **contenance, his rewards, his authorities**…此处 King's contenance, his rewards, his authorities 三个名词短语构成的排比辞格。

②明喻。He keeps them, **like** an ape, in the corner of his jaw; first mouth'd, to be last swallowed. 此处 Hamlet 将 Claudius 利用两个朋友收集信息的行为，比喻为猩猩先把食物放到嘴里，后期再慢慢享用。

③隐喻。When he needs what you have **gleaned**, …此处 Hamlet 将收集情报信息和在收割后的田野上拾捡稻穗相比。

④拟人。A knavish speech **sleeps** in a foolish ear. 此处 Hamlet 将自己说讽刺的话，Rosencrantz 无法理解，比拟为这些话在他的耳朵里睡眠，不起任何作用。

Hamlet: The body is with the King, but the King is not with the body. The King is a thing. ①

Guildenstern: A thing, my lord?

Hamlet: Of nothing. Bring me to him. Hide fox, and all after.

[Exeunt.]

Act IV, Scene 3

Elsinore. A room in the Castle. Enter King.

Claudius: I have sent to seek him and to find the body.
How dangerous is it that this man goes loose!
Yet must not we put the strong law on him:
He's loved of the distracted multitude,
Who like not in their judgment but their eyes, ②
And where 'tis so, th' offender's scourge is weighed,
But never the offence. ③ To bear all smooth and even
This sudden sending him away must seem

【辞格辨析】

①隐喻。The King **is a thing**. 此处 Hamlet 将 Claudius 比喻为一件事物，为对他的侮辱。

②借代。…who like not in their judgment, but their **eyes**. 此处 Claudius 用 eyes 来指代群众对 hamlet 外貌的喜爱多于对王子的理性判断。

③换说。… and where 'tis so, **th' offender's** scourge is weigh'd, /but never the offence. 此处 Claudius 用 the offender 来指代 Hamlet。

Deliberate pause. Diseases desperate grown
By desperate appliance are relieved, ①
Or not at all.   [Enter Rosencrantz.]
How now? O What hath befallen?
Rosencrantz: Where the dead body is bestowed, my lord,
We cannot get from him.
Claudius: But where is he?
Rosencrantz: Without, my lord, guarded, to know your pleasure. ②
Claudius: Bring him before us.
Rosencrantz: Ho! Bring in the lord.

[Enter Hamlet and Guildenstern with Attendants.]
Claudius: Now, Hamlet, where's Polonius?
Hamlet: At supper. ③
Claudius: At supper? Where?

【辞格辨析】

①隐喻和头韵。**Diseases desperate** grown/by **desperate** appliance are relieved. 此处 Claudius 用 disease（生病）来比喻 Hamlet 的杀人犯法；此外，此处的 disease 和 desperate 也一起构成头韵辞格。

②省略。But where is he? /**Without**, my lord, **guarded**, to know your pleasure. 此处为少了主谓的省略辞格，完整应为"Hamlet is without (outside) and being guarded."。

③省略。Now, Hamlet, where's Polonius? /**At supper**. 此处为少了主谓的省略辞格，完整表述应为"Polonius is at supper."。

Hamlet: Not where he eats, but where he is eaten. A certain convocation of politic worms are e'en at him. Your worm is your only emperor for diet. ① We fat all creatures else to fat us, and we fat ourselves for maggots. ② Your fat king and your lean beggar is but variable service—two dishes, but to one table. ③ That's the end.

Claudius: Alas, alas!

Hamlet: A man may fish with the worm that hath eat of a king and eat of the fish that hath fed of that worm. ④

Claudius: What dost thou mean by this?

Hamlet: Nothing but to show you how a king may go a progress through the guts of a beggar. ⑤

【辞格辨析】

①隐喻。**Your worm is your only emperor** for diet. 此处Hamlet将蛆虫比喻为餐食中的王者。

②普通重复。We **fat** all creatures else to **fat** us, and we **fat** ourselves for maggots. 此处的三个fat构成重复辞格。

③隐喻。Your fat king and your lean beggar is but variable **service—two dishes**, but to one table. Hamlet将国王和乞丐比喻为蛆虫要吃的两碟不同的菜肴。

④同根异形重复。A man may **fish** with the worm …of the **fish** that hath fed of that worm. 此处第一个fish为动词,第二处为名词。

⑤隐喻。Nothing but to show you how a king may **go a progress** through the guts of a beggar. 此处将国王被蛆虫食用后,蛆虫被用来钓鱼,鱼又被乞丐吃掉整个过程比喻为国王的巡视。

第四章 《哈姆雷特》辞格辨析

Claudius: Where is Polonius?

Hamlet: In heaven. Send thither to see. If your messenger find him not there, seek him i' th' other place yourself. But indeed, if you find him not within this month, you shall nose him as you go up the stair into the lobby.

Claudius: Go seek him there. 　　　　　[To Attendants.]

Hamlet: He will stay till you come. 　　[Exeunt Attendants.]

Claudius: Hamlet, this deed, for thine especial safety—

Which we do tender, as we dearly grieve

For that which thou hast done—must send thee hence

With fiery quickness. ① Therefore prepare thyself.

The bark is ready and the wind at help,

Th' associates tend and everything is bent

For England. ②

Hamlet: 　　　　For England?

Claudius: 　　　　　　　　Ay, Hamlet.

Hamlet: 　　　　　　　　　　　Good.

【辞格辨析】

①插说。…**which we do tender as we dearly grieve/for that which thou hast done**，…此处插说表达了 Claudius 即将遣送 Hamlet 到英国的原因。

②排比和拟人。**The bark is ready** and **the wind at help**，/ **th' associates tend**, and **everything is bent**/for England. 此处四处主谓结构构成了排比辞格；此外，the wind at help 则将 wind 赋予生命，能够为这趟旅程提供协助。

255

莎剧《哈姆雷特》辞格辨析与文体鉴赏

Claudius: So is it, if thou knewst our purposes.
Hamlet: I see a cherub that sees them. But come, for England!
Farewell, dear mother.
Claudius: Thy loving father, Hamlet.
Hamlet: My mother! Father and mother is man and wife.
Man and wife is one flesh. ① So—my mother.
Come, for England!   [Exit.]
Claudius: Follow him at foot;
Tempt him with speed aboard.
Delay it not; I'll have him hence tonight.
Away! for everything is sealed and done
That else leans on th' affair. Pray you make haste.

　　　　　　[Exeunt Rosencrantz and Guildenstern]
And England, if my love thou hold'st at aught
As my great power thereof may give thee sense
Since yet thy cicatrice looks raw and red
After the Danish sword, ② and thy free awe

【辞格辨析】

　　①隐喻。Man and wife is one **flesh**. 此处源自《圣经》，即将丈夫和妻子之间的亲密关系比喻为同一个肉体。

　　②拟人和头韵。And, **England**, if my love thou hold'st at aught, /…/Since yet **thy cicatrice looks raw and red**/after the Danish sword, …此处 Claudius 将英国比拟为人，将英国被丹麦击败比喻为被伤口仍没有愈合，依然鲜红疼痛；这一句中的 raw 和 red 也构成头韵，起到对伤口特点的强调作用。

Pays homage to us, thou mayst not coldly set
Our sovereign process, which imports at full
By letters congruing to that effect
The present death of Hamlet. Do it, England!
For like the hectic in my blood he rages
And thou must cure me. ① Till I know 'tis done,
Howe'er my haps, my joys were ne'er begun. ②　　[Exit.]

Act IV, Scene 4

Near Elsinore. Enter Fortinbras with his Army over the stage.

Fortinbras: Go, Captain, from me greet the Danish king.
Tell him that by his license Fortinbras
Craves the conveyance of a promis'd march
Over his kingdom. You know the rendezvous.
If that his Majesty would aught with us
We shall express our duty in his eye, ③

【辞格辨析】

①明喻。For **like the hectic in my blood** he rages, /And thou must **cure** me. 此处 Claudius 将 Hamlet 对他的关系, 比喻为疠病, 只有英国将 Hamlet 处死才能治疗这疠病。

②尾韵。Till I know 'tis **done**, /howe'er my haps, my joys were ne'er **begun**. 此处的 done 和 begun 构成尾韵, 表示本场结束。

③提喻。We shall express our duty **in his eye**, …此处用 eye 指代国王, in his eye 指代当面向国王致谢, 为提喻辞格。

莎剧《哈姆雷特》辞格辨析与文体鉴赏

And let him know so.

Norwegian Captain: I will do't, my lord.

Fortinbras: Go softly on.   [Exeunt all but the Captain.]

  [Enter Hamlet, Rosencrantz, Guildenstern, and others.]

Hamlet: Good sir, whose powers are these? ①

Norwegian Captain: They are of Norway, sir.

Hamlet: How purposed, sir, I pray you?

Norwegian Captain: Against some part of Poland.

Hamlet: Who commands them, sir?

Norwegian Captain: The nephew to old Norway, Fortinbras.

Hamlet: Goes it against the main of Poland, sir,

Or for some frontier?

Norwegian Captain: Truly to speak, and with no addition,

We go to gain a little patch of ground

That hath in it no profit but the name.

To pay five ducats, five, I would not farm it, ②

Nor will it yield to Norway or the Pole

A ranker rate, should it be sold in fee.

Hamlet: Why, then the Polack never will defend it.

Norwegian Captain: Yes, it is already garrisoned.

Hamlet: Two thousand souls and twenty thousand ducats

【辞格辨析】

①借代。Good sir, **whose powers** are these。此处用 powers（军力）这一相关性的特征指代军队。

②间隔重复。To pay **five** ducats, **five**, I would not farm it. 此处为间隔重复，重复了词语 five，起到对该词的强调作用。

Will not debate the question of this straw. ①
This is th' imposthume of much wealth and peace
That inward breaks, and shows no cause without
Why the man dies. ② I humbly thank you, sir.
Norwegian Captain: God b' wi' you, sir.

[Exit.]

Rosencrantz: Will't please you go, my lord?
Hamlet: I'll be with you straight. Go a little before.

[Exeunt all but Hamlet]

How all occasions do inform against me
And spur my dull revenge! ③ What is a man
If his chief good and market of his time
Be but to sleep and feed? A beast, no more. ④

【辞格辨析】

①提喻和隐喻。Two thousand **souls** and twenty thousand ducats/will not debate the question of this **straw**. 此处用 soul（灵魂）指代士兵；此外，Hamlet 将为了莫须有的原因发动战争去争夺不毛之地比喻为如一根稻草般没有价值。

②隐喻。This is th' **imposthume** of much wealth and peace, /that inward breaks, ... 此处 Hamlet 将在富足和和平年代发动战争比喻为一个脓肿的破裂。

③拟人。How all occasions do inform against me/and spur my **dull revenge**! 此处 Hamlet 将他自己延迟的复仇行为比拟为一个迟钝和呆滞的主体。

④省略。... **A beast, no more.** 此句问题的答语为省略辞格，完整应该为"The man is a beast."。

Sure he that made us with such large discourse,
Looking before and after, gave us not
That capability and godlike reason
To fust in us unused. ① Now, whether it be
Bestial oblivion, or some craven scruple
Of thinking too precisely on th' event—
A thought which, quartered, hath but one part wisdom
And ever three parts coward, —I do not know
Why yet I live to say 'This thing's to do,' ②
Sith I have cause, and will, and strength, and means
To do't. ③ Examples gross as earth exhort me. ④
Witness this army of such mass and charge
Led by a delicate and tender prince
Whose spirit, with divine ambition puffed,

【辞格辨析】

　　①隐喻。…and godlike reason/to **fust** in us unused. 此处将 reason 比喻为能够 fust（腐烂）的事物，表示不好好利用理性就好比让理性自行腐烂。

　　②插说和隐喻。Of thinking too precisely on the event, —/**A thought which, quarter'd, hath but one part wisdom/and ever three parts coward**, …此处 Hamlet 将 thought（思想）比喻为一种事物，可分为由智慧和懦弱构成的几份。

　　③排比。Sith I have **cause**, and **will**, and **strength**, and **means**/to do't. 此处的四个名词构成了排比辞格。

　　④拟人。Examples gross as earth exhort me. 此处 Hamlet 将 earth（大地）拟人化，赋予其能够劝说他复仇的能力。

Makes mouths at the invisible event

Exposing what is mortal and unsure

To all that fortune, death, and danger dare

Even for an eggshell. ① Rightly to be great

Is not to stir without great argument

But greatly to find quarrel in a straw ②

When honour's at the stake. How stand I then,

That have a father killed, a mother stained,

Excitements of my reason and my blood,

And let all sleep; ③ while to my shame I see

The imminent death of twenty thousand men

That for a fantasy and trick of fame

Go to their graves like beds, ④ fight for a plot

【辞格辨析】

①排比和隐喻。…to all that **fortune**, **death**, and **danger** dare, /even **for an eggshell**. 此处的 fortune，death 和 danger 三个名词构成排比辞格；此外，Hamlet 在这里还将微不足道的目的比喻为 eggshell（蛋壳）。

②同根异形重复。Rightly to be **great**/Is not to stir without **great** argument, /but **greatly** to find …此处的 great 和 greatly 构成了同根异形重复。

③隐喻。…/and **let all sleep**. Hamlet 此处将自己的不作为，比喻为让各种亟待报仇的事物沉睡。

④明喻。…go to their graves **like** beds. 此处 Hamlet 将为了一些莫须有的名声而慷慨赴死，比喻为像奔向床睡觉那般毫不畏惧地走进坟墓。

Whereon the numbers cannot try the cause,
Which is not tomb enough and continent
To hide the slain? O, from this time forth,
My thoughts be bloody, or be nothing worth!　　　　　[Exit.]

Act IV, Scene 5

Elsinore. A room in the Castle. Enter Horatio, Queen, and a Gentleman.

Gertrude: I will not speak with her.

Gentleman: She is importunate, indeed distract.
Her mood will needs be pitied.

Gertrude:　　　　　　　　What would she have?

Gentleman: She speaks much of her father, says she hears
There's tricks i' th' world, and hems and beats her heart;
Spurns enviously at straws, speaks things in doubt
That carry but half sense. ① Her speech is nothing,
Yet the unshaped use of it doth move
The hearers to collection. They aim at it,
And botch the words up fit to their own thoughts

【辞格辨析】

①排比。She speaks much of her father, says she **hears**/ There's tricks i' th' world, and **hems** and **beats** her heart, /**spurns** enviously at straws; **speaks** things in doubt...此处列出 Ophelia 发疯后的一系列行为，在句中通过五个动词和动宾短语的使用，构成排比辞格。

262

Which, as her winks and nods and gestures yield them,
Indeed would make one think there might be thought, ①
Though nothing sure, yet much unhappily.
Horatio: 'Twere good she were spoken with, for she may strew
Dangerous conjectures in ill-breeding minds.
Gertrude: Let her come in.　　　　　　[Exit Gentleman]
[Aside] To my sick soul (as sin's true nature is)
Each toy seems Prologue to some great amiss. ②
So full of artless jealousy is guilt
It spills itself in fearing to be spilt. ③

　　　　　　　　　　　[Enter Ophelia distracted.]

【辞格辨析】

①隐喻和排比。They aim at it, /and **botch the words up** fit to their own thoughts/which, as her **winks** and **nods** and **gestures** yield them, …此处 botch the words up 将群众对 Ophelia 发疯时的只言片语串起来理解，比喻为修补拼凑一件被破坏的物体；另外，wink、nod 和 gesture 三个动词构成排比辞格。

②隐喻。…each toy seems **Prologue** to some great amiss. 此处 Gertrude 将每一处 toy（小事件）比喻为大差错的 prologue（前言）。

③拟人，同根异形重复和尾韵。So full of artless jealousy is **guilt**/it **spills** itself in fearing to be **spilt**. 此处 Gertrude 将 guilt（内疚）赋予生命，拥有恐惧的心理以及能做出自我破坏的动作；另外，spills 和 spilt 为同根词语的不同形态，构成同根异形重复辞格；guilt 和 spilt 也构成尾韵辞格。

Ophelia: Where is the beauteous Majesty of Denmark?

Gertrude: How now, Ophelia?

Ophelia: [sings]

How should I your true-love know

From another one?

By his cockle hat and staff

And his sandal shoon. ①

Gertrude: Alas, sweet lady, what imports this song?

Ophelia: Say you? Nay, pray You mark.

(Sings) He is dead and gone, lady,

He is dead and gone;

At his head a grass-green turf,

At his heels a stone. ②

O, ho!

Gertrude: Nay, but Ophelia—

Ophelia: Pray you mark.

(Sings) White his shroud as the mountain snow— ③

[Enter King.]

【辞格辨析】

①借代和隐喻（Thomson & Taylor, 2007: 375）。By his **cockle hat and staff** /and **his sandal** shoon. 此处使用 cockle hat（船形帽），staff（木杖）和 sandal shoon（便鞋）指代朝圣者。而朝圣者又经常用来比喻求爱的人。

②尾韵。…he is dead and **gone**. /…at his heels a **stone**. 此处歌谣中，gone 和 stone 构成尾韵。

③明喻。White his shroud **as** the mountain snow. 此处歌谣中，Ophelia 将裹尸布比喻为如雪山一般洁白。

第四章 《哈姆雷特》辞格辨析

Gertrude: Alas, look here, my lord!

Ophelia:〔Sings〕

Larded all with sweet flowers

Which bewept to the grave did not go

With true-love showers. ①

Claudius: How do you, pretty lady?

Ophelia: Well, God dild you! They say the owl was a baker's daughter. Lord, we know what we are, but know not what we may be. God be at your table!

Claudius: Conceit upon her father.

Ophelia: Pray let's have no words of this; but when they ask you what it means, say you this:

(Sings) To-morrow is Saint Valentine's day,

All in the morning bedtime,

And I a maid at your window

To be your Valentine.

Then up he rose and donned his clothes

And dupped the chamber door—

【辞格辨析】

①尾韵和隐喻。White his shroud as the mountain **snow**/…/ **larded with** sweet **flowers**, /which bewept to the grave did not **go**, /with true love **showers**. 此处的 snow 和 go, flowers 和 showers 构成尾韵；另外，此处的 lard with（给……上猪油调味）是一处包含烹饪意象的隐喻，表示裹尸布上用鲜花点缀。

Let in the maid, that out a maid ①
Never departed more.
Claudius: Pretty Ophelia!
Ophelia: Indeed, la, without an oath, I'll make an end on't!
[Sings] By Gis and by Saint Charity,
Alack, and fie for shame!
Young men will do't if they come to't
By Cock, they are to blame. ②
Quoth she, 'Before you tumbled me,
You promised me to wed.'
He answers:
'So would I 'a' done, by yonder sun
An thou hadst not come to my bed.' ③

【辞格辨析】

①尾韵。... all in the morning **betime**, /... /to be your **Valentine**. /Then up he **rose** and donned his **clothes**/and dupped the chamber **door**, /...that out a **maid**/never departed **more**. 这里 betime 和 Valentine，rose 和 clothes，door 和 more 构成尾韵辞格。

②谐音双关。By **Cock**, they are to blame. 此处 Cock 和 God 为谐音双关，表示青年将自己的随意归咎于欲望和天意。

③尾韵（1）—（4）。...and fie for **shame**! /young men will **do't** if they come **to't**/... they are to **blame**. /... /you promised me to **wed**, /... /so would I 'a' **done**, by yonder **sun**, /...come to my **bed**. 此处歌谣中的 shame 和 blame，do't 和 to't，wed 和 bed，done 和 sun 等构成尾韵。

Claudius: How long hath she been thus?

Ophelia: I hope all will be well. We must be patient. But I cannot choose but weep to think they would lay him i' th' cold ground. My brother shall know of it. And so I thank you for your good counsel. Come, my coach! Good night, ladies. Good night, sweet ladies. Good night, good night. ①

[Exit]

Claudius: Follow her close; give her good watch, I pray you.

[Exit Horatio]

O, this is the poison of deep grief. ② It springs
All from her father's death. O Gertrude, Gertrude,
When sorrows come, they come not single spies
But in battalions! ③ First, her father slain;
Next, your son gone, and he most violent author
Of his own just remove; the people muddied, ④

【辞格辨析】

①间隔重复。**Good night**, ladies. **Good night**, sweet ladies. **Good night, good night.** Good night 构成间隔重复。

②隐喻。O, this is the **poison** of deep grief. Claudius 将悲伤比喻为毒药,认为发疯是受到悲伤这一毒药毒害的结果。

③拟人。When **sorrows come**, they come not **single spies/but in battalions!** 此处 Claudius 将 sorrows(悲伤)比喻为士兵,当悲伤到来的时候,不是单个士兵出发,而是整个兵团到来,形容各种不幸的事情接踵而来。

④隐喻。The people **muddied**, …此处 Claudius 将不辨真相的群众比喻为沾上厚厚的泥土。

莎剧《哈姆雷特》辞格辨析与文体鉴赏

Thick and and unwholesome in their thoughts and whispers
For good Polonius' death, and we have done but greenly
In hugger-mugger to inter him; poor Ophelia
Divided from herself and her fair judgment,
Without the which we are pictures or mere beasts; ①
Last, and as much containing as all these,
Her brother is in secret come from France,
Feeds on his wonder, keeps himself in clouds
And wants not buzzers to infect his ear
With pestilent speeches of his father's death, ②
Wherein necessity, of matter beggared,
Will nothing stick our person to arraign
In ear and ear. O my dear Gertrude, this,
Like to a murd'ring piece, in many places
Give me superfluous death.

[A noise within.]

Gertrude: Alack, what noise is this?

【辞格辨析】

①隐喻（1）（2）（Thomson & Taylor, 2007: 380）。Without the which we are **pictures** or mere beasts. 此处 Claudius 将失去判断力的人比喻为一张画像或一头猛兽。

②排比和隐喻。...**feeds** on his wonder, **keeps**, himself in clouds, /and **wants** not buzzers to **infect his ear**/with pestilent speeches of his father's death. 此处的动词 feed, keep 和 want 构成了排比辞格；另外，infect his ear 这里，Claudius 将流言比喻为传染病，将流言干扰视听比喻为疾病感染了耳朵。

Claudius: Where are my Switzers? Let them guard the door.

[Enter a Messenger]

What is the matter?

Messenger: Save yourself, my lord.

The ocean, overpeering of his list

Eats not the flats with more impetuous haste

Than young Laertes in a riotous head

O'erbears your offices. ① The rabble call him lord

And, as the world were now but to begin,

Antiquity forgot, custom not known,

The ratifiers and props of every word,

They cry 'Choose we! Laertes shall be king!'

Caps, hands, and tongues applaud it to the clouds, ②

'Laertes shall be king! Laertes king!' ③　　[A noise within.]

【辞格辨析】

①明喻。The **ocean, overpeering** of his list, /… /**than young Laertes** …, /o'erbears your offices. 此处通过比较级将 Laertes 带兵攻进皇宫的气势, 比喻为海水卷向岸边。

②排比, 借代 (1) (2) (3) 和夸张。**Caps, hands, and tongues** applaud it **to the clouds**. 此处由 caps, hands 和 tongues 构成的排比; 这三个名词也同时指代帽子高飞, 鼓掌和欢呼的兴奋的场景, 为借代辞格; 第三处是由 to the clouds 表示呼叫声直冲云霄, 属于夸张的辞格。

③间隔重复。**Laertes shall be king!** /…/ '**Laertes shall be king! Laertes king!** 此处三个 Laertes (shall be) king 构成间隔重复辞格。

Gertrude: How cheerfully on the false trail they cry!
O, this is counter, you false Danish dogs!　①
Claudius: The doors are broke.　　　[Enter Laertes with others.]
Laertes: Where is this king? —Sirs, staid you all without.
Followers: No, let's come in!
Laertes:　　　　　　　　I pray you give me leave.
Followers: We will, we will!
Laertes: I thank you. Keep the door.

　　　　　　　　　　　　　[Exeunt his Followers.]
　　　　　　　　　　O thou vile king,
Give me my father!
Gertrude:　　　　　Calmly, good Laertes.
Laertes: That drop of blood that's calm proclaims me bastard,
Cries cuckold to my father, brands the harlot
Even here between the chaste unsmirched brows
Of my true mother.　②
Claudius:　　　　What is the cause, Laertes,
That thy rebellion looks so giantlike?
Let him go, Gertrude. Do not fear our person.

【辞格辨析】

①隐喻。How cheerfully on **the false trail they cry**! /...you false Danish **dogs**! Gertrude 将不明就里却大声呼叫的群众比喻为跟踪错的嗅迹而乱吠的猎狗。

②排比。That drop of blood that's calm **proclaims** me bastard; /**cries** cuckold to my father; **brands** the harlot/...此处 proclaim, cry 和 brand 引领的动宾结构构成排比辞格。

There's such divinity doth hedge a king

That treason can but peep to what it would,

Acts little of his will. ① Tell me, Laertes,

Why thou art thus incensed. Let him go, Gertrude.

Speak, man.

Laertes: Where is my father?

Claudius: Dead. ②

Gertrude: But not by him!

Claudius: Let him demand his fill.

Laertes: How came he dead? I'll not be juggled with.

To hell allegiance, vows, to the blackest devil,

Conscience and grace to the profoundest pit. ③

I dare damnation. To this point I stand,

That both the world, I give to negligence,

Let come what comes; only I'll be revenged

Most throughly for my father.

Claudius: Who shall stay you?

【辞格辨析】

①拟人。That **treason** can but peep to what it would, /acts little of his will. 此处 Claudius 将 treason（叛变）比拟为人，对皇权只能 peep（偷窥），而做不了大的行动。

②省略。Where is my father? /**Dead.** 此处 dead 为省略辞格，完整的句子是"Your father is dead."。

③排比。**To hell**, allegiance! Vows, **to the blackest devil/conscience and grace**, **to the profoundest pit**. 此处 Laertes 重复了三个 to 引起的短语，构成排比辞格。

271

莎剧《哈姆雷特》辞格辨析与文体鉴赏

Laertes: My will, not all the world's!
And for my means I'll husband them so well
They shall go far with little.
Claudius: Good Laertes,
If you desire to know the certainty
Of your dear father's death, is't writ in your revenge
That sweepstake you will draw both friend and foe, ①
Winner and loser?
Laertes: None but his enemies.
Claudius: Will you know them then?
Laertes: To his good friends thus wide I'll ope my arms
And, like the kind life-rendering pelican,
Repast them with my blood. ②
Claudius: Why, now You speak
Like a good child and a true gentleman.
That I am guiltless of your father's death
And am most sensibly in grief for it
It shall as level to your judgment 'pear

【辞格辨析】

①隐喻。...that **sweepstake** you will draw both friend and foe, ...辞格 Claudius 将 Laertes 的复仇行为比喻为赌博,将他不分敌友地报复比喻为赌徒无差别地吞下所有赌注。

②明喻。...and, **like** the kind life-rend'ring pelican, /repast them with my blood. 此处 Laertes 表明自己在复仇过程对朋友会如同鹈鹕一般,用自己对鲜血来喂养他们。

As day does to your eye. ①

　　　　　　　　　　　　［A noise within：'Let her come in.'］

Laertes：How now? What noise is that? 　　［Enter Ophelia.］

O heat, dry up my brains! Tears seven times salt

Burn out the sense and virtue of mine eye!

By heaven, thy madness shall be paid by weight

Till our scale turn the beam. ② O rose of May! ③

Dear maid, kind sister, sweet Ophelia!

O heavens! Is't possible a young maid's wits

Should be as mortal as an old man's life? ④

Nature is fine in love, and where 'tis fine,

It sends some precious instance of itself

【辞格辨析】

①明喻。…it shall **as** level to your **judgment 'pear**/as day does to your eye. 此处 Claudius 将 Laertes 所判断到的自己的清白，比喻为如同眼睛对白昼的认知一样清晰。

②隐喻（1）（2）。Tears seven times salt/**burn out** the sense and virtue of mine eye! /…/till our **scale turn the beam**. 此处 Laertes 将悲伤的眼泪比喻为比盐水咸七倍，能够将眼睛的感知和美德烧尽；另一处隐喻是将替 Ophelia 报仇和赢得公正比喻为天平的一端高高翘起。

③换说。O **rose of May**! …这里 Laertes 用 rose of May（五月的玫瑰）来指代美丽的 Ophelia。

④反问句。O heavens! Is't possible a young maid's wits/should be as mortal as an old man's life? 此处为 Laertes 对上天的反问，表示他的不忿。

After the thing it loves. ①

Ophelia:［sings］

They bore him barefaced on the bier

(Hey non nony, nony, hey nony)

And in his grave rained many a tear. ②

Fare you well, my dove!

Laertes: Hadst thou thy wits, and didst persuade revenge

It could not move thus.

Ophelia: You must sing 'A-down a-down, and you call him a-down-a.' O, how the wheel becomes it! It is the false steward, that stole his master's daughter.

Laertes: This nothing's more than matter.

Ophelia: There's rosemary, that's for remembrance. Pray you, love, remember. And there is pansies, that's for thoughts.

Laertes: A document in madness! Thoughts and remembrance fitted.

Ophelia: There's fennel for you, and columbines. There's rue for you, and here's some for me. We may call it herb of grace o' Sundays.

【辞格辨析】

①拟人。**Nature is fine in love**, … /it sends some precious instance of itself/after the thing it loves. 此处 Laertes 将 nature（自然）比拟为拥有人的感情，会将自己最珍贵的部分赠与深爱的人或物。这里表示 Laertes 认为 Ophelia 深爱其父亲，因此在他去世后，也将自己最宝贵的理智送给了父亲。

②尾韵和隐喻。…on the **bier**, /… /and in his grave **rain'd many a tear**. 此处的 bier 和 tear 构成尾韵；另外 rained many a tear 则将流泪比喻为下雨。

O, you must wear your rue with a difference! ① There's a daisy. I would give you some violets, but they withered all when my father died. ② They say he made a good end.

[Sings] For bonny sweet Robin is all my joy.

Laertes: Thought and affliction, passion, hell itself
She turns to favour and to prettiness.

Ophelia: [sings]
And will he not come again?
And will he not come again?
No, no, he is dead,
Go to thy deathbed.
He never will come again.
His beard was as white as snow,
All flaxen was his poll.
He is gone, he is gone,

【辞格辨析】

①一笔双叙双关（1）（2）。O, you must wear your **rue** with a **difference**！此处 rue 构成一笔双叙双关，即将 rue 理解为茴香花或者悔恨；第二，difference 可以理解为"不同"，也可以理解为宗谱徽章上的图案的差异。这句话有两种解读，一是 Ophelia 表示她和其他人同时佩戴茴香花，必须佩戴方式有所区别；另一个是表示他们两人都有悔恨悲伤，但种类有别。

②一笔双叙（1）（2）。There's a **daisy**. I would give you some **violets**, …daisy（雏菊）代表感情的掩饰，Ophelia 留给自己作为对爱情的引以为戒；violet（紫罗兰）代表忠诚，在父亲离世时枯萎了，表示世上忠诚已经不复存在。

■ 莎剧《哈姆雷特》辞格辨析与文体鉴赏

And we cast away moan.
God 'a' mercy on his soul! ①
And of all Christian souls, I pray God. God b' wi' you.

[Exit.]

Laertes: Do you see this, O God?
Claudius: Laertes, I must commune with your grief
Or you deny me right. Go but apart,
Make choice of whom your wisest friends you will,
And they shall hear and judge 'twixt you and me.
If by direct or by collateral hand
They find us touched, we will our kingdom give—
Our crown, our life, and all that we call ours—
To you in satisfaction. ② But if not,
Be you content to lend your patience to us

【辞格辨析】

①直接重复（1）（2）和尾韵。And **will a not come again**? /**and will a not come again**? /no, no, he is **dead**, /go to thy **deathbed**, /... /His beard **as white as snow**, /all flaxen was his **poll**. / **He is gone, he is gone**, /and we cast away **moan**. /God 'a' mercy on his **soul**! 此处 and will he not come again 和 he is gone 分别构成两处直接重复，为歌谣的咏唱；此外，二个 again, dead 和 deathbed, snow, poll 和 soul, 以及 gone 和 moan, 构成了尾韵。

②排比。...we will **our kingdom** give, /**our crown, our life**, and **all that we call ours**, ...此处名词短语构成排比。

And we shall jointly labour with your soul
To give it due content. ①
Laertes：　　　　　Let this be so.
His means of death, his obscure funeral—
No trophy, sword, nor hatchment o'er his bones,
No noble rite nor formal ostentation— ②
Cry to be heard as 'twere from heaven to earth
That I must call't in question.
Claudius：　　　　　So you shall;
And where th' offence is let the great axe fall. ③
I pray you go with me.　　　　　　　　　［Exeunt］

Act IV, Scene 6

Elsinore. Another room in the Castle. Enter Horatio with a Gentleman.

【辞格辨析】

①拟人。And we shall jointly labour with your soul/to **give it due content**. 此处 Claudius 将 Laertes 的 soul 比拟为有感情的主体，能够感到对他们给出的答案感到满意。

②同位语和排比。… his obscure funeral—/**No** trophy, sword, **nor** hatchment o'er his bones, /**No** noble rite **nor** formal ostentation—… 此处有两处辞格，即 no trophy, … nor formal ostentation 构成 his obscure funeral 的同位语；另外是这处同位语中四个由 no/nor 引领的名词短语构成的排比辞格。

③尾韵和借代。So you **shall**; /and where th' offence is let **the great axe fall**. 此处的 shall 和 fall 构成尾韵；另外，用 the great axe fall（大斧头的掉落）指代砍头的刑罚。

Horatio: What are they that would speak with me?

Gentleman: Seafaring men, sir. They say they have letters for you.

Horatio: Let them come in.　　　　　　　[Exit Gentleman.]
I do not know from what part of the world I should be greeted if not from Lord Hamlet.　　　　　　　　　　　　　[Enter Sailors.]

Sailor: God bless you, sir.

Horatio: Let him bless thee too.

Sailor: 'A shall, sir, an't please him. There's a letter for you, sir, —it comes from th' ambassador that was bound for England—if your name be Horatio, as I am let to know it is.

Horatio: [reads the letter] *Horatio, when thou shalt have overlook'd this, give these fellows some means to the King. They have letters for him. Ere we were two days old at sea, a pirate of very warlike appointment gave us chase. Finding ourselves too slow of sail, we put on a compelled valour and in the grapple I boarded them. On the instant they got clear of our ship, so I alone became their prisoner. They have dealt with me like thieves of mercy, but they knew what they did: I am to do a good turn for them. Let the King have the letters I have sent, and repair thou to me with as much speed as thou wouldst fly death.* ① *I have words to speak in thine ear will make thee dumb.*

【辞格辨析】

①明喻。And repair thou to me with **as much speed as thou wouldst fly death.** 此处 Hamlet 要求 Horatio 尽快来见他,将期望他到来的速度与逃避死亡威胁的速度相比。

Yet are they much too light for the bore of the matter. ① These good fellows will bring thee where I am. Rosencrantz and Guildenstern hold their course for England. Of them I have much to tell thee. Farewell. He that thou knowest thine, Hamlet.
Come, I will give you way for these your letters,
And do't the speedier that you may direct me
To him from whom you brought them.　　　　　[Exeunt.]

Act IV, Scene 7
Elsinore. Another room in the Castle. Enter King and Laertes.

Claudius: Now must your conscience my acquittance seal ②
And you must put me in your heart for friend
Sith you have heard, and with a knowing ear
That he which hath your noble father slain
Pursued my life.
Laertes:　　　　It well appears. But tell me

【辞格辨析】

①隐喻（黄国彬，2013：554）。…yet are they much **too light for the bore of the matter**. 此处为军事隐喻，即将自己的语言比喻为小枪弹，将事情的真实面貌比喻为巨大的炮膛，表示语言已无法表达事态的严重性。

②隐喻。Now must your conscience **my acquittance seal**, /…Claudius 向 Laertes 解释自己没有杀害 Polonius，并比喻为还清借款，把 Laertes 的信任比喻为在清还单上盖章。

莎剧《哈姆雷特》辞格辨析与文体鉴赏

Why you proceeded not against these feats
So crimeful and so capital in nature,
As by your safety, wisdom, all things else,
You mainly were stirred up. ①
Claudius: O, for two special reasons
Which may to you, perhaps, seem much unsinewed
But yet to me they are strong. The Queen his mother
Lives almost by his looks, and for myself, —
My virtue or my plague, be it either which, —
She's so conjunctive to my life and soul
That, as the star moves not but in his sphere
I could not but by her. ② The other motive
Why to a public count I might not go
Is the great love the general gender bear him,
Who, dipping all his faults in their affection,

【辞格辨析】

①排比。As by your **safety**, **wisdom**, all **things** else, /you mainly were stir'd up. 此处的三个名词构成了排比辞格。

②插说（1）（2）和明喻。And for myself, -/**my virtue or my plague, be it either which**, —/She's so conjunctive to my life and soul/that, **as the star moves not but in his sphere**, /I could not but by her. 此处 my virtue…be it either which 和 as the star moves not but in his sphere 为两处插说辞格，表示补充信息和表明态度；另外，as the star moves not but in his sphere 也为明喻辞格，Claudius 把自己比喻为围绕 Gertrude 转动的行星，表达了 Gertrude 对他的重要性。

Would, like the spring that turneth wood to stone,
Convert his gyves to graces, ① so that my arrows,
Too slightly timbered for so loud a wind,
Would have reverted to my bow again
And not where I had aimed them. ②
Laertes: And so have I a noble father lost,
A sister driven into desp'rate terms
Whose worth, if praises may go back again,
Stood challenger on mount of all the age ③

【辞格辨析】

①隐喻,明喻,借代和头韵。…who, **dipping** all his faults in their affection, /would, **like the spring that turneth wood to stone**, /convert his **gyves** to **graces**. 此处有四种辞格:第一处为隐喻,Claudius 将群众的爱戴之情比喻为液体,将他们对 Hamlet 的爱戴之情比喻为将他浸泡在情感中;第二处为明喻,将群众无视 Hamlet 的违法行为,将他的 gyves(罪行)转变为 graces(魅力),与能够将木头变为石头的魔法泉水相比;第三处为借代,即用 gyves(脚镣)指代罪行;第四处为 gyves 和 graces 构成的头韵。

②隐喻。…so that my **arrows**, /too slightly timber'd for so loud a wind, /would have reverted to my bow again. Claudius 将自己惩罚 Hamlet 的想法,比喻为往靶子射箭,而将群众对 Hamlet 的爱戴,比喻为大风,将他射出去的箭吹回来。

③隐喻和夸张。…a sister … /… /**stood challenger on mount of all the age**…此处 Laertes 将 Ophelia 的美貌比喻为位于众山顶端;也将其美貌夸大为时代之首,属于夸张辞格。

For her perfections. But my revenge will come.

Claudius: Break not your sleeps for that; you must not think
That we are made of stuff so flat and dull
That we can let our beard be shook with danger
And think it pastime. You shortly shall hear more.
I loved your father, and we love ourself,
And that, I hope, will teach you to imagine—

[Enter a Messenger with letters.]

How now? What news?

Messenger: Letters, my lord, from Hamlet.
This to your Majesty; this to the Queen.

Claudius: From Hamlet? Who brought them?

Messenger: Sailors, my lord, they say; I saw them not.
They were given me by Claudio; he received them
Of him that brought them.

Claudius: Laertes, you shall hear them.
Leave us. [Exit Messenger.]

[Reads] *High and Mighty, —You shall know I am set naked on your kingdom. Tomorrow shall I beg leave to see your kingly eyes. When I shall (first asking your pardon) thereunto recount the occasion of my sudden and more strange return. Hamlet.*

What should this mean? Are all the rest come back?
Or is it some abuse, and no such thing?

Laertes: Know you the hand?

Claudius: 'Tis Hamlet's character. 'Naked!'
And in a postscript here, he says 'alone.'
Can you devise me?

Laertes: I am lost in it, my lord. But let him come.
It warms the very sickness in my heart
That I shall live and tell him to his teeth
'Thus didest thou.'
Claudius: If it be so, Laertes
(As how should it be so? how otherwise?),
Will you be ruled by me? ①
Laertes: Ay my lord,
So you will not o'errule me to a peace.
Claudius: To thine own peace. If he be now returned
As checking at his voyage, ② and that he means
No more to undertake it, I will work him
To an exploit. Now ripe in my device, ③
Under the which he shall not choose but fall;
And for his death no wind shall breathe ④

【辞格辨析】

①插说。If it be so, Laertes/（**As how should it be so? how otherwise**?），/will you be rul'd by me? 此处插说表达了 Claudius 的对 Hamlet 归来的疑惑。

②明喻。If he be now returned/**as** checking at his voyage. 此处 Claudius 将 Hamlet 的归来比喻为猎鹰在追捕猎物过程中受到干扰而返回。

③隐喻。Now **ripe** in my device. 此处 Claudius 将自己想到一个周全的计谋比喻为果实成熟。

④隐喻。And for his death no **wind** shall breathe. 此处 Claudius 将群众的评论比喻为风。

But even his mother shall uncharge the practice

And call it accident.

Laertes:　　　　　My lord, I will be ruled;

The rather, if you could devise it so

That I might be the organ. ①

Claudius:　　　　　It falls right.

You have been talked of since your travel much,

And that in Hamlet's hearing, for a quality

Wherein they say you shine, Your sum of parts

Did not together pluck such envy from him

As did that one; and that, in my regard

Of the unworthiest siege.

Laertes: What part is that, my lord?

Claudius: A very riband in the cap of youth.

Yet needfull too; ② for youth no less becomes

The light and careless livery that it wears

Than settled age his sables and his weeds, ③

【辞格辨析】

①隐喻。…the rather, if you could devise it so/that I might be the **organ**. Laertes 将自己比喻为仪器，服从 Claudius 的操作和安排。

②隐喻。**A very riband in the cap of youth**. 此处 Claudius 将剑术比喻为青年帽顶的绸带，对青年人来说，其重要性就如同年长者的衣物，是身份的一种象征。

③借代。…than **settled age** his sables and his weeds, … Settled age 为借代辞格，即用年龄来指代年长者。

Importing health and graveness. Two months since
Here was a gentleman of Normandy.
I have seen myself, and served against, the French,
And they can well on horseback; but this gallant
Had witchcraft in't. He grew unto his seat ①
And to such wondrous doing brought his horse
As had he been incorpsed and demi-natured
With the brave beast. ② So far he topp'd my thought
That I, in forgery of shapes and tricks,
Come short of what he did.

Laertes: A Norman was't?

Claudius: A Norman.

Laertes: Upon my life, Lamound.

Claudius: The very same.

Laertes: I know him well. He is the brooch indeed
And gem of all the nation. ③

Claudius: He made confession of you;

【辞格辨析】

①隐喻。**He grew unto his seat**, /…Claudius 将精通马术的人比喻为长到了马背上一般。

②借代。… with **the brave beast**. 此处用 the brave beast 来指代马。

③隐喻。He is the **brooch indeed/and gem** of all the nation. 此处将优秀的马术师比喻为国家的胸针和宝石。

■ 莎剧《哈姆雷特》辞格辨析与文体鉴赏

And gave you such a masterly report
For art and exercise in your defence,
And for your rapier most especially,
That he cried out 'twould be a sight indeed
If one could match you. The scrimers of their nation
He swore had neither motion, guard, nor eye
If you opposed them. ① Sir, this report of his
Did Hamlet so envenom with his envy
That he could nothing do but wish and beg
Your sudden coming o'er to play with you.
Now, out of this—

Laertes:　　　　What out of this, my lord?
Claudius: Laertes, was your father dear to you?
Or are you like the painting of a sorrow,
A face without a heart? ②
Laertes:　　　　Why ask you this?
Claudius: Not that I think you did not love your father
But that I know love is begun by time

【辞格辨析】

①排比和借代。…he swore had neither **motion**, **guard**, nor **eye**, /if you oppos'd them. 此处为三个名词构成的排比辞格；另外，eye 在这里指代 Laertes 的外形，属于借代辞格。

②明喻（Thomson & Taylor, 2007：402）。Or are you **like the painting of a sorrow**, /a face without a heart? Claudius 将空有外表没有真心的悲痛，比喻为表情悲惨的画像。

第四章 《哈姆雷特》辞格辨析

And that I see, in passages of proof
Time qualifies the spark and fire of it.
There lives within the very flame of love
A kind of wick or snuff that will abate it, ①
And nothing is at a like goodness still,
For goodness, growing to a plurisy
Dies in his own too-much. ② That we would do
We should do when we would; for this 'would' changes
And hath abatements and delays as many
As there are tongues, are hands, are accidents, ③
And then this 'should' is like a spendthrift sigh ④

【辞格辨析】

①隐喻。...time qualifies **the spark and fire** of it. /There lives within the very **flame of love**, /a kind of **wick or snuff** that will abate it. 此处 Claudius 将一个人的感情，如此处 Laertes 对自己父亲 Polonius 的爱比喻为烛火，但也提出这些火焰中的灯芯中也隐含着让自身熄灭的因素。

②隐喻。For goodness, growing to a **plurisy**, /dies in his own too-much. 此处 Claudius 将 goodness（良善）比喻为胸膜炎，最终因为（胸部）膨胀而消亡。

③排比和借代（1）（2）。...as there **are tongues, are hands, are accidents**. 此处的三处谓语结构构成排比；另外，tongues 和 hands 也分别指代语言和行为，是借代辞格。

④明喻。...**like a spendthrift sigh**, /that hurts by easing. 此处 Claudius 将发誓要报仇的行为，比喻为赌徒的忏悔，仅仅为了安抚内心的愧疚但于事无补。

That hurts by easing. But to the quick o' th' ulcer! ①
Hamlet comes back. What would you undertake
To show yourself your father's son in deed
More than in words?

Laertes： To cut his throat i' th' church!
Claudius：No place indeed should murther sanctuarize.
Revenge should have no bounds. But, good Laertes,
Will you do this? Keep close within your chamber.
Hamlet returned shall know you are come home.
We'll put on those shall praise your excellence
And set a double varnish on the fame ②
The Frenchman gave you; bring you in fine together
And wager on your heads. He, being remiss,
Most generous, and free from all contriving,
Will not peruse the foils, so that with ease,
Or with a little shuffling, you may choose
A sword unbated, and, in a pass of practice ③
Requite him for your father.

【辞格辨析】

①隐喻。But **to the quick o' th' ulcer!** 此处 Claudius 将回到说话的主题比喻为直接触碰溃疡的伤口。

②隐喻。…and set **a double varnish on the fame**…此处 Claudius 将夸大 Laertes 的剑术水平比喻为给名声上漆，使其更有光泽。

③头韵。…and, in a **pass of practice**, …此处的 pass 和 practice 构成头韵。

Laertes：　　　　　　　I will do't!
And for that purpose I'll anoint my sword.
I bought an unction of a mountebank,
So mortal that, but dip a knife in it,
Where it draws blood no cataplasm so rare,
Collected from all simples that have virtue
Under the moon, can save the thing from death
This is but scratched withal. I'll touch my point
With this contagion, that, if I gall him slightly,
It may be death.

Claudius：　　　Let's further think of this,
Weigh what convenience both of time and means
May fit us to our shape. If this should fall,
And that our drift look through our bad performance
'Twere better not essayed. Therefore this project
Should have a back or second that might hold
If this did blast in proof. ① Soft! let me see.
We'll make a solemn wager on your cunnings—
I ha't!
When in your motion you are hot and dry—
As make your bouts more violent to that end—

【辞格辨析】

①隐喻（Wilson, 2009：263；Hibbard, 1987：318）。... if this did **blast in proof**. 此处 Claudius 将计划失败比喻为爆炸，即点燃大炮的意象。

■ 莎剧《哈姆雷特》辞格辨析与文体鉴赏

And that he calls for drink, I'll have prepared him
A chalice for the nonce, whereon but sipping,
If he by chance escape your venomed stuck,
Our purpose may hold there. —But stay, what noise?

〔Enter Queen.〕

How now, sweet Queen?
Gertrude: One woe doth tread upon another's heel,
So fast they follow. ① Your sister's drowned, Laertes.
Laertes: Drowned! O, where? ②
Gertrude: There is a willow grows aslant a brook
That shows his hoar leaves in the glassy stream. ③
There with fantastic garlands did she come
Of crowflowers, nettles, daisies, and long purples, ④
That liberal shepherds give a grosser name,

【辞格辨析】

①拟人。**One woe doth tread upon another's heel**, /so fast they follow. 此处 Gertrude 将 woe（悲哀）拟人化，将连续发生的悲伤事件比喻为悲哀的接踵而来。

②省略。Your sister's drowned, Laertes. /Drowned! O, **where**? 此处为省略辞格，完整句子为 "Where did she drowned?"。此处的省略有助于突出人物惊讶的情感。

③隐喻。There is a willow grows aslant a brook, /that shows his hoar leaves in **the glassy stream**. 此处将平静而清澈的湖面比喻为玻璃一般。

④排比。… of **crowflowers**, **nettles**, **daisies**, and **long purples**,…此处的各种植物花名字构成排比辞格。

But our cold maids do dead men's fingers call them.
There on the pendant boughs her coronet weeds
Clambering to hang, an envious sliver broke,
When down her weedy trophies and herself
Fell in the weeping brook. Her clothes spread wide
And, mermaid-like awhile they bore her up, ①
Which time she chaunted snatches of old tunes,
As one incapable of her own distress,
Or like a creature native and indued
Unto that element. But long it could not be
Till that her garments, heavy with their drink,
Pulled the poor wretch from her melodious lay
To muddy death. ②

Laertes: Alas, then she is drowned?
Gertrude: Drowned, drowned.
Laertes: Too much of water hast thou, poor Ophelia,
And therefore I forbid my tears; but yet
It is our trick; nature her custom holds,

【辞格辨析】

①明喻。And, **mermaid-like**, awhile they bore her up. 此处 Gertrude 将落下水，衣裙展开的的 Ophelia 的形象，比喻为美人鱼。

②拟人。…that her garments, **heavy with their drink**, / pull'd the poor wretch from her melodious lay…此处 Gertrude 将 Ophelia 的衣物拟人化，看作喝水的主体。

Let shame say what it will.　① When these are gone
The woman will be out.　② Adieu, my lord.
I have a speech of fire that fain would blaze
But that this folly drowns it.　③　　　　　　　　　[Exit.]
Claudius:　　　　　Let's follow, Gertrude.
How much I had to do to calm his rage I
Now fear I this will give it start again;
Therefore let's follow.　　　　　　　　　　　　　[Exeunt.]

第五幕

Act V, Scene 1

Elsinore. A churchyard. Enter two Clowns, [with spades and pickaxes].

First Clown: Is she to be buried in Christian burial

【辞格辨析】

①拟人。Let shame **say** what it will. 此处 Laertes 将 shame （羞耻）比拟为人，能够表达自己的意愿。

②借代。When these are gone, /the **woman** will be out. 此处 Laertes 用 woman 指代他软弱的一面，为借代辞格。

③隐喻。I have **a speech of fire**, that fain would **blaze**/but that this folly **drowns** it. 此处 Laertes 将自己要表达的愤怒的语言比喻为火焰，而悲伤的眼泪可将这些火焰浇灭。

when she wilfully seeks her own salvation? ①

Second Clown: I tell thee she is. Therefore make her grave straight. The crowner hath sate on her and finds it Christian burial.

First Clown: How can that be, unless she drowned herself in her own defence?

Second Clown: Why, 'tis found so.

First Clown: It must be *se offendendo*; ② it cannot be else. For here lies the point: if I drown myself wittingly, it argues an act, and an act hath three branches ③ —it is to act, to do, and to perform. Argal, she drowned herself wittingly.

Second Clown: Nay, but hear you, Goodman Delver!

First Clown: Give me leave. Here lies the water—good. Here stands the man—good. If the man go to this water and drown himself, it is, will he nill he, he goes. —Mark you that. But if the water come to him and drown him, he drowns not himself. Argal, he that is not guilty of his own death shortens not his own life.

【辞格辨析】

①换说。…when she **wilfully seeks her own salvation**? 此处的 wilfully seeks her own salvation 是自杀的另一种说法，属于换说辞格。

②谐音双关。It must be **se offendendo**. 此处 se offendendo 意思为'so offended'（冒犯），其英文拼写和拉丁文'se defendendo'（正当防卫）相似，构成谐音双关，也侧面反映出 first clown 的教育水平较低。

③隐喻。…and an act hath three **branches**. 此处将行为的分类比喻为树枝的枝干。

■ 莎剧《哈姆雷特》辞格辨析与文体鉴赏

Second Clown: But is this law?

First Clown: Ay, marry, is't. Crowner's quest law.

Second Clown: Will you ha' the truth on't? If this had not been a gentlewoman, she should have been buried out o' Christian burial.

First Clown: Why, there thou say'st! And the more pity that great folk should have countenance in this world to drown or hang themselves more than their even-Christian. Come, my spade! There is no ancient gentlemen but gardeners, ditchers, and grave-makers. They hold up Adam's profession.

Second Clown: Was he a gentleman?

First Clown: He was the first that ever bore arms.

Second Clown: Why, he had none.

First Clown: What, art a heathen? How dost thou understand the Scripture? The Scripture says Adam digged. Could he dig without arms? ① I'll put another question to thee. If thou answerest me not to the purpose, confess thyself.

Second Clown: Go to!

First Clown: What is he that builds stronger than either the mason, the shipwright, or the carpenter?

【辞格辨析】

①换义双关。He was the first that ever bore **arms**. /…/ could he dig without **arms**? 此处的 arms 为换义双关。第一处 arms 取的是"徽章"的意思；第二处取"手臂"的意思，两者构成换义双关。

Second Clown: The gallows-maker, for that frame outlives a thousand tenants. ①

First Clown: I like thy wit well, in good faith. The gallows does well. But how does it well? It does well to those that do ill. Now, thou dost ill to say the gallows is built stronger than the church. Argal, the gallows may do well to thee. To't again, come!

Second Clown: Who builds stronger than a mason, a shipwright, or a carpenter?

First Clown: Ay, tell me that and unyoke. ②

Second Clown: Marry, now I can tell!

First Clown: To't.

Second Clown: Mass, I cannot tell.

[Enter Hamlet and Horatio afar off.]

First Clown: Cudgel thy brains no more about it, for your dull ass will not mend his pace with beating. ③ And when you are asked this question next, say 'a grave-maker.' The houses he makes lasts till doomsday.

【辞格辨析】

①拟人和隐喻。The gallows-maker, for that **frame outlives a thousand tenants**. 此处将 gallows（绞刑架）赋予生命，会比其 tenants（房客）活得更长；第二处将被处以死刑的人比喻为绞刑架上的房客。

②隐喻（Wilson, 2009: 289）。... and **unyoke**. 此处 unyoke 为农田犁地的意象，即将牛轭卸下来，指停止劳动。

③隐喻。... for your **dull ass** will not mend his pace with beating. 此处将笨拙的脑瓜比喻为 dull ass（笨驴），认为即使鞭打它也不会让它跑得更快。

■ 莎剧《哈姆雷特》辞格辨析与文体鉴赏

Go, get thee in and fetch me a stoup of liquor.

[Exit Second Clown, First Clown digs and sings.]

First Clown: In youth when I did love, did love,

Methought it was very sweet

To contract-a the time for-a my behove,

O, methought there-a was nothing-a-meet.

Hamlet: Has this fellow no feeling of his business that he sings at grave-making?

Horatio: Custom hath made it in him a property of easiness.

Hamlet: 'Tis e'en so. The hand of little employment hath the daintier sense.

First Clown: [sings]

But age with his stealing steps

Hath clawed me in his clutch

And hath shipped me into the land, ①

As if I had never been such.   [Throws up a skull.]

Hamlet: That skull had a tongue in it, and could sing once. How the knave jowls it to the ground, as if 'twere Cain's jawbone, that did the first murther. ② This might be the pate of a politician, which this ass now o'erreaches;

【辞格辨析】

①隐喻。But age, with his stealing steps, /hath clawed me in his clutch, /and hath shipped me into the land, …此处 first clown 的歌词中，将 age（时间）比喻为有爪子的动物，将人抓住并送往其他地方（即死亡）。

②换说。…that did **the first murther**! 此处 the first murther 指代亚当和夏娃的儿子 Cain（该隐），他杀害了自己的兄弟。

296

one that would circumvent God, might it not?

Horatio: It might, my Lord.

Hamlet: Or of a courtier, which could say 'Good morrow, sweet lord! How dost thou, good lord?' This might be my Lord Such-a-one, that praised my Lord Such-a-one's horse when he meant to beg it-might it not? ①

Horatio: Ay, my Lord.

Hamlet: Why, e'en so! And now my Lady Worm's, chapless, and knock'd about the mazzard with a sexton's spade. ② Here's fine revolution, and we had the trick to see't. Did these bones cost no more the breeding but to play at loggets with 'em? ③ Mine ache to think on't.

First Clown: [Sings]

A pickaxe and a spade, a spade,

For and a shrouding sheet,

O, a pit of clay for to be made

【辞格辨析】

①反问句（1）（2）。This might be the pate of a politician …, **might it not**? /…/…This might be my Lord Such-a-one, …, **might it not**? 此两处为反问句，强调所说内容。

②隐喻。And now my Lady Worm's, chapless, and knock'd about **the mazzard** with a sexton's spade. 此处 Hamlet 将头盖骨比喻为 mazzard（mazer 大杯子）。

③隐喻和反问句。Did these bones cost no more the breeding but to **play at loggets with 'em**? 此处有两处辞格：第一处是 Hamlet 将 first clown 随处扔出骨头的行为和九柱游戏扔小柱相比。第二处反问句则突显出 clown 对生死的淡漠。

■ 莎剧《哈姆雷特》辞格辨析与文体鉴赏

For such a guest is meet. ①　　　　[Throws up another skull].
Hamlet: There's another. Why, may not that be the skull of a lawyer? Where be his quiddits now, his quillets, his cases, his tenures, and his tricks? ② Why does he suffer this mad knave now to knock him about the sconce with a dirty shovel and will not tell him of his action of battery? ③ Hum! This fellow might be in's time a great buyer of land, with his statutes, his recognizances, his fines, his double vouchers, his recoveries. ④ Is this the fine of his fines, and the recovery of his recoveries, to have his fine pate full of fine dirt? Will his vouchers vouch him no more of his purchases and double ones too,

【辞格辨析】

①尾韵（1）　（2）。… **spade**, /… **sheet**; /… **made**/… **meet**. 此处歌谣中，spade 和 made，sheet 和 meet 构成了尾韵辞格。

②排比。Where be **his quiddits** now, **his quillets**, **his cases**, **his tenures**, and **his tricks**? 此处 Hamlet 列举了律师生前相关的各种事物，quiddits（雄辩），quillets（诡辩），cases（案件），tenures（头衔），和 tricks（诡计）这五处名词短语构成排比辞格。

③反问句。Why …, and will not tell him of his action of battery? 此处为反问句，强调所说内容。

④排比。… with **his statutes**, **his recognizances**, **his fines**, **his double vouchers**, **his recoveries**. 此处 Hamlet 列举了地产交易商生前相关的各种事物，statutes（法规），recognizances（保证书），fines（赔偿金），double vouchers（证明人）和 recoveries（赔偿），构成排比辞格。

than the length and breadth of a pair of indentures? ①
The very conveyances of his lands will scarcely lie in this box; and must th' inheritor himself have no more, ha? ②

Horatio: Not a jot more, my Lord.
Hamlet: Is not parchment made of sheepskins?
Horatio: Ay, my lord, And of calveskins too.
Hamlet: They are sheep and calves which seek out assurance in that. ③

【辞格辨析】

①反问句（1）(2)，同根异形重复（1）—（4）和双关换义双关（Thomson & Taylor, 2007: 417）。…his **fines**, his double vouchers, his **recoveries**. Is this the **fine** of his **fines** and the **recovery** of his **recoveries**, to have his **fine** pate full of **fine** dirt? Will his **vouchers vouch** him …, and double ones too than the length and breadth of a pair of indentures? 此处有三种六处辞格："Is this the fine…of fine dirt?"和"Will his vouchers…a pair of indentures?"分别构成两处反问辞格，突出 Hamlet 的思考和强调的内容；fine, recovery 和 vouch 分别构成三处同根异形重复；其中 to have his fine pate full of fine dirt 中的 fine 也构成了换义双关辞格，表示"好头骨"和"细小的泥土"。

②一笔双叙双关和反问句。…scarcely lie in **this box**; and must th' inheritor himself have no more, ha? 此处有两处辞格，this box 可以同时理解为棺材和装合约的盒子，构成一笔双叙双关；此处同时也是反问句。

③隐喻。They are **sheep and calves** which …此处 Hamlet 将相信合约条款的人比喻为 sheep（绵羊）和 calves（小牛），表示"愚蠢"的意思。

莎剧《哈姆雷特》辞格辨析与文体鉴赏

I will speak to this fellow. Whose grave's this, sirrah?

First Clown: Mine, sir.

[Sings] O, a pit of clay for to be made

For such a guest is meet.

Hamlet: I think it be thine indeed, for thou liest in't.

First Clown: You lie out on't, sir, and therefore 'tis not yours. For my part, I do not lie in't, yet it is mine.

Hamlet: Thou dost lie in't, to be in't and say it is thine. 'Tis for the dead, not for the quick; therefore thou liest.

First Clown: 'Tis a quick lie, sir; 'twill away again from me to you.

Hamlet: What man dost thou dig it for?

First Clown: For no man, sir.

Hamlet: What woman then?

First Clown: For none neither. ②

【辞格辨析】

①换义双关（1）（2）。For thou **liest** in't. /You **lie** out on't, sir, …I do not **lie** in't, … /Thou dost **lie** in't, … 'Tis for the dead, not for the **quick**; therefore thou **liest**. /'Tis a **quick lie**, sir; …此处由 lie 和 quick 构成两处换义双关。其中，lie 在 thou liest in't 和 you lie out on't 中取的是"躺，位于"的意思，表示 first clown 站在墓穴中，在 'Tis a quick lie 中，则取"撒谎"的意思；quick 在 not for the quick 表示"生者"的意思，与"死者"相对，在 'Tis a quick lie 则表示"（反应）快速"的意思。

②省略（1）（2）。… for no man, sir. /… /For none neither. 此处两处回答都是省略，完整的句子分别是 "I dig for no man." 和 "I dig for none neither."。

Hamlet: Who is to be buried in't?

First Clown: One that was a woman, sir; but, rest her soul, she's dead.

Hamlet: How absolute the knave is! We must speak by the card, or equivocation will undo us. ① By the Lord, Horatio, this three years I have taken note of it, the age is grown so picked that the toe of the peasant comes so near the heel of the courtier he galls his kibe. ② —How long hast thou been a grave-maker?

First Clown: Of all the days i' th' year, I came to't that day that our last king Hamlet overcame Fortinbras.

Hamlet: How long is that since?

First Clown: Cannot you tell that? Every fool can tell that.

【辞格辨析】

①隐喻和一笔双叙双关（Thomson & Taylor, 2007：419）。We must **speak by the card**, or **equivocation** will undo us. 此处 card（罗盘）使用了来自航海的意象，Hamlet 将和 first clown 对话过程需要斟词酌句比喻为如船员行船需要严格按照罗盘的方向来行驶；第二处 equivocation 可以同时表示法庭辩论中使用模凌两可的话语，也可以理解为说笑表演过程中使用的含糊语言，构成一笔双叙双关辞格。

②隐喻。The age is grown so picked that the toe of the peasant **comes so near the heel of the courtier he galls his kibe**. Hamlet 在此处将掘墓者（代表社会较低阶层的人）对他（代表社会较高阶层的人）说俏皮话时表现出来的不尊重，比喻为人们走路时，由于过于紧前行者，而踩到对方脚后跟的冻疮的行为，表现出他不满的情绪，为隐喻辞格。

It was the very day that young Hamlet was born—he that is mad, and sent into England.

Hamlet: Ay, marry, why was be sent into England?

First Clown: Why, because 'a was mad. 'A shall recover his wits there; or, if 'a do not, 'tis no great matter there.

Hamlet: Why?

First Clown: 'Twill not he seen in him there. There the men are as mad as he.

Hamlet: How came he mad?

First Clown: Very strangely, they say.

Hamlet: How strangely?

First Clown: Faith, e'en with losing his wits.

Hamlet: Upon what ground?

First Clown: Why, here in Denmark. ① I have been sexton here, man and boy thirty years.

Hamlet: How long will a man lie i' th' earth ere he rot?

First Clown: Faith, if 'a be not rotten before 'a die (as we have many pocky corses now-a-days that will scarce hold the laying in) ② 'a will last you some eight year or nine year. A tanner will last you nine year.

【辞格辨析】

①一笔双叙双关。Upon what **ground**?/Why, here in Denmark. Hamlet 发问取的是 ground "原因"的意思，而 first clown 则表示"什么地方"，构成一笔双叙双关。

②插说。…（as we have many pocky corses now-a-days that will scarce hold the laying in）…此处为插说，补充信息。

Hamlet: Why he more than another?

First Clown: Why, sir, his hide is so tanned with his trade that 'a will keep out water a great while; and your water is a sore decayer of your whoreson dead body. Here's a skull now. This skull hath lien you i' th' earth three-and-twenty years.

Hamlet: Whose was it?

First Clown: A whoreson mad fellow's it was. Whose do you think it was?

Hamlet: Nay, I know not.

First Clown: A pestilence on him for a mad rogue! 'A poured a flagon of Rhenish on my head once. This same skull, sir, was Yorick's skull, the King's jester.

Hamlet: This?

First Clown: E'en that.

Hamlet: Let me see. [Takes the skull.] Alas, poor Yorick! I knew him, Horatio. A fellow of infinite jest, of most excellent fancy. He hath borne me on his back a thousand times. And now how abhorred in my imagination it is! My gorge rises at it. Here hung those lips that I have kissed I know not how oft. Where be your gibes now—your gambols, your songs, your flashes of merriment that were wont to set the table on a roar? ① Not one now, to mock your own grinning? Quite chap-fallen?

【辞格辨析】

①排比。Where be your gibes now—**your gambols, your songs, your flashes** of merriment …此处三处名词短语，即your gambols（把戏），your songs（歌声），your flashes of merriment（嬉戏），构成了排比辞格。

303

Now get you to my lady's chamber and tell her, let her paint an inch thick, to this favour she must come. Make her laugh at that. Prithee, Horatio, tell me one thing.

Horatio: What's that, my Lord?

Hamlet: Dost thou think Alexander looked o' this fashion i' th' earth?

Horatio: E'en so.

Hamlet: And smelt so? Pah! ［Puts down the skull.］

Horatio: E'en so, my Lord.

Hamlet: To what base uses we may return, Horatio! Why may not imagination trace the noble dust of Alexander till he find it stopping a bunghole?

Horatio: 'Twere to consider too curiously, to consider so.

Hamlet: No, faith, not a jot; but to follow him thither with modesty enough, and likelihood to lead it, as thus: Alexander died, Alexander was buried, Alexander returneth into dust, the dust is earth, of earth we make loam, and why of that loam (whereto he was converted) might they not stop a beer barrel? ①

Imperious Caesar, dead and turned to clay,

Might stop a hole to keep the wind away.

【辞格辨析】

①首语重复和链形重复。**Alexander** died, **Alexander** was buried, **Alexander** returneth into **dust**; **the dust** is **earth**; **of earth** we make **loam**, and why of that **loam**（whereto he was converted）might they not stop a beerbarrel? 此处 Alexander died, Alexander was buried, Alexander returneth into dust 构成首语重复辞格；dust, earth 和 loam 等则构成了链形重复辞格。

O, that that earth which kept the world in awe
Should patch a wall t' expel the winter's flaw! ①
But soft! But soft! Aside! Here comes the King—
[Enter priests with a coffin in funeral procession, King, Queen, Laertes, with Lords attendant.]
The Queen, the courtiers. Who is this they follow?
And with such maimed rites? This doth betoken
The corse they follow did with desperate hand
Fordo it own life. 'Twas of some estate.
Couch we awhile, and mark.　　　　　[Retires with Horatio.]
Laertes: What ceremony else?
Hamlet: That is Laertes, a very noble youth. ② Mark.
Laertes: What ceremony else?
Priest: Her obsequies have been as far enlarged
As we have warranty. Her death was doubtful;
And but that great command o'ersways the order
She should in ground unsanctified have lodged

【辞格辨析】

①借代和尾韵 (1)(2)。Imperial Caesar, dead and turned to **clay**, /...to keep the wind **away**. /O, that **that earth** which kept the world in **awe**, /...t' expel the winter's **flaw**! 此处的 that earth 指的是 Caesar 的尸体, 是借代辞格; 此外, clay 和 away, awe 和 flaw 构成尾韵辞格。

②同位语。That is Laertes, **a very noble youth**. 此处为同位语, 对 Laertes 的信息补充。

305

Till the last trumpet. ① For charitable prayers,
Shards, flints, and pebbles should be thrown on her. ②
Yet here she is allowed her virgin rites,
Her maiden strewments, and the bringing home
Of bell and burial. ③
Laertes: Must there no more be done?
Priest: No more be done.
We should profane the service of the dead
To sing a requiem and such rest to her
As to peace-parted souls. ④
Laertes: Lay her i' th' earth;
And from her fair and unpolluted flesh
May violets spring! I tell thee, churlish priest,

【辞格辨析】

①借代。She should in ground unsanctified have lodged/till **the last trumpet**. 此处用 the last trumpet 指代世界末日（Thomson & Taylor, 2007: 426）。

②排比。For charitable prayers, /**shards**, **flints**, and **pebbles** should be thrown on her. 此处 shards, flints 和 pebbles 三个名词构成排比结构。

③排比和头韵。Yet here she is allowed **her virgin rites**, / **her maiden strewments**, and **the bringing home/of bell and burial**. 此处三个名词短语构成排比辞格；另外，bell 和 burial 另构成头韵辞格。

④头韵。...to sing a requiem and such rest to her/as to **peace-parted** souls. 此处的 peach 和 parted 构成头韵。

A ministering angel shall my sister be

When thou liest howling.

Hamlet： What, the fair Ophelia?

Gertrude：Sweets to the sweet! ① Farewell.

[Scatters flowers.]

I hoped thou shouldst have been my Hamlet's wife;

I thought thy bride-bed to have decked, ② sweet maid,

And not have strewed thy grave.

Laertes： O, treble woe

Fall ten times treble on that cursed head ③

Whose wicked deed thy most ingenious sense

Deprived thee of! Hold off the earth awhile,

Till I have caught her once more in mine arms.

[Leaps in the grave.]

Now pile your dust upon the quick and dead

Till of this flat a mountain you have made

【辞格辨析】

①换义双关。**Sweets** to the **sweet**. 此处第一处 sweet 指洒下的花朵，第二处指 Ophelia，即后文的 sweet maid，构成换义双关。

②头韵。I thought thy **bride-bed** to have decked. 此处的 bride 和 bed 构成头韵。

③换说。O, treble woe, /fall ten times treble on **that cursed head**…此处 Laertes 用 that cursed head 指代导致 Ophelia 发疯的人，即 Hamlet，为换说辞格。

307

■ 莎剧《哈姆雷特》辞格辨析与文体鉴赏

T' o'ertop old Pelion or the skyish head
Of blue Olympus. ①
Hamlet:〔comes forward〕What is he whose grief
Bears such an emphasis? Whose phrase of sorrow
Conjures the wand'ring stars, and makes them stand
Like wonder-wounded hearers? ② This is I,
Hamlet the Dane.   〔Leaps in after Laertes.〕
Laertes: The devil take thy soul!
                    〔Grapples with him.〕

【辞格辨析】

①夸张和拟人。Now pile your dust upon the quick and dead/ till of **this flat a mountain you have made/t' o'ertop old Pelion, or the skyish head/of blue Olympus**. 此处 Laertes 要求众人将他和 Ophelia 一起埋葬,让坟墓高度赛过 the Pelion(希腊皮利翁山)和 Olympus(希腊奥林匹克山),为夸张辞格;另外 the skyish head of blue Olympus 则采用拟人手法,将高山比喻为拥有头部的人。

②夸张,拟人和头韵。What is he whose grief/bears such an emphasis? **Whose phrase of sorrow/conjures the wand'ring stars**, and makes them stand/like **wonder-wounded** hearers? 这一句有三处辞格:Ophelia 去世给 Hamlet 造成的悲痛能让行星驻足,为夸张辞格;此处也将 star(行星)赋予人的特征,会有好奇的心理,并会驻足听人诉说,为拟人辞格;此外,句中的 wonder-wounded 则构成头韵辞格。

第四章 《哈姆雷特》辞格辨析

Hamlet: Thou pray'st not well.
I prithee take thy fingers from my throat,
For, though I am not splenitive and rash,
Yet have I in me something dangerous,
Which let thy wisdom fear. Hold off thy hand!
Claudius: Pluck them asunder.
Gertrude: Hamlet, Hamlet!
Lords: Gentlemen!
Horatio: Good my lord, be quiet.
[The Attendants part them, and they come out of the grave.]
Hamlet: Why, I will fight with him upon this theme
Until my eyelids will no longer wag. ①
Gertrude: O my son, what theme?
Hamlet: I loved Ophelia. Forty thousand brothers
Could not with all their quantity of love
Make up my sum. ② What wilt thou do for her?
Claudius: O, he is mad, Laertes.
Gertrude: For love of God, forbear him!

【辞格辨析】

①借代。I will fight with him upon this theme/until **my eyelids will no longer wag**. 此处 Hamlet 用 my eyelid will no longer wag（眼睑不再眨）表示死亡，为借代辞格。

②夸张。I loved Ophelia. **Forty thousand brothers/could not with all their quantity of love/make up my sum**. 此句 Hamlet 将自己对 Ophelia 的爱与四万份来自 Laertes 这位哥哥的爱相比，为夸张辞格。

■ 莎剧《哈姆雷特》辞格辨析与文体鉴赏

Hamlet: 'Swounds, show me what thou't do.
Woul't weep? Woul't fight? Woul't fast? Woul't tear thyself?
Woul't drink up eisel? Eat a crocodile? ①
I'll do't. Dost thou come here to whine,
To outface me with leaping in her grave?
Be buried quick with her, and so will I.
And if thou prate of mountains, let them throw
Millions of acres on us, till our ground,
Singeing his pate against the burning zone,
Make Ossa like a wart! ② Nay, an thou'lt mouth,
I'll rant as well as thou.

Gertrude: This is mere madness;
And thus a while the fit will work on him.
Anon, as patient as the female dove
When thather golden couplets are disclosed,

【辞格辨析】

①排比。**Woul't weep? Woul't fight? Woul't fast? Woul't tear thyself?** /**Woul't drink up eisel? Eat a crocodile?** 此处五个问句构成排比辞格。

②夸张，借代和明喻。…let them throw/millions of acres on us, till our ground, /singeing his pate against **the burning zone**, /make Ossa like a wart. 此处 Hamlet 继续使用夸张的手法，将覆盖在他身上的万顷泥土将大地堆砌到如太阳那般高耸；第二处用 the burning zone 指代太阳，为借代辞格；最后一处将 Ossa（希腊奥萨山）比喻为一颗肉赘，突出刚堆砌的山的高度。

310

His silence will sit drooping. ①

Hamlet: Hear you, sir!
What is the reason that you use me thus?
I loved you ever. But it is no matter.
Let Hercules himself do what he may,
The cat will mew and dog will have his day. ②　　[Exit.]
Claudius: I pray thee, good Horatio, wait upon him.

[Exit Horatio.]

[To Laertes] Strengthen your patience in our last night's speech.
We'll put the matter to the present push. —
Good Gertrude, set some watch over your son. —
This grave shall have a living monument.
An hour of quiet shortly shall we see;
Till then in patience our proceeding be. ③　　[Exeunt.]

Act V, Scene 2

Elsinore. A hall in the Castle. Enter Hamlet and Horatio.

【辞格辨析】

①明喻。Anon, **as patient as the female dove**/when that her golden couplets are disclosed, /his silence will sit drooping. 此处 Claudius 将 Hamlet 歇斯底里之后的状态,比喻为孵蛋的鸽子,当小鸽子被孵出来便会安静下来。

②尾韵。Let Hercules himself do what he **may**, /…and dog will have his **day**. 此处 may 和 day 构成尾韵辞格。

③尾韵。An hour of quiet shortly shall we **see**; /till then in patience our proceeding **be**. 此处 see 和 be 构成尾韵辞格。

Hamlet: So much for this, sir. Now shall you see the other.
You do remember all the circumstance?
Horatio: Remember it, my Lord!
Hamlet: Sir, in my heart there was a kind of fighting
That would not let me sleep. Methought I lay
Worse than the mutinies in the bilboes. Rashly—
And praised be rashness for it— ① let us know,
Our indiscretion sometime serves us well
When our deep plots do fall—and that should learn us
There's a divinity that shapes our ends,
Rough-hew them how we will. ②
Horatio: That is most certain.
Hamlet: Up from my cabin,
My sea-gown scarf'd about me, in the dark
Groped I to find out them; had my desire,
Finger'd their packet, and in fine withdrew ③
To mine own room again, making so bold

【辞格辨析】

①同根异形重复。**Rashly**—/And praised be **rashness** for it;…此处的 rashly 和 rashness 构成同根异形重复辞格。

②隐喻（Thomson & Taylor, 2007: 434）。… **rough-hew them how we will.** 此处 rough-hew 为隐喻辞格，Hamlet 将命运的安排比喻为粗糙地将树砍树砍倒。

③提喻。Had my desire,/**finger'd their packet**, and in fine withdrew…此处用手指指代用手偷窃，为提喻辞格。

(My fears forgetting manners) to unseal
Their grand commission; where I found, Horatio
(O royal knavery!), an exact command, ①
Larded with many several sorts of reasons,
Importing Denmark's health, and England's too, ②
With, hoo! —such bugs and goblins in my life—
That, on the supervise, no leisure bated,
No, not to stay the grinding of the axe,
My head should be struck off. ③
Horatio: Is't possible?

【辞格辨析】

①拟人和插说（1）（2）。Making so bold/ (**My fears forgetting manners**) to unseal/…/ (**O royal knavery!**), …此处的 my fear forgetting manners 将 fear（忧虑）拟人化，在偷看信件这件事上，忘记了教养，为拟人辞格；另外，my fear forgetting manners 和 O royal knavery 也分别构成两处插说，第一处补充信息，第二处为表达 Hamlet 此刻愤怒的感情。

②隐喻和拟人。**Larded with** many several sorts of reasons, /importing **Denmark's health and England's too**. 此处将 Claudius 在信中添加各种理由比喻为在食物上涂猪油调味；此处也将丹麦和英国两个国家拟人化，将国家的正常运行比喻为人的身体健康。

③夸张。… no, **not to stay the grinding of the axe**, /my head should be struck off. 此处 Hamlet 将 Claudius 命令英国见到 Hamlet 之后立即处死他，表达为连磨斧头的时间都没有，为夸张辞格。

Hamlet: Here's the commission; read it at more leisure.
But wilt thou bear me how I did proceed?
Horatio: I beseech you.
Hamlet: Being thus benetted round with villanies,
Or I could make a prologue to my brains
They had begun the play. ① I sat me down,
Devised a new commission; wrote it fair.
I once did hold it, as our statists do
A baseness to write fair, and laboured much
How to forget that learning, but, sir, now
It did me yeoman's service. Wilt thou know
Th' effect of what I wrote?
Horatio: Ay, good my Lord.
Hamlet: An earnest conjuration from the King,
As England was his faithful tributary,
As love between them like the palm should flourish,
As peace should still her wheaten garland wear

【辞格辨析】

① 隐喻和拟人。Being thus **benetted round with villanies**, /or I could make a prologue to my **brains**, /they had **begun the play**. 此处 Hamlet 将自己身处恶人的包围之中，比喻为被网所围困，为隐喻；另外，Hamlet 也将 brain（头脑，思考）拟人化，认为在他还没有周详计划之前，它们已经开始下一步的行动，突出了他接下来行为的本能性质。

And stand a comma 'tween their amities, ①
And many such-like as's of great charge,
That, on the view and knowing of these contents,
Without debatement further, more or less,
He should the bearers put to sudden death,
Not shriving time allowed.

Horatio: How was this sealed?
Hamlet: Why, even in that was heaven ordinant.
I had my father's signet in my purse—
Which was the model of that Danish seal—
Folded the writ up in the form of th' other,
Subscribed it, gave't th' impression, placed it safely,

【辞格辨析】

①首语重复，排比，明喻，拟人，借代和隐喻。**As England …as** love between them **like the palm should flourish**，/**as peace should still her wheaten garland wear**/and **stand a comma 'tween their amities**. 此处有六种辞格：第一和第二处是通过三个 as 构成首语重复辞格和由这三句话构成的排比辞格；第三处是在 love between them like the palm should flourish 中，将国家之间的友好情谊比喻为如棕榈树一般茂盛生长；第四处为拟人辞格，即在 peace should still… /and make…一句中，将和平拟人化；第五处为用 wheaten garland（麦穗花环）指代和平带来的富庶，为借代辞格；最后将两国之间的友谊比喻为两国中间只有一个逗号那么短的停顿，表示友谊不间断，为隐喻辞格。

The changeling never known. ① Now, the next day
Was our sea-fight; and what to this was sequent
Thou know'st already.
Horatio: So Guildenstern and Rosencrantz go to't.
Hamlet: Why, man, they did make love to this employment!
They are not near my conscience; their defeat
Does by their own insinuation grow.
'Tis dangerous when the baser nature comes
Between the pass and fell incensed points
Of mighty opposites. ②
Horatio: Why, what a king is this!

【辞格辨析】

①排比。Foulded the **writ up** in the form of th' other, / **subscribed** it, **give't** th'impression, **placed** it safely, /the changeling never known. 此处由四个动词构成排比辞格, 描述了一系列的行为动作。

②借代 (1) (2) 和隐喻 (Thomson & Taylor, 2007: 438)。'Tis dangerous when **the baser nature** comes/between the pass and fell incensed points/of **mighty opposites**. 此处有两种三处辞格: 第一处和第二处为借代, 即分别由 the baser nature 和 mighty opposites 分别指代身份低下和身份高贵的两个人群, 在上下文中 the baser nature 指 Ronsencrantz 和 Guildenstern, the mighty opposites 指 Hamlet 和 Claudius; 第三处为隐喻, Hamlet 将两个朋友介入他和 Claudius 之间的明争暗斗比喻为这两人处于两个强敌的激烈争斗之间。

第四章 《哈姆雷特》辞格辨析

Hamlet: Does it not, thinks't thee, stand me now upon—
He that hath killed my king, and whored my mother;
Popped in between th' election and my hopes;
Thrown out his angle for my proper life, ①
And with such cozenage—is't not perfect conscience
To quit him with this arm? ② And is't not to be damned
To let this canker of our nature come
In further evil? ③
Horatio: It must be shortly known to him from England
What is the issue of the business there.
Hamlet: It will be short. The interim is mine,

【辞格辨析】

①排比和隐喻。He that hath **killed** my king and **whored** my mother; /**popped** in between the election and my hopes; /**thrown out his angle for my proper life**, …此句由四个动词短语构成排比辞格;此外,throw out his angle for my proper life 则是一处钓鱼意象的隐喻,Hamlet 将 Claudius 对他的试探和陷害,比喻为向鱼扔出鱼钩。

②反问句(Bloom, 2003: 230)。Is it not perfect conscience/to quit him with this arm? 此处为反问句,为了增强对询问内容的强调。

③隐喻和反问句。And is't not to be damned/to **let this canker of our nature** come/in further evil? 此处 Hamlet 将 Claudius 比喻为国家的溃疡;另外,这句话也是反问句,起到强调的作用。

And a man's life is no more than to say 'one.' ①
But I am very sorry, good Horatio,
That to Laertes I forgot myself,
For by the image of my cause I see
The portraiture of his. I'll court his favours;
But sure the bravery of his grief did put me
Into a tow'ring passion.

Horatio:　　　　　　Peace! Who comes here?

　　　　　　　　　　[Enter young Osric, a courtier.]

Osric: Your lordship is right welcome back to Denmark.

Hamlet: I humbly thank you, sir. [Aside to Horatio] Dost know this waterfly? ②

Horatio: [aside to Hamlet] No, my good Lord.

Hamlet: [aside to Horatio] Thy state is the more gracious, for 'tis a vice to know him. He hath much land, and fertile. Let a beast be lord of beasts, and his crib shall stand at the king's mess. 'Tis a chough ③ but, as I say, spacious in the possession of dirt.

【辞格辨析】

①夸张。And a man's life is no more than to say 'one.' 此处 Hamlet 使用夸张的手法，将人的生命与说出"one"这个字的时间相对比，强调生命的短暂。

②隐喻。Dost know this/**waterfly**. 此处 Hamlet 将 Osric 比喻为一只水苍蝇。

③隐喻（1）（2）。Let **a beast** be lord of beasts, and **his crib** shall stand at the king's mess.' Tis a **chough**. 此处 Hamlet 将这些依靠财产购买官位的人比喻为 beast（畜生）；将 Osric 比喻为会学舌的寒鸦。

第四章 《哈姆雷特》辞格辨析

Osric: Sweet lord, if your lordship were at leisure, I should impart a thing to you from his Majesty.

Hamlet: I will receive it, sir, with all diligence of spirit. Put your bonnet to his right use. 'Tis for the head.

Osric: I thank your lordship, it is very hot.

Hamlet: No, believe me, 'tis very cold; the wind is northerly.

Osric: It is indifferent cold, my lord, indeed.

Hamlet: But yet methinks it is very sultry and hot for my complexion.

Osric: Exceedingly, my Lord, it is very sultry, as 'twere—I cannot tell how. But, my lord, his Majesty bade me signify to you that he has laid a great wager on your head. Sir, this is the matter—

Hamlet: I beseech you remember.

[Hamlet moves him to put on his hat.]

Osric: Nay, good my lord; for mine ease, in good faith. Sir, here is newly come to court Laertes—believe me, an absolute gentleman, full of most excellent differences, of very soft society and great showing. Indeed, to speak feelingly of him, he is the card or calendar of gentry, ① for you shall find in him the continent of what part a gentleman would see.

【辞格辨析】

①隐喻（Wilson, 2009: 245; Thomson & Taylor, 2007: 440-441）。He is the **card** or **calendar** of gentry. 此处 Osric 将 Laertes 的表率行为比喻为航海的罗盘和指南针。此处为航海意象的隐喻。

319

Hamlet: Sir, his definement suffers no perdition in you, though, I know, to divide him inventorially would dozy th'arithmetic of memory and yet but yaw neither in respect of his quick sail. ①
But, in the verity of extolment, I take him to be a soul of great article and his infusion of such dearth and rareness as, to make true diction of him, his semblable is his mirror, and who else would trace him, his umbrage, nothing more. ②

Osric: Your lordship speaks most infallibly of him.

Hamlet: The concernancy, sir? Why do we wrap the gentleman in our more rawer breath? ③

【辞格辨析】

①隐喻（1）（2）（Wilson, 2009: 245）。I know, to **divide him inventorially** …, and yet but **yaw** neither in respect of his **quick sail**. 此处把 Laertes 的各种过人之处比喻条目众多的账本，条目多到令计算的人发困；此外，Hamlet 也将 Laertes 比喻为一艘满帆的船，而将自己和其他人比喻为偏离航道的船只，无法与 Laertes 的速度相比。

②隐喻（1）—（3）和插说。I take him to be **a soul of great article**, …, **as**, **to make true diction of him, his semblable is his mirror**, and **who else would trace him, his umbrage**, nothing more. 此处 Hamlet 延续前面账本的意象，将 Laertes 比喻为重要的条款；另外，将模仿他的人分别比喻为 mirror（镜子）和 umbrage（影子）；to make true diction of him 为插说，表达了 Hamlet 对自己的评价真实度的强调。

③隐喻和借代。Why do we **wrap** … in our **more rawer breath**? 此处将赞美的语言比喻为被粗俗的气息包裹；more rawer breath（粗俗的气息）也指代语言，是借代辞格。

第四章 《哈姆雷特》辞格辨析

Osric: Sir?

Horatio: [aside to Hamlet] Is't not possible to understand in another tongue? ① You will do't, sir, really.

Hamlet: What imports the nomination of this gentleman?

Osric: Of Laertes?

Horatio: [aside] His purse is empty already. All's golden words are spent. ②

Hamlet: Of him, sir.

Osric: I know you are not ignorant— ③

Hamlet: I would you did, sir; yet, in faith, if you did, it would not much approve me. Well, sir?

Osric: You are not ignorant of what excellence Laertes is—

Hamlet: I dare not confess that, lest I should compare with him in excellence; but to know a man well were to know himself.

Osric: I mean, sir, for his weapon. But in the imputation laid on him by them, in his meed he's unfellowed.

【辞格辨析】

①借代。Is't not possible to understand in another **tongue**? 此处 Horatio 用 another tongue 指代另一个人说出来的话。这里暗指 Osric 无法理解 Hamlet 模仿他的语气所说出来的话。

②隐喻。His **purse** is empty already. All's golden words are spent. 此处 Horatio 将 Osric 用完了学来的优雅语言，无法再继续和 Hamlet 对话比喻为花光钱袋中的钱。

③弱陈。I know you are not ignorant—…此处 Osric 用 not 和 ignorant 表示他确信 Hamlet 听说过 Laertes 的能力。

321

■ 莎剧《哈姆雷特》辞格辨析与文体鉴赏

Hamlet: What's his weapon?

Osric: Rapier and dagger.

Hamlet: That's two of his weapons—but well.

Osric: The King, sir, hath wager'd with him six Barbary horses, against the which he has impawned, as I take it, six French rapiers and poniards, with their assigns, as girdle, hangers, and so. Three of the carriages, in faith, are very dear to fancy, very responsive to the hilts, most delicate carriages, and of very liberal conceit.

Hamlet: What call you the carriages?

Horatio: [aside to Hamlet] I knew you must be edified by the margin ere you had done. ①

Osric: The carriages, sir, are the hangers.

Hamlet: The phrase would be more germane to the matter if we could carry cannon by our sides. I would it might be hangers till then. But on! Six Barbary horses against six French swords, their assigns, and three liberal-conceited carriages: that's the French bet against the Danish. Why is this all impawned, as you call it?

Osric: The King, sir, hath laid that, in a dozen passes between yourself and him he shall not exceed you three hits. He hath laid on twelve for nine, and it would come to immediate trial if your lordship would vouchsafe the answer.

【辞格辨析】

①隐喻。I knew you must be **edified by the margin** ere you had done. 此处 Horatio 将 Hamlet 无法明白 Osric 的语言和阅读过程无法理解相比，将其需要解释比喻为需要在书的边沿加注释。

第四章 《哈姆雷特》辞格辨析

Hamlet：How if I answer no?

Osric：I mean, my lord, the opposition of your person in trial.

Hamlet：Sir, I will walk here in the hall. If it please his Majesty, it is the breathing time of day with me. Let the foils be brought, the gentleman willing and the King hold his purpose—I will win for him if I can; if not, I will gain nothing but my shame and the odd hits.

Osric：Shall I redeliver you so?

Hamlet：To this effect, sir, after what flourish your nature will. ①

Osric：I commend my duty to your lordship.

Hamlet：Yours, yours. [Exit Osric.] He does well to commend it himself; there are no tongues else for's turn.

Horatio：This lapwing runs away with the shell on his head. ②

Hamlet：He did comply with his dug before he sucked it. Thus has he, and many more of the same breed that I know the drossy age dotes on, only got the tune of the time and outward habit of encounter ③—a kind of yeasty collection, which carries them through and through the most fannd and winnowed opinions; and do but blow them to their trial—

【辞格辨析】

①隐喻。To this effect, sir, **after what flourish your nature will**. 此处 Hamlet 将修饰语言、点缀措辞比喻让植物更加繁茂生长。

②隐喻。This **lapwing** runs away **with the shell** on his head. 此处将戴着大帽子的 Osric 比喻为顶着蛋壳的麦鸡。

③隐喻。Only got **the tune of the time** and …此处为将时代流行的事物和做法比喻为时代的音调。

the bubbles are out. ① 　　　　　　　[Enter a Lord.]

Lord: My lord, his Majesty commended him to you by young Osric, who brings back to him that you attend him in the hall. He sends to know if your pleasure hold to play with Laertes, or that you will take longer time.

Hamlet: I am constant to my purposes. They follow the King's pleasure. If his fitness speaks, mine is ready. Now or whensoever, provided I be so able as now.

Lord: The King and Queen and all are coming down.

Hamlet: In happy time. ②

Lord: The Queen desires you to use some gentle entertainment to Laertes before you fall to play.

Hamlet: She well instructs me. 　　　　　　[Exit Lord.]

【辞格辨析】

①隐喻（1）(2)（Wilson, 2009: 248; Hibbard, 1987: 343-344）。... a kind of **yeasty collection**, which carries them through and through **the most fanned and winnowed opinions**; and do but **blow them to their trial—the bubbles are out**. 此处有两处隐喻辞格：第一处是将虚夸花巧的语言比喻为 yeasty collection（发酵起泡的混合物），为酿酒的意象，而这些浮夸的奉承语言就如同酒缸上面发酵产生的 bubbles（泡沫），一吹便破，比喻如 Osric 这一批没有真才实学，依靠鹦鹉学舌的方法习得一些上流社会的用语，终究会被识破；第二处将一些精挑细选的有学之士比喻为经过扬谷器筛选过的饱实的种子。

②省略。In happy time. 此处的完整句子应该是"It is in happy time."。

324

Horatio: You will lose this wager, my Lord.

Hamlet: I do not think so. Since he went into France I have been in continual practice. I shall win at the odds. But thou wouldst not think how ill all's here about my heart. But it is no matter.

Horatio: Nay, good my Lord—

Hamlet: It is but foolery; but it is such a kind of gaingiving as would perhaps trouble a woman.

Horatio: If your mind dislike anything, obey it. I will forestall their repair hither and say you are not fit.

Hamlet: Not a whit, we defy augury. There's a special providence in the fall of a sparrow. If it be now, 'tis not to come; if it be not to come, it will be now; if it be not now, yet it will come. ① The readiness is all. Since no man knows aught of what he leaves, what is't to leave betimes? Let be.

[Enter King, Queen, Laertes, Osric, and Lords, with other Attendants with foils and gauntlets. A table and flagons of wine on it.]

Claudius: Come, Hamlet, come, and take this hand from me.

[The King puts Laertes' hand into Hamlet's.]

Hamlet: Give me your pardon, sir. I have done you wrong,
But pardon't, as you are a gentleman.

【辞格辨析】

①排比。**If** it be now, 'tis not to come; **if** it be not to come, it will be now; **if** it be not now, yet it will come. 此处为由三个 if 引领的条件从句构成的排比句。

This presence knows, and you must needs have heard,
How I am punished with sore distraction.
What I have done
That might your nature, honour, and exception
Roughly awake, I here proclaim was madness. ①
Was't Hamlet wronged Laertes? Never Hamlet.
If Hamlet from himself be taken away,
And when he's not himself does wrong Laertes,
Then Hamlet does it not, Hamlet denies it.
Who does it, then? His madness. If't be so,
Hamlet is of the faction that is wronged;
His madness is poor Hamlet's enemy. ②
Sir, in this audience,
Let my disclaiming from a purposed evil
Free me so far in your most generous thoughts
That I have shot my arrow o'er the house
And hurt my brother.

【辞格辨析】

①排比。What I have done/that might your **nature**, **honour**, and **exception**/roughly awake, …此处三个名词构成排比。

②普通重复和拟人。Was't **Hamlet** wronged Laertes? Never **Hamlet**. /If **Hamlet** from himself be taken away, /… /then **Hamlet** does it not, **Hamlet** denies it. /… /**Hamlet** is of the faction … /His madness is poor **Hamlet**'s enemy. 此处为由 Hamlet 名字构成的重复；Hamlet 也将发疯比拟为自己的敌人，是拟人辞格。

Laertes: I am satisfied in nature,
Whose motive in this case should stir me most
To my revenge. But in my terms of honour
I stand aloof, and will no reconcilement
Till by some elder masters of known honour
I have a voice and precedent of peace
To keep my name ungored. But till that time
I do receive your offered love like love,
And will not wrong it.
Hamlet: I embrace it freely
And will this brother's wager frankly play.
Give us the foils. Come on.
Laertes: Come, one for me.
Hamlet: I'll be your foil, Laertes. ① In mine ignorance
Your skill shall, like a star i' th' darkest night,
Stick fiery off indeed. ②
Laertes: You mock me, sir.
Hamlet: No, by this hand.
Claudius: Give them the foils, young Osric. Cousin Hamlet,

【辞格辨析】

①换义双关。Give us the **foils**. Come on. /... /I'll be your **foil**, Laertes. 此处 Hamlet 利用 foil 的多义性构成换义双关，第一个 foil 指的是击剑比赛的剑，第二个 foil 则意思为"衬托"。

②明喻。Your skill shall, **like a star i' th' darkest night**, / stick fiery off indeed. 此处 Hamlet 将 Laertes 的剑术比喻为星星，闪亮整个夜空。

You know the wager?

Hamlet: Very well, my Lord.

Your Grace has laid the odds o' th' weaker side.

Claudius: I do not fear it, I have seen you both

But since he is better'd, we have therefore odds.

Laertes: This is too heavy; let me see another.

Hamlet: This likes me well. These foils have all a length?

Osric: Ay, my good Lord.

Claudius: Set me the stoups of wine upon that table.

If Hamlet give the first or second hit

Or quit in answer of the third exchange

Let all the battlements their ordnance fire.

The King shall drink to Hamlet's better breath

And in the cup an union shall he throw

Richer than that which four successive kings

In Denmark's crown have worn. Give me the cups,

And let the kettle to the trumpet speak,

The trumpet to the cannoneer without,

The cannons to the heavens, the heaven to earth. ①

【辞格辨析】

①链形重复，拟人和省略。And let the kettle to **the trumpet speak**, /**the trumpet** to the **cannoneer** without, /the **cannons** to the **heavens**, the **heaven** to earth. 此处为由 trumpet, cannon 和 heaven 构成链形重复；这三种事物的响声也被比拟为向对方说话；三个 to 引领介宾短语省略了谓语动词。

第四章 《哈姆雷特》辞格辨析

'Now the King drinks to Hamlet.' Come, begin.
And you the judges, bear a wary eye.
Hamlet: Come on, sir.
Laertes: Come, my Lord.
Hamlet: One.
Laertes: No.
Hamlet: Judgment!
Osric: A hit, a very palpable hit.
Laertes: Well, again!
Claudius: Stay, give me drink. Hamlet, this pearl is thine;
Here's to thy health.
[Drum; trumpets sound; a piece goes off.]
Give him the cup.
Hamlet: I'll play this bout first. Set it by awhile.
Come. [They play.] Another hit. What say you?
Laertes: A touch, a touch; I do confess't.
Claudius: Our son shall win.
Gertrude: He's fat and scant of breath.
Here, Hamlet, take my napkin, rub thy brows.
The Queen carouses to thy fortune, Hamlet.
Hamlet: Good madam!
Claudius: Gertrude, do not drink.
Gertrude: I will, my Lord; I pray you pardon me. [Drinks.]
Claudius: [aside] It is the poisoned cup; it is too late.
Hamlet: I dare not drink yet, madam; by-and-by.
Gertrude: Come, let me wipe thy face.

Laertes: My lord, I'll hit him now.

Claudius: I do not think't.

Laertes: [aside] And yet it is almost against my conscience.

Hamlet: Come for the third, Laertes! You but dally.

Pray you pass with your best violence;

I am afeard you make a wanton of me.

Laertes: Say you so? Come on.   [Play.]

Osric: Nothing neither way.

Laertes: Have at you now!

[Laertes wounds Hamlet; then in scuffling, they change rapiers, and Hamlet wounds Laertes.]

Claudius: Part them! They are incensed.

Hamlet: Nay come! again!   [The Queen falls.]

Osric: Look to the Queen there, ho!

Horatio: They bleed on both sides. How is it, my Lord?

Osric: How is't, Laertes?

Laertes: Why, as a woodcock to mine own springe, Osric,

I am justly killed with mine own treachery. ①

Hamlet: How does the Queen?

Claudius: She sounds to see them bleed.

Gertrude: No, no! The drink, the drink! O my dear Hamlet!

【辞格辨析】

①明喻。Why, **as a woodcock to mine own springe**, Osric, /I am justly kill'd with mine own treachery. 此处 Laertes 将被自己涂毒的剑刺伤比喻为被丘鹬中了圈套。

The drink, the drink! I am poisoned. ①   [Dies.]
Hamlet: O villany! Ho! let the door be locked.
Treachery! Seek it out.   [Laertes falls.]
Laertes: It is here, Hamlet, thou art slain.
No medicine in the world can do thee good:
In thee there is not half an hour of life;
The treacherous instrument is in thy hand
Unbated and envenomed. The foul practice
Hath turned itself on me. Lo, here I lie,
Never to rise again. Thy mother's poisoned.
I can no more. The King, the King's to blame.
Hamlet: The point envenomed too? Then, venom, to thy work.
[Hurts the King.]
Lords: Treason! Treason!
Claudius: O, yet defend me, friends! I am but hurt.
Hamlet: Here, thou incestuous, murderous, damned Dane,
Drink off this potion! Is thy union here?
Follow my mother.   [King dies.]
Laertes: He is justly served.
It is a poison tempered by himself.
Exchange forgiveness with me, noble Hamlet,
Mine and my father's death come not upon thee,

【辞格辨析】

①直接重复和间隔重复。No, no! **The drink, the drink! O my dear Hamlet! /the drink, the drink!** I am poison'd. 此处的 the drink 构成直接和间接重复辞格。

莎剧《哈姆雷特》辞格辨析与文体鉴赏

Nor thine on me! [Dies.]
Hamlet: Heaven make thee free of it! I follow thee.
I am dead, Horatio. Wretched queen, adieu!
You that look pale and tremble at this chance,
That are but mutes or audience to this act,
Had I but time (as this fell sergeant Death,
Is strict in his arrest) O, I could tell you—
But let it be. ① Horatio, I am dead.
Thou liv'st; report me and my cause aright
To the unsatisfied.

Horatio: Never believe it.
I am more an antique Roman than a Dane.
Here's yet some liquor left.

Hamlet: As th'art a man,
Give me the cup. Let go! By heaven, I'll ha't.
O good Horatio, what a wounded name
(Things standing thus unknown) shall live behind me! ②

【辞格辨析】

①隐喻和插说。Had I but time (**as this fell sergeant Death, /is strict in his arrest**) O, I could tell you—/but let it be. 此处 this fell sergeant Death 将死神比喻为在紧密逮捕犯人的军士,说明死期已到;这一句话也是插说,表达了说话过程产生的想法。

②插说。What a wounded name/ (**Things standing thus unknown**) shall live behind me! 此处 Hamlet 通过插说,补充条件信息。

332

第四章 《哈姆雷特》辞格辨析

If thou didst ever hold me in thy heart
Absent thee from felicity awhile
And in this harsh world draw thy breath in pain
To tell my story.　　　　　[March afar off, and shot within.]
What warlike noise is this?
Osric: Young Fortinbras, with conquest come from Poland
To the ambassadors of England gives
This warlike volley.
Hamlet:　　　　O, I die, Horatio!
The potent poison quite o'ercrows my spirit. ①
I cannot live to hear the news from England,
But I do prophesy th' election lights
On Fortinbras. He has my dying voice. ②
So tell him, with th' occurrents, more and less,
Which have solicited—the rest is silence.　　　　[Dies.]
Horatio: Now cracks a noble heart. ③ Good night, sweet prince,
And flights of angels sing thee to thy rest!

【辞格辨析】

①隐喻（Thompson & Taylor, 2007: 459）O, I die, Horatio!/The potent poison quite **o'ercrows** my spirit. 此处隐喻为斗鸡的意象，表示毒性如同取胜的斗鸡一般得意洋洋，耀武扬威。

②借代。On Fortinbras. He has my dying **voice**. 此处Hamlet用voice指代他的遗嘱，为借代辞格。

③隐喻（Thompson & Taylor, 2007: 460）。Now **cracks** a noble heart. 此处为乐器意象的隐喻，将人的心脏比喻为竖琴，把心脏停止跳动比喻为琴弦断了。

莎剧《哈姆雷特》辞格辨析与文体鉴赏

Why does the drum come hither? [March within.]
[Enter Fortinbras and English Ambassadors, with Drum, Colours, and Attendants.]

Fortinbras: Where is this sight?
Horatio: What is it you will see?
If aught of woe or wonder, cease your search. ①
Fortinbras: This quarry cries on havoc. ② O proud Death,
What feast is toward in thine eternal cell ③
That thou so many princes at a shot
So bloodily hast struck.
Ambassador: The sight is dismal
And our affairs from England come too late.
The ears are senseless that should give us hearing
To tell him his commandment is fulfilled
That Rosencrantz and Guildenstern are dead.

【辞格辨析】

①头韵。If aught of **woe** or **wonder**, cease your search. 此处的 woe 和 wonder 构成头韵辞格。

②隐喻(Wilson, 2009: 258; Hibbard, 1987: 353)。**This quarry cries on havoc.** 此处使用打猎的意象。Fortinbras 将多人去世的场景与打猎后猎物成堆的意象相比喻。

③拟人(Thomson & Taylor, 2007: 461)。O proud death, /what **feast** is toward in thine eternal cell…此处将死神拟人化,将类似屠杀的场面比拟为死神在家设宴。

Where should we have our thanks?

Horatio: Not from his mouth,
Had it th' ability of life to thank you.
He never gave commandment for their death.
But since, so jump upon this bloody question
You from the Polack wars and you from England
Are here arrived, give order that these bodies
High on a stage be placed to the view,
And let me speak to the yet unknowing world
How these things came about. So shall you hear
Of carnal, bloody and unnatural acts,
Of accidental judgments, casual slaughters,
Of deaths put on by cunning and forc'd cause, ①
And, in this upshot, purposes mistook
Fall'n on th' inventors' heads. All this can I
Truly deliver.

Fortinbras: Let us haste to hear it,
And call the noblest to the audience.

【辞格辨析】

①排比（1）—（3）。So shall you hear/**of carnal, bloody, and unnatural acts,/of accidental judgements, casual slaughters,/of** deaths put on by cunning and forced cause;…此处 Horatio 用了由 of 引领的三个名词短语，诉说丹麦国发生的事情，构成排比辞格；其中，修饰 act 的三个形容词，以及 acts, judgements 和 slaughters 也分别构成两处排比。

For me, with sorrow I embrace my fortune. ①
I have some rights of memory in this kingdom
Which now, to claim my vantage doth invite me.
Horatio: Of that I shall have also cause to speak
And from his mouth whose voice will draw on more.
But let this same be presently performed,
Even while men's minds are wild, lest more mischance
On plots and errors happen.
Fortinbras: Let four captains
Bear Hamlet like a soldier to the stage,
For he was likely, had he been put on,
To have proved most royally. And for his passage
The soldiers' music and the rites of war
Speak loudly for him.
Take up the bodies. Such a sight as this
Becomes the field but here shows much amiss. ②

【辞格辨析】

①谐音双关。For me, with sorrow I em**brace** my **fortune**. 此处的 embrace 和 fortune 两个词同时谐音 Fortinbras,构成谐音双关。

②隐喻和尾韵。Such a sight as **this**/becomes **the field**, but here shows much **amiss**. 此处 Fortinbras 将宫廷中横尸的景象比喻为战场;另外 this 和 amiss 也构成尾韵辞格。

第五章 辞格文体鉴赏

第四章主要针对辞格在局部行文中的文体效果，对莎剧《哈姆雷特》全剧出现的常见辞格做了辨析。从第四章可以看到莎士比亚辞格使用频繁。关于莎士比亚的修辞使用，约瑟夫（Joseph）有如下一段表述：

> 鉴于对修辞理论的分析，非常明显的是，第一，莎士比亚对其作品的主题发展和在戏剧和诗歌中的表达方式是其所在时代的特色；第二，他充分利用了当时的所有思想话题和语言资源；第三，他个人的天赋使得其在遵循这些规则创作时，超越了同时代的人，创作出属于所有时代的作品（1962：4）。

可以说，莎剧中辞格的频繁使用，可以看作是来自莎士比亚生活的英国伊丽莎白时代的烙印，并非他个人的写作特色；然而，莎剧能够在世界流传，成为经典文学，则与莎士比亚对这些辞格的富于天赋的应用相关。如第一章提到的，沃尔夫冈·克莱门（Wolfgang H. Clemen）（1966）认为，修辞在莎士比亚手中已经成为有效的文学创作工具,在主题表达和人物塑造方面起到了决定性作用。换言之,莎士比亚的作品是他生活时代推崇修辞使用的缩影,但他比同时期大部分作家出色的地方,在于他不仅仅将修辞运用到局部增添语言生动性上,而且将修辞运用到整体的主题创设和人物塑造上。前文第四章已经对《哈姆雷特》一剧在辞格使用方面做了"局部"分析,主要揭示的是莎剧中辞格出现的频率和文体效果,以展示这一部诞生于伊丽莎白时期的莎剧的时代特点;本章则尝试从整体的角度,分析这些辞格如何促进该剧的主题渲染以及人物塑造,揭示莎士比亚在辞格使用方面的过人天赋。

第一节 《哈姆雷特》辞格使用概述

基于第四章的辨析可以发现,莎士比亚在《哈姆雷特》戏剧中,共使用了常见辞格约 950 次。根据该剧牛津版的排版,该剧共有约 3800 行,换言之,基本上每 4 行,即 40 个音节,就会出现 1 处辞格。在莎士比亚的笔下,辞格的使用不是为了简单地追求行文生动。保罗·康托尔(Paul Cantor)总结说,"这部戏剧(即《哈姆雷特》)在诗和戏剧两个方面都一样出名。但总体来说,莎士比亚将诗的部分从属于戏剧,换言之,他将诗歌用来服务于戏剧方面的目的"(2004:71)。可以说,莎士比亚笔下辞格的使用,不仅是为了迎合时代的潮流,也不仅是为了行文符合抑扬五步格的写作需求,而是服务于戏剧创作。下文将从不同辞格的文体效果讨论莎士比亚使用辞格创造行文的多重解读可能性和多重语域的文体特点。

辞格的频繁使用,不仅使莎剧行文语言生动,还是莎剧的另一个典型的特点——文本的多重解读——的创设手段,即在一个语境中,同一句话,甚至同一场会话语境,存在多种解读效果。在这部剧中,多重解读效果主要通过使用双关和隐喻辞格来实现的,如下面例1:

例1:

Claudius:

How fares our cousin Hamlet?

Hamlet:

Excellent, i' faith; of the chameleon's dish. I eat the air, promise-crammed. You cannot feed capons so.

Claudius:

I have nothing with this answer, Hamlet. These words are not mine.

例1中包含两处双关,第一处为fares,在句中有表达"问候"的意思,该词也有表示"用餐"的意思,是一处一笔双叙双关。在此,哈姆雷特在回答克劳狄斯的见面问候语,取了该词"用餐"的意思,可理解为询问他的进食情况,与后面的eat the air(吃空气)形成延续呼应;第二处为air,该词的读音谐音heir(继承人),构成谐音双关。但做谐音处理时,eat the air也可以理解为eat the heir(吃掉继承人),即是对克劳狄斯暗杀老哈姆雷特,又通过娶嫂夺取哈姆雷特的王位继承权的一种暗指。借助这个谐音双关,这处上下文因此有以下两种解读:

第一种,克劳狄斯见到哈姆雷特,并对他做了最基本的问候,哈姆雷特却回答吃的是变色龙的食物,变色龙是以空气为生的生物（此为英语文化的传说），每天被空气塞得比阉鸡还饱。这一层理解会使读者觉得莫名其妙，这也体现在克劳狄斯的"I have nothing with this answer"（我无法理解这个回答）的回答中。这一种解读反映了哈姆雷特假装疯癫，语言答非所问的一面。第二种解读则是选择双关辞格所指的另一层意思，即理解为暗指克劳狄斯用空口的承诺（如第一幕第二场提到的将哈姆雷特作为王位最直接的继承人，并给予他与亲生父亲一般的关爱）将哈姆雷特塞饱，而其实则想方设法谋害他这一王位继承人。第一种理解体现的是一种疯疯癫癫的对话，创造答非所问的戏剧效果；第二种理解则是哈姆雷特对克劳狄斯的意图的揭发，是哈姆雷特以疯癫为遮掩的反抗。

可见，这些双关类辞格的应用，使行文具备多种解读，富有戏剧性，更耐人寻味。除了双关，相似类辞格也是莎士比亚常用的修辞手法，他对辞格的扩展使用更是炉火纯青。有时，扩展辞格甚至与双关辞格相结合，使得解读的层次更为多元，如例2：

例2：
Polonius：

                           In few, Ophelia,
Do not believe his vows, for <u>they are brokers</u>
Not of that <u>dye</u> which their <u>investments</u> show
But mere <u>implorators</u> of unholy <u>suits</u>
Breathing like sanctified and pious <u>bonds</u>
The better to beguile.

例2的主体是一处拟人的相似类辞格，即将哈姆雷特对莪菲莉娅的爱情盟誓比喻为 brokers，并和接下来的 investments，implorators，suits，和 bonds 等构成扩展隐喻。除了这处隐喻辞格之外，这里列出的这五个词语同时也是多义词，在上下文中构成一笔双叙的双关效果。这五个词语至少有两种解读：第一种，broker 可以理解为生意的中间人，随着这个理解，与行文中 implorators，suits 和 bonds 等词语构成商业意象的扩展隐喻，这三个词也随之可以理解为"投资""仲裁者""诉求"和"债券"，整句话可以理解为"誓言就如同生意中间人一般，兜售各种看似可靠的债券来从中牟利"；第二种，broker 也可以理解为销售旧衣服的商人，与行文的三个词语 dye，investment 和 suit，构成与衣物意象相关的扩展隐喻，这三个词也可以分别将理解为"颜色""衣服"和"套装"，整句话又可以解读为"誓言就像兜售旧衣物的商人一样，所卖的衣物并不是外在所染颜色所展示的"。

辞格的使用不仅为莎剧的行文带来多重解读的可能，也是莎士比亚创设多种语体的有效手段，形成另一个重要的语言特点——多重语体效果。"莎士比亚的天赋体现在他为剧中几乎所有主要角色，以及个别次要角色，都创造了个性化的语言"（Cantor，2004：71）。在《哈姆雷特》一剧中，他使用排比、对仗等辞格，为克劳狄斯创造了一种严肃的朝堂语体，如例3：

例3：
Claudius：
Though yet of Hamlet <u>our dear brother's</u> death
The memory be green, and that it us befitted
To bear our hearts in grief, and <u>our whole kingdom</u>

To be contracted in one brow of woe,
Yet so far hath discretion fought with nature
That we with <u>wisest sorrow</u> think on him
Together with remembrance of ourselves.
Therefore <u>our sometime sister</u>, <u>now our queen</u>,
<u>Th' imperial jointress to this warlike state</u>,
Have we, as 'twere with <u>a defeated joy</u>,
<u>With an auspicious, and a dropping eye</u>,
<u>With mirth in funeral, and with dirge in marriage</u>,
In equal scale weighing delight and dole,
Taken to wife. Nor have we herein <u>barred</u>
Your better wisdoms, which have freely gone
With this affair along. For all, our thanks.

例3为新王克劳狄斯即位后第一次面对朝臣的讲话。精心设计的句法结构和迂回的表达方式，是英语朝堂语言的文体特点（ibid.：71），而莎士比亚则借助不同的辞格来实现这些文体效果。在例3中的16行诗行中，共有同位语、对仗、排比和插说等形变辞格，以及拟人、提喻、逆喻和隐喻等义变辞格。其中，同位语和插说很好地实现行文的迂回推诿又不失庄重的效果。如"Though yet of Hamlet our dear brother's death/the memory be green"中，our dear brother（我们亲爱的兄长）是Hamlet的同位语，起到补充信息的作用；"Therefore our sometime sister, now our queen, /th' imperial jointress to this warlike state"中，后半句也是同位语，补充王后的身份信息。这两处插入语不但补充了人物的背景信息，也强调了克劳狄斯与老王哈姆雷特的兄弟关系，以及王后对王国的继承权，将听众对世俗中叔嫂乱伦的关注转移到对兄弟关系,对继承权,以及对国家面临战争的现状的关注。行文的推诿措辞也体现在插说辞格的使用上,克劳狄斯在表达与先王王后结婚的过程中,在句子"Have we taken to wife."中间,插入 as 'twere with a defeated joy, /With an auspicious, and a dropping eye, /With mirth in funeral, and with dirge in marriage, /In equal scale weighing delight and dole 这四行内容,在这些内容中,又借助逆喻辞格表达了悲喜交集的感情,也较为迂回地、刻意又不失严肃庄重地表达了这种行为背后的欣喜与无奈的矛盾心理。

朝堂语体的严肃性还体现在排比和对仗的使用。这两种辞格通过整齐的句法结构增强语言气势。如上文的插说辞格内容,均为使用对仗的手法,凸显悲和喜的对比;同时借用以"with + 名词短语"引领的整齐结构,构成排比,使语言达到一气呵成的效果,塑造了较高格调的正式语体。

即使是正式语体,莎士比亚在《哈姆雷特》一剧中,也有不同形式的体现。例如,普隆涅斯的正式语体就和克劳狄斯有一定的区别。在第二幕第二场,即前文第三章的例 24 中,当普隆涅斯向克劳狄斯和葛特露分享自己的发现前,他开始了大段的陈述,连用了由 what 和 why 等疑问词引领的排比辞格,以及隐喻、拟人和间接重复等辞格,也是属于辞格频繁使用的一个小篇章,然而,其效果却不尽然,不仅没有庄重的文体效果,而且还使得葛特露觉得不耐烦,提醒他需要"More matter, with less art."(多实质内容,少些艺术手法),这一例子可以看作是正式语体的一种不符合场景的使用案例。类似情况还有奥斯利克(Osric)对正式语体的使用。如果说普隆涅斯是辞格使用和场景匹配的失败导致修辞效果的失败,那么,奥斯利克的"正式"语体使用则体现出他捉襟见肘的语言能力和刻意模仿的毛病。在第五幕第二场，奥斯利克向哈姆雷特描绘勒替斯的才能时，虽然学会了使用辞格这些被哈姆雷特称为 the tune of the time（世人醉心的音调）和 yeasty collection（发酵起泡的混合物）的语言，但由于没有真才实学，在听了哈姆雷特带着嘲讽的、刻意堆砌修辞的回答之后，便变得没有招架之力了，最后不得不转为平白无奇的口语体。

除了正式语体之外，剧中也借助辞格创设了一些诙谐，甚至是粗俗的语体。如在第三幕第二场戏中戏开始之前，哈姆雷特和莪菲莉娅之间的对话，便是使用双关辞格来体现情侣之间的调情嬉戏。在这部戏剧中，通过克劳狄斯严肃又嫌迂回的朝堂正式语体，普隆涅斯的适得其反的正式语体，奥斯利克鹦鹉学舌的正式语体，哈姆雷特的反讽式的正式语体，抑或是哈姆雷特和莪菲莉娅之间的充满性暗示的粗俗语体，莎士比亚为读者展示了如何使用不同辞格创设不同语体效果，以及展示了如何使用同一辞格创设同一类语体的不同文体效果。

第二节　辞格与主题渲染

如第一节所述，莎士比亚借用辞格的使用，实现了文本多重解读的可能性和多重语体效果等局部作用，此外，从整体来看，辞格还扮演着渲染主题的作用。

1980 年，乔治·莱卡夫（George Lakoff）和马克·琼生（Mark Johnson）发表了《我们赖以生存的隐喻》（*Metaphors We Live By*），开启了从认知语言学视角看隐喻的先河。在该书的开篇，他们便观点鲜明地提出，隐喻现象不仅出现在语言中，而且出现在思想和行为中。"我们平常赖以思考和行动的认知体系，本质上是隐喻性的"（1980：4），并通过"Your claims are indefensible."和"I've never won an argument with him."等包含"死隐喻"的句子，证明在认知当中，辩论概念经常被比喻为战争，即 ARGUMENT IS WAR 这一隐喻认知机制。本书也借助这一思路来理解《哈姆雷特》剧中的意象，并总结出不同主题紧密相关的意象，以揭示莎士比亚对剧中角色或话题的认知。与莱卡夫和琼生不同，本书不以"死隐喻"为观察对象，而以包含意象的辞格，即隐喻、明喻和拟人等，作为分析对象。从这一系列包含意象的辞格中可以发现莎士比亚在《哈姆雷特》一剧中是如何使用这些辞格所包含的意象渲染主题的。

通过对该剧的意象分析，可以发现有以下三种话题经常和同一类意象相结合，起到烘托主题的作用。这三种话题可以概括为：丹麦王国是花园，道德沦丧是生病，以及试探循迹是狩猎。

一、丹麦王国是花园

在第一幕第二场中，当朝堂中庆祝克劳狄斯新王即位的人们都离去的时候，哈姆雷特说出例4的话：

例4：
Hamlet：
…
How weary, stale, flat, and unprofitable
Seem to me all the uses of this world!
Fie on't! ah, fie! 'Tis an unweeded garden
That grows to seed; things rank and gross in nature

>   Possess it merely. That it should come thus:
>   …

在这段话中，哈姆雷特用 an unweeded garden（一座未除杂草的花园）这一意象来比喻丹麦国，这一个扩展隐喻又与后文的 grows to seeds, rank and gross 等词相呼应，形成一个较为连贯的画面，整体可以解读为"丹麦国是花园，花园里杂草丛生，未经修剪"，这些长在花园中的杂草，也即是丹麦国中的人和事。因此，这一扩展隐喻又可以进一步解读为"丹麦国中不道德的人犹如杂草一般，占据整个花园，四处滋生腐烂"。这一意象表达了哈姆雷特对他母亲葛特露在老哈姆雷特去世不久便改嫁叔父克劳狄斯这一不伦行为的愤怒。剧中将人比喻为丛生和腐烂的杂草的案例还有例5：

例5：

Hamlet：
Haste me to know't that I with wings as swift
As meditation or the thoughts of love
May sweep to my revenge.
Father's Ghost：
                                I find thee apt.
And duller shouldst <u>thou be than the fat weed</u>
That rots itself in ease on Lethe wharf
Wouldst thou not stir in this.

例5中，老哈姆雷特的鬼魂对哈姆雷特决意报仇的样子表示宽慰，将听说父亲被害而无动于衷的人比喻为阴间肥腻的杂草,悠然自得地在遗忘河旁腐烂消亡。类似的将道德败坏的人和事与丛生的腐烂植物类比的,在剧中还有克劳狄斯在第三幕第三场最后的祷告,他承认说"My offence is rank! It smells to heaven."(我的罪行臭气熏天);在第三幕第四场,哈姆雷特质问母亲葛特露的时候,将已故父亲的伟岸形象和今王克劳狄斯相比,得出"Here is your husband, like a mildew'd ear/Blasting his wholesome brother."(这是你的丈夫,如发霉的玉米穗,也感染他的兄弟,使他枯萎),并要求他母亲从此拒绝与克劳狄斯见面,"Do not spread the compost over the weeds/To make them ranker."(不要往杂草上施肥,使之更加繁茂)。

除了杂草,剧中也提及其他的植物。在第四幕第五场中,莪菲莉娅发疯后,她从野外摘了各种的花草,分配给不同的人,每一种野花也都暗指不同角色的特点和命运,见例6:

例6:
Ophelia:
There's <u>rosemary</u>, that's for remembrance. Pray you, love, remember. And there is <u>pansies</u>, that's for thoughts.
…
There's <u>fennel</u> for you, and <u>columbines</u>. There's <u>rue</u> for you, and here's some for me. We may call it herb of grace o' Sundays. O, you must wear your rue with a difference! There's a <u>daisy</u>. I would give you some <u>violets</u>, but they wither'd all when my father died. They say he made a good end.

例6中各种花草都有隐含的意义,构成双关类辞格。根据威尔逊（Wilson）的分析，rosemary（迷迭香）代表记忆，也是西方婚礼和葬礼的常用植物，莪菲莉娅送给了哥哥勒替斯；pansies（三色堇）代表思想或爱的想念，她留给了自己；fennel（茴香）和columbine（漏斗花）分别代表谄媚和通奸，送给了克劳狄斯；rue（芸香）代表悲伤和悔过，莪菲莉娅送给葛特露和自己；daisy（雏菊）代表感情的掩饰，莪菲莉娅留给自己作为对爱情和誓言的引以为戒；最后的violet（紫罗兰）代表忠诚，在她父亲离世的时候都枯萎了，表示世上忠诚已经不复存在（2009：226）。正如勒替斯所说的，"This nothing's more than matter."（无意识的话语比正言更具威力），莪菲莉娅在疯癫的情况下，用花语道出了每个人的特点和命运。

从以上各种意象可以看到，莎士比亚在创作过程中，以丹麦王国为花园这一主题隐喻为基础，借助该隐喻的扩展，将丹麦国中生活的人比喻为花园中各种各样的花草。从对这一隐喻的进一步扩展中，也可以总结出，他将道德有缺陷的角色，比喻为滋长腐烂的杂草，而用各种不同的花，代表人物的其他品质，使"丹麦王国是花园"的主题比喻在行文过程进一步得到渲染和巩固。

二、道德沦丧是生病

《哈姆雷特》中另一处常见的意象是疾病。在第二场第二幕，哈姆雷特告诉好友"My wit is diseased."（我的心智生病了），将一个人的心智赋予生命，比拟为会生病的主体。在剧中，哈姆雷特和克劳狄斯两个角色频繁使用了该类疾病意象。对哈姆雷特来说，他使用疾病最多的两个对象是葛特露和克劳狄斯，如例7和例8：

例7：

Hamlet：

Mother, for love of grace,
Lay not that flattering unction to your soul
That not your trespass but my madness speaks.
It will but skin and film the ulcerous place,
Whiles rank corruption, mining all within,
Infects unseen.

例8：

Hamlet：

Before mine uncle. I'll observe his looks;
I'll tent him to the quick.

  对哈姆雷特来说，葛特露和克劳狄斯是剧中道德沦丧的两个角色，在和他们的对话中，他时常使用一些疾病的意象。如例7中，当他在训斥母亲和克劳狄斯的乱伦关系时，将这一道德沦陷比喻为溃疡疾病，警告母亲不要以哈姆雷特发疯为由，为这一道德伤口涂上膏药，因为即使如此，这处溃疡也只是表面被覆盖，而内部依然继续溃烂。在第二幕第二场中，在剧中剧表演之前，哈姆雷特和霍拉旭商量如何观察克劳狄斯观剧的表现，用了例8的语言，"I'll tent him to the quick."（我会查看他伤疤里的嫩肉），即表示观察他是否暴露了自己犯罪的痕迹。这里哈姆雷特将克劳狄斯掩饰的罪行，比喻为掩盖在结痂里面的伤口。相类似的，当他发现克劳狄斯在祷告，无法下手杀他时，说出"This physic but prolongs thy sickly days."，将祷告比喻为治疗疾病的药物。第三幕第二场中，哈姆雷特将克劳狄斯观看剧中剧被冒犯生气比喻为酗酒后胆病发作（见第三章例50），也都使用疾病的意象来暗指克劳狄斯的罪行。

在哈姆雷特将克劳狄斯的道德败坏比喻为疾病的同时，克劳狄斯也将哈姆雷特比喻为自己心中的病痛，在第四幕第三场中，他说出了"For like the hectic in my blood he rages, /And thou must cure me."，将哈姆雷特比喻为自己的痨热病，将英国国王帮他处死哈姆雷特比喻治疗疾病，因为"Diseases desperate grown/By desperate appliance are relieved."（疾病的疯狂发展必须使用疯狂的方式才能减轻），相似的地方还有例9：

例9：

Claudius：

But so much was our love

We would not understand what was most fit,

But, like the owner of a foul disease,

To keep it from divulging, let it feed

Even on the pith of life.

在第四幕第一场中，克劳狄斯在听说哈姆雷特误杀了普隆涅斯之后，将自己和葛特露比喻为 the owner of a foul disease（疾病的宿主），如果在这个时刻保护哈姆雷特不受惩罚，即如病人为了避免病情暴露给其他人，只能任由疾病蚕食自己的生命一般。

从这些例子可以看到，莎士比亚在使用系列疾病意象的同时，形象地将哈姆雷特和克劳狄斯这对仇人塑造为彼此的疾病。对哈姆雷特来说，克劳狄斯毒死自己的父亲，娶了自己的母亲，还夺去了自己的王位继承权，是道德沦丧之人，如身患各种疾病的主体一般；而克劳狄斯因为忌惮哈姆雷特发现自己的罪行，向自己实施报复，所以对哈姆雷特有一种天然的抵触，也将他看作自己的恶疾。从这两个角色对疾病意象的使用中，可以看到，哈姆雷特对疾病意象的使用，更多是站在道德的角度来量度，而克劳狄斯则从自身的安危来确定，两个角色之间的品格高低也透过对疾病意象的使用一目了然。

三、试探循迹是狩猎

在本书第一章提到，《哈姆雷特》一剧的其中一个主题就是试探，如哈姆雷特对克劳狄斯的罪行试探，普隆涅斯利用女儿对哈姆雷特的爱情试探，哈姆雷特两位好友对哈姆雷特的内在意图试探等。莎士比亚在对这些试探行为的描述过程，经常用到狩猎的意象，形成"试探循迹是狩猎"这种认知效果。

当哈姆雷特准备利用剧中剧来试探克劳狄斯时，他说出例10 的内容：

例 10：
Hamlet：
I prithee, when thou seest that act afoot,
Even with the very comment of thy soul
Observe my uncle. If his occulted guilt
Do not itself unkennel in one speech
It is a damned ghost that we have seen,
……

例 10 中，哈姆雷特将克劳狄斯的罪恶，比喻为躲藏起来的猎物（根据威尔逊的说法是狐狸），而剧中剧的作用就是刺激克劳狄斯,使其以各种方式透露自己的罪行,就如同狩猎过程,将猎物从洞穴中逼迫出来。而在第三幕第二场中,当哈姆雷特了解到自己的两名好友为克劳狄斯派来监视他的时候,也用了一处狩猎的意象来隐晦地揭发他们的意图,用了例11的比喻:

例11:

Rosencrantz:

How can that be, when you have the voice of the King himself for your succession in Denmark?

Hamlet:

Ay, sir, but 'while the grass grows'——the proverb is something musty. O, the recorders! Let me see one. To withdraw with you——why do you go about to recover the wind of me, as if you would drive me into a toil?

在例11中,他将两名好友对他的各种无休无止的试探,比喻为打猎的过程,猎人故意站在风口,让猎物嗅到猎人味道后,往猎人设定好的陷阱方向逃走。他以此来表示两个好友通过各种设定好的对话内容,引诱自己透露发疯的原由,或者复仇的计谋。

除了哈姆雷特,其他试探的主体也使用了同类的意象。普隆涅斯在向克劳狄斯和葛特露表明自己已经发现哈姆雷特发疯的根源时,并说如果他有失误,则"Or else this brain of mine/ Hunts not the trail of policy so sure/As it hat us'd to do."(如果我的脑袋不如以往那般,能像猎狗一样精准地寻味狩猎),在这里,普隆涅斯将能够准确判断情况,挖掘哈姆雷特发疯的隐情比喻为猎狗依靠气味狩猎。在下文中,普隆涅斯提出让女儿莪菲莉娅来让哈姆雷特道出真言的时候,也说出 "I'll loose my daughter to him."(我会将我女儿放出来去见他),也是充满了引诱猎物上钩的意味。

上文分别梳理了《哈姆雷特》剧中,辞格传递出来的系列意象所构成的更深一层的解读。从意象的使用中,可以看到,莎士比亚对辞格,以及辞格中传递的意象的使用并不随意,也不是简单地为了行文的生动性;辞格使用对莎士比亚来说,更是一种主题的渲染,以及更深层次解读的传递。通过一系列植物的意象,他告诉读者丹麦王国就是一座花园,丹麦王国中的人是花园中各种花草;通过一系列疾病辞格的使用,他又向读者展示道德的堕落就好比疾病发作;最通过狩猎意象的使用,则形象地将试探行为和狩猎过程结合起来。这些意象在表面上使行文更加生动,而深层上则使戏剧主题更加深厚。

第三节 辞格与人物塑造

在莎士比亚笔下,辞格同时也是人物塑造的工具。从辞格的使用多寡,读者可以体会到角色社会地位的高低;从辞格使用的深刻与否,读者也能体会到角色的思想深浅。同时通过辞格的使用,甚至是辞格的错误使用,莎士比亚也为读者塑造了不同的人物性格形象。下文将从辞格与人物身份,以及辞格与人物性格两个方面来陈述。

一、辞格与人物身份

辞格的使用是莎剧中人物身份的一种评判标准,这可以从辞格的使用频率和使用深浅度来解读。

　　莎剧表达人物身份的方式多种多样，比如诗体和散文体的使用就是其中的一项标准，一般来说，诸如克劳狄斯等贵族身份的角色，都是以诗体（即抑扬五步格）为主，而普通的侍卫和小丑则以散文体为主。哈姆雷特则是一个例外。在剧中同时使用了诗体和散文体，且散文体的表达也不逊色于诗体，如第二幕第二场中，向两位新来的好友表明自己近期心境萎靡时，就大地、苍穹和人类所发出的那段感慨，被许多学者称赞不亚于诗作。除了诗体和散文体，通过对辞格的分析也发现，辞格的使用情况也体现了剧中人物的身份。通过统计发现，在剧中，哈姆雷特为使用辞格种类和次数最多的角色。在他著名的 to be or not to be 的 33 行独白中，共使用 7 种 19 处辞格，使用频率高达每行 57%。辞格使用频率较高的其他角色还包括国王克劳狄斯等。朝臣普隆涅斯、霍拉旭和勒替斯等，辞格的使用频率也较高，而剧中的侍卫和小丑，则比例最低。在文艺复兴时期，使用修辞是一个人教育程度的象征，莎士比亚也将这一标准应用到戏剧的创作中，赋予剧中主角或身份较高的角色以各种修辞的能力，而身份较低的，则较少使用修辞手段。

　　此外，虽然不同角色都使用修辞，但通过对这些修辞的分析也可以看到，不同的角色，对修辞的使用复杂程度不一。哈姆雷特为剧中的主角，在他所使用的辞格中，也较多出现扩展隐喻的现象，如例 12：

　　　　例 12：

　　　　Hamlet：

　　　　He did comply with his dug before he suck'd it. Thus has he, and many more of the same bevy that I know the drossy age dotes on, only got the tune of the time and outward habit of encounter—a kind of yeasty collection, which carries them through and through the most fann'd and winnowed opinions; and do but blow them to their trial—the bubbles are out.

在例 12 中,哈姆雷特使用了酿酒的意象来描述奥斯利克鹦鹉学舌的现象。此处哈姆雷特讽刺时代流行的学习浮夸文体现象,以及这些如奥斯利克的朝臣,没有真才实学,依靠模仿学到朝堂虚夸语言,就如同酿酒过程,由于发酵的关系,酒缸上面漂浮的那些沫屑,经不起一阵风吹过就都爆破了。其中,drossy(浮渣)、yeasty collection(发酵起泡)和 bubbles(气泡)等意象相互呼应,虽然存在多处隐喻,但同一类别的意象使得整个语篇成为一个整体。这些扩展隐喻的使用,表现了说话人严谨的思维模式。

亚里士多德认为,能够在不同的事物之间发现相似点是天才的体现。而为了塑造哈姆雷特这一思想深邃而思维敏锐的王子形象,莎士比亚也赋予了他使用较多原创性隐喻的能力,如例 13:

例 13:

Hamlet:

Let the candied tongue lick the absurd pomp,
And crook the pregnant hinges of the knee
Where thrift may follow fawning.

在隐喻辞格中,以动词或形容词形式引起的较为隐晦。在例 13 中,哈姆雷特将没有志气和尊严、容易为蝇头小利屈服的人，比喻为膝盖如同铰链般容易启合，属于非常新颖的意象。相比之下，其他角色，如侍卫等，所使用的辞格则相对比较简单和直接，剧中除了侍卫博纳多（Bernado）使用的隐喻辞格较为复杂之外（见第三章例35），其他辞格的使用都相对比较直接，如马塞勒斯（Marcellus）在询问霍拉旭有关丹麦国上下近日忧心忡忡的现象时，使用了排比辞格等。辞格使用的频率和复杂度高低是刻画人物的一种手段，除此之外，辞格使用的熟练程度也是一个人物身份高低的参数。在剧中，哈姆雷特对辞格的使用几乎信手拈来，即使有时候刻意而为之，有过度使用修辞之嫌，如与奥斯利克对话部分，也是为了讥讽他的迂腐；反之，其他社会层次较低的角色，在使用辞格时，则漏洞百出，如掘墓人将 se defendendo 说成 se offendendo，这处谐音双关则反映了掘墓人对该表达似懂非懂，体现出他教育水平较低的特点。

二、辞格与人物性格

除了借助辞格体现人物身份的贵贱高低，莎士比亚也借助辞格来塑造剧中各种人物的不同形象。哈姆雷特自不必说，莎士比亚不仅赋予他最多的台词，使用最多最复杂的辞格，也让他使用多种语体，能够说出充满哲理的独白，也能够随口而出各种猥亵语和粗话。难怪康托尔（Cantor）便提到，"莎士比亚赋予哈姆雷特自己的语言才能比其他他创造的角色都要多。当其他角色都倾向于用一种特有的调子说话时，哈姆雷特的语言则几乎上下覆盖各个类型"（2004：74）。通过这些语言手段，莎士比亚塑造了一个近乎"全人"的王子形象。剧中其他的角色，则都有自己的较为突出和确切的特征，下文主要介绍克劳狄斯和普隆涅斯。

克劳狄斯出场的第一次演讲（见本章第一节例3）频繁使用各类辞格。其中，借助逆喻辞格，克劳狄斯表达自己的矛盾之情，也颇有技巧地将自己与嫂子乱伦的本质给掩饰过去，而使自己的即位显得理所当然。此外，作为国王，为了展示自己的气势，克劳狄斯也极力使用有利于增强语势的排比辞格，如例14：

例14：

Claudius：

…

But to persever

In obstinate condolement is a course

Of impious stubbornness. 'Tis unmanly grief；

It shows a will most incorrect to heaven，

A heart unfortified, a mind impatient,

An understanding simple and unschooled；

For what we know must be, and is as common

As any the most vulgar thing to sense,

Why should we in our peevish opposition

Take it to heart? Fie! 'tis a fault to heaven,

A fault against the dead, a fault to nature,

To reason most absurd, whose common theme

Is death of fathers, and who still hath cried,

From the first corse till he that died to-day,

'This must be so. '

例14为克劳狄斯对哈姆雷特的过度悲伤的训斥，在此选段中，共使用了两处排比辞格，两者所表达的内容均为从自然和理性的角度，对过度悲伤之情进行了批判。这些排比句式所创设出来的气势，甚至连哈姆雷特在当下都无以反驳，只能屈从于他。可以说，"莎士比亚第一次展示克劳狄斯作为国王的掌管能力是通过体现他对语言的掌管能力开始的"（Cantor, 2004: 71）。

此外，通过分析克劳狄斯的语言，也发现莎士比亚在塑造这个人物时，赋予他使用插说辞格的特殊能力。一般来说，插说辞格的主要功能为补充行文信息，其补充的成分，在整个句子中，也属于次要的部分。然而，通过分析克劳狄斯使用的插说辞格可以发现，该辞格在克劳狄斯手中，则是一种伪辩的手段，在他使用该辞格的语境中，插说部分甚至比正文内容更多，更重要。如前文例3中，借助插说辞格，克劳狄斯创设一种迂回的句法结构，在过程中增添了各种理由和无奈，将娶嫂这一事件变得轻描淡写。相似的例子还有例15和例16：

例15：

Claudius：

Hamlet, this deed, for thine especial safety, ——
Which we do tender as we dearly grieve
For that which thou hast done, ——must send thee hence
With fiery quickness.

例16：

Claudius：

…

The Queen his mother

Lives almost by his looks; and for myself, —
My virtue or my plague, be it either which, —
She's so conjunctive to my life and soul
That, as the star moves not but in his sphere,
I could not but by her.

例15中,与其直接告诉哈姆雷特他将被遣送到英国,克劳狄斯使用插说辞格,先说明他对哈姆雷特杀死普隆涅斯行为的悲痛,最后才将遣送他到英国的决定说出;相类似地,在例16中,克劳狄斯在向勒替斯解释自己无法直接惩罚哈姆雷特的原因时,同时使用了两处插说。在第一处中,克劳狄斯陈述他对王后葛特露的深爱之情,通过插说补充了对这种爱情是好是坏都全盘接纳的态度;第二处插说中,克劳狄斯使用了一个明喻辞格,将自己对王后的迷恋比喻为行星围绕恒星轨道旋转。这两处插说,虽然从语法的角度来看,都属于行文的附属添加部分,但从修辞效果来说,则通过貌似不经意的策略,将听众的注意力从最关键的事件中引开。如果说,插说为克劳狄斯的语言特点,可能也不为过,然而通过分析克劳狄斯的几处自白可以发现,在私下的语言中,克劳狄斯几乎没有使用任何插说辞格,行文都比较直截了当。可以粗略地总结,莎士比亚在这里,借用插说辞格的创造性使用,给读者塑造了一个藏巧于拙,老于世故的形象。

与克劳狄斯相比,普隆涅斯对修辞的使用则没有那么恰如其分,莎士比亚通过这一角色使用修辞的方式,塑造了另一种人物形象。同样使用朝堂语体,普隆涅斯的技巧没有克劳狄斯熟练,如上文讨论过的第三章的例24,普隆涅斯不仅没有因为使用排比和重复辞格而让行文显得庄严,反而因为不合时宜而受到嫌弃。同样的,在第三章例 29 中,普隆涅斯借助 defect,defective 和 effect 等词构成同根异形重复辞格,但依然没有达到庄重的修辞效果。普隆涅斯对修辞的过度使用,还体现在例 17 中:

例 17:
Polonius:
Marry, I will teach you! Think yourself a baby
That you have ta'en these <u>tenders</u> for true pay,
Which are not sterling. <u>Tender</u> yourself more dearly,
<u>Or (not to crack the wind of the poor phrase,
Running it thus)</u> you'll <u>tender</u> me a fool.

例 17 中,普隆涅斯共使用了不同意思的 tender 创造了换义双关,三处 tender 的使用分别表示"清偿""照顾"和"使变成……"。然而,在使用过程中,普隆涅斯对自己的过度使用辞格其实心存自知之明,随着使用插说补充了 not to crack the wind of the poor phrase(不让驱赶各词语像驱赶小马一样,让它气喘吁吁)。可见,同样是使用插说辞格,普隆涅斯尚未如克劳狄斯般了解该辞格的精髓所在,而是一味地重复,特别是当他说出"I have a daughter (have while she is mine)."时,插说辞格的使用更显得多余。值得指出的是,莎士比亚塑造普隆涅斯这一人物,并不是简单为了衬托其他人对辞格的熟练使用,而是通过这些辞格的不合时宜的使用方法,塑造出一个絮絮叨叨、卖弄才学甚至有些自欺欺人的朝臣形象,同时也创造一种诙谐的戏剧效果,为该部戏剧带来片刻的轻松时光。

本章主要从整体的视角，分析辞格的使用在莎剧中产生的文体效果。从分析中可以看到，辞格的使用不仅有助于增加局部行文的生动性，从整部戏剧来看，辞格也是莎士比亚构建多重解读、多重语域的手段；同时，通过创造性地使用辞格，莎士比亚也将辞格的使用与主题的渲染和人物塑造紧密结合。从分析中也可以看到，莎士比亚在该剧中对辞格的使用已经达到挥洒自如、出神入化的程度，这也是莎剧，特别是《哈姆雷特》，能够成为经典的文学作品的重要原因之一。

第六章 结语

本书从讨论西方修辞学的发展到聚焦辞格的分类，从讨论莎剧的修辞语言到分析这些修辞的文体效果，从对莎剧《哈姆雷特》剧中局部的、微观的辞格辨析，到对辞格在该剧中整体的、宏观的修辞文体效果的讨论，全部都是围绕修辞与语言使用最为直接相关的辞格来展开。

莎士比亚戏剧一直都是文学爱好者喜欢的阅读对象，也是研究者热衷的研究话题，不仅因为莎士比亚戏剧中深邃的主旨和各形各色的角色，也因为莎士比亚对英语语言的使用，总能让读者和研究者耳目一新。从本书辞格角度的辨析和分析也可以看到，莎士比亚戏剧行文中，辞格使用频率之高，使用方式之巧妙，以及使用目的之深沉，都能给人以深刻的印象。在《哈姆雷特》一剧中，辞格的使用，不仅是莎士比亚让行文更加生动有趣的工具，更是他用来深化主题，渲染氛围和塑造人物的法宝。正是他对辞格的创造性使用能力，使得他从其他同样频繁使用辞格的文艺复兴作家中脱颖而出；也正是他通过这些创造性语言所塑造出来的深邃的主题和个性的角色，使得他的作品成为世界文学经典。

第六章 结语

然而，聚焦辞格辨析也有其自身的一些问题和困难：

首先是语言变化带来的困难。由于莎剧创作于16世纪，其英语语言与现、当代存在一定的区别，这也会给部分辞格的判断带来困难。例如"Fear me not."在现在的辞格判断标准来说，有倒装的因素，而在伊丽莎白时期，却是常见的语序，因此，为了避免这类因为语言的历史发展带来的错误判断，本书没有对诸如倒装这些可能存在受到时代因素影响的辞格做辨析。同时，辞格的使用或者对辞格的敏感度也与历史因素相关。威尔逊便曾提到，"莎士比亚不是给读者，而是给听众写剧本，这些人根本没有时间或者好奇心去考虑莎士比亚对隐喻的使用"（Wilson, 2009：xxxviii）。这个论述其中一部分因为伊丽莎白时期的莎剧观众，特别是受过教育的观众，都是接受过系统的修辞训练的，辞格的使用和判断是他们一种极其熟练的能力，并不需要如现当代读者般大费周章地来辨析；而对现当代读者来说，由于时代文科教育重点从修辞学中转移开，对修辞的陌生感也增强了，也许在伊丽莎白时期耳熟能详的修辞手段，在现在都变成了充满新意的表达；对他们来说是"死"的隐喻或表达，对现当代读者来说仍然具有吸引力。这些时代带来的变化，也给辞格的判断带来一定的困难。

其次是跨文化因素带来的困难。不同的文化对世界的认识不尽相同。例如，在莎剧中存在一部分隐喻，它们对于母语者来说，可能已经变成习以为常的"死隐喻"（dead metaphor），母语读者可能已经不容易从它们的使用中感受到修辞的效果，而对外语读者来说，则依然存在新鲜感。例如，该剧开头有一句"Stand and unfold yourself.", 其中unfold对大部分母语读者为死隐喻，在看到该词时，基本不会想到它是来自衣物折叠这一意象的隐喻。然而，对汉语读者来说，却还具有一定的意

363

象新鲜感,即用打开衣物的动作比喻说出身份。对于这类辞格,本书以"新颖性"作为主要标准,如果对辨析者来说仍有新意,且能透过意象获得一定文体效果的,则都纳入辞格中。相反,由于跨文化因素的影响,有一些对母语读者来说很清晰的意象,则对汉语读者来说较难理解。例如,当哈姆雷特将普隆涅斯比喻为 fishmonger(鱼贩子)后,说到"Then I would you were so honest a man."(那我希望你是一个忠实的人),哈罗德·詹金斯(Harold Jenkins)认为 honest 为双关词,一方面鱼贩子是老实人的行业,另一方面鱼贩子本身也纵欲,且令其他人纵欲(1982:246),关于 fishmonger 和 honest 两个词结合后的这一层双关的解读,对汉语读者来说需要一定的文化背景知识,理解起来也比较困难。对这一类的辞格辨析,则难免存在遗漏。

最后是情景和经验依赖性带来的困难。对情景依赖性的辞格包括但不局限于讽刺辞格(irony)。正如科贝特(Corbett)讨论讽刺辞格时所说,"如果作者误判了他的听众的理解力,他就会发现,他的听众只能理解到表层的意思,而不是有意传递的相反的意思"(1999:446)。对于这类对语境依赖性太强,需要一些主观色彩来解读的辞格,本书也没有纳入辨析中。这方面的案例主要体现在不同版本的《哈姆雷特》中,不同读者对同一处用语经常有不同的解读,每个人的解读都依赖自己的经验和知识,因此给出来的辞格判断也有出入。如在第一幕中,当哈姆雷特对鬼魂说,"I am bound to hear.",斯宾塞(T. Spencer)将其中的 bound 理解为"obliged"(必须的)(1980:237),而汤姆森和泰勒(Thompson & Taylor)则理解为"destined"(命中注定的)。

受到上述的各种因素的影响,对辞格的辨析也不可避免地

第六章 结语

多少具有一定的主观色彩。同时，由于在辨析过程对情景的解读不同，或由于知识经验不足，也可能产生对辞格的遗漏等问题，但是，这些消极因素都不足以阻止我们对莎剧语言魅力的探索。

现在各种各样的莎剧研究专著琳琅满目，莎士比亚的语言也是大部分著作经常提及的主题，特别是莎士比亚的辞格使用这一话题，论著更是层出不穷。然而，纵观这些著作，大部分以所有莎剧作为分析的数据库，从不同的戏剧中寻找出不同的修辞例子来说明莎士比亚的语言特征。本书则希望以最为经典的《哈姆雷特》一剧为例，一方面给读者展示莎士比亚在经典作品中的辞格使用情况，另一方面也想以较为系统的方式，让读者对莎士比亚辞格使用频率之高有更为直观的体验，以及对其辞格使用技巧之炉火纯青有更深刻的体会。

参考文献

ARISTOTLE. On Rhetoric: A Theory of Civic Discourse [M]. 2nd edition. Translated by George Kennedy. New York and Oxford: Oxford University Press, 2007.

BALDWIN W. William Shakespeare's Small Latine and Lesse Greeke (vol. 2) [M]. Champaign: University of Illinois Press, 1944.

BLOOM H. An Essay by Harold Bloom [C] //RAFFEL B. The tragedy of Hamlet, Prince of Denmark (the Annotated Shakespeare). New Haven and London: Yale University Press, 2003: 229-243.

BURKE K. Rhetoric—Old and New [J]. The Journal of General Education, 1951, 5: 202-209.

BURKE K. A Rhetoric of Motives [M]. Berkeley and Los Angeles: University of California Press, 1969.

CARTER B. Introduction [M] //BOBCOCK W. Hamlet—a Tragedy of Errors. West Lafayette: Purdue University Press, 1961: 13.

CANTOR P. Shakespeare Hamlet: A Study Guide [M]. New York: Cambridge University Press, 2004.

CATHCART C. Hamlet Date and Early Afterlife [J]. The Review of English Studies, 2001, 52: 341-359.

CLEMEN W. The Development of Shakespeare's Imagey [M]. London: Methun, 1966.

CORBETT E., CONNORS R. Classical Rhetoric for Modern Student [M]. New York and Oxford: Oxford University Press, 1999.

CROWLEY S, HAWHEE D. Ancient Rhetorics for Contemporary Students [M]. New York: Pearson, 2004.

EVANS I. The Language of Shakespeare's Plays [M]. London: Methuen, 1964.

EVANS R. The Osier Cage: Rhetorical Devices in Romeo and Juliet [M]. Lexington: University of Kentucky Press, 1966.

GREENBLATT S, COHEN W, HOWARD J, MAUS K. The Norton Shakespeare [M]. New York and London: W. W. Norton & Company, 2005.

HARRIS R. Writing with Clarity and Style: A Guide to Rhetorical Devices for Contemporary Writers [M]. London and New York: Routledge, 2018.

HARRISON G B. Introducing Shakespeare [M]. Harmondsworth: Penguin, 1959.

HERRICK J. The History and Theory of Rhetoric [M]. 4th edition. Boston: Allyn and Bacon, 2008.

HIBBARD G R. Hamlet [M]. By William Shakespeare. Oxford World's Classics. Oxford: Oxford University Press, 1987.

HONIGMANN E A J. The Date of Hamlet [J]. Shakespeare Survey, 1956, 9: 24 -34.

HORVEI H. The Che'vril Glove: A Study in Shakespearean Rhetoric [M]. Bergen, 1984.

JENKINS H. Hamlet [M]. By William Shakespeare. The Arden Shakespeare. London: Methuen and Co. , Ltd, 1982.

JOHNSTON B. Poems of Ben Johnson [M]. London and New York: Routledge, 1954.

JOSEPH M. Rhetoric in Shakespeare's Time—Literary Theory of Renaissance Europe [M]. New York and Burlingame: Harbinger Book, 1962.

KERMODE F. Shakespeare's Language [M]. New York: Farrar, Straus, and Giroux, 2000.

LAKOFF G, JOHNSON M. Metaphors We Live By [M]. Chicago: University of Chicago Press, 1980.

LEECH G. Linguistics and the Figures of Rhetoric [C] // FOWLER R. Essays on Style and Language: Linguistic and Critical Approaches to Literary Style. Oxford: Alden Press Ltd, 1966: 135 -156.

NASHE T. From the Anatomie of Absurditie [C] //SMITH G. Elizabethan Critical Essays (Vol. 1). London: Oxford University Press, 1950: 321 -337.

PLETT H. Figures of Speech [M] //SLOANE T. Encyclopedia of Rhetoric. Oxford: Oxford University Press, 2001.

PUTTENHAM G. The Art of English Poesy [M]. Ithaca and London: Cornell University Press, 2007.

QUINTILIAN. The Institutio Oratoria of Quintilian (III) [M].

Translated by BUTLER H. Cambridge: Harvard University Press/London: William Heinemann Ltd, 1959.

RAFFEL B. The Tragedy of Hamlet, Prince of Denmark [M]. The Annotated Shakespeare. New Haven and London: Yale University Press, 2003.

SHAPIRO J. 1599: A Year in the Life of William Shakespeare [M]. London: Faber and Faber, 2006.

SPENCER T J B. Hamlet [M]. By William Shakespeare. New Penguin Shakespeare. With an Introduction by Anne Barton. Harmondsworth: Penguin Books, 1980.

THOMPSON A, TAYLOR N. Hamlet [M]. By William Shakespeare. The Arden Shakespeare. London: Thomson Learning High Holborn House, 2007.

VICKERS B. Shakespeare's Use of Rhetoric [C]//MUIR K., SCHOENBAUM S. A New Companion to Shakespeare Studies. Cambridge: Cambridge University Press, 1971: 83-98.

WILSON D. Hamlet: The Cambridge Dover Wilson Shakespeare [M]. New York: Cambridge University Press, 1952/2009.

卞之琳. 关于我译的莎士比亚悲剧《哈姆雷特》: 有书无序 [J]. 外国文学研究, 1980 (1): 41-42.

郝田虎. 发明莎士比亚 [J]. 江西社会科学, 2014 (1): 82-88.

胡曙中. 英汉修辞跨文化研究 [M]. 青岛: 青岛出版社, 2008.

黄国彬. 解读《哈姆雷特》——莎士比亚原著汉译及详注（上/下）[M]. 北京: 清华大学出版社, 2013.

梁启超. 饮冰室诗话 [M]. 长春: 时代文艺出版社, 1998.

鲁迅. 科学史教篇 [M]. 鲁迅文选. 上海: 上海远东出版社,

2011: 1 – 10.

马常纲. 英汉对照莎士比亚名言录 [M]. 西安: 陕西人民教育出版社, 1992.

孟宪强. 中国莎学简史 [M]. 长春: 东北师范大学出版社, 1994.

裘克安. 莎士比亚年谱 [M]. 北京: 商务印书馆, 1988.

吾文泉. 莎士比亚: 语言与艺术 [M]. 南京: 江苏文艺出版社, 2002.

徐鹏. 莎士比亚的修辞手段 [M]. 苏州: 苏州大学出版社, 2001.

严复. 天演论 [M]. 北京: 华夏出版社, 2002.

张泗洋. 莎士比亚戏剧研究 [M]. 长春: 时代文艺出版社, 1991.